I'm Tired of Zombies
Book Four:
End Game
By James W. Murphy

Table of Contents

I'm Tired of Zombies: Book 4,

Valley Vengeance

Cast of Characters

Douglas Sutton – Main character; born in Maine; world traveler; educated University of Wyoming.

Paradise Valley – The place Doug bought and made his ranch, a swathe of Wyoming two by six miles in diameter; location of the Underground.

The Underground – A marvel of the mind of Doug Sutton; a complex built underground, encompassing more than 5,000 square feet of living space, replete with storeroom, kitchen, den, gymnasium and three bedrooms.

David Malone – Deputy Sheriff, Albany County, Wyoming; Doug's great friend.

Julia Malone – Wife of David Malone; Registered Nurse with hospital in Laramie.

Gill Meadows – The ammo guy; lived in Centennial; a Marine; served in Korea and two tours in Vietnam.

Ruth – Young lady Doug ran into on a scavenging outing, now Mrs. Sutton

Darrell and Jeff – The bad boy brothers.

Erskine Little – The sniper; young boy found by the foursome in Fort Collins, Colorado.

Zach Horn – Deputy Sheriff, Albany County, Wyoming; murdered by the bad boy brothers.

Sam Burke – The old man of the valley; a Marine, served in Korea; rancher; PhDs in Electrical and Physical Engineering.

Anne Burke – Wife of the old man of the valley; author of well-known western novels.

Doctor Steven Roche, PhD – Colorado facility employee; a convincing yet false individual.

Doctor Miller – Associate of Dr. Roche; the director of the underground research facility near Wellington, Colorado.

Judith – The child the Zombie Signal is named for, The Judith Signal attracts zombies.

Chet Bost – The young stranger who, out of nowhere, knocked on the Sutton's door.

Daniel ('Nemo'), Dan Norris – U.S. Marine, cowboy, adventurer, traveler

Jeffrey ('Ski') Jablonski – U. S. Marine, cowboy, traveler, companion of Nemo

Jack ('Keger') Kagel – U. S. Marine, cowboy, traveler, companion of Nemo and Jeff

Thomas John Gerill – Sheriff, Albany County, Wyoming; 'TJ'.

June Gerill – Sister of TJ Gerill; lives in Scottsbluff, Nebraska.

Jamie O'Donnell – 'Friend' of June Gerill; Ammunition manufacturer.

Miss Donna Peckham – Wyoming native; cowgirl; ultimately TJ's wife.

David Douglas Sutton – **DD**; son of Doug and Ruth Sutton.

Howard Mason – Staff Sergeant, U.S. Army; one of the captives from the Colorado complex.

Donnie Phillips – Private, U.S. Army; one of the captives from the Colorado complex.

Timothy Sandoval - Private, U.S. Army; one of the captives from the Colorado complex.

Chapter 1: Working the Ground

Spring was upon Centennial Valley, Wyoming. The grass was lush and green. The birds sang their melodies, the geese honking in the creek, the ducks doing likewise. Eagles soared. The aspens were quaking in the breeze. Deer and Elk frolicked in the meadows of the valley meadows. Cattle roamed and sheep grazed. The mares had colts.

Thomas John Gerill, dubbed TJ by family and friends, the Sheriff of Albany County, Wyoming, tall and lanky, stepped from his home in Paradise Valley. His valley ranch was located in Centennial Valley, Albany County, Wyoming. He was on the front porch stretching, took in a deep breath of fresh mountain air. Fresh air – TJ had been taking it for granted for nearly three years now. The plague that had begun in Africa almost wiping out humankind nearly a decade ago, had had a significant positive change on the planet - the earth had begun to recover from man's use and abuse.

The air had become much fresher since millions upon millions of automobiles, trucks, trains, airplanes, ships, and other motorized contraptions were no longer moving and leaving behind exhaust gasses blanketing the planet. The trees and grass were greener than he'd ever seen before. There were more birds, more deer, more elk, and more of every kind of critter. The ground seemed to have become richer, maybe it too, was recovering from mankind's legacy.

TJ pulled an Adirondack chair up near the leading edge of the porch, sat down, propped his big cowboy-booted feet up on the railing and sipped his coffee. He turned in his Holy Bible to Paul's letter to the Ephesians, chapter two and read, "As for you, you were dead in your transgressions and sins, in which you used to live when you followed the ways of this world and of the ruler of the kingdom of the air, the spirit who is now at work in those who are disobedient. All of us also lived among them at one time, gratifying the cravings of our sinful nature and following its desires and thoughts. Like the rest, we were by nature objects of wrath. But because of his great love of us, God, who is rich in mercy, made us alive with Christ even when we were dead in transgressions – it is by grace you have been saved."

TJ sat the Bible in his lap and looked out over Paradise Valley and was positive God's grace allowed the world and this valley to recover as it had. And it was God's grace that had indeed saved those that lived in peace together and enjoyed the fruits this valley He made provided. It wasn't The Garden of Eden, but was, in TJ's mind, a very close second.

The day was clear and sunny, with a light breeze, and, according to the thermometer on the porch, a pleasant seventy-two degrees Fahrenheit. TJ couldn't think of anything that would make the day more perfect than it already was, until Donna, TJ's wife, came out and pulled the other Adirondack up next to him and put her cowgirl-booted feet up on the rail alongside his. She too, had brought her coffee and a smile that would melt butter.

She saw the Bible on TJ's lap and asked, "What are you reading this morning?"

TJ closed his eyes, tilting his head back and recited, "Paul's letter to the Ephesians, 'But because of his great love of us, God, who is rich in mercy, made us alive with Christ even when we were dead in transgressions – it is by grace you have been saved.' It's from chapter two," he answered.

"Fitting, looking out over the valley," she said.

"I thought that, also," TJ admitted looking at his wife and smiling.

They sipped their coffee in silence, appreciating the mood of the day. Today was a rest day. Tomorrow the two would Z up, that is go with a sidearm, a rifle, and a shotgun, and go to TJ's birthplace, Rock River, Wyoming. They were scheduled to go to the apple orchard and scavenge apple trees to transplant in the valley. Jack Kagel, also known as Keger, a

Marine (all prior service people that were Marines, are always and forever Marines, by the way), was going to tag along just to get out and about.

Jack was one of three Marines that had shown up in the valley almost a year before TJ's arrival. The other two, Daniel Norris and Jeff Jablonski, also known as Nemo and Ski, had moved into three homes on the southern ridge of the valley, a place that had a commanding view of the lands to the north, east and west. The southern ridges above their homes were heavily tree-covered, steep, and craggy in places, resulting in natural fortifications for their three small ranches.

TJ happened upon the scene just after the valley had gone through a fierce battle, where Douglas Sutton, owner of Paradise Valley, and David Malone, TJ's Deputy Sheriff, had tragically been murdered by members of the infamous Colorado complex people. After the battle proper, while returning from an errand, Douglas Sutton was killed by a sniper while driving his ATV back to the ranch. He had his wife, Ruth, and Dave's wife, Julia Malone, on board. The subsequent ATV crash threw the two ladies from the vehicle, literally saving their lives as the attackers raked the little vehicle with automatic weapons fire. Ruth and Julia quickly crawled into an aspen grove and hid until the three Marines and finally, TJ, had arrived and put a stop to the fighting.

Sadly, Doug had been killed before being told his wife, Ruth, was pregnant with their first child. The surprise announcement about the baby, literally minutes after the father had been killed, was an emotionally trying time for everyone. They did not know whether to be saddened or elated by the news. The baby was born on the seventh of March the following year, and that became a celebration day the seven remaining adults would not soon forget.

After the valley residents settled down, they began in earnest to plan and then execute an attack on the Colorado complex where the men who attacked them came from. In that attack, they destroyed every building, every satellite dish, tower antennae, and, they hoped, their last drone and the hanger for the things. The attack had gone off without a hitch and was devastating. The valley attack team, made up of Dan, Jack, Jeff, Julia, Donna, and TJ, completed a total surprise assault against the people of the Colorado complex, and they didn't even have a chance to fire weapons during the one-sided sneak attack. It was now early spring, and the battle had been five months ago.

TJ heard a horn honk down the lane and looking up saw the ATV the Marines had. He got up and opening the door to the house, hit the button on the remote mounted on the wall that opened the gate. The ATV pulled up near the front steps and Nemo, Daniel Norris, got out, and said, "Howdy up there. How ya doin'?"

"Doing well," TJ said with a smile. "Coffee?"

"I'm a Marine, we need coffee by IV if we can get it," he answered, laughing.

"Come on up and I'll pour you a mug," TJ offered.

Nemo gave Donna a wave and followed TJ inside. Donna stayed on the porch enjoying the morning. Once inside, TJ gave Nemo a mug of joe and asked, "What's up?"

"I've been thinkin'," Nemo answered.

"Uh oh, the national debt just doubled," TJ said, giving a humorous chuckle and worried look.

Nemo chuckled and said, "No, nothing that bad." He turned and went back outside on the porch and leaned against the rail. TJ followed and sat back down in his Adirondack. It was quiet other than the sounds of nature.

TJ looked at Nemo and caught his eye, gave him a sideways glance, and raised his coffee mug towards him, giving him a nudge, so-to-speak, to continue.

"Okay, I'm nervous," Nemo admitted.

"About what? DD, Ruth, and Julia doing okay?" TJ asked with concern in his voice.

"It's not them, they're fine," he happily answered. "Brother, it's been five months since we took out that complex and I'm thinking if they had an escape tunnel from that underground portion of the place, we could be seeing them any time. It's on my mind's all."

"What do you think we should do about it," Donna asked him.

He took another long sip of his coffee and kept his gaze on the sky. They could tell he was thinking about the issue and knew by the look it would impact the whole valley.

"My Marine senses are telling me to get ready, to prepare. For what, I don't know, but it's driving me nuts. Jeff's nipples are itching, too."

TJ choked on his coffee and Donna busted into a hearty laugh at that, as it was a well-known fact that Jeff's nipples did itch during weather changes and other odd things from time-to-time, including using that bodily torment to forecast possible enemy action – they all had come to rely on Jeff's amusing affliction.

Nemo chuckled too, and continued, "Seriously, we all suddenly have 'feelings'," he said making quote signs with his hands, "…and we're getting the urge to get ready…again. For what I don't know, but I feel like we need to prepare. Even Jack is getting antsy."

TJ continued to chuckle and nodded his understanding, holding his hand up for Dan to stop talking so he could catch his breath from chocking and laughing so hard. "That was too much this early in the morning," he said continuing to chuckle.

"I'm good for the day, too," Donna agreed, laughing again.

"It's okay, it's okay, I've been feeling like I need to look over my shoulder for over a week now," TJ admitted.

"You?" Dan asked, surprised.

"Yeah, I got the feeling Tuesday a week ago that I was being watched. Thought it was her," pointing at Donna, "but it wasn't as she came out of the barn right then. Didn't even know I was standing there. I still had the feeling after she went inside the house. I looked for a drone, but couldn't see one, then looked all around the property, even going up to the high ground on the Underground. Didn't see a thing. It continues, though, and that bugs me even more since you, Jack, and nipple-boy are having those feelings as well."

The 'nipple-boy' comment brought another round of chuckles by the trio. Donna got up and collecting mugs went inside to refill with coffee. Dan looked at TJ after she'd gone in and said, "So what are we going to do, Sheriff?"

"Uh-oh, you're pulling the Sheriff card for this, huh? That ain't right."

"Sure, it is. You know Albany County like the back of your hand, much better than the rest of us, so you know where we should go to look, or at least go to keep watch."

"I'll have to get the maps out and take a look at the topography, 'specially to the southeast. Yes, I know Albany County very well, but not all the sweet spots. And this valley is relatively new to me from an 'I really know it' standpoint."

"I'll help. I know how to read maps and can plot a dime you dropped fifty miles away."

TJ harrumphed, but said, "I'd love the help. I'll talk to Donna and see when our social calendar is open, and we'll schedule a dinner."

"Schedule a what?" Donna asked coming out of the house balancing the coffee mugs.

TJ chuckled again and answered her, saying, "We need to have the valley over for dinner one evening for a valley strategy, and tactics powwow. When's the soonest we're open? Menu options are open, too."

She squinted and looked up at Nemo and said, "I think the next opening on the social calendar is tomorrow night and menu should be beef tips on pasta with gravy, corn, and fresh bread."

Dan stood up and said, "Mouth's waterin' already, lady…I'll alert the others. What time should we all meet?"

"How about everyone come over around two and we'll take it from there?" TJ said.

"I'll let everyone know," Dan said, then looked at Donna and with a smile and a wink said, "I'm taking the mug – bring it back tomorrow. See you guys later," he finished and jumped back in the ATV and left for Marine Hill to the south.

TJ got up and closed the gate after Dan had pulled through and went back inside.

"What 'cha doin'?" Donna asked.

"Going to get maps out and get the ones for this valley and the surrounding areas. I think I'll try to print that satellite view off the computer Doug had and see if it'll give us a good view of the valley and the surrounding area."

"I'll help. I like doing research, you know that."

He did indeed, remembering the incident at the Laramie public library a few years prior. He chuckled with the memory.

"What's so funny?" Donna asked.

"Spider – all those legs…" TJ laughed holding his empty hand up in a gesture to fend off an imaginary eight-legged critter.

"I can't believe you remember that," she said disgusted.

He said, rather loudly, "How could I forget that blood-curdling scream you delivered that day?"

She gave him a smack on the back-side and said, "Get! Get in there and get those maps!"

"Yes, ma'am," he answered laughing again. Going into the library, TJ opened the drawer holding the maps and began going through the stack looking for anything from Albany and neighboring Laramie Counties. The topo maps were the ones he kept out and one National Forest map in Albany County. Together, the topo and National Forest maps would show most of the standing structures in the county. TJ decided he would draw in the structures not shown on the topo map that were on the National Forest map.

It only took him a few minutes to draw in the structures he found and put the National Forest map away then printed the satellite image off the computer. He got a pad of paper and a few pencils and took them out to the table. He stood next to it thinking and decided he would add the topo maps of the

Colorado complex area. He put them on the table then put in the table leaves and getting a glass of ice water, went back out on the porch to relax and enjoy the day.

He had taken care of the animals early that morning and could hear the dairy cow he'd found, out in the pasture mooing. She was probably chewing her cud and mad that one of the other animals got too close, probably Dusty. The chickens gave him more than a dozen eggs and he was happy about that. He thought about saddling their two horses and taking a ride with Donna up the western canyon for a picnic but remembered she had already made plans for lunch over with Julia and Ruth. TJ put his feet back up on the porch rail and got comfortable, sipped his water, and promptly fell asleep.

Dan got back to his place on Marine Hill and called for Jack and Jeff to come over. Jeff complained Nemo had a mug of Donna's coffee and didn't bring he and Jack a mug full. Nemo gave Jeff a sly look and a smile that said, 'too bad, Charlie,' and told them about the powwow and dinner at Paradise Valley tomorrow beginning at two in the afternoon.

"What's the topic?" Jack asked.

"What's the menu," Jeff asked always interested in a meal.

"The Colorado complex and the feelings we've been having lately. TJ said he'd been tense like he was being watched, for the past week or so himself. Said he looked for a drone but didn't see one. So, we're not alone with the being watched feelings. I didn't talk to him about not seeing any Zs for over a month and for me, I find that disturbing."

Jeff asked, "Why do you suppose that is?"

"Got me, brother. I'm tired of zombies and glad we're not seeing any, but I still find it strange. I wonder, deep down, if that facility has done something new with the zombie population."

"Yeah, breeding them," Jeff said sniggering afterwards.

Jack and Dan shook their heads, and Dan continued with, "Yeah, right. Keep it logical, brother. Any decent suggestions?"

Jack and Jeff both shook their heads. "We can speculate all day long, but most likely won't have the real answer," Jack mumbled. He looked over to Dan and asked, "Recon?"

"Frankly, I think we should," Dan said. "At least get close and launch a drone of our own and take a look for another entrance to that place. I think it'd be quieter and less likely we'd be seen. I positively want to know if they have another drone or even more than one if we can get that information."

"I like sneaking around, you know," Jeff offered.

"Yes, we know you do," Jack said.

"That may very well be the thing we need to do," Dan said chin in hand. "You think you're still as quiet as you used to be?"

"I guess I'll find out, huh?" Jeff answered with a sideways glance and a sly grin.

"We'll keep this under our hats tonight, save it to let TJ know you're going. He has more intel about the area than we do, and his information will be valuable. He's reconed the place before."

"If you remember, I was with him and Donna when they did that recon and I've seen the area," Jeff said. "I want to go in from the northwest and west and see what's out those directions. See if they have an exit from that basement out there somewhere near the base of the mountains. With the area as large as it is, I'd say a week…maybe ten days to go over it well enough."

"I'll go along as support, too," Jack volunteered. "I'll be the camp gofer and keep the coffee hot."

"When do you want to go?" Dan asked Jeff.

"Depends on what we get tomorrow night in the meeting, I guess," Jeff said.

"Well, for one, I think the meeting will set the groundwork for the next year or so," Jack contemplated.

"Probably, let's pack it up and get back to whatever it was you were doing," Dan said.

"Guess I won't be going for apple trees," Jack said unhappily.

The three gathered weapons, ammo, and the scotch the next afternoon and headed towards TJ and Donna's place. They could see Julia, Ruth, and DD, getting in their truck so knew they would be along in a few minutes. With the community meeting and then dinner, it was going to be a nice afternoon and evening with the gathering of the valley residents at TJ and Donna's home site.

The gate was already open, so the men pulled up to the house and parked on the north side next to the garage. They got out and sauntered up to the porch steps where Donna and TJ welcomed them. Dan gave TJ the bottle of scotch and Donna went to get some tumblers for the men. Since the day was another beautiful one, TJ had pulled out all the deck chairs and set them all over the porch and invited the three Marines to have a seat. When Donna came out with the tumblers, TJ did the honors and poured two fingers in each and passed them out, setting the partially empty bottle on the coffee table.

"Here's to a nice community gathering and dinner, to the cook and the host," Jack announced as a toast.

"Here-here," Dan and Jeff said in unison.

The four men clinked glasses and sipped the amber liquor. Julia, Ruth, and DD pulled up about then and everyone got up and went to greet the ladies and the little man. They all stood around in the front of the house hugging, chatting, and passing DD around the group. The baby was always the center of attention for the group when they gathered. He was the valley pride and joy.

They climbed the steps onto the porch and the men gathered the chairs into a sort of circle. Ruth put DD in a bouncy chair with a blanket next to the table in the middle and Donna served wine to the ladies. The small talk centered on everyone's health and well-being and, of course, on David Douglas Sutton, DD. After several minutes, Dan interrupted the group and asked TJ why he'd called the group together.

"If you don't already know, Dan came to see me yesterday and voiced his concern about the feelings he, Jack and Jeff were having of late," TJ began. "The feeling they were being watched from time-to-time and needing to prepare – for what, they're not sure. I told him I'd been having the same feelings for over a week myself. How about you ladies," TJ asked, motioning to Ruth and Julia, "any uneasy feelings with you?"

Ruth was first to respond, saying, "I haven't felt that I was being watched, but have been watching to the southeast for a while. Don't know why, really, just an uneasy feeling and thinking we may be getting Zs coming over the hill by Highway 47. I haven't seen anything but have been keeping a closer watch that direction for some reason."

Julia was next adding, "I've felt like I've been watched. It's a creepy feeling, reminding me of the old scary movies where someone was looking through a window at you or something. I've scanned the skies several times thinking a drone might be up there but haven't seen anything either."

"I've been watching for drones myself," TJ added. "So, that's why I've asked everyone to gather today. Almost all of us have a sudden uneasiness that's bothering us. Dan, yesterday, said he was bothered by the feeling so much that he feels we should get ready for something. Make sure our weapons and ammunition are up to snuff and ready at all times, the vehicles fueled at all times, the bug-out kits are ready to go, equipment packed, and extra clothing and food stocked."

"I agree," Julia said. "I've already begun and have been getting things ready for several days now over at our place."

"I was wondering what you were doing," Ruth said surprised. "You should have told me; I would have helped pack."

Julia smiled at her and said, "You've got your hands full," she said, pointing at DD.

"Not when he's napping, I could help then," Ruth said.

"No, when he's napping, you should, too," Julia told her.

"She's right," Jeff agreed. "Heck, he's not even a year old and both of you need your rest after the ordeal you went through. And then helping with the attack…you're one strong lady, but you've got to take care of yourself and DD."

"Okay, okay, I know when I'm over-ruled," Ruth gave in, smiling.

The group chuckled and Dan said, "We need to agree on a bug-out location and TJ mentioned the Ranger's shack west of Centennial. That sounds like a good place as there will be shelter enough for all of us, fresh water with the pump and extra equipment that is already there and the materials we can add in case of trouble."

"That is a good place as it has roadway access, too, and with all those tall Lodge Pole pine trees surrounding the place, somewhat protected from aerial attack," Ruth observed. "We should also consider the lodge up at Albany. It's still useful, has a water supply and there is more than enough room for all of us. We should add supplies and equipment there, too."

"That's a good suggestion," TJ agreed. "That's two places…want to opt for a third?"

"The airport terminal," Jeff said. "I was up there looking it over on one of my scouting forays and thought it would make a good bug-out place. Lots of room, good views for defense and loads of materials we can use. Don't know about water, though."

"Another sound idea and we can research the water issue," TJ said agreeing with Jeff. "Okay, votes or just ready all three places?"

A chorus of all three rang out so that order of business settled TJ asked the Marines what the residents should do about the valley as a whole. "Do we need to set watches and keep an eye out all the time or if someone gets one of the feelings we're being watched, alert everyone and we'll all go try to find who or whatever is out there?"

Jack looked at him and said, "Not enough of us to cover the valley effectively. We should be mindful enough to stop and look around with binos or NVGs at night. Just be extra cautious and take the time to look around our areas.”

“Too bad we didn’t have some motion sensors and stuff to set around the valley on the roads,” Jeff said deviously. “Not much we can do about the sky without radar.”

“Still not enough people even for that,” Dan said. “We just need to be aware. If one of us sees anything out of the ordinary, let everyone know and as a team we’ll go check it out. What else everyone?”

“Driveway sensors,” Jack suggested.

Julie asked, “What, Jack?”

“Driveway sensors,” he answered her. “You set them up at the beginning of your driveway and when someone breaks the invisible electronic beam, a signal alarms in the house letting the residents know someone is coming. Kind of like a long-range doorbell. We can get those readily and figure out their range. Maybe they’ll give us an extra minute or two to react.”

Every set of eyes, save DD’s, were on Jack. It was a novel and great idea.

“What made you think of that?” Dan asked him.

“Remember that rancher up near Osage we worked with that time for spring roundup?” Jack countered. “He had one and I thought it a neat thing.”

“We’ll definitely need to put that on the list of things to get and play with,” TJ said to the group. “If the range is a good way off, then we should place the sensors out at the extreme range to give us as much time as possible, say on both the road to Centennial from here and over on Eleven and one on Highway 47. That’ll give us three alarms.”

“Good idea, Jack,” TJ said with a smile, “anything else from anyone?”

“Doing a recon on the Colorado complex again to see if they’ve begun repairing the facility,” Jack answered quickly. “We need to know. And if they are rebuilding, then I think we’ll answer the surveillance question. I want to know for sure. I’ve always thought they had an out somewhere, an emergency exit from the underground whatever they may have. Remember the building with the elevator penthouse?" Nods from everyone. "That was the second floor if you remember. So, why an elevator in a single-story building? It must have an underground facility the elevator serviced. We don't know how deep it went so that's a mystery. If it's like anything else underground, it'll have an emergency exit somewhere…out there," he ended with a wave.

"I agree," Jeff said. "We need to check out the west side as well."

"Me, too - agreeing that is – and I think we need to fly a high-altitude drone all over the place and photograph everything," Jack seconded.

"I'm in and can fly that drone, Jack," Julia added.

"I'm in, too," Dan said. "We'll fly several drones and save time."

"That leaves me and Donna to take care of the valley and DD, while you're gone on the mission," Ruth said with a smile.

"Ohh, I'm in with that," Donna said. "Alone time with the jet tub…you bet!"

"And a bottle of wine I'd wager," TJ said smiling and the others chuckling.

"But of course," Donna said in a flamboyant manner and a prissy wave of her hand.

Everyone broke into laughter at her response. Friendlily chiding each other and laughter continued for several minutes but finally, TJ brought the group back under control with, "When do we go, what do we take, and how long will we be gone?"

Dan answered first, "As soon as possible, Z'd up to the hilt, adding a pair of fifties and we'll take the bomber drones we didn't need to use during the last attack. We just might need them this time. I figure three to five days for the recon."

TJ stood and went inside, coming out a few minutes later with the maps he'd gathered for the group. He spread them on the outdoor coffee table and said, "With the five of us and a couple of those drones we can cover a lot of ground. I think we should go out several miles in all directions and do a search with the drones, filming everything. If we don't see any signs of activity, we can come back here and go over the films in detail."

"While we're there," Julia said, "I can stay in the bunker complex at the NG base and be the camp gofer. I can watch for their drone or drones if they have any and use a Stinger."

"We'll take two trucks then and one trailer with fuel," Dan said. "We'll plan for three to five days but take additional supplies for two weeks just in case.   Julia, you'll be medic…update and fill the kit. If anyone needs anything, make a list and we'll try and get it on the way back."

TJ swung a map around to face himself and looking at it said, "We should go down on Highway 85 and not use I-25. The team with the truck and trailer will take Julia to the NG bunkers. The second team will continue south to Ault, then turn west on Highway 33. They can go under I-25 to College Avenue, turn north, and launch a drone from the south side of this lake. They'll be about five miles south of the complex so well enough away to be comfortable about launching. I'd say fly out to the extreme range of the drone and fly a pattern around the area south of the complex and to the west. We'll rendezvous at the NG bunkers no later than five in the afternoon everyday we're out. We'll cover as much ground as we can in the time allotted. Everyone doing ground recon use cameras and photograph everything. Remember fresh batteries and new cards in the cameras."

"At least a ten-mile radius around the complex proper," Dan mused. "I suggest going as far west as the mountains and focus there…that just seems logical to me."

Jeff looked at Jack, gave him a punch on the arm, and said, "Told ya." Then, "We can do that," pointing at Jack. "The big drones have a range of twenty-five miles, fifty for a round trip so we can cover a lot of ground," Jeff said.

"Without a load, right?" TJ asked.

"Yep, but, if we find something and want to take it out, we'll take the bombs with us and load 'em as necessary," Jeff said with that evil grin of his.

"Whoa, Tex, let's not go making a lot of noise until we know what we're facing," Dan said.

Donna got up and went inside, Ruth on her heels. They went into the kitchen and started dinner.

The five scooted closer together on the porch TJ pouring more scotch for everyone and wine for Julia.

"So, this is strictly going to be a recon unless we run into trouble, right?" Jack asked. "No heroics or loose cannon stuff, right?"

"Correct," TJ answered. "We're strictly going for the recon...no trouble unless we're forced - we're just going to look around, quietly."

They all turned and looked at Jeff.

"What?" he said looking at all of them as they gazed at him.

"Just recon," Dan added.

"I got it," Jeff said with finality and a feigned hurt look.

"When do we go?" TJ asked the group.

"As soon as we all get packed, say three days from now," Dan said.

Everyone agreed so they discussed supplies and equipment they would take. The list made up mostly of weapons and ammunition, was long. Five adults needed a lot of water and food for a possible two week stay and they all hoped they would be outta there in the five days they wanted to use. Each truck would have the usual loadout of weapons and ammo, along with clothing, sleeping supplies, toiletries, and water...everything they hoped would be needed.

"Who's hungry," Ruth said opening the door. The group of five stood as one and headed inside for dinner. Dan collected DD and took him in, TJ collected the maps.

Dinner was good and the banter was even better. The evening came to an end and the guests left for their homes. Donna and TJ finished cleaning the kitchen and sat back out on the porch to enjoy the early evening. TJ had a glass of iced tea and Donna had another glass of wine. They sat quietly enjoying the sounds, the birds, the geese and ducks, the horses and cattle calling, and an elk bugling to the west somewhere behind the house.

"This is wonderful," Donna said.

"Yes, it is," TJ agreed. "I love sitting out here or up on the deck or up on the Underground and just looking and listening. It's so peaceful and relaxing."

"Do you miss people?" Donna suddenly asked.

"What?" TJ returned, not quite understanding.

"People…do you miss them?" she asked again.

"Oh, yeah, I do," he answered solemnly. "I sometimes miss the noise, the hustle and bustle of life as it was. I miss hearing a horn honk in traffic, the screech of breaks, kids laughing and playing, college kids arguing and debating. I miss hearing horses all the time and airplanes and I really miss *Fox and Friends* in the mornings. I miss my friends and now my sister and Jamie." His head hung and he once again felt the grief of losing his sister and good friend. Their deaths were hard on TJ.

"I'm sorry I upset you," Donna said placing a hand on his shoulder. "I miss my family, too, and a lot of the things you talked about. Airplanes flying overhead, for one. I liked *Fox and Friends*, too. I miss the farm report on TV, and I miss the internet."

"Wasn't much of a fan of the internet. It became a useful tool doing police work, but just something that wasted one's time if you ask me."

"You know what I miss the most?" she asked him.

"What's that?" he returned.

"Church. You know, gathering to worship and singing, getting a good sermon, one that made us think and could apply to our daily lives. It's so - neat is the word I guess - that the Bible applies to our lives right now but was written so many years ago. And the potlucks! I really miss those. I loved getting together after church like that and everyone would bring something and the whole congregation would get together for a Sunday afternoon of food, friends, laughter, and play. I really do miss that."

"Come to think of it I really miss it, too. I was in Cheyenne one Sunday and stopped in a church called Meadowbrooke – I think it was in 2019. The pastor, I think his name was Keith, gave a sermon on 'Ruth', and I've thought of that several times since meeting Ruth Sutton. Don't know why, but she reminds me of that sermon. Maybe because she's a fighter, fighting on the side of what's just and right."

"You see things differently than the rest of us, you know that?"

"No, not really. I mean, I want what the people of this valley want - to live in peace and friendship together. To enjoy each other's stories, thoughts, and ideas. To help each other live, planting crops and taking care of the animals. Getting together like we do and discuss things, not fight over them. The reason I think the way I do is my upbringing and training, I guess. I look at things for the better, even though I know I need to keep watch for the bad or evil side. I fight with myself all the time over right and wrong and my own sin."

"How so?"

"Those men murdered Dave and Doug and have tried on several occasions to kill all of us. I want to go erase them so we can live out our lives peacefully. I fight with myself over the right and wrong of that. I know in the Bible it says there are two kinds of anger – righteous anger and sinful anger – and I hope the anger I hold against whoever these people are is right and not sinful in nature." He turned and looked at her and said, "Because I do have anger, a seething anger for them and it makes me want to go and get them. Is that right or wrong?"

Donna looked TJ in the eyes and said, "Remember the Bible tells us even Jesus got angry and acted – remember the time he beat the money dealers in the temple? Sometimes we need to act. If they would leave us alone and live peacefully together, you wouldn't feel this way. But they prefer to attack us every chance they get, and for what reason or reasons, we may never know. That's sinful in my book. Protecting ourselves even to the point of going after those people like we did and will do…that's not wrong. It's a justification for us really, saying that we will fight for peace, moral character, and survival."

"I think I'll go in and read my Bible for a while," TJ said standing. He bent over, gave her a kiss, and went inside leaving Donna on the porch. He got his Bible out and sitting in the library, placed the Bible in his lap and said a short, silent prayer, *'Father in Heaven, I am troubled. I have anger towards the people that attack us, and I fight with myself to control my emotions. I need Your help, Father, and ask You to help me discern if my anger is just or sinful and if the latter, help me to control it; not to give in to it. I give it to You, Father. Help us, in Jesus' name, thank You, Amen.'*

TJ wasn't one to 'guess' at things, but on this occasion, he opened the Bible and stuck his finger on the page, thinking God would guide his hand to the right passage. He closed his eyes for a moment then looked where his finger had landed – Psalm chapter four, verse four, and read, "In your anger do not sin; when you are on your beds, search your hearts and be silent." TJ got a cold chill, and the goose bumps came up on his arms and neck. It appeared God was indeed listening. TJ read verse five, "Offer right sacrifices, and trust in the Lord." He took in a deep breath and closed his Bible. *Don't let my anger be sinful, search my heart, be silent, in other words think, and trust in the Lord,* TJ thought. He looked up at the wall of books across from where he was sitting and went into heavy thinking mode.

Donna came in and seeing TJ in the library, went over and looked at him through the doorway. She could see he was in deep thought – his thousand-yard stare - looking at the wall of books but not seeing anything, so she silently turned for the kitchen, poured herself some tea and went back out on the porch. She would leave him be knowing his mind was in a far-off place.

After almost fifteen minutes, TJ opened his Bible again and pointing once again, noted he was in the New Testament book of James, chapter one, verse nineteen and read, "My dear brothers, take note of this: Everyone should be quick to listen, slow to speak, and slow to become angry, for man's anger does not bring about the righteous life that God desires." Then verse twenty said, "Therefore, get rid of all moral filth and the evil that is so prevalent and humbly accept the word planted in you, which can save you."

Two for two! He read verse twenty-three - "Do not merely listen to the word and do deceive yourselves. Do what it says." TJ looked up at the wall again and thought, *'Maybe my anger is wrong. Maybe we've done enough to those people and God's telling me to back off, that the continuation of my anger towards them is wrong."*

He sat staring at the wall again, thinking for quite some time, finally getting up and with his Bible in hand, gathered his Henry and Colt, then taking a few quick food items, namely jerky, left the house, told Donna he was going riding to think, gave her a kiss and headed for the barn. He saddled Dusty, tied a bedroll to his saddle bags, added a few water bottles, put his Henry in the scabbard after ensuring it was loaded, mounted, and rode out, giving a wave to Donna as he rode by.

Donna just nodded and returned the hand-kiss TJ gave her. She had watched him go to the barn and come out with Dusty a few minutes later. She knew he was troubled over something and let him be. Growing up with her father and four brothers, she knew the mood TJ was in and knew he needed space and to be alone. She quietly watched him ride down the hill towards the southeast pasture, knowing he would cross the creek and go someplace to be alone and work it out. With it being late, she worried about his safety but let him go. She knew he needed time…and solitude.

TJ turned Dusty for the creek and crossed where Doug had built the emergency crossing. Once on the other side, he rode across the pasture, crossed the main road turning Dusty to the north in the valley flats. He gave Dusty the reigns and let him go. The two rode in silence, with Dusty's hooves making little or no noise in the thick, moist early spring grass of the valley.

After a while, Dusty came to a stop in the little meadow where Doug had built the fire ring. TJ snapped out of his thinking, realizing they'd stopped, and seeing they were in the meadow and smiling, reached down and gave Dusty a pat on the neck. The animal, by instinct, knew TJ's mood and that he needed time, and this was the place for it. TJ dismounted with his Bible and Henry, built himself a fire, and laid out his bedroll. He unsaddled Dusty then sat cross-legged, leaning against his saddle, with his Henry across his lap and his Bible in his hands. He said another quick, silent prayer asking for God's direction and opened the book.

His finger found John, chapter fourteen and began with verse one, and Jesus was speaking, saying, "Do not let your hearts be troubled. Trust in God; trust also in me." TJ thought to himself: *Well, that was rather blunt, Father in Heaven…You know I trust in you and especially in Your Son.* He turned more pages and his finger found Paul's letter to the Romans, chapter two, verse eight which said, "But for those who are self-seeking and who reject the truth and follow evil, there will be wrath and anger." Now a different turn – *who's going to give the wrath and anger? God…me…Jesus…the Marines?* He felt confused.

TJ thought about that for a while and throwing more wood on the fire he turned pages in his Bible again and his finger found Paul's letter to the Ephesians, chapter four, verse twenty-six and read, "In your anger do not sin. Do not let the sun go down while you are still angry, and do not give the devil a foothold."

He felt he was getting mixed signals. He knew he needed to watch his anger and not let it develop into a sinful state. He knew he needed to trust in the Lord Jesus. He knew God used people on earth to do his bidding against evil, just look at

Joshua in the Old Testament and the story of David and Goliath. But TJ felt he was being held back for some reason. Maybe he wasn't supposed to go on the recon, let the other four go by themselves…. He just wasn't sure.

He turned pages in his Bible once again and read from Hebrews, chapter three, verse eleven, "So I declare on oath in my anger, 'They shall never enter my rest.'" What? TJ was worried now, thinking his anger was sinful. He turned to the middle of the book and slammed his finger down, his anger rising at God and His word, and landed on Psalm forty-six, verse ten, "Be still, and know I am God." He felt as though he could bend nails with his fingers. *Be still…*' okay, he could be still and contemplate what he'd read.

He angrily got up and threw five more logs on the fire, stood there, and watched the flames catch on the new fuel. He walked around the small meadow a few times, actually stomped, and just because he could, he grabbed his Bible and turned again to a page, this time placing his finger on it instead of slamming it down, and read from the Gospel of Mark, chapter six, and saw in red letters, Jesus saying, "Come with me by yourselves to a quiet place and get some rest."

Well, he was at a quiet place and knew he could rest. He looked at Dusty, who just happened to be looking at TJ, shook his head, and said, "Come on boy; let me give you a rub down. We're staying the night." TJ let the horse roam the small meadow, browsing on the lush grass. TJ had laid out the saddle blanket from Dusty, readjusted the saddle on it, and was using it again as a back rest. He settled in once again and with his head down, staring at the flames dancing in the moss-rock fire ring, and thought about the Bible verses he'd read.

Donna, with her binoculars, climbed out of the eastern portal of the Underground and moved to the eastern lip of the mountain. She brought the binos up and scanned the valley below, searching for TJ. She was worried he and Dusty had not returned. She spotted the tendril of smoke climbing out of the aspen stand and rightly assumed it was TJ, and that he had set up camp for the night. She did remember he had a bedroll on the back of his saddle. Satisfied, but still worried, she gave a small harrumph and went back inside.

TJ woke startled and freezing. The fire had died down to a few embers and night had fallen. TJ was thirsty and somewhat hungry. First things first, he placed a healthy amount of wood on the embers, fanning them with his Stetson until a flame caught, adding some tender and soon had the fire going once again. He retrieved a water bottle and drained half of the fluid, then got out some jerky and granola. He sat quietly and munched on his make-shift meal, sipping water from time-to-time.

He felt God had a funny way of communicating with humans. In the past, TJ had prayed for guidance and on occasion received clear direction in some form or another. A few occasions it was as if the phone wasn't connected at all and received no indication on what to do. On this occasion, however, the message was, he felt, somewhat garbled. Told to not be angry and to be still, to think about what he needed to do. He wondered if he was supposed to go on the recon to Colorado or not. And what about his angry feelings towards the Colorado issue?

He turned and got his Bible again, adjusted the saddle so he could use the flames from the fire as a light, and opened the precious book and placed his finger on a passage. It was Proverbs, chapter twenty-eight, verse five, which said, "Evil men do not understand justice, but those who seek the Lord understand it fully." *Am I evil, or are they?* TJ thought to himself. He looked at the Bible again and his eyes came to rest on the previous chapter of Proverbs, twenty-seven, verse twelve and read, "The prudent see danger and take refuge."

Okay, perhaps God was telling him what to do. He'd told him to be still, to find a quiet place, and now to take refuge. He closed his Bible and placing it in the saddlebags, reached over and put more wood on the fire, got comfortable watching the flames and covered up with his bedroll. He would rest tonight and decide on what to do tomorrow morning after praying. He said a prayer thanking God for His words and thanked Jesus for His guidance and asked the Holy Spirit to watch over him as he slept. He prayed for blessings for his friends and Donna, and asked God to give some direction to those people in Colorado. Maybe God can make them understand what peace is.

The birds woke TJ the next morning. A heavy fog enveloped the area and the fire had died to almost nothing. He looked around the meadow and Dusty was staring at him as if to say, 'bout time you got up'. "Morning, boy, you get any sleep?" TJ asked the horse. TJ sat up and put several pieces of wood on the embers left in the fire pit, gave them a few fans and seeing the wood smoking, got up and relieved himself in the aspens.

Back at the fire pit, he saw the flames begin and got his last water bottle out of his saddlebags along with several strips of jerky for his breakfast. He stood, staring at the flames, eating the jerky and sipping water, thinking about the things he'd read in the Bible the day before. He felt he had established that he was not to go to Colorado, but to stay in the valley, a quiet place for the most part. He was to rest and contemplate the Lord. The verse from Psalm kept rolling around in his head, "Be still, and know I am God." Be still…*Okay, Lord, I'll be still. But I didn't get anything that said I wasn't supposed to send the other four to recon in Colorado so I'm going to let them go. I'll stay and rest and contemplate You, Father."*

TJ took a last sip of water and a final bite of jerky, pulled his Henry from the saddle scabbard, and told Dusty to stay in camp. He eased into the aspen stand and quietly headed for the river. When he broke out of the trees, a beam of sunlight hit him full in the face. Everywhere else the fog was thick, but this small hole in the blanket of cover put a beam of sunlight on him, warming him. He stood there with his arms outstretched; the Henry in his right hand, eyes closed and facing the sunlight, letting it bathe him in warmth. It was as if the moment was for him and him alone. He felt honored by God to have this beam of sunlight as his very own.

He heard Dusty whinny and stomp a few times. He smiled turning and eased back through the aspens to the meadow. He saddled Dusty, then went back to the river and filled both empty water bottles and used that to douse what remained of the fire. He policed up the area and mounted Dusty and turned for Paradise Valley.

He had work to do, breaking ground for the spring planting, making a dug-out area for the underground greenhouses and doing some other repairs around the barn and garage. He would make time for rest and contemplation up on the Underground also. As he rode for home, he felt more and more confident he was doing what God wanted. By the time he reached the barn, he knew indeed he was not to go on the recon, but also knew he was to send the others. Once inside, he said a quick prayer thanking God for His input then happily unsaddled Dusty, giving him a rub down and fed him. TJ gathered the morning's eggs and left the barn for the house.

Chapter 2: Chores and Recon

Dusty got a half can of grain along with two flakes of hay, some fresh water, and a nice rub-down from TJ. After gathering the eggs from the chickens, TJ headed for the house. He had seen smoke rising from the chimney so knew Donna was up, and that meant the coffee was probably ready also.

Opening the door to the house, he found Donna standing there with her hands on her hips. Uh-oh, a clear sign she wasn't too happy. "Morning babe - you sleep well?" TJ asked, meekly.

"Could have been warmer…if my man had been in the bed with me that is," she answered sharply.

"Uh, Dusty and I slept down near the river," he told her.

"Get some coffee and put those eggs up and that Henry," she told him.

"You want me to fix you a couple of these?" he asked her, leaning his Henry against the door jamb.

"Sure, over easy with sausage and toast," she answered.

He turned for the kitchen, put the eggs in the refrigerator, save four, and poured himself a mug of coffee. He noted she had gone over to the fireplace and put in a few logs and sat on the couch. He'd make breakfast and keep his mouth shut until she was cooled down…or warmed up by the fire. He put the Henry on the rifle rack, his Stetson on the hat peg then concentrated on breakfast and keeping quiet. Surely this isn't what God had meant about being quiet!

Breakfast ready, he set the table and called her over. He said a quick prayer of thanks for the food and took his first bite.

"Where did you go?" she asked.

He held up a finger while finishing a bite of sausage then answered, "Dusty and I rode around the flats for a bit and camped by the river."

"Did I do something wrong?" she sternly asked.

"No," he almost yelled. "I needed some time to think, and I was reading my Bible a lot."

"What were you thinking about?"

His fork was mid-way to his mouth when the question came. He stopped and said, "I've had a lot on my mind about drones, Colorado, and black hummers and what to do about them – and my anger towards them. I prayed and asked God for guidance." He quickly brought up the fork-full of eggs to his mouth wanting to eat while the food was hot.

"What did you learn from the Bible and your prayer?"

He finished chewing and answered, "I need to take a step back. I'm sure God doesn't want me to go on the recon with Dan, Julia, Jack, and Jeff. I got a clear indication that I needed to stay in the valley, rest, think about the Bible readings and God, and get control of my anger towards the Colorado group."

"You got all that from praying?"

"And reading the Bible; I'm still a bit confused on what I need to do on a few issues, but I got a clear understanding that I needed to take control of my anger, not to let it turn into something sinful. I really got an indication that I needed to slow down, rest, and contemplate God, Jesus, and the Holy Spirit. I know for sure that is one of the directions I need to take."

"So, what are you going to do, and what are you going to tell Dan and them?"

"I got a green light indication for them to go so I think they'll be fine going to do the recon. I'm sure Dan and Julia will understand. They're pretty level-headed and will know where I'm coming from when I explain my reasoning."

"When are you going to tell them?"

He finished chewing a bite of toast he'd put egg on and said, "I'm going over in just a bit. You want to tag along just to get out?"

"Yes."

"Afterwards, I'm coming back and begin digging the pits for the underground greenhouses. That should give me plenty of time to think about the messages I got. I'm going to read the Bible some more, too. When I take breaks and such, I'll open and read it some."

He got up and picking up their dishes, washed and dried them and put them away. He went out and opened the garage and pulled out the ATV and made sure it had all the necessary supplies and equipment they took every time they went out.

Donna came out after getting Z'd up and got in the ATV. TJ pulled his Colt and made sure it was loaded, checked his M4 and got in himself and pulled out. They took a left on the road and went the long way around. Going around the 'block' as they called it, served several purposes: it let her cool off, let him think a little more on what he would say to Dan and the others, and let them get a bit of a recon of the valley done to report to the others.

After they'd turned south on Highway 11, TJ got on the citizens band radio and called Dan and told him to meet them at Julia and Ruth's for a quick meeting.

"What's up?" Dan asked him.

"I have news and will be there in five," TJ answered.

"Okay, brother, heading over now, out," Dan said over the net.

TJ and Donna pulled into the ladies' drive and parked just as Dan walked up - perfect timing. Donna got out and gave Dan a hug and went up the steps to the porch, knocking on the door. TJ and Dan shook hands and followed Donna up the steps.

Ruth answered the door and said, "I thought I heard your ATV pulling in. Glad to see you, what's up?"

Donna said, "TJ needs to talk to Julia and Dan, so I tagged along to see you and DD. How's he doing?"

"He's coming along fine, growing like a weed," Ruth said. "Come on in everyone. Julia – company's here!"

Julia came down the stairs smiling, and welcomed everyone and asked, "Everyone for a mug of coffee?"

Head nods from everyone except Donna, as she had gone for DD and picked him up. The little tyke giggled every time she did that. "You know your Aunt Donna is here, don't you boy?"

Julia poured Dan, TJ, Ruth, and herself a mug of Joe and passed them out and asked, "What's up?"

"I need to talk to you and Dan for a few minutes if I may," TJ explained, motioning to the front porch. Ruth went into the living room with Donna and DD.

Out on the porch, Julia sat in one of the deck chairs as did Dan, and TJ began explaining what had happened to him and why. The two listened to him attentively and from time-to-time nodded understanding. After he finished explaining everything, he asked if they had questions. Both said they didn't, and both fully understood his reasoning.

Dan said, "I think you're doing the right thing. I think the four of us can cover the area in two teams and with the drones. I still think the plan we have is a good one and haven't thought any changes are needed. We'll be leaving tomorrow morning and I think we need to offer to Ruth that she and DD might want to consider moving in with you guys while we're gone, if that'd be okay with you."

"I think it would be wonderful," TJ said with a smile. "I'd love to have DD over for a week or so. It would be a great scenery change around our place to have a baby in the house."

Julia laughed as did Dan. Julia said, "I don't think she will, but we'll see." She stood and said, "Come on in, guys."

They went back inside and posed the question to Ruth. She thought for a minute and said, "I think that would be a welcomed change, like a mini vacation of sorts. I'll pack some things for the two of us and we'll be over in the morning with the others – that okay?"

Donna said, "Absolutely. We're going to have a blast," she exclaimed holding DD up above her head. He giggled with his baby's laugh. Everyone smiled. Donna handed DD back to Ruth and asked if she could help pack their things. Ruth was happy for the offer, agreeing, and they headed up the stairs together.

TJ looked at Julia and Dan and asked, "Is there anything we have you need for the recon? If so, I'll have it ready for you in the morning."

Dan shook his head and said, "I can't think of anything, other than Donna's coffee. We've already loaded the two trucks and hooked up the trailer."

"I can't think of anything either," Julia said. "If I do between now and tomorrow morning, I'll let you know."

"Yeah, what she said," Dan said with a chuckle.

"When you get back, we'll have a feast at our place," TJ promised. "What do you want to have?"

Julia was first saying, "Comfort food that you and Donna make. I love her fried chicken and your fresh bread."

"Oh, I'm in on that, too," Dan said. "And have a bottle of your finest ready to go, too."

"That'll be no problem," TJ said with a smile. "Comfort food and scotch it is and the coffee for tomorrow morning."

"What are you going to do while we're gone?" Donna asked.

"I'm going to start the pits for the underground greenhouses," TJ answered. "I may even go over to Laramie and get those windows like we'd planned. I'll pick up some more PVC piping, too, and some more lumber for the supports and floors."

"Pallets," Dan said.

"What?" TJ returned.

"Pallets for the floor," Dan answered. "I'd use pallets for the floor. If they rot, we can easily replace them and there are zillions of them lying about. A ready-made floor if you ask me."

"That's a great idea," TJ said. "I'll take a trailer and bring a load back. Good idea and simple. I'll lay a floor of pallets then build the plant stands on top."

"Now you're talking," Dan said.

Ruth and Donna came down then and said DD was down for a nap. They said their farewells and that they would see them in the morning got back in the ATV and TJ and Donna went home. Once there, Donna made dinner and after they ate, they sat together in the living room, TJ holding his Bible in his lap.

"You going to open that and read, or just hold it?" Donna asked him.

"Yes," TJ answered.

She gave him a questioning look and said, "Yes, what?"

"Yes, I'm going to open it. Yes, I'm going to read it. Yes, I'm going to hold it."

"I'm not trying to be argumentative, just wondering what's up with you – you've got me concerned. I mean, yesterday you took off and were gone overnight. Today we go to a mystery meeting you had with Julia and Dan. Then I learn you're not going on the Colorado recon. What's going on? You sick or something?"

"No, not sick. I'm not getting answers. Not about us, no problems between us. I'm just getting mixed signals about what I need to do about the Colorado issue," TJ explained. He went ahead and told her the whole story, about the scripture he read, the prayers, the feelings…everything.

She snuggled in closer to him. They stayed like that for a while. Finally, TJ opened the Bible and turned to the Gospel of John, chapter three and read his favorite verse, sixteen: "For God so loved the world that he gave his one and only Son, that whoever believes in him shall not perish but have eternal life." He looked at Donna curled up next to him and said, "I really believe in Jesus and that He is God's Son."

"I do, too," Donna mumbled. She was obviously about to fall asleep, so TJ became quiet, keeping his reading and his thoughts to himself.

TJ wondered if God had him stay behind for a reason and if so, for what purpose, for what reason. TJ took about a half of the pages in the Bible in his fingers and turned the bulk of pages to his right and found himself reading Psalm, chapter one thirty-eight, verse eight, "The Lord will fulfill his purpose for me: your love, O Lord, endures forever – do not abandon the works of your hands."

TJ looked up at the flames in the fire and thought *I am the works of God's hands, along with the earth. He made both - everything. His purpose for me will be fulfilled by Him. I guess I'm just along for the ride. NO! That's wrong. I still have to make a conscious choice. It may be His will, but it's a choice I have to decide to make – I think.*

He woke Donna and throwing two logs on the fire and placing the screen in front of the flames, the pair went to bed. The next day would be a long one, what with the team leaving on the recon early then TJ beginning work on the underground greenhouses.

The alarm went off at three thirty in the morning, jarring TJ, and Donna out of deep sleep. TJ rolled over and turned it off, got up, went into the bath, relieved himself then washed up and brushed his teeth. He would wait to take a shower until after the dirty work for the greenhouses was done. He thought he might even take a jet-tub bath tonight as hot as he could get it just to soak and relax.

He went downstairs, turned the coffee on, and went out the front door, standing on the porch. The morning was quiet, and bazillions of stars were twinkling in the heavens. Since the power grid failed, the night sky was more brilliant than TJ had ever seen it. He always marveled at the sight of the Milky Way's great expanse in the night sky and it sometimes scared him knowing God had spoken it into existence. Too, he marveled that out of the whole expanse of space, he and his fellow humans were the most important things to God, Jesus, and the Holy Spirit. Still, even with that knowledge, he felt rather small in the scheme of things.

He noticed light on the southern ridge and could see two sets of lights making their way down the ridge. That would be the team and they would be here in ten minutes or so. TJ went back inside and poured himself a mug of coffee and saw Donna coming down the stairs in her robe.

"After they leave, I'm going back to bed," she announced.

"You want some coffee?" TJ asked her.

"No, not yet - later, thanks - but I better make that batch Dan wants," she answered. She came into the kitchen and TJ gave her a kiss. She made coffee for the travelers then together they went outside and stood on the porch.

TJ pointed up and said, "Isn't it beautiful?"

Donna looked up and said, "Yes, it is. I can't believe how brilliant it has become since the lights went out and the air pollution has dissipated. I guess the light pollution, as they called it, had a greater impact on viewing stars than I knew. It's amazing how brilliant it is. It's beautiful, huh?"

"Makes me feel small…real small," TJ admitted. "I sometimes have a hard time wrapping my mind around the fact that out of all of that, we mere humans are the most important thing to God. Really makes me feel small. Reminds me of a video of a sermon I saw called, '*How Great is Our God*,' by Loui Giglio. That was a great video and gave a whole new meaning to what I thought of a golf ball."

"I haven't seen that. You'll have to tell me about the golf ball sometime. We'll have to find the video then watch it and we'll talk about it more. Here they come," Donna said pointing down the lane.

TJ reached inside the door and pushed the remote button, opening the gate. The two trucks pulled into the front yard and stopped. Dan got out as did Jeff, and together they sauntered over to the porch. Dan quietly said, "Mornin'. You two okay?"

"Right as rain," TJ answered. "You're ready to go I see."

"Yep, ready as we'll ever be," Dan replied.

"You have everything you need? Anything we have you thought you might need other than this coffee?" Donna asked handing him two thermoses of her brew.

"Thank you…we're set and I'm confident we have everything we need," Dan told them. "We've decided to go down Highway 287 into Fort Collins. We're going to get another trailer at the farm store and another fuel tank outfit down there. That'll benefit us all around getting another set, especially if we have to bug out."

"Good thinking," TJ said.

"Well, the travel mugs are full so we should head out," Jeff said. Thanks for everything. Ruth said they would be over later on this afternoon. Come on, boss, let's get on the road," he said to Dan and turned for his truck. They paused together and said a prayer for the protection and safe return of the team.

Dan shook TJ's hand and gave Donna a peck on the cheek and turned for his truck. Donna ran up to Julia's window and gave her a hug and told her to be careful. TJ shook hands with Jack and Jeff and told Jack they would go get those apple trees when he got back. They all waved, and the team left the valley.

TJ closed the gate then went inside and topped off his coffee mug. He and Donna kissed each other, and she went back upstairs to the bedroom, he leaving the house going to the barn and taking care of the animals. Dusty barely gave him notice as he entered. TJ took care of the barn chores and collected what eggs there were in the coop. He took them to the kitchen and placed them in the basket on the counter.

He quietly left the house and going to the garage, went inside and gathered the plans they had drawn up for the greenhouses and studied them some more. He would first go out and using stakes measure and stakeout the dimensions of the complex at the site they'd chosen. He had several cans of orange paint he would use to mark the ground in preparation for the backhoe work. Other preparatory work he'd already done was to fell several trees on the east side of the yard, near the barn. This is where he would dump the dirt he dug out. It would extend the front yard by several meters and he would brace the dirt by building a retaining wall of stone.

He got the stakes and put them in the back of the ATV, then the paint cans, his gloves, and several water bottles. The backhoe was already parked near the site and had a full fuel tank. He went back and studied the plans once more, and getting a hundred-foot tape measure, put it in the ATV. To help keep his lines straight when he used the paint, he had some string he would tie to the stakes about an inch off the ground, paint the lines, and then dig.

By the time he was finished painting lines, he was in the mood for breakfast so went into the house. Donna was up and cooking as he came in.

"Coffee's fresh," she told him, "wash up, get a mug, and sit down."

"Aye, captain," he said washing up at the kitchen sink. She gave him a smack on the backside, and he said, "What was that for?"

"Just because."

"I could arrest you for assaulting a peace officer you know."

"Try it buster…you may be the Sheriff in these here parts, but I'm the boss."

"Gotta give you that, you're one bossy lady."

"So, sit down, cowboy and I'll bring your breakfast over."

They discussed their plans for the day and after cleaning the dishes, he went back outside to begin digging the pit for the first greenhouse. Donna went upstairs to clean up, dress and then she would go out to help.

The southern sides of the two pits would have a ramp TJ had cut into the ends. These would be used to haul supplies and equipment down into the pit until completed then a stairway would be built for access in place of the ramps.

Ruth called them on the radio and said DD was 'in a foul mood' and would wait until the following day to come over.

Relieved, Donna was thankful she wouldn't have to cook a big dinner for their guests but missed them, nonetheless.

By the end of the day, TJ had the first pit dug and the second begun. They had previously collected pine straw and used it as a base covering for the floor. Next, they sat the French-drain into the trench he'd dug in the center of the pit. It, along with the one from the other pit, would connect and drain into the Little Laramie River. Donna then spread gravel they got from the quarry to fill in the channel space and covered the lot with another layer of pine straw. Using the ATV, she then began collecting the pine straw and stone to complete the floor in the second pit. They would go to Laramie and get a load of pallets to make the floors in a day or two.

As the sun went down over the western ridge, the two stopped working and trudged inside after stowing the vehicles. Both were whipped and decided to have sandwiches and fruit for dinner, along with some wine and a jet-tub soaking. They were in bed and out like lights shortly after the bath.

The next day, they began by praying for the recon team and thanked the Lord for giving them the good health they enjoyed. Then back to work and by the end of the second day, were ready to begin building the plant stands for the greenhouses. They would need to run into town, Laramie, for more wood and the pallets. TJ decided they would need additional hardware and nail-gun nails to complete the project and planned to leave the next morning after breakfast.

Ruth and DD had arrived, and Donna asked Ruth if she needed anything from Laramie. Together they made a list and Donna said she and TJ would be back in time to have a movie with popcorn after dinner. Ruth said that would be great and volunteered to fix dinner. What a great lady.

The next morning, TJ and Donna pulled the truck and trailer into the hardware store's lot and parked. They looked around and not seeing any Zs ambling about, got out and went in. They were able to get almost everything on their list and took as much lumber they felt safe to load on the truck and trailer and topped off the load with pallets. TJ felt more than enough to complete the project.

They were in the back of the store in the fenced in area when TJ noticed a Z plodding along the fence line, attracted by the noise they were making loading the pallets. It had been a while since they had seen or were threatened by a Z and that made TJ, the policeman TJ that is, wonder why. Where had they all gone? Not all of them could have been taken out by the eight nuclear weapons detonated around the nation. Maybe they took out a great many of them, but he knew they didn't take out almost three-hundred million. The population of the United States at the time of the pandemic was around three hundred and twenty-five million or so. No way the eight nukes, could take out that many humans or Zs.

TJ got Donna's attention and motioned towards the Z. She drew her suppressed nine and took careful aim. TJ watched as her bullet hit just above the right eye. The creature dropped in its tracks. No sooner than the thing dropped, TJ noticed another Z coming from the same direction as the first. He drew his suppressed nine and got ready.

Donna eased up next to him and together they watched the Z approach. They were not in any real danger as they had closed the gate to the rear of the store. But these days, it paid to take care of any Zs they encountered as a public safety measure more than anything else.

TJ was about to pull the trigger on the thing when Donna poked him in the side. He looked at her and she pointed behind the Z, and following her finger, he saw several more Zs approaching. Again, the cop in TJ brought up more questions, one of which was where were these things coming from?

The two humans moved closer to the fence line for better shooting and got down to business. TJ fired first and the closest Z dropped with a round to the head. Donna put in her ear plugs just in case and motioned for TJ to do the same. Hearing protection in, TJ brought his nine up once again and fired into the crowd of Zs coming their way. One dropped, as did another with the next round.

Now a mass of Zs had gathered and was getting too close. Together, they may have been enough to topple the fence, so Donna opened fire with her twelve-gauge shotgun and with the first shot several dropped. That was all well and good, however the report from the shotgun definitely woke up the area. They no longer faced just a few Zs, but now it looked as if a horde was forming and that being the case, they were in real danger.

TJ ran back to the truck and grabbed their M4s and magazine vests and ran back to Donna. He handed her a set and they got ready. TJ was quicker and began firing with his M4 into the throng nearing their position. Donna quickly followed suite but using her shotgun instead. They fired round after round and still the mass of creatures continued forming at the fence. TJ yelled, "We may need to retreat into the store if they begin to wobble that fence."

"I was already thinking that," Donna yelled back after firing another round of buckshot into the mass. "You want me to go and get the door open and something to block it with?"

"Let's fire another mag full then run," TJ yelled back.

She quickly reloaded her twelve and he switched out his spent mag and inserted another. TJ cut loose with his fire and dropping the closest Zs to the fence noted they were beginning to pile up. Donna fired rapidly into the greater mass of the creatures dropping many. The remainder were having trouble negotiating the bodies piling up to their front.

TJ emptied his mag and pulled two grenades. He waited until Donna emptied her twelve and told her to get inside and he would be along in a second. He pulled the pins on the grenades and threw them into the largest congregation of zombies. He ran to the rear store entrance and Donna slammed the door as he slid through the doorway. As he turned to help brace and lock the door, they heard the two grenades explode.

"To the front so we can see what they're doing," TJ said. They ran to the front and peering around the corner through the glass front, saw the grenades he'd thrown had dropped more of the things, but there were still well over fifty of the creatures heading for the fence – which was weakening. Behind those, many more were ambling along and congregating with the others. TJ and Donna were now in grave danger.

"You think we'll be safe enough in here?" Donna asked.

"I think so; haven't heard of any of them busting through glass so maybe," he answered.

"Where do you think they came from?"

"I've been wondering that myself. Looking at their clothing, not too many are farm or ranch people. Most look like city workers, office types, you know?"

"I suppose. How are you on ammo?"

He patted his chest rig and said, "Five full mags, two more grenades, almost a full load of nine and a full load of twelve-gauge, since I haven't used it yet. How about you?"

"I'm about out of twelve-gauge, almost a full load of nine, full load for the M4, and four grenades."

"That should do us for a while. There's a good amount of extra ammo in the truck, but it could be dicey getting to it later. Come on, let's go back to the break area and see if we can find some water. I could use a bottle. Anyway, if we go back there and get quiet, those things will lose interest and move away. Afterwards we can clear enough bodies to get the truck out."

They went to the back of the store and found some water bottles and drank their fill, sitting at a small table. Neither spoke, keeping their thoughts to themselves.

TJ was the one that broke the silence saying, "We should wait an hour or so and let them get bored with trying to find us and move on…hopefully. We'll just wait it out here and rest."

Donna agreed and got out of the chair and lay on the floor to nap. TJ told her he would go back to the front to watch.

The Zs were still focusing on the fence line as he peered out the window. There were now at least hundred or more of the things and he could see more moving into the parking lot from the west. Even if they wanted to drive out, they would have to clear the mounds of bodies before they could pass. For now, the fence was holding. For how long, he didn't have a guess. He thought about other ways of drawing the Zs away but had no immediate answers. It was perplexing the creatures were continuing to mass at the fence even though there was no longer any noise being made. TJ felt they should be leaving by now. He moved back into the store and sitting behind a counter watched the front.

By mid-afternoon, the mass of Zs had swelled to well over two hundred. The fence still held but was weakening as TJ and Donna could see it waver.

"I've never seen them stay this focused on something this long before, have you?" Donna asked.

"No, and that bothers me," TJ answered. "It's as if they suddenly have reasoning power again. If they do, then all of mankind is in trouble. If these things can think now, the world is woefully in trouble. Do you know if there is another way out of the back so we can get the truck and trailer out?"

"No, sorry, I don't. Let's take a look out the front and see if we can see one."

They moved back peered around the side of the window. From what they could see on the west, north and east sides, the fence, which was about twelve feet in height, ran completely around the rear of the store. They didn't have a view to the south so moved to that side of the store to see if they could view that direction. They could find no doors or windows so had no idea what was there or if they could drive out that route.

Back near the front, they could see more Zs trooping in from the west. TJ looked at Donna and said, "We're definitely in trouble. There's got to be near three hundred of 'em out there now. The fence is weakening. If we're going to make a move, it'll need to be soon. I think I should try to get out the back and move to the south and see what's there and if we can get out that way. It may be our only hope."

"Let's think this through for a minute. I agree with you we need to see what's to the south, but let's think about going out the back. I'm thinking there may be another way."

"What's that?"

"The roof - maybe there's access from inside the store to the roof and we could look from there."

"Now you're thinking outta the box – come on."

The two ran to the rear of the store and looked for an access stairway or ladder. Donna was the fortunate one and found a ladder leading up to a hatchway that had a lock. She climbed up and tried the lock, which was secured tightly. She called for TJ and he saw the ladder and the cover, so went up and pulled and yanked on the lock to no avail. He pulled his nine and hesitated. In the hemmed in space, he may be in danger of getting hit by the ricocheting bullet.

He was about to pull the trigger when he felt a tug on his leg. Looking down, he saw Donna standing there holding up a crowbar to him. He holstered his nine, took the crowbar, and used it to dislodge the lock. It took several heaves, but it finally gave, and TJ opened the access panel to the roof and climbed out, and Donna quickly followed. They moved over to the south side and although the fence went completely around to the corner of the building, a space was clear enough for them to get the truck through the fence. They looked at each other and smiled.

Donna asked, "Will the truck be able to bust through that fence?"

"I'm sure it will, but I think we need to give it some help by cutting the tie-down wires holding it to the poles. That should free the tension enough for us to push through and under the wire. You have everything you wanted from here?"

"Yes, let's get outta here."

They went back inside, closing the roof access panel and went to the back door. TJ told Donna to wait there, and he ran to the front to see what the Zs were doing and if the fence still held. He ran back to Donna and told her it was holding for the time being and he suggested when they go out, he would run and cut the wires on the fence while she threw grenades into the mass of creatures, ducking behind the truck as they went off. Once he got back, they would get in the truck and pull out. Sounded like a good plan.

TJ ran and got a heavy-duty pair of bolt cutters, not taking any chances, and ran back to Donna. She had taped paper and cut up boxes to the glass in the door so the creatures wouldn't be able to see TJ slip out and go around to the south side. He smiled and gave her a thumb up. They made sure their weapons were loaded and she loosened the grenades she had in her chest rig. TJ handed her his last two and she slowly opened the door for TJ to slip out.

He scooted around the end of the building on the south side and got to the fence and began cutting the wire holding the fencing to the poles. He reached as high as his arms would allow and had both sides and along the crossbar cut in no time. He ran back to the corner of the building and seeing Donna peering from the slightly ajar door, he counted with his fingers - one, two, three, and he made for the truck. Donna stepped out with pins already pulled from two of her grenades and threw them over the fence, ducking behind the truck. When they blew, she threw two more and heard TJ starting the truck.

Her two grenades went off and she got up, opened the passenger door, threw the last grenades, jumped in, and ducked behind the dash. TJ pulled the truck into a tight turn in the space they had and pulled around to the south side. Donna pulled the pouch with the extra grenades from the back and put four in her vest and handed four more to TJ.

He pulled the truck up near the fence and looking at her said, "Here goes nothing," and pressed on the gas pedal. They went through with horrible scraping and squealing sounds - the truck would need a paint job - and they lost several pallets. TJ turned to the east and headed down the avenue to the big mart store to finish getting the things on their list.

There wasn't much left on the list and most of it was for the baby and mother back in the valley. Donna would make the mad dash inside, gather the materials, and get back out to the truck as fast as she could. TJ parked at the entrance and after looking around, Donna jumped out and went inside after unlocking the chain.

She grabbed two carts and flew down the aisles to the baby department.   It took her about fifteen minutes but had everything on the list and added as many packs of the diapers as she could handle on the two carts.

Back outside, as soon as she pushed the carts out, TJ grabbed one and began unloading the supplies into the truck's back seat. Donna locked the chain and helped with the second cart. As they finished, they could see Zs coming down the avenue towards them. They got back in the cab, started the truck, and continued east, pulling out onto I-80, and steering for home.

As they turned onto Highway 130 and heading west, they began to breathe easier. "That was close," TJ said.

"No foolin'," Donna agreed. "Makes me wonder where they all came from. We should have brought one of the dogs. They may have warned us well before we got into that situation."

"Next time we will," TJ agreed. He floored the truck as Ruth and DD would be fixing dinner, so they wanted to be home on time. If not, they knew she would worry. "I've never seen the Zs do that before – it was as if they had thought processes again or were being controlled some way to focus on us. I'm wondering if those nuts from the Colorado complex, did something to the Judith signal to make these things converge like that."

"Next time, huh…I'm not sure I want a next time. That's the most zombies we've seen in quite a while. It doesn't make sense does it? And if it is something from that complex, we may really be in danger."

"No, it doesn't make sense. Scary if you ask me."

"I'm with you there.   I wonder if they migrated or something, maybe from Cheyenne or Fort Collins or somewhere."

"Your guess is as good as mine, my lady," TJ responded. "Everything about the plague and the aftermath is a big unanswered question if you ask me. We cannot predict what they do, how they act or react, where they all come from. The list of questions goes on and on. Looking at the clothing most of those things wore, they weren't from around here," the Sheriff in TJ contemplated out loud.

"I do wonder if the Colorado complex had anything to do with that."

TJ almost wrecked the truck. He stopped in the middle of the highway and looked at Donna; "What?" she said.

"What you just said, about the complex in Colorado. What if they've planted transmitters around Laramie and turned that signal on over here somewhere and that's what's bringing them in?"

Now she was looking at him with wide eyes and wonder. It seemed to be the most logical explanation they could come up with as they both stared at each other. "We gotta get back quick and talk with Ruth about this since she knows more about it than we do," TJ said, starting the truck and moving once again. He floored the truck and sped back to the valley, flying into and up their lane.

They dropped the trailer near the construction site and unloaded the truck at the garage as fast as they could, and Donna went inside to help with dinner and talk with Ruth. Ruth and DD were already working on dinner. TJ left all the baby supplies and the other things Ruth wanted on the porch.

He went inside to wash up and told the ladies dinner smelled great. He and Donna told Ruth about the danger from the zombie threat. Then during dinner, Ruth told them everything she knew about the Judith signal and the things the Doc had discussed with them about the Zombie threat. The information, for the most part, was info TJ and Donna were already aware of so very little was helpful. They did know that if the Colorado people were up to something they needed to find out quickly and try to combat it.

Until he knew for sure they were safe beyond a shadow of a doubt, TJ decided he would increase security measures around the ranch to their fullest. That meant weapons and ammunition near every door, additional munitions up to the Underground, and he would have to ride the fence line the next day to check for damage. If he needed to he would put the construction project on hold so he could improve the defenses around Paradise Valley and around Ruth's and DD's home. The greenhouses would have to wait.

Chapter 3: Danger Afoot

TJ returned from cleaning up and grabbed DD and held him up above his head, an action one could tell the little tyke enjoyed to no end by the amount of giggling and the smiles he always had when held aloft. "Kid's going to love high places when he gets older. You won't be able to keep him out of trees," he told Ruth.

"Don't I know it. And with a sheriff and three Marines for surrogate fathers and grandfathers, heaven only knows what he'll be doing by the time he's ten," Ruth said with a chuckle.

TJ quickly said, "I'm gonna make a Ranger outta him."

Donna came over and gave Ruth a hug and held out her hands to TJ for the baby. "No," TJ said flatly. "He's playing with Uncle TJ right now."

"We'll see," Donna said to him with a leer. "Get to the table; dinner will be ready in a few minutes."

"Yes, oh maternal one," he said and scooted towards the table.

Ruth followed Donna into the kitchen saying, "What can I do to help?"

"Would you set the table?"

"Love to. You and TJ doing okay?"

"Yes, well maybe not today."

"What…what happened?" Ruth asked suddenly worried.

"We ran into a horde in Laramie and had a touch and go situation there for a while. We killed about fifty of them but there were still around three hundred or more when we escaped."

Ruth was looking at Donna wide eyed, with her mouth open in surprise. She swallowed and said, "We haven't been in that kind of danger for a long, long time. Where did they come from?"

"We asked each other that very question and want to talk to you about it more over dinner."

TJ walked up and said, "Talk about what?"

"I was telling her about what happened in Laramie," Donna told him, "and told her we wanted to talk about it over dinner."

"It was a close one, that's for sure," TJ said.

Ruth looked at TJ and asked, "Where do you think they came from and for that matter, what do you think is going on to bring them in like that?"

"Donna and I have a gut feeling that since we've been so fortunate with our attacks and defense against the Colorado people, we think they've gone on the offensive against us by setting off that Judith signal somewhere close by. I have a feeling that's what's bringing the Zs in. The number of them we saw I haven't seen in quite some time. It was a real horde of around four-hundred creatures, with more coming in, and they were definitely coming for us. I've never seen Zs be so focused before and for such an extended period of time. We think the noise we were making loading the lumber brought them in and it just escalated from there. But now that I've been thinking about it, it may be that the Colorado people have figured out a way to control those things and drive or steer them in a direction they want."

"I guess that makes the only sense, the Judith signal drawing them in that is. I hope it's not what you say, and they've found a way to control them. That would put us and the rest of the remaining humans in extreme danger. I hope the team is alright," Ruth whispered.

"That's been on my mind, too," TJ agreed. "Hopefully, they made it through before the horde formed. We certainly didn't see them when we went in, nor as we left town. Have your dog's been acting funny lately?" TJ asked Ruth.

"Not really, Little Bit was staring at something to the east the other day when we were out, but the other dog didn't react," Ruth answered. "I thought it might be a rabbit or something. He goes ballistic when a rabbit is around."

"Dinner's ready," Donna said placing the pork chops on the table. The adults sat down, and TJ invited Ruth to say a blessing.

Dinner's conversation was the new zombie outbreak in Laramie and the theories they all made. Most focused on where the creatures had come from, and were the things being controlled in some way. They talked about the dogs' reaction, staring to the east, but came to a dead-end conclusion. Theories were all they had, but with no concrete evidence, they would not know for sure.

So, they put ideas for taking care of the threat out on the table. First up was using the bombers to saturate the horde with explosives. Next was a group effort once the recon team was back, where they would mount M240 Bravos on the hummer and two trucks and hit the threat head on in a running gun battle of sorts, using grenades, thumpers, and the machineguns to reduce the threat. Next, use of saltwater squirt guns and balloons was discussed. But they rejected that as extremely hazardous since they would needlessly allow the creatures to get dangerously close for the saltwater munitions to be effective.

TJ decided that tomorrow he would drive up to the airport and launch a long-range drone and look around Laramie. He knew Laramie very well, even the far eastern edge, which was only about six miles from the airport so the long-range drone would have more than enough range and time on station to look around. He would take two drones with fully charged battery packs, and two additional battery packs in case he found something interesting to observe. As soon as he finished his dinner he would go out to the garage and plug in the packs and Z up the truck with additional AR and twelve-gauge ammo and grenades. He would take his full chest rig as well.

"Tomorrow when I go to the airport, I'll keep the radio on," TJ told Donna. "If you need me or if I need you, we can get in touch with each other."

"I'm going with you," Donna said flatly.

TJ looked at her and after a moment said, "With the threat such as it is, I think you, Ruth and DD should stay here. It would be much safer. Anyway, I'll be in that compound that's just east of the airport. It's fenced in and I'll be safe there. Ruth - you and DD might want to consider staying with Donna and I for a few more days, at least until the others get home. I would feel better knowing you're not alone over at your place."

Ruth looked down at her plate and a moment later said, "I'll go over and pack a few more things. I'll be happy for the two of us to vacation with you for a few more days – it makes too much sense, Sheriff, so I'll be happy to stay. I'll be another gun anyway. After dinner, Donna, would you tag along with me and help me pack a few things?"

"I'd love to," Donna answered.

"I'll keep DD here with me until you get back," TJ said with a smile. "We'll have some fun."

"You just volunteered to feed him then," Ruth said. She got up and rummaging in her bag, brought out some home-made baby food and a bottle for DD, handing the works to TJ. "Here you go."

Donna got up and began taking the dishes off the table. Ruth helped and TJ began to feed the little man of the valley. What a mess, but both were having fun since TJ was doing the 'airplane' thing feeding DD.

"We're going now," Donna said giving TJ a kiss. "We'll be back shortly." She had her chest rig, shotgun, M4 and a nine ready to go. She had even gotten out another shotgun and a bandolier of rounds for Ruth, along with another nine with seven additional magazines.

"Take the truck, it'll be safer," TJ advised.

"I have mine here, TJ," Ruth said with a grin.

"Just be careful and keep your radio on," he said getting up and warming up the base station. "Get," he told the two and went back to feeding DD. The two women left giggling.

"Just you and me, little man," TJ said to DD. "We're going to finish dinner, burp a little, then you can have some of your bottle and I will have some of mine," intending to pour himself a tumbler of scotch. "We'll sit on the front porch and enjoy the view, how's that?"

That's where they were when the ladies returned. DD sound asleep in TJ's lap, wrapped in his blanket, with TJ rocking the boy gently in a rocking chair. TJ reached over getting his tumbler and raised it in a toast to the ladies as they pulled up.

"Well, ain't you a pair," Ruth said with a huge grin on her face.

"He's been a perfect gentleman," TJ quietly told them. "He ate and drank his fill and was out like a light in no time once we got out here." TJ got up with the baby and went inside, laid him on his blanket on the couch and went back out to help the ladies bring in luggage.

When they were finished, they looked on the couch and DD hadn't moved a muscle. Uncle TJ had done a good job and Ruth was impressed.

"Ruth, where do you want to bed down tonight?" Donna asked.

"Guest bedroom ready?" she returned.

"Yep, as always; you sit with DD and TJ and I'll take your stuff up," Donna said with a smile. "Come on, TJ, let's get her room ready."

After they got Ruth and DD situated, TJ went out into the garage, plugged in four sets of battery packs for the drones, and got the machines out. He went over each one with a fine-tooth comb, ensuring the pair was prepared to fly extended missions. He got out four data cards and loaded two and put two in his kit.

He opened the ammo locker and put in a satchel of twelve grenades, two ammo cans of twelve-gauge, double-aught buckshot, a can of .556 caliber ammo along with another filled with full magazines, and one more filled with nine-millimeter ammo. He decided to load a forty-millimeter thumper, adding a box with twenty-five rounds for the weapon. He was ready to go to war if necessary.

Back inside, he got his chest rig, M4, shotgun and nine out and gave them the once over, ensuring they were ready to rock. He checked all the mags making sure they were fully loaded, checked the frags in the vest and gave his combat knife a few licks with a whetstone then reinserted it in the sheath on the left shoulder strap of his chest rig. He took the lot and set it near the door.

"You're ready, I see," Donna said.

"Yeah, I put a bunch of extra ammo and a forty in the truck just in case. I have enough to fight a small war," TJ told her.

"You taking a fifty?" she asked.

"No, don't think that'll be necessary. Have double loads of mags for the M4 and nine, with an extra can of each, two cans of twelve and a full satchel of grenades plus the ones in my vest. I'm good."

She nodded and asked, "Leaving at daylight?" He nodded. "When do you think you'll be back?"

"'Bout noon I figure, maybe sooner."

"I'll fix you a to-go pack then," Donna said.

Smiling he motioned to the stairs and they went to bed.

The next morning found TJ pulling out in the early morning darkness; that time just before the dim light from sunrise began. Donna had gotten up with him fixing him a pot of coffee, a breakfast, the to-go pack of treats, bottled water, and food, and then gave him a free lesson on safety. He really appreciated her concern. She gave him a hug and a kiss and said she was going back to bed.

It took him twenty minutes to get to the enclosure at the airport where he wanted to launch the drones, and once inside, got his equipment and materials out, inserting the battery packs into the drones and preparing both for launch. He had his weapons arrayed around him: shotgun in its sheath on his back right shoulder, M4 on its single point sling hanging to his right, the suppressed nine in its holster, and the forty-millimeter grenade launcher sitting on the hood of the truck along with a few rounds of canister shot…just in case.

He sat in the passenger's seat sipping his coffee, waiting for the sun to peek over the eastern mountain ridge so he could see enough to launch the drone and fly to Laramie safely. The sky was clear, and he could still see stars twinkling in the heavens, but the eastern sky was getting lighter, dimming the star view.

TJ raised his binoculars and looked around. He didn't see any humans or Zs and that was a good thing. He intently looked in the distance for black hummers, trucks, or lights and seeing none of those, prepared the first drone, setting it out thirty feet or so from the truck. He started the engines letting them warm. After a moment, he lifted off to about fifty feet and let the drone hover for a moment, checking the connections and video feed. Everything was in the green, so he turned the craft to the northeast and as he flew, made the craft rise in altitude.

He leveled off at forty-five hundred feet above ground level and flew to the north end of town. By the time the craft reached Laramie, it was light enough for the camera to pick up details. He flew east/west patterns back and forth above Laramie and from north to south. He closely watched the video feed for signs of either Zs or the black vehicles. He'd been flying for almost a half hour and was about ready to turn back to the truck when he saw a mass of Zs in a park in the middle of Laramie. They were massed on the northwest side of the park near some ball fields. There were hundreds of them, possibly a thousand by the looks, congregating around a large tree in between the ball fields. More were pouring in from all directions.

He hovered above the mass for a moment then flew the drone back to where he was and landed. He prepared the second drone making sure the battery pack was fresh and repacked the first. The second drone launch went as planned and after his hover, rose in altitude to five thousand feet AGL, and headed back to the park. Along the way he kept a sharp eye out for black hummers or other vehicles.

Arriving over the park, TJ circled the drone slowly, looking for signs of the people from Colorado. He had the drone hovering over an auto salvage yard that had rows and rows of wrecked or abandoned vehicles and saw in the midst of the bulk of dilapidated cars and trucks, a group of several that were somewhat out of place. They were all black, grouped together similar to wagons circling on the northern end. TJ counted six vehicles. Bingo. He zoomed the camera lens as close as it would allow and watched as men moved about the vehicles. *Too bad I don't have any of the bombers loaded up, I could fix this problem right now,* he thought to himself.

TJ quickly flew the drone back to his position as fast as the craft would fly. After landing, he placed everything in his truck and the police officer literally floored the accelerator to get home. As he got to the bottom of the hill on Highway 130, he radioed the house and Donna answered quickly.

"Get the bombers ready and you get Z'd up. We're going in for a fight."

"What did you find?" she radioed back.

"The mother lode so to speak - be there in a few minutes," he answered and sped on.

After explaining what he'd found when he arrived, they left Ruth, and DD at the house and after loading the bomber drones, he and Donna sped back to the enclosure near the airport. As he parked, he told Donna to get her binoculars out and scan the sky for a drone if the Colorado crew had one. He had packed a Stinger just for the possibility and was ready to use it if need be.

TJ unloaded the bomber drones. They'd brought four with four of their homemade bombs each. The two of them would fly one each, taking eight bombs all together to begin with. Driving over, they discussed tactics and she would follow his drone with hers until they got to the salvage yard. They would hover together to let her get a bird's eye view of the area they were to bomb. Once she had the target identified, they would split, with her flying to the south and TJ staying to the west.

They would bomb the site with her bombing from south to north and vice versa and TJ doing the same from west to east. TJ reminded Donna that the men would be armed so she needed to bob and weave when pulling away from a bombing run. Each would drop two bombs per run.

They had everything ready. Donna had not seen any other drones flying around so they launched their bombers. TJ rose to an altitude of four-thousand feet with Donna flying in formation with him. They headed east, Donna trailing so she could keep his drone in sight with her camera. As he got closer, he could see the rail yard, TJ told Donna he was slowing and to pan her camera due east until she saw the railroad cars lined up.

She found them and said so and he told her to look just past the trains to the east and asked if she could see the wrecking yard. She said she did, and he told her where the black vehicles were congregated on the north side. She had them in view and as they hovered to the west of the salvage yard, he looked at her, smiled and winked then flew his drone to just a bit to the north and she to the south end of the wrecking yard.

They had decided it was to be ladies first so as Donna got about a mile to the south, she turned her drone, spotted the vehicles again, then began her dive. She got to her release point and quickly pressed the button for two of the bombs to drop. As soon as the light showed green for both, she pulled up, jinking her control stick to make her drone bob and weave on the pull-out.

TJ was in a hover and saw Donna's drone dive. He watched as she released the two bombs and followed them down. The first impacted just to the north of the group of vehicles and sent shrapnel and debris everywhere. The second hit between a hummer and a truck and the resulting explosion was a sight. The truck, not as heavy as the hummer, flipped onto its driver side and began to burn.

TJ, after a ten count, flew his drone towards the east and began his dive, making his aim point a bit south of where Donna had released. She would be waiting to the north, watching, and filming the results of his bombing run. He reached his release point and in one second, released his two bombs and began wobbling his control lever making his drone bob and weave on the pull out.

Donna watched the two bombs fall into the parked black vehicles. Several men had jumped out of a panel truck in the group, and she could see them looking around. The first bomb landed in their midst and they disappeared in the explosion of dust, shrapnel, and debris. TJ's second bomb landed next to the panel truck and it exploded into a mass of burning wreckage.

Donna waited for a ten count then dove on her second bombing run. She lined up on the vehicles on the southern side of the group and could see men firing their weapons at her. She jinked her drone a few times but steadied as she neared her release point, dropping her last two bombs then bobbing and weaving as she pulled out.

TJ watched her bombs fly true, with the first landing between two vehicles blowing both onto their sides, one burning. The second bomb hit in the midst of the men firing at her drone and detonated, ending that threat.

TJ gave a ten count and began his second run, deciding to drop his bombs into the middle of the group. He could now see at least four of the six vehicles burning, and one on its driver's side burning next to a hummer. The hummer and one other vehicle appeared to be intact, so TJ made the attempt to hit both. Releasing his first bomb on the western most truck and his second a half-second later at the hummer then pulled out of his dive weaving as best he could.

Donna, in her hover, watched as TJ's first bomb landed between a burning vehicle and a truck. She saw the explosion flip the truck onto its top and immediately begin to burn. She didn't see the second hit but saw the result as the hummer on the north side lifted onto its rear bumper and turn into a burning heap. It now appeared as though the entire mass of vehicles were ablaze. Thick black smoke rose from the site and small explosions could be seen in the conflagration.

TJ turned his drone and watched the remainder of the action for a moment then headed back to the truck for his next drone. Donna had already turned for the airport and landed her bomber next to the truck, shutting it down as TJ landed next to her.

"We need the second set?" she asked.

"Just to be sure let's go let them have another dose. I want to keep two bombs each to drop on that tree as I think that's where the Judith signal is being transmitted. We'll take out a bunch of those Zs at the same time."

"Ready," she said.

"So am I - let's go," TJ said and lifted off. They flew straight to the wrecking yard and hovered watching for a few moments before beginning their runs. The vehicles in the group continued burning. TJ and Donna watched and saw several men congregating to the south and TJ said that is where he would drop. They would both bomb from west to east with TJ dropping first while Donna filmed. TJ would fly back to altitude and film Donna's run.

TJ said, "Ready?"

"All set; let's hit 'em," Donna said.

TJ began his dive, focusing on the group of men. He released one bomb and corrected just a bit and dropped his second bomb on the vehicles then pulled out, jinking left and right. Donna watched as the first bomb blew just to the south of the men. She could see several lifted off their feet and flying through the air landing in the midst of the fiery vehicles, with parts of others following. *Gross* she thought. She did her ten-count and began her dive, focusing on the vehicles as there was no need to aim for the men again.

TJ turned to watch Donna's run and saw both of her bombs go off in the heart of the vehicles adding to the carnage. TJ and Donna both decided the group of vehicles and the men they once held had had enough. Donna joined up with TJ's drone and together they flew to the east until they came to the horde of Zs massing around the tree.

"You see how they're gathering around that tree?" TJ asked.

"Yes, that has to be where the signal is transmitting from," Donna answered.

"My thought also. Let's hit that tree, one bomb at a time this time, okay?"

"Let 'er rip my lover."

TJ shook his head, smiling, and made his first dive, releasing his bomb at the proper time and pulling out of his dive. Donna filmed the hit and was pleased to see Zs, both whole and in parts, flying out from the impact site near the tree. She waited for the ten seconds and began her dive.

TJ was in position and filming her run. He watched as her bomb hit, falling through the branches of the tree, and detonating above ground in the midst of the branches. The result was spectacular as it flattened many Zs, but the greatest result was it caused the tree to catch fire. The flames quickly spread from limb to limb, the leaves adding fuel to the quickly spreading destruction. He paused for several minutes watching the tree burn.

Donna pulled out of her dive and as she neared TJ, turned to see the result of her bomb, and saw the tree was a mass of flames looking like a huge torch might. She looked at TJ and said, "We need to hit it again?"

"May as well just to be sure," TJ answered and began his dive. His bomb landed on the ground next to the east side of the tree and exploded, sending Zs and pieces of Zs in all directions. Donna watched as the tree shook and swayed but stood its ground.

TJ pulled up, turned his drone, and said, "Go for it."

Donna went into her dive and dropping her last bomb, pulled out and upwards. TJ's drone filmed the result and he watched as her bomb, once again, dropped through the remaining branches and exploded near the 'Y' made by the larger branches splitting off from the main trunk. The result was just what the doctor ordered as the two main branches of the tree splintered in the explosion, sending splinters of wood flying in all directions, mowing down many more Zs.

TJ looked at Donna with a satisfied smile and said, "Great hit - mission accomplished."

"Yeah, baby!" Donna yelled.

They flew their drones back and allowing the two to cool before loading. Donna poured some coffee from the thermos, and they sat, leaning back against the truck and sipped the brew, enjoying a successful mission.

"How many men you think we got with that?" Donna asked.

TJ thought a while and said, "At least six since that was the number of vehicles in the group, but probably more. Sad they were doing this. I sort of feel like that panel truck you blew up was the place they were transmitting the Judith signal. I want to wait a while and fly another drone over there to see if the Zs have begun to disperse. If so, then we'll know for sure if the signal has stopped."

"That's a good idea, how about a sandwich and some carrot sticks?"

"I'd love some and some more coffee, thank you."

Donna got up reaching in the truck to get the bag with sandwiches and other food. She sat beside TJ again and handed him a sandwich and a handful of carrot sticks. He leaned over and gave her a kiss saying thank you.

They sat together in the midmorning sun watching the two smoke tendrils rising in the east, thinking about what they had just done and were thankful TJ had come out earlier to investigate the new zombie threat. His actions may have literally saved the valley from a horde invasion.

Thinking of that, Donna was suddenly surprised and with a startled look, quickly turned, sitting up straighter, and looking at TJ with wide eyes and a surprised expression. He, being startled by her actions, looked at her, and said, "What!" and quickly looked around thinking they were in danger.

"You," she said in an almost whisper.

"What…what about me," TJ said looking at his lap, legs and chest now thinking something was crawling on him.

"You…you, and God," she said with a stunned expression. "This is why you couldn't go with the team and recon the Colorado complex."

He looked at her not understanding and asked, "What are you talking about?"

"The other day when you were getting mixed signals, reading your Bible and camping out. This mission is the reason you were not to go with them. God held you back so we could take care of this situation."

TJ's face went slack as he realized what she was saying. He turned his gaze to the ground and thought a minute, then rotated until he was on his knees, motioning for Donna to do the same, and he began praying a prayer of thanks and wonder at God's ways. He was about to say Amen when Donna broke in and prayed for a time herself. When she finished and became quiet, TJ ended their prayer session with, "In Jesus' name, Amen."

"I'm going to make that flight over there now and see what the Zs are doing," TJ said getting up and changing out a battery pack in a drone. He lifted off, hovered a moment, then flew the drone eastward and up. When he reached four-thousand feet AGL, he leveled off and sped towards the two spires of smoke tendrils rising from Laramie, attesting to their attack.

TJ first paused above the site of the black vehicles and watched for movement. All six of the vehicles were destroyed and a few were still burning. He could see bodies and pieces of bodies lying around the vehicles and counted eight that were for the most part whole. He turned his aircraft to the east and flew over to the remnant of the tree and the zombies had indeed begun to disperse, spreading in every direction they were capable of ambling. He flew on to the east looking at his town, what was left of it. When he reached the eastern edge of Laramie, he turned to the south, flew over I-80, and turned to the west. He flew a zig-zag pattern on his return flight to the truck and other than the number of Zs, did not see any other signs of threat that is no black vehicles.

"Bringing it back now," TJ said. "I didn't see any other sign of danger other than the enormous number of Zs in the area."

"Think we should pack up and go into town and check out those vehicles and the bodies; try and get some intel on what they were doing?" Donna asked him, placing a drone in the back of the truck.

"No, not right now," he answered. "It'll be way too hot and the threat of all the Zs is a real danger. We should avoid Laramie for a while. Maybe in a few days. If necessary, we can go to Fort Collins for goods." He landed the drone near the back of the truck, undid the battery pack and placing the pack in the charging bin, lifted it, and packed it. He put the drone in the back of the truck, and they headed home to Paradise Valley.

Ruth and DD were on the front porch as Donna and TJ pulled up to the house. DD was on a blanket with a few stuffed animals and toys, gooing and laughing, trying to grab the playthings. "How did you do?" Ruth asked, rising from her Adirondack chair.

"Complete success on two accounts," Donna answered.

"Two? What was the second?" Ruth asked.

Donna deferred to TJ and he explained, "After bombing the vehicles, I felt the Judith signal was coming from a tree all the Zs were congregating around so we kept a few bombs and blew the tree up. It worked as I took another flight over the town a little later to see, and they were scattering all over, so it must have worked.”

“That’s great,” Ruth said happily. “Did you see any other danger?”

“No, no other vehicles or anything other than the enormous number of Zs in town. We’ll have to avoid Laramie for a while or go in loaded to the hilt for action. If we really have to go in, we’ll need to take some fireworks like you guys have in the past.”

“Yeah, that does work. You think the team will be able to get through okay?” she asked, concerned.

TJ looked at her and his silence was answer enough, but he said, “I really don’t know. They’ve been gone three days now and should return day after tomorrow. Two days of scattering on the zombie horde’s part might be okay. I just don’t know for sure. Donna and I can load up another round of bombs for the bombers and go over and wait. When we see them coming down the pass, we can call them on the radio and warn them and give support with the bombers if needed.”

“I’m sorry I can’t be part of your efforts, but that sounds like a good idea,” Ruth said with sadness in her tone. “I’d say take a fifty with you just in case. Never know what you might run into, like black hummers.”

“Yeah, maybe two,” Donna agreed. “With both of us having cannons, we can really cause some damage.”

“I suppose so,” TJ answered with a grin. *Maybe I’ll stay here in the valley with DD and sic those two on the world* he thought. He chuckled.

“What’s so amusing?” Donna asked him.

“You two…I was just thinking maybe I’ll stay home with DD and send you two to cover them. The world won’t know how to react.”

“That’s rich,” Ruth said. “You know, that’s not such a bad idea. I could use a day off; maybe do some shopping and looking around. We could take some super-soaking squirt guns with salt water and hose a few Zs while we’re out, you know, make the trip interesting. We can take a nice lunch with us and have a picnic somewhere where we can keep an eye on the pass for the team."

TJ didn't know if she was for real or being sarcastic. He hadn't been around Ruth enough to read her yet.

Donna immediately chimed in saying, "I think that's a great idea, even if you really didn't mean all that. You do need a break and TJ loves DD. He can handle him for a day while we have a lady's day out. They can go hunting or riding Dusty or something."

The three sat together on the front porch with fresh mugs of coffee. DD had fallen asleep on the blanket. All three adults were lost in their own thoughts. TJ thinking about what he and Donna had just accomplished and if that is what God had really intended. Donna thinking about taking a break in the jet tub with a good glass or two of wine. Ruth was seriously thinking about having that lady's day out with Donna and leaving DD with TJ for a guy's day alone.

The bath won over for Donna and she said so, getting up, and going inside leaving the three to themselves on the front porch. She did stop by the freezer and took out a chicken placing it on the counter to thaw. They would have baked chicken with potato cubes, carrot slices, and onion for dinner. She readied the vegetables and giving a nod of approval, turned for the stairs.

"You really think Donna and I can go to Laramie and leave you and DD alone?" Ruth asked TJ.

"It makes me a little nervous, but that's the chauvinist coming out in me. The more I think about it, you both need a break. The only issue is the zombie threat, which you've both faced down on several occasions. It's just me worrying about the two of you is all, but again, the chauvinist is popping out."

Ruth began laughing and said, "I haven't thought of chauvinism in so long. It just surprised me hearing you confess like that, sorry."

TJ chuckled, too, and said, "Don't worry about it. I'm a bit old-fashioned when it comes to the ladies. My mom and dad taught us that kind of respect."

"Did they teach you your work ethic also?" she asked.

"Yes, always taught us to do the best we could. Especially if we were working for someone else being paid with another's money for the work asked of us. Dad always taught us to excel in everything we did, to be the one people went to for guidance. He said that would make us good leaders and that is what the world needed, leaders with Godly morals and ethics that knew their stuff."

"Good ethics to live by if you ask me," Ruth said. "So, you settled down about the two of us going to Laramie?"

"Yeah, I suppose. If it's okay with you, I'm still gonna worry while you're gone – just the way I am," TJ confessed.

"I reckon; if you didn't, I'd be worried," she returned with a grin. "We'll be okay. Both of us have been through some tough scrapes and come out okay. We know when to stand and fight and when to turn tail and run like the dickens. I promise we'll haul it if the need arises."

"Good enough for me," TJ said rising. "I think I'm going to hit the sack for a nap; I've got a lot of work to do tomorrow so need the rest."

"We'll be in shortly, you have a nice nap, TJ," Ruth said as he went inside. She looked out over the valley and the memories of she and Doug sitting out here on the porch in the evenings came to mind and she was saddened. She missed him terribly. Shaking off the melancholy, she rose and collected DD and went inside to begin dinner preparations.

TJ had almost completed the second pit by noon the following day. He still had to dig the center-line ditch for the French drain system. After that, he would begin bringing in the pine straw, the French drain itself, the gravel, lumber for the framing, and the pallets for the floor. Lunch first.

He went inside and Donna, DD, and Ruth were at the table waiting with sandwiches and carrot sticks ready for the mid-day meal. TJ smiled and washed up.

"We're going to Laramie tomorrow, mid-morning," Donna said. "First thing we'll do is stop at the airport, launch a drone, and take a look at the zombie situation. If it's reasonably clear, we'll go in, do our thing, and find a place to wait for the recon team. I want to see if any of those black vehicles are running around anyway. That'll be good information to know. We'll watch for the team and get ready to cover them. Both of us are taking a full load out along with fifties. You know we both like those things. I've already loaded my truck with all the extra ammo, grenades and my fifty and a can of loaded mags for it. We'll be ready for just about anything."

"Take a Stinger along just in case you see a drone and go over to that wrecking yard and look through those vehicles and see if anything's left for intel," TJ directed.

"Stinger's already in and that we can do," Ruth said.

TJ shook his head, said a blessing, and took a bite of his leftover chicken sandwich.

After lunch, he got back on the frontend loader and dug the trench in the second greenhouse pit. He lay the pine straw, installed, and connected the French drain system, covered it with a layer of gravel then another of pine straw, then built the floor from the pallets. The work was good, keeping his mind off what would happen the following day.

He had put in the last pallet and the floors of both pits were complete. The French drains were in and would work as planned. Now he would haul the lumber to build the framework for the plant stands and to hold the glass that would be installed for the roof. He figured with the break tomorrow, keeping a watch on DD, he would go over his measurements for the remainder of the project. These twelve-hundred square foot underground facilities would grow a wide variety of fresh produce for the valley residents all year long. That was a good thing.

Donna had talked Ruth into preparing her famous pork chops for dinner, along with boiled potatoes and carrots, instead of more chicken. The dinner conversation, begun by

Donna, not TJ, quickly went to the following day's events. She asked TJ if there was anything he needed from Laramie as far as the greenhouse project went.

"Maybe more three-inch screws and nails, preferably the outdoor decking type screws if you can find any," TJ answered her.

"We're going to the big mart first," Ruth said. "You know if there was any left there?"

"I don't recall seeing any, but that doesn't mean they're not there, maybe in the storeroom," TJ replied.

"If we have to, we'll go to the ranch store – bound to be more there," Donna said.

TJ looked at her shaking his head and said, "After the last trip there, please be careful if you do go. Heck, it would probably be better for you to go around and look in people's garages for them instead. Might be safer and we'll probably be doing that sooner rather than later as we've just about used up the supplies in the stores."

"We may not have time for all that," Ruth observed. "We'll make a quick stop at the big mart then get set up and watch for the team returning. I think by that time, the drone's battery pack will be completely recharged, and I can fly it up over the pass and watch for the team. I hope we don't run into any trouble."

"Please be careful," TJ said to both. "I think I'll pack DD up and go to Lake Owen for some fishing. Did you bring the baby pack with you?"

"Yes, he'll love being outside," Ruth said.

They finished dinner and TJ and Donna did the dishes and cleaned up. Ruth and DD were on the couch and the couple joined them after the kitchen work. They discussed final thoughts for the ladies trip the following day. TJ reminded them about the fireworks and Donna said they were already loaded.

"I hope the team got some good intel on the Colorado complex. It'll be good to know what those rascals are doing if anything," Ruth observed.

"The team's going to crap when they hear about what we did and the zombie threat," Donna said.

"Are you two leaving at sunrise or midmorning?" TJ asked.

"We want to get an early start so right after breakfast," Donna told him.

"What time will you come back here if the team doesn't show?" he queried.

"If they don't show, it'll be close to dark, maybe a little after," Ruth answered.

"Depends on them, really," Donna said. "If they show, that's what time we'll be heading back so maybe earlier."

"Okay, I'll take DD fishing for a couple of hours in the morning after he's fed and cleaned up," TJ told them. "That way I'll be here whenever you get back."

They broke for the evening and went to bed after saying a round of goodnight wishes and a prayer. TJ went out on the second-floor balcony and gazed at the night sky and the valley below. It was a peaceful evening with stars in abundance. He was about to turn to go back inside when off in the distance to the northwest, an elk bugled, a long squealing bugle probably to call the herd together for the night. To TJ it was a good sign. TJ smiled and thanked God for letting him live in a place like the valley.

Chapter 4: Recon Team

Julia, Dan, Jack, and Jeff were beat. The reconnaissance mission had been running for days and the crew, tired from both the exertions and the stress, were happy to be heading home. Sneaking around all over the area was stressful to say the least. Covered in mud and grime, clothing torn and stiff with filth, the four had given their all. Both trucks were packed, and the team pulled out and began their journey home.

Jeff was riding shotgun for Julia and Jack was for Dan. The group was exhausted and wanted nothing more than to get home and bathe or shower, get a good hot meal in them along with good wine and scotch, then crash. All four felt they could sleep for a week.

The team was heading north on U.S. Highway 85, having met in Greeley, Colorado. They had just passed through Ault, Colorado, heading towards Nunn. The day began before sunrise and packing their sleeping mats and bags, quickly filled coffee mugs, and pulled out without lights on. The morning sun was just beginning to provide light enough for the foursome to see as they sped northwards.

Dan was keeping a steady speed of seventy miles per hour, concentrating on the road while Jack kept watch from side to side and in the air. They had not encountered any drones on their scouting missions and were immensely grateful for that. Julia followed along, concentrating on keeping Dan in her vision. Jeff scanned the sides and sky.

Dan was crossing Colorado County Road 100 and saw movement ahead and slowed rapidly. Julia almost hit him from behind, not realizing he was slowing since they'd removed their break lights. Dan pointed and Jack squinted in the early morning light trying to make out what was moving ahead.

Jeff came over the radio saying, "What's up fellers?"

Jack grabbed the mike and responded, "Something moving up ahead, slow down and get ready for anything. Julia, watch for areas to pull over into fast."

After a few more moments of moving forward slowly, Dan and Jack could finally make out what was moving - a herd of buffalo was crossing the highway from east to west.

Jack keyed his mike and said, "It's a herd of buffalo crossing the road."

Jeff looked at Julia and she, him, and he keyed his mike and said, "A what?"

"A herd of buffalo is crossing the highway in front of us. We need to stop until they've crossed," Jack told them.

Dan had slowed enough and moved to his right so Julia could pull up next to them and together they stopped and watched the site. Before the plague there was a small buffalo herd of about five hundred animals on a ranch in southern Wyoming, and this must be the herd, which now numbered well over a thousand of the beasts.

Jeff looked at Dan and said, "One of those would fill everyone's freezers for a while…how 'bout it?"

After some thought, Dan looked at Jeff with a smile and said, "I think we're out of ear shot of the complex. Go ahead and drop one."

Jeff got his Remington 700 SPSX sniper rifle out, chambered a round after getting out of the truck, and taking careful aim, fired at one of the largest animals he could safely shoot. The animal fell forward and tumbled. The rest of the herd picked up speed and quickly moved to the west. "Dibs on the hide," Jeff quickly said.

It took the four over an hour to field dress the animal then manhandle the twenty-five-hundred-pound beast onto the trailer. It would indeed fill several freezers with meat. The crew cleaned up and got back on the road. This time they didn't stop until they reached the pass and Julia called for a bathroom break.

They stopped at the Lincoln Monument rest stop on the apex of Monument Pass on I-80, knowing there were several 'facilities' scattered around the small park. The four walked around the area, which was becoming overgrown with plant life now, and enjoyed the moment.

As Julia and Jeff approached their truck, they heard Ruth's voice come over the radio, "Recon team, this is home base, are you close, over?"

Jeff ran for the radio and keying the mike said, "This is recon, we're at Lincoln's house, over. What's up lady?"

"It's great to hear your voice," Ruth said with glee. "Are all of you okay?"

"Other than tired and ready for a hot bath and a hot meal, never better my dear," Jeff said with a smile.

"Great news. Situation is red alert in Laramie. Z horde of several thousand nearby. Use extreme caution and we'll meet you by number two," referring to the second exit in Laramie.

"Copy red alert in Laramie and see you at two in twenty, out," Jeff said ending his transmission. He looked for Jack and Dan, whistled to get their attention, and raising his hand with his index finger up in the air and twirling it around, called the two over.

"Just got a radio call from Ruth and she says its red alert in Laramie as there is a Z horde of several thousand creatures there. Said she'd meet us at the second exit," Jeff explained to the two.

"Z up everyone," Dan ordered and the four quickly donned their chest rigs and readied shotguns, M4s and handguns. Prepared for God only knew what, they got back in their trucks and began the final stage of their journey, pulling out on the downhill side of the pass going west down Telephone Pass to Laramie.

It took seven minutes instead of twenty, but they could see Ruth's truck sitting just off the interstate, perched on the on-ramp, ready to go. Dan pulled up and stopped with Julia right behind him. They all piled out and greeted each other. Both groups were happy to see each other.

Dan, the leader in him taking over, said, "Ruth, what's this about a horde?"

"It's a long story…way too long for here," she answered. "You know you stink! Get in the trucks and let's get you guys home and cleaned up. We'll discuss everything from both sides over a good dinner tonight at Paradise Valley. That's where DD and I've been living for the past few days for safety reasons. Come on, let's go."

Jeff said, "I'm buying dinner. We're having buffalo steaks," he said pointing back to the trailer. They would save the story for back in the valley so everyone could hear it.

They piled back into the trucks and left Laramie. When they got to the hill, the four that had been away for a while felt a great relief at seeing their valley home below. It was a satisfying feeling knowing they had come through a perilous mission unscathed. They followed Ruth and Donna as they led them to Paradise Valley. TJ had already opened the gate and the three trucks pulled in and parked in the front yard.

TJ, with DD in his arms, waited on the porch, a huge smile on his face as he'd heard the transmissions between Ruth and Jeff earlier and knew everyone was safe. The group climbed out of their vehicles with moans and groans and stretching, pleased the journey was over.

"What the heck is that thing?" TJ asked pointing at the trailer.

Jeff said, "A buffalo I shot. It'll fill all our freezers for a while and that's what we're having for dinner tonight, buffalo steaks."

TJ looked at him with a surprised expression on his face and to himself thought, *the stories are going to be great tonight.* He went down the steps and gave Donna a kiss then handed DD to Ruth. He gave Julia a hug and each of the three Marines a handshake and a smack on the back, glad to have them all home safely. He, too, commented on their 'odor.'

After unloading the buffalo and skinning it, they cut several large steaks for dinner then hung it in the cooler and TJ said, "Okay, you guys get in the house and get cleaned up 'cause you stink something awful and we'll get dinner and the drinks started. Now scoot. We'll worry about the unloading the trucks and things later," he finished as they all climbed the porch steps and went inside. Donna and Ruth began dinner and TJ, after sitting DD in his bouncy chair, went in the library and got a new bottle of eighteen-year-old Glenfiddich scotch and a bunch of tumblers.

Ruth had promised to make her pork chops for their welcome home, but the buffalo steaks would be a real treat. She and Donna worked on dinner and had everything well underway when the crew began streaming down the stairs somewhat refreshed after their baths and showers. Dan was down first and accepted a tumbler of scotch from TJ, giving him a smile and a small toasting lift of his glass before sipping the liquid.

Jeff and Jack were next, also accepting tumblers of scotch and Julia came down last. She opted for a glass of red wine. TJ served Donna and Ruth some wine then poured himself a few fingers of scotch.

After getting his drink ready, TJ turned to his guests and said, "Ladies and gentlemen, first thing I'd like to do is pray." They all gathered in the middle of the room and TJ said a prayer of thanks for the safe return of all six of the people from the valley. He thanked the Lord for letting him complete the digging portion of the greenhouses without incident, and he thanked the Lord for their safety. After he said Amen, he toasted the group for their safe return, and they responded 'here - here' and took sips of their drinks.

Dan, TJ, Jack, and Jeff gathered in front of the fireplace and the Marines asked TJ about the greenhouse project. He explained what he'd done so far and what he would be doing in the next few days, depending on what the recon team reported after dinner.

Dan looked at him and shook his head with a sad continence on his face. TJ got the message that the news from the recon wasn't going to be good.

TJ slapped Jeff on the back and said, "Got to take DD fishing this morning and we caught several nice ones. If they were less than twenty inches, we threw them back."

"Where'd you go?" Jeff asked.

"Lake Owen since its close," TJ answered. "We took the ATV and had a swell time. Saw two moose and several deer – mule deer, no whitetail. Saw a bald eagle, too."

"What bait were you using?" Jeff asked.

"Mosquito flies and they didn't last long," TJ said to him. "The fish are getting bigger and more of them, too - same with the animals. I'm seeing more deer, elk, moose, bear, birds, eagles…just about everything. I guess the world is healing without billions of humans running around."

"Yeah," Jeff interjected, "I've been looking at the stars at night lately and they are very bright again, kind of like when we were in Nam. The air is fresher and when we were down in Colorado, there was no more of that brown cloud down there. The sky and air are cleaning up nicely."

Dan, looking down into his glass of scotch mused, "Maybe this was God's way of cleaning house so-to-speak." The other three men looked up at him and saw the forlorn look on his face as he contemplated his scotch.

Jeff quietly said, "I reckon so."

"I'm not sure God had anything to do with this, guys," TJ said morosely. Heads nodded in agreement.

"Dinner's up," Ruth called out, breaking the men's musing.

They gathered at the table, seating the ladies first then sitting. TJ asked Jeff to say the blessing and afterwards they ate heartily, and the atmosphere was happy. Small talk was rampant and more questions about the greenhouse and the fishing and the shopping flew all around the repast. The buffalo steaks were an exceptional treat for the valley residents.

After dinner and cleaning up the dishes and kitchen, the people of the valley gathered in the living room with fresh drinks and began their discussion of the previous week's happenings. TJ began by saying he was thankful everyone was home safe and sound then looked at Dan and Julia and asked them to tell what happened in Colorado.

"Well, like we decided, we split in Laramie with Jack and Jeff going down Highway 287 and Julia and I going over to Cheyenne and going down Highway 85. Julia and I set up in the National Guard bunkers and began our recon early the next morning, parking the truck near where you did on I-25," he said pointing at TJ. "We hiked west being cautious and didn't see or hear anything at all. It was almost too quiet. The complex is still destroyed and there were no signs of it being repaired or rebuilt anywhere. The towers and satellite dishes are still toast. That building with the elevator shaft was blown to bits. The destruction was complete on that complex.

"Together we hiked around that lake and went into the complex itself. Yes, we were nervous and our heads on a swivel, M4s up and ready. We stood next to the building and watched and listened. Didn't hear a thing save the wind and didn't see one person. I climbed into the debris and listened for quite a while where the elevator shaft was but didn't hear anything at all. The only Z we saw was walking to the north, just beyond the complex and it didn't see us.

"Julia went around to the south and I moved to the west and we met at what was the hanger. Those three connex boxes you hit, TJ, held ammo as we saw the evidence. That's what caused that big explosion. The hanger was just as destroyed. We assumed there had to have been secondary explosions as there was evidence of several impact points other than the mortar rounds – bigger and deeper holes – and we figured that was from missiles they had stored in there with the drones."

Julia continued, "We continued to the west, scouting the western slope away from the complex. There was another small lake to the south, just beyond the complex and seeing that I told Dan I would go around it and look around. We turned on our mikes as we'd be out of sight of each other, and I moved out. I skirted the lake and the three homes that were nearby; I entered and scouted through them. Two had substantial supplies we could use so keep that in mind for later and I marked them on the map…here and here. I didn't see any exits from the complex, or any signs of recent habitation anywhere."

Dan said, "I went a little northwest from the complex and found an unusual…lake, I guess. Anyway, it was about two hundred by one-hundred fifty yards and had an island. It reminded me more like an old castle's grounds with a moat than anything. If we could see it from the air, it would resemble an eye because of its shape and the island - it would look like a pupil. Anyway, it had a pier but no boats. I found one container box, locked, and one connex box also locked. I didn't have the tools necessary to open them. The island was interesting, and I skirted the entire lake area. Some of the area on the island looked swampy and it was definitely swampy on the west and southwest sides. I came out a mess. I didn't see any buildings or construction on the island, but since other than swimming out to it, I had no way of getting out there to look closer. We saved that for a drone recon later.

"To the northeast was a small ranch and after scouting that out and not seeing anything of interest, I moved down the road coming out on County Road 15 and turned to the south to rejoin with Julia. I didn't see any signs of movement, construction, fire, or habitation along the route I took."

Dan pointed to Jack and he began, "We drove south on that Road 15 and camped northwest of the complex. We figured Dan and Julia would take the complex the first day, so we concentrated on the western slopes and the north. I went due east, covering the north side of the area and in two days of scouting, didn't see any sign of habitation or people and only had to drop one Z - using my suppressed nine on it. Thing was going a little west of north when I dropped it. I covered two lakes, skirting both completely and didn't see anything of interest around them. I did find a vet's office and there are a multitude of supplies in there we could use - another thing to keep in mind - and I marked it on the map, uh…here. I went all the way east to I-25 then moved about a mile to the north and turned back to the west and didn't see a thing."

"I went due west," Jeff said. "From where we camped, I headed for a line of broken ridges, and thinking if they had a tunnel exit somewhere, that would be the logical place. I started on the north end, near another vet's office, and worked my way south following the ridge line. I found a place to cross using Highway 21C and moved to the north. I hadn't gone a half mile when the road turned into Highway 287. I kept that bit of information up front on my mind. Anyway, I moved along the western side of the ridgeline, working my way north.

"I found them about a mile up." Ruth, Donna, and TJ shifted in their seats with that announcement and became attentive. "The tunnel exit was well hidden, and I might have missed it if it hadn't been for the smoker. It's funny, none of us smoke and I haven't thought about that in so long that it was quite the surprise when I smelled it – almost made me cough." A few chuckled. "I cautiously moved forward and saw the entrance…or exit. The smoker was dressed in a gray kind of clothing that camouflaged him in the rocks very well. He probably would have had me if not for the smoke. I backed off and came to an arroyo and getting down inside it, followed it to the west until it went under 287. I came out on the other side, climbed up and crawled over the road and using my binos, found the tunnel exit. It's really hard to see, so I marked the spot on the map…here," he indicated on the map.

"How big is the tunnel entrance?" Donna asked.

"Big enough for a hummer or a large pickup to use. It cuts diagonally into the rock face, making it hard to see, and from that entrance it runs on a heading of zero-one-zero degrees and about fifty meters or so inside it hangs a right that I could see from my vantage point. Looking at the topography, it looks like the tunnel runs between two lakes almost due east of the entrance: a bit northeast of this little airport, which is being used as the grass had fresh indentations. From that point it's a beeline to the complex we destroyed. The reason I say the entrance is big enough for a hummer is one pulled up to the entrance, made a guard change, turned around then went back inside. It was 1300 hours when the guard change was made. I watched for several hours and just before dark, made my way south along the west side of 287 to where I originally found the Highway, and made my way back towards camp. The next morning, I told Jack what I'd found and marked it on the maps we had as best as I could. Like I said, I marked the location on 287, a stack of stones on the east side of the Highway, pointing to the north. If you take a compass fix from the stones, the entrance is on a heading of zero-eight-six degrees, and on a reciprocal heading is a ridge that we can use as a mortar position as it's only two miles distant. As I was heading back to camp, I saw that airstrip and using my compass, it's on a heading of one-one-five degrees from the tunnel entrance. It looks like it has been used a lot recently as I saw vehicle tracks in the grass. The north end of the strip had a building, but I didn't get a chance to go look at it. There are two runways, the longest running north to south and the shortest from east to west. The short one is about five hundred yards long and the long one is about a half-mile long. It's definitely big enough for a small plane and the short one more than enough for a drone."

"It was day three when Jeff and I hooked back up," Jack explained. "We snuck back up to the area where the tunnel is and took a bunch of compass readings, photos, and marked our maps accordingly. By the end of day four, we packed up and drove to the rally point that night and slept in the truck to wait for Dan and Julia."

"Julia, did you find anything to the south?" TJ asked.

"No, nothing to speak of. I skirted another lake down there and got messed up in a boggy area. There's another vet's office near Highway 1. I saw it as I went by and marked it on my map…uh…here. I made my way back to the complex, met up with Dan and together we went back to the truck on I-25, and drove back to the bunkers, ate a good meal, slept, and met with Jack and Jeff at the rally point the next morning and came home."

"Questions anyone?" Dan asked.

"What are we going to do about the tunnel?" Ruth asked.

"I think we should think about that for a few days and get back together for another meeting…say day after tomorrow," TJ advised. "We can discuss it then."

"What happed while we were away?" Julia asked.

The three left behind laughed together and then told the recon team what had happened over the five days they'd been away. The shopping, the horde, the bombing, the recon in Laramie…. All of them were laughing afterwards and Jeff said he'd missed all the fun – "figures", he complained out loud.

Donna told them about their shopping trip and told them about going to the wrecking yard where she and TJ had bombed the black vehicles. The six vehicles were completely destroyed, burned. They found very little from an intel standpoint, but did find one piece of interesting information, which she brought out to show. It was six sheets of information stapled together and gave instructions on where to set Judith transmitters in Laramie and the surrounding area. This piece of intel would be very important as the residents would be able to locate these transmitters and re-use them elsewhere. It was a nice find.

Donna said they dispatched a half-dozen Zs which were crawling around the vehicles. They were dressed in black fatigues and were obviously from the Colorado complex. She said they had searched the bodies and found nothing in their pockets. Materials in the vehicles had been completely destroyed by fire so nothing else of interest was found.

Her final bit of information was to tell the team they had gone around town hunting Zs, using the saltwater guns on the ones they got close enough to. She indicated it had been a nice shopping day.

They broke for the evening with the recon team going to the underground to turn in. Everyone was out within an hour and they all slept soundly that night, very thankful everyone had returned to the valley unharmed.

Next morning woke everyone with the aroma of bacon and sausage permeating the air. Everyone cleaned up and met in the kitchen area, sipping mugs of steaming coffee and with small talk. The men gathered in one area discussing TJ's activities later with the greenhouse construction. The women looked like busy bees in the kitchen, cooking the bacon, sausage, eggs, and toast and getting everything ready to serve. Paper plates, plastic stemware, and paper towels were used. The only 'real' dishware used were the coffee mugs.

Donna finally called everyone together and TJ said a blessing. They all sat down and began eating and watching Ruth giving DD a bit of the scrambled eggs to gum on. The kid really liked eggs since every time she removed the spoon from his mouth, his arms would fly out to the side, and his eyes would almost bulge, as if to say, 'where are you going with that'.

After breakfast, the men refilled their go-mugs and broke for the garage, leaving the women and DD to their wants. TJ told the guys he was going to be moving the lumber to the worksite, then the saw and other tools he would need to complete the project. He was adamant about needing their help when it came to the point of installing the glass. He would not be able to do that alone and the Marines said they would be there to help.

Before they began to load, Dan looked at TJ and said, "I want to see those six vehicles that you guys bombed."

"No problem, we have them on video," TJ said.

"No, I want to go see them," Dan corrected. "I want to look them over and see what we might find to use as intel. Our observations might prove different since we've been trained as investigators."

"That's a good idea, how about later this afternoon? The four of us can Z up and go over for a recon."

"That'll work," Dan said getting nods from Jack and Jeff.

By noon they had stacked the lumber in both underground sections and began building. The construction was going well with the four of them working together, much smoother than TJ had anticipated. The ladies would come out from time-to-time and refill their mugs or give them bottles of water and Donna said they would break for lunch and have a picnic near the construction site.

Shortly after one, the ladies and DD showed up with baskets full of food and water and called the men up for lunch. They sat on blankets spread out with DD in the middle gooing and goggling at everyone, arms flailing. Julia had made chicken salad sandwiches, and they'd cut carrot, celery, and cucumber spears to go along.

Dan told the ladies he and the men would be heading to Laramie after lunch to do another recon on the bombed vehicles. They would Z up and take additional materials due to the Z threat. Dan told the group he didn't want to stay more than a few hours and if needed, they would make another trip the following day.

Ruth said that would be fine as they would be having buffalo steaks for dinner again and that Dan was cooking the meat on the grill, so he had to be back by five. "You just been 'voluntold' dude," Jeff told him to a round of laughs from everyone.

The day was sunny and bright with a gentle breeze coming out of the southwest. It was about seventy degrees and a very pleasant day from a weather standpoint. Dan was giving Jeff grief over the 'voluntold' statement when TJ put his hand out and called for everyone to be quiet. Seven sets of ears suddenly became sound absorbing antenna.

"To the southeast," Ruth said, "a drone it sounds like."

"Everyone in the house – now!" Dan yelled. Everyone was up in an instant with Ruth grabbing DD and scrambling for the back entrance. Jack went straight to the armory and brought out a Stinger. Jeff and TJ went in and came out with AR-10s and several magazines each and another stinger. Dan went inside and came out with a fifty-caliber rifle and two magazines then the men headed for the front door.

TJ raised his hand as he got to the door and quietly opened it a crack and listened. "It's still to the southeast. Dan, you should go up to the Underground and come out the east portal…take Jack with you. Jeff, get the other Stinger and meet me on the porch."

The men broke with that and went to their assigned positions. The women gathered a few things and went into the library, with Donna giving TJ a kiss as she went by. When Jeff returned with the Stinger, he and TJ went out on the porch and got ready. It was only a few minutes more and they heard a whistle from above, announcing Dan and Jack were ready to rock. If the drone came within range, Jack would be first to fire.

The four men held their collective breaths and waited. TJ was first to notice the change in pitch of the drone's engine and gave a sharp whistle, signaling the men up on the Underground the things approach. All four got ready, with Jack rising and engaging the radar ranger on the Stinger, Dan readying the fifty to fire, TJ chambering a round into his AR-10 as did Jeff. Jeff also readied his Stinger, short of arming the missile.

Jeff looked at TJ and gave him a nod signaling his readiness and TJ returned the gesture. That's when they heard the Stinger from up on the Underground launch, the whooshing sound erasing all other sounds from the valley. The two on the porch just did catch sight of the missile as it streaked to the south over the barn. They waited and several seconds later, heard the explosion as the missile detonated. Once again, they waited. They no longer heard anything; the valley became quiet.

TJ walked to the north end of the porch and looked up the mountain towards the Underground and saw Dan giving a thumb up gesture. He had a smile on his face as well. "They got it, Dan's up there giving a thumb up signal and has a big smile. Another drone down."

"I think, if you don't mind, that I'll take the ATV and run over to our place right quick and check things out. I'm hoping they didn't drop something on our places."

"Go for it. Want to wait for one of the others just in case; maybe we'll leave for Laramie from there?" TJ asked.

"I'd better," he answered. He went for the garage and opening the door, pulled the ATV out, and made a run up the east trail to the Underground. A few moments later, it sped down with Dan riding shotgun and flew down the lane. TJ had already opened the gate and they blew through, turning right on the road.

TJ went back inside the house and leaning his AR-10 against the door jamb, looked at the ladies, and said they got the drone. "Dan and Jeff are going to check your places out – see if they dropped anything on them. I'm hoping not, but we'll see."

"How many more of those Stingers do we have?" Julia asked.

"Six. I think a trip up to Guernsey may be in order to look for more. We'll see," he said and turned for the door. Outside he was surprised to see Jack coming down the east road from the Underground. He had the fifty slung over his shoulder, along with his M4 and ammo.

"You see the hit?" Jack asked with a smile as he reached the porch.

"No, trees in the way, was it a good one?" TJ returned.

"It made a big splat in the sky and another when it hit near the road to Albany. Are the boys going to check it out?"

"No, going to see if it dropped anything on any of your places. Not sure what they'll do after that."

"Knowing those two, probably go fishing or something."

TJ laughed and picked up the Stinger Jeff had left on the porch. He redid the safeties and leaned the weapon against the door jamb next to his AR-10. He sat with Jack on the steps and said, "So much for going to Laramie today."

"Yeah, I agree with you there, brother. The excitement from this engagement will wear us all out after the adrenalin wears off," Jack agreed. "And just think, only one shot fired. Technology…beats me," Jack said shaking his head and got up ambling over to the barn and going in.

Donna came out and sat next to TJ and cuddled up to him. He put his arm around her and held her close. Ruth and Julia came out and sat on the steps with them. Julia looked at TJ and asked, "Did they go to look at the drone?"

He shook his head and said, "No, they went to see if the drone dropped anything on your places."

"You think they did?" she asked lifting up taller, looking in the direction of their home site.

"That's what they went to find out," TJ said, not knowing. "Jack said that afterwards, knowing those two, they just may go fishing or something." The girls laughed and the cheerfulness was refreshing. Tensions eased some.

"TJ," Ruth asked," why do you suppose these people still try to attack us? I mean, after what we did to the complex and to their people several times before that, and what you did to them in Laramie just the other day, you'd think they would get the message we mean business and to leave us alone. All we want to do is live in peace here in our valley."

"Ruth, I believe all of us want the same thing, peace in our valley," TJ said. "And I'm sorry, but I don't have any answers to your questions about the Colorado folks. I wish I did know the reason behind their attacks. But I do know that I will continue to protect our liberty here in the valley from these people and against anyone or anything else that tries to take our peace away."

"Ooh-rah," Jack said as he came up. "Sorry; heard what you said TJ and I agree. Our liberty is a gift the way I see it. A gift from God and we need to protect that gift. If you read the Bible, then you know in many places people had to fight to protect their liberty. The way I see it, God doesn't like wimps. He doesn't want us to give up – lay down and coward out. He wants us to be strong and fight for what's right. I think like it says in Micah*, in the Old Testament, that soon we'll beat our swords and weapons into plowshares and pruning hooks and we'll war with no one any longer. But right now, because those people from the complex are doing something evil and wrong, we still need to fight, and that means keeping our weapons close. They try to kill us every time they see us. They instigate the hostilities, not us. I'd rather them leave us alone, like Ruth said. Let us live in peace and we'll leave them alone to live in…whatever it is they live in."

The four of them looked at Jack in stunned silence as that

*Micha, Chapter 4, verses 1-5

had been the longest dissertation any of them had ever heard from him.   He stood there leaning against the porch rail. He'd put a blade of straw in his mouth and was picking his teeth with it, mulling over the situation they were in, his cowboy boot covered feet crossed, his Stetson tipped back on his head some.   He looked every bit, the cowboy from Wyoming.

TJ broke from his gaping at Jack and said, "Jack thanks for being here. I thank God every day for the three of you being with us. We are honored by your friendship and presence."

Jack's eyes came up and met TJ's. Sincerity was written on both men's faces. Jack straightened up and held out his hand and shook TJ's. It was a gesture both men knew to be one of respect and understanding, sealing their friendship and comradeship for all time. Forevermore they were brothers.

When their hands parted, TJ asked, "What were you doing in the barn?"

"I took care of the animals for you," he replied. "Seemed like something I should do. We don't have any critters yet and I miss caring for 'em. I like being a cowboy and taking care of livestock and animals in general. They're pretty straight forward, you know."

"I know what you mean," TJ answered.

"Were there eggs?" Donna asked.

"Yes, ma'am - a few - I left 'em for you," he answered her.

She got up and said, "May as well go get 'em."

Julia and Ruth rose and followed her to the barn leaving Jack and TJ by the porch. "How much more time you think you'll need on the greenhouses?" Jack asked TJ.

"Two or three days at least," he replied. "If you want to help, you're more than welcome to stay here while we do the work. Donna and I would be glad to have you."

"I think I'll take you up on that," Jack said. "I could use some home-cooked meals. Living with two other Marines can be hard on the pallet, if you know what I mean."

TJ chuckled and said, "I suppose it could be tough. You get many varieties?"

It was Jack's turn to chuckle and said, "Yeah, two - cooked and burnt." That caused both men to laugh. "Naw, it ain't too bad. We have steaks, hamburger you've made, soup with vegetables you grew, I shoot a grouse every now and then, and we've had duck and geese a time or two."

"That buffalo you brought home was a treat," TJ said. "Those steaks are great."

"You should a seen that herd that crossed the road in front of us. Must a been a thousand of the critters but I may be exaggeratin' a bit. We had to wait it out as they passed. Jeff got the idea to drop one…I think it was him. Anyway, you're right, it was a good meal."

"I figure I'll finish the butchering after I get the greenhouses finished. We should be able to fill everyone's freezers with that much meat. How much burger you think I should make with the leftovers?"

"As much as you can I think," Jack answered. "We'll put it in the freezers for sure. It should make for some great chili and stuff."

The ladies came back with a basket of eggs right then and TJ told Donna about Jack staying for a few days to help out with the greenhouses. She said that would be great and a big help. Ruth and Julia said they needed to get home and they all went into the house.

Ruth packed up their things and got DD ready to go. Julia brought their truck around and after the goodbyes were all said and done, they left for their place, leaving the three sitting on the porch enjoying a glass of iced tea.

They'd been sitting for about a half-hour when they heard the ATV coming. TJ got up and opened the gate and the machine sped up the hill and stopped in front of the house. Jeff and Dan got out and stretched and said they'd seen Ruth and Julia and told them their place was okay. All their places were okay. Dan explained they went to the drone, found, and smashed the tracking device and looked over the wreckage. It had four missiles and he pointed to the three Hellfire missiles that had not been destroyed in the back of the ATV.

"I figure we can make a command detonation device for them and use them as IEDs (Improvised Explosive Devices)," Dan explained. "We can use them as mines or something."

"Too bad we can't fire them," Jack said. "We could line them up and shoot them at that tunnel entrance. They'd take care of that problem right quick."

That brought surprised looks from the other three as that seemed to be a great idea. If they could figure out how to fire the things electronically, maybe they could use them on the tunnel. They would have to research that one.

Jack said, "I'm going to be staying here for a few days and help TJ with those greenhouses so I'm taking the ATV over to my place and pack a few things. Be right back," and he jumped in after he and Jeff took the missiles out of the back and took off.

"Can we help, too?" Jeff asked.

"Certainly," TJ told him. "We'd love the help – the more the merrier and the faster the work'll get done and the growing begun."

"I've already started a bunch of plants in buckets and baskets," Donna said. "We'll be transplanting for the most part."

Dan asked, "What time you want us here every day until the project is done – we'll be here."

"Between nine and ten will be fine," TJ said. "That way everyone can get some rest and a good breakfast in before the work begins. I figure with four…five of us working together, it'll take two, maybe three days to finish up. It's just a matter of building the plant stands, installing the stairs and doors, and placing the glass in the framework. Shouldn't take long at all."

Dan laughed and said, "Famous last words – remember Murphy and that law of his?"

Chuckles from everyone then TJ looked at him and said, "Hey, it should be a piece of cake."

Dan gave a nod of his head and said, "Okay, let's get to it then. We still have some daylight left we can at least get something done. But tomorrow I want to go to Laramie and check out those vehicles you took out. I think we'll find some important information…at least."

"I agree," TJ said. "All the materials for the greenhouses are out there, even the screws, nails, and fasteners, duct tape, bailing wire…"

"…bailing wire?" Jeff asked.

"Just in case, stuff, you know," TJ answered. "I've even got all the plumbing materials out there ready to go. I guess we could run the line from river connection I've already put into the dispersal point, split the line, and connect it to the watering system. If we have it ready to go, when the project is built and the ladies have the plants in, we can turn the water on and see what happens."

"Plumbing it is then," Jeff said getting up and stretching. Dan got up also and TJ followed as they went around to the greenhouse sites, picked up the PVC piping, connectors and a few cans of the bonding glue and climbed the bank to the river where TJ had already installed the river connection. Jeff cut the retaining lines on the PVC and began laying the pipe along the lines chosen to the greenhouses.

The sun had gone down over the mountain and darkness was setting in when the men finished running the lines to both greenhouse locations. Jeff and Dan headed back to their places. Jack went up to the Underground, where he would be staying for the duration of the construction project, and TJ went in the house. He and Jack would clean up and have dinner with Donna. It would be a nice quiet evening after a long day.

The MQ-1A Predator long-range drone found Laramie and turned due west. It found the fertile valley of the Laramie River valley to the west of Laramie and dropped to two hundred feet above ground level (AGL) and flew southwest. As it found Sevenmile Lakes, it turned almost due west again, remaining at the two-hundred-foot AGL level. It flew over Twin Buttes Lake and the pilot back in Colorado in his underground bunker, readied the two weapons the drone held, Hellfire missiles. Both activated, the pilot's console read the activation by noting two green lights beaming from the panel. By that time, the drone reached Lake Hattie Reservoir and as it neared the western most shore, turned to a heading of two four five degrees and began a slow climb.

It crossed Lake Hattie continuing on the same heading and continued rising in altitude. It as it passed the western shore, the drone suddenly began rising at a steeper angle, quickly ascending to 10,000 feet AGL. The pilot activated several cameras and focused the long-range lens on the far ridge beyond Sheep Mountain. The pilot could see the juncture of Highways 11 and 47 and steered to a heading of two-five-zero degrees true, found the structure in the camera and fired the first missile.

He readjusted the camera and finding the second structure, fired the second missile, and immediately began a diving turn to the southeast not hanging around to view the hits. The first missile would have a flight of nine point eight seconds before hitting the first structure and detonating. The second would have just over another second and a half of additional flight time before it hit and detonated in the second structure.

Julia had just pulled her blankets up and got comfortable in her bed after saying a prayer. She was getting warm, settling in when the Hellfire missile tore through the east wall of the home she, Ruth, and DD lived in. It flew through the entire home and detonated just outside Julia's window on the west side of the house. She died instantly as the missile's exploding shock wave and concussion blew in her window and collapsed the bedroom wall.

Ruth was thrown from her bed and DD's crib slammed against the eastern wall in their room. DD immediately began screaming. Ruth knew they were in trouble and crawled over to DD, picked him up and headed for the bedroom door. She heard the second explosion and wondered what was happening, knowing the Colorado people were attacking in some manner. As she opened her door, she saw flames coming from under Julia's door and knew her friend wouldn't be joining them anymore. She flew down the stairs, stepping in glass and debris, and out the back door and looking to the west, saw Jack's home in flames. She ran that direction.

Dan and Jeff both heard the first explosion and jumped, gathering weapons knowing they were in trouble. Before both flew out of their homes the second missile hit. They ran down their drives and met each other at the juncture of the three and saw Julia and Ruth's, and Jack's places in flames. Thank God Jack was with Donna and TJ. They began running towards Julia and Ruth's place and held up short as they saw Ruth carrying DD heading their way.

"What happened?" she yelled, panting, out of breath with the exertion; DD continued to cry and clung to his mother for dear life.

"Don't know," Jeff answered. "We heard the first explosion – guess that was your place – grabbed our gear and before we got out heard the second. Where's Julia?"

Ruth looked at the ground and they knew, "She won't be coming anymore," Ruth sadly answered then began to cry, falling to her knees.

"Come on, let's get under cover," Dan said draping his arm around Ruth and DD, lifting and leading them towards the aspen stand.

"What about the houses?" Jeff asked.

"Let 'em burn. We don't have the capability of fighting a fire like that anyway," Dan said and began heading for the aspens near Jeff's place.

DD began to settle down as they entered the trees. The three adults stood back in the aspen grove, shoulders slumped and saddened by the loss of Julia. But hardness was there, too, along with resolve and determination. Dan looked at Jeff and both knew it was time to end the war. This - game - had to come to an end.

They saw the headlights of a truck coming up Highway 11 and knew it was TJ, Donna, and Jack. They flew into the turn and sped up the ridge and stopped near Jack's place, which was still burning fiercely, and his stores of ammunition had begun cooking off.

Jeff stepped out of the aspens, whistled, and gave a sign Jack knew meant safe and the trio drove up the hill to the aspens, got out weapons ready. "What happened," TJ said, panting.

Dan looked at him and answered, "I think it was missiles, fired from a long way off, I think over Sheep Mountain from the east. The first hit their house," pointing at Ruth and DD, "and the second hit Jack's place; we're all glad you were at Paradise Valley or we would have lost you, too."

Donna put her hand over her mouth and practically screamed, "What do you mean by that?"

Ruth, disheartened, answered, "Julia's gone, dear."

Donna dropped to her knees and began crying, softly at first, then sobbing. Ruth handed DD to Jeff and kneeling next to her, began to cry. The four men and DD stood together, surrounding the women and the look of fierce determination they saw in each other's faces told the story. They let the ladies grieve.

Finally, TJ moved away from the group. Secondary explosions had begun coming from both homes, the ammunition stores cooking off as the places burned. He watched the flames and as Dan came up beside him, the reflected flames in TJ's eyes brought a fleeting moment of fear to Dan. There was going to be hell to pay for this and the Sheriff, and the Ranger in him, and the Marines were going to be the ones dealing death.

TJ grimly ordered Dan, "Get all the supplies you need packed for a long expedition. Pack every round you can carry, every grenade, everything…. We're going to war. Meet us back at Paradise Valley and we'll plan. Make it quick as we don't know if we're about to be hit again or not."

Dan looked TJ in the eye and said, "We'll bring everything we can carry - no quarter this time." TJ looked back and simply nodded.

Chapter 5: Preparations & Action

The fires were smoldering by the time the trio were loaded and ready to depart for Paradise Valley. They took the time to find and wrap Julia's body. They would take her along and bury her with Dave. The Marines were shedding tears the entire time. It was a dismal procession as they reverently carried her body to the truck.

They decided to load all three of the trucks the Marines had and attached their trailers also. One had a fuel tank and they filled it and the trucks from the tanker they'd brought over from Dave and Julia's. With weapons and ammo, food, bedding, clothing, and other supplies loaded, they looked around their slice of heaven on the southern ridge and together, said a group prayer then moved to their vehicles.

TJ heard the horn from Dan's truck and used the remote to open the gate for them, closing it as Jeff pulled through. He met the Marines in the front yard and gave an appreciative nod seeing the supplies they had readied on their trailers.

Dan was first out and seeing TJ, said, "We have Julia on my trailer. We need to put her next to Dave.

The look TJ gave him was hard. The mixture of anger and sadness made Dan's eyes water. Dan knew Julia was like a baby sister to TJ. After a moment, TJ settled down and shook his head and turned for the frontend loader. Dan led the other Marines into the house, and they poured themselves mugs of coffee and waited for TJ, knowing he would rather be alone preparing Julia's grave next to her husband's.

TJ did just that and had tears streaming down his cheeks the whole time he dug. He had Julia's final resting place beside Dave, Doug, and Erskine ready in less than an hour. He backed the frontend loader to a spot out of the way and shut it down, sitting there alone for a while in his own thoughts, sadness, anger, and tears.

As he sat in silence, the sadness slowly turned to seething anger. The tears dried upon his hot cheeks. His hands balled into white-fleshed fists of steel and he hit the dash of the loader several times. He stood up, looked at the grave then back at the home he and Donna lived in, climbed down from the loader, and purposefully strode back to the front porch.

He found the Marines sitting in the Adirondacks, sipping coffee. "It's done," TJ said in a sort of defiant tone.

"Say an hour then, to gather for the interment?" Dan asked.

"Fine," was the one-worded answer from TJ, who then strode into the house, ran upstairs to clean up.

An hour later, Ruth with DD, Donna, Dan, Jack, and Jeff waited on the front porch. TJ still had not come down. Jeff looked at Donna and gave her a questioning look without saying a word. She looked at him, shrugged her shoulders slightly, and shook her head, frowning.

Dan stood to go inside and see what was keeping TJ and froze in mid-stride, hearing, along with the others, the heavy footsteps coming downstairs. It was time. Everyone else on the porch stood and waited. The front door opened, and TJ stood there in his Sherriff's full ceremony uniform, Colt on his hip and Stetson worn just so, Bible in his left hand tucked into his chest near his badge. He looked at Dan and nodded then led the heartbroken procession down the stairs.

Jack had already placed the truck with Julia's remains near the grave site and the four men gently pulled her from the truck and walked her to the site. TJ looked at Donna, and she began to pray. The prayer spread from person to person and when it seemed everyone was done, TJ took the lead, said a final prayer for Julia's spirit, and said Amen.

TJ looked up from his prayer and saw everyone with tears. He looked back at Dan, Jack, and Jeff, nodded and the four of them lowered Julia. Ruth and Donna both began softly crying. The men pulled the ropes leaving Julia next to her husband and TJ turned and proffered his arm for Donna. Jack did the same for Ruth and the group made their way back to the house. Jeff went up to TJ and asked, "May I finish?" pointing to the back where the aspen stand was. TJ nodded.

A half-hour later, Jeff returned with a tear-streaked, grief ridden face. Donna handed him a glass of sweet tea. He downed it and using his sleeve gave the impression he was wiping his mouth when in actuality he was wiping tears.

The six remaining adults of Centennial Valley, Wyoming, stood together on the front porch. It was a quiet time. TJ finally cleared his throat and said, "I'm not going to say mean and hateful things right now. That'll come. I just want us all to remember Julia and Dave as they were, a happy Christian couple that loved the world and everyone in it. Their memories will be with us always and remember, we'll be seeing them again, and that will be a most happy time." He stopped then as the grief overcame him and the Sheriff softly cried, along with the others, without shame.

That evening, Donna and Ruth got together and made some soup and sandwiches. They all sat quietly at the table. Ruth said a prayer and dinner was a quiet affair. Jeff, broke the mood by posing the question, "What're we gonna do?"

"Like we said we were going to do last year, we're gonna kill 'em all," Donna answered resolutely.

"How many Stingers we have left," TJ asked.

"We have three - one was blown at Jack's place," Dan answered.

"How many mortar rounds," TJ asked again.

"'Bout four hundred-twenty or so," Jack said.

"So, we have four mortars with that many rounds, three Stingers and I have four AT-6s up in the Underground,' TJ said.

"That enough to do it?" Ruth asked.

"Probably not," TJ answered her.

"We don't have enough intel either," Dan said. "We don't know what all is in that underground facility. We can guess a lot of things because from what you say, the tunnel is at least

101

five miles long with no telling how many side branches and other exits. They could have a hundred branches in there full of supplies and equipment and heaven only knows what. And we don't really know how many troops they have either."

"Too bad we didn't have a biological weapon of some kind we could roll in there," Jeff mused.

"That would be rich," Donna said.

"He does have a point though," TJ said. "We could drop in tear gas…a lot of it and see what kind of roaches that flushes and where…"

It got quiet around the table as they thought about that. Tear gas was easy to get, and TJ probably had a ready supply along with masks back in Laramie at the Sherriff's office. Maybe the Air Force base had more they could find and even the Cheyenne PD might have a supply they could get.

"That's not a bad thought," Jack said. "If we at least drove them back, then we could fire those AT-6s down the tunnel from the entrance and blow it. Who knows, maybe that is the only exit?"

"Doubtful," Dan said. "But a good idea and we can make it better by pumping gasoline down the thing before firing the AT-6s. Fry the lot of them."

"I like the tear gas idea," Jeff said. "Drive them back then attack. The four of us could take 'em."

"Not in our lifetimes," TJ said. "We'd need a hundred men to try and take a facility like that, especially with all the unknowns."

"My emotions talking, sorry," Jeff said downtrodden.

"Mine, too, my friend," TJ said. "I'm suddenly thinkin' right now that we don't have time for emotion. We have to think logically and come up with a viable plan of action."

"Leave," Dan said.

Immediately Ruth added, "Yes, leave."

TJ looked at both of them and asked, "Leave what…here?"

"Yes," they said in unison.

Dan looked at Ruth and she nodded so he continued, "We need to leave the valley for our own safety. I think the

Ranger's shack would be best. It has a sustainable water supply and a good enough building to hold us comfortably. It has the outhouse, too."

"We could run supplies every day, trying to save as much as we can before they completely destroy our homes," Donna said.

"And we can store most of the stuff in that warehouse building on the west side of Centennial," Jack thought out loud.

"After we move as much material as we can, we can begin our study of the tunnel entrance, the surrounding topography and plan another recon and possibly an attack," TJ said. "Once and for all take that place out and kill 'em all."

"I'd like to get one of them alive and have a chat with 'em," Jeff said with a grim, nasty look on his face.

"Now that I do like," Jack said sitting up with the same kind of look.

"Me, too," Ruth commented with a faraway look on her face that sent a chill down Donna's spine.

Silence brought the group together thinking about that, taking a prisoner, and 'chatting' with the person. They would be able to get valuable intelligence and possibly some idea of how large the facility was underground and maybe, just maybe, find out why they wanted to kill the valley residents.

Jeff looked at Dan and said, "The little airport. I bet that's where they launch the drones so I bet we could get one of them there. Maybe two or three even."

Dan looked at TJ and saw the grim smile on his face. Now they were talking. Taking one or more of their people as prisoners and milking them for information was a not only a good way to get intel but would lift their morale greatly. Just knowing they could do something constructive lifted spirits.

TJ said, "I think that is a great idea and feel we need to act on it. Dan, what do you say we do first?" TJ asked him, giving him the lead on this one.

"Move out, taking as much of our supplies as we can get out of here before the next attack. We need to have someone on watch duty when we're loading materials. That way if they do attempt another drone attack, we can use a Stinger on them."

"I wish we had more of those," Jack said more to himself than the group.

"Maybe we will have more," TJ said. "I think we have several missions to work up. Moving to a safer location with our supplies and materials is first priority, then going shopping for more firepower, then going on a scouting mission to get a prisoner or two would be next. We could split forces, so to speak, and Donna, Ruth, DD, and I can go to Guernsey and the Air Force base in Cheyenne for more war fighting supplies, concentrating on explosives, shoulder fired missiles and mortars and rounds. Dan, Jack, and Jeff can go for the prisoner since they have Special Forces combat experience."

"I like his way of thinking," Jeff said, looking at Dan.

"All agree?" Dan asked the group. He got a round of nods from everyone in agreement and said, "Then hop to it everyone. Jack, Jeff; take your rigs to the Ranger Station and unload then go to the ridge and load up everything you can and take it to the warehouse. TJ, Donna and Ruth; you begin here, and I'll help. We need to concentrate on survival materials first, food, clothing, and bedding supplies. Next are weapons, ammo, and explosives." He got nods from everyone again, so he ended with, "First thing in the morning then."

"I'll take the first watch," Jack said and got up heading for the door.

"Stingers are in the truck," Jeff said.

Outside, Jack, with Jeff's help, got the Stingers and put them in the ATV and Jack said, "I'll wake you at midnight. Sleep in the room closest to the eastern portal as that'll be where I set up."

"Got it, see you in a while," Jeff said turning for the house.

Jack fired up the ATV and drove up the eastern trail to the portal and readied two of their three Stingers. He arranged his

AR-10 and his M4, got one of the lawn chairs and a set of binos and got comfortable scanning the sky for unwanted guests. He soon had tears running down his cheeks again, thinking about Julia. He stood up and began to pace back and forth along the edge, *Payback time* he thought to himself.

Dawn found Jeff yawning and stretching trying to stay awake. Jack had seen nothing flying last night and Jeff hadn't seen anything through the early morning hours either. It was almost six and a chill had come in, but Jeff was prepared and had his coat on. He brought his binos up and was looking to the southeast when the eastern portal opened, and Dan climbed out. He had two mugs of steaming hot coffee with him.

"Morning; see anything?" Dan asked handing a mug to Jeff.

"No, and thanks," he answered, taking a healthy sip of the hot liquid. "Thank you for this," he said holding up his mug.

"You're welcome, thought you'd need it," Dan said quietly. "Got chilly."

"Yeah, came in about three hours ago," Jeff said setting his mug down and looking through his binoculars again.

"Why don't you go get some shut-eye and I'll stand watch 'till noon. I asked TJ to spell me then."

"Nah, I'm awake now that the sun's coming up. Won't be able to sleep and you know it. I'll help Jack at the houses. He up yet?"

"Yeah, he's up. Go get some breakfast and I'll see you guys later."

Jeff handed Dan the binoculars and turned for the portal. Dan began his watch by scanning the sky with the binos, doing a 360-degree scan of the morning sky. Even though he knew they were ready, he checked the Stingers and the other weapons ensuring they were and sat in the lawn chair.

Noon came and TJ took over the watch. The groups had moved a significant number of supplies to both the Ranger shack and the warehouse in the six hours since Dan had begun his watch.

Dan said, "I've been scanning in a 360 all morning. I'm thinking someone down there is thinking out of the box and that's why they got those two shots in like they did. We weren't expecting something like that, so we need to think out of the box, too. I got a feeling the next attack will come from the west or southwest. Here," he said getting a map out, "take a look at this." He set the map out on the back tailgate of the ATV and TJ followed Dan's finger as it made a track from the tunnel, up the front range mountains following Highway 287, turning west near the border, and finding Highway 230, turning almost due north until it hit Fox Park, Wyoming. His finger followed a line to Rob Roy Reservoir. As his finger got to Cinnabar Park, Dan said, "This is where I'd heat up the weapons then follow this track until I got to the river valley, following the river to about here and fire the missiles. They would each go to the Underground and your home. That release point gives the drone ample time to turn out to the south and head home."

"You've given this some thought," TJ said still looking at the map.

"Yep, been thinking about it all night and day. They could come from the south, but then they'd have to watch out for the mountain. Same to the north. Best chance of getting the Underground and your home is from the west, I'd say."

TJ straightened up and looked to the west and asked Dan, "What's the range on these things?" pointing at the Stingers.

"About five miles or so, maybe a little less than five, but well over four, why?"

"Cinnabar Park is only two miles or so from here, so they'll be in range as soon as they hit the river. If we see one coming first, we'll have a good chance to save the place if they come from that direction. These things need to hit the target to kill it?"

"No, these are FIM 92K models and have a proximity fuse, so if they get close, they'll blow, and the shrapnel will take out the target. They'll do the job. They may be sneaky enough to send two drones if they have them, so if you fire the first, get the second up and running quickly. Might just save the day."

TJ nodded understanding. He took the binos from Dan and scanned to the west, then made his 360. Dan climbed down the portal leaving TJ to his watch duty.

The remainder of the day went well for everyone. Jack and Jeff had taken all the supplies from Marine Hill to the new encampment and storage areas and had begun helping the others take materials from Paradise Valley. They would do the Underground next and use the two remaining ATVs to haul materials down the mountain.

It was getting late. The wind was up, and a cold overcast had come in from the northwest. It was going to be a chilly evening and night. The valley group met for dinner just after six in the evening. They had stopped for the night and would have dinner then relax for a while before going to bed. Jack was up on the eastern portal doing his tour on watch. Dan and TJ had both told him to keep a good watch to the west and their reasoning why.

They had put up a ten-foot by ten-foot canopy for cover in case the cloud cover brought in rain, or worse, snow. It had cooled considerably since the clouds had rolled in. Jack was bundled up in his coat, gloves, and a balaclava, and had a mug full of steaming coffee and two thermoses full for the night. He used his binoculars frequently looking mostly to the west but scanning 360 degrees often. He was tired of losing his friends and just couldn't understand why the Colorado people were attacking the way they were. The questions just kept coming for all the valley residents.

Midnight came and the change of the watch took place with Jeff taking over. He knew about the probability of the next attack coming from the west and concentrated his viewing on that direction. He, too, was dressed in a heavy coat, gloves, and head covering and had an ample supply of hot coffee. The cold was jarring, and he walked back and forth on the lip of the

Underground to keep warm. He considered a fire but didn't want to advertise his position.

The drone launched at 0245 hours from the short, grass runway. It launched from east to west. As the crow flew, the target was sixty-five miles to the northwest from the little airstrip. However, after liftoff, the drone was turned and flown directly north, then to the northwest, following Highway 287. At the Colorado/Wyoming border, the craft turned due west until it came to Highway 230, turning until it found the intersection for Fox Park and then to Rob Roy Reservoir. As it reached Cinnabar Park, the pilot, deep underground, armed the Hellfire missiles slung underneath the wings of the drone once again getting the two green lights on his panel.

Jeff saw the thing as it began its turn to the east over the river. He quickly activated the first Stinger and lifted it to his shoulder, found the drone and fired. He dropped the spent tube and picked up the second Stinger, activating it. He brought it up to his shoulder and found the drone and saw his missile make a direct hit blowing the drone into several pieces, burning as it fell. He saw one missile cook-off from the flaming wreckage and soar to the south, arching high into the night sky, turning towards the ground, and speeding to earth.

The noise of the Stinger launch brought the others out of the Underground and the house, all brandishing weapons of some kind. TJ and Jack came up the western portal and asked what had transpired and Jack explained his action and the result, all the while keeping watch with the second Stinger on his shoulder.

Dan yelled down the mountain to the folks below, "It came from the west like we talked about! Jack got it before it launched its missiles."

"Way to shoot!" came from TJ.

"We're going to stay up and watch. You guys get some sleep," Dan yelled down.

"How many more of those things you think they have?" Jeff asked.

"No telling, and that's one reason we need to move outta here for a while. At least until we get them taken care of," Dan said.

"We're down to two Stingers," Jeff observed.

"Maybe TJ'll find some more in Guernsey," Jack said.

"I hope so," Dan said. "I hope they find some good stuff. With the three of them taking trucks and trailers, they should be able to bring back some good materials. I'm making a list of things for them to watch for, and since TJ was a Ranger, he'll know what we'll need if he sees it."

"We were lucky again, weren't we?" Jeff asked.

"Yes," Dan answered somberly.

By dinner time the next day the group had moved most of the supplies and equipment out of the Underground and out of the root cellar in the house. The following day they would complete the movement of materials and move into the Ranger shack.

TJ, Donna and Ruth, prepared for their mission to the military bases for supplies. They would take three trucks with trailers, one with fuel, and first go to the Air Force base near Cheyenne, then to Guernsey if necessary. They had decided to make it two separate missions, returning to the Ranger station after gathering what they could from Cheyenne, and off-loading those supplies into the warehouse. Then they would rest and resupply then head north to Guernsey.

The Marines prepared for their mission to attempt capture of one or more of the men from the Colorado group. They would depart in two trucks and take along the two remaining Stingers. All three would be fully decked out with their weapons of choice and plenty of ammunition. They would drive to Cheyenne then turn south on Highway 85 and come in from the east. Since they had already done the recon of the area, they knew best where to set up for their covert mission.

With five trucks and trailers loaded with the last of the supplies, weapons and ammunition, the valley residents reluctantly departed Paradise Valley and drove the short distance to both the warehouse and the Ranger station. The men emptied the trucks at the warehouse and the ladies drove up to the station and began unloading there. They took time to discuss actions and reactions to their situation and decided they were doing the right thing with the Marines going south to Colorado, and TJ and the rest going for war-fighting supplies and equipment at the Air Force base and Guernsey.

That night in the station, they held a group prayer session. Most prayed for safety for everyone on their missions. Several prayed for good health and a bountiful harvest in the fall. Positive thinking, as if there would be a fall for the valley residents and a harvest at all. The outlook for them was at best doubtful at this point. With an unknown number of enemies trying to kill them, supplies were dwindling and because of the harassment from the Colorado complex, the valley residents were not able to plant crops like they wanted and needed. The upcoming winter looked dismal indeed.

But they continued to pray, asking for deliverance, assistance, and guidance with their continued fight for life. Dan asked for guidance while on their mission to Colorado and asked for a sign they were doing the right thing. They all had doubts about their actions – were they right in God's eyes or not. The Bible had many stories of men fighting for God and doing right by fighting and sometimes killing millions to get the job done. Dan and TJ had talked about this on a few occasions and came to the mutual understanding that God didn't want wimps - He wanted people to fight for what was morally correct, right, and just. This, the group knew, was what they were fighting for.

Chapter 6: Ladies Day Out

The change in plans put everyone on edge. TJ, Donna, Jack, and Jeff had been gone for several days on their second outing for war supplies and equipment. They had gone to Guernsey two days prior and were to be returning in three. Upon their return, the three Marines would deploy to Colorado with the specific task of capturing one or more of their adversaries. They would take three trucks loaded with supplies and equipment and store the lot in a school they decided to use as a basing facility. It would hold all five trucks in the garage structure and the school itself would be a perfect bivouac area.

Dan and Ruth had been caring for DD and having a swell time at the Ranger's Station. It was a pleasant summer day and they had DD on a blanket out by one of the picnic tables the facility had on site. Both were sipping coffee and watching DD cooing while playing with his toys. From time-to-time one or the other would snicker at the little tykes' actions. DD was beginning to crawl and that brought an increase in awareness and watchfulness from the adults. The little scooter was very inquisitive and got into everything.

"Dan, may I ask you a personal question?" Ruth asked.

"Sure, go ahead," Dan answered looking her way.

"Did you ever marry?"

"No, never did," he answered with a shake of his head.

"Why is that?"

After a several moments of thought he answered," I suppose I never found the right woman. Too, Vietnam changed me…changed everyone who was there."

"How so?"

"When I came back to the world - America that is - I saw life differently. It seemed…well…cheap. I have no idea how many of those people I killed – a lot – and when I got back, I had to re-learn what life was all about and what it meant. I wandered for a while working odd cowboy jobs all over Wyoming, northern Colorado, Montana, and some in Nebraska, and one day went into a church in Cheyenne in 2004. The pastor – I think his name was Billy something – anyway, he was talking about family and those families who were having troubles. He said it rarely got better and it just seemed to always worsen. But he had a good answer at the end, and it revolved around the love of Christ. All things were able to be forgiven - everything. He said forgiveness was a choice. That to let go of something that was bothering you was a matter of choice. You either chose to let it go and forgive, or let it fester and therefore you would make the choice to allow your anger and uncaring attitude and unloving life carry on. We have to give the pain and anger to God, and that led again to that word 'choice'.

"It got me to thinkin' about choice and specifically, my choices in my life. I decided to go somewhere and think, so I packed what little I had, and I drove out into the Medicine Bow. I had my backpack and took along some water, a few freeze-dried meals, a bedroll, and a few other things, and standing there by my truck, looked around. I prayed and asked the Lord to send me in a direction He wanted me to go. I started out and an elk bugled over my left shoulder and for some reason, I turned and went towards that bugle. After about an hour or so of hiking, I came to a little canyon that came down a small mountain. I went up into it and found a nice place up on a promontory to look out over the forest. I sat up there for quite a while reading my Bible and thinking.

Sitting on that rocky outcropping, I realized I had chosen to let the war direct the person I had become. Frankly, I was tired of it, so I 'chose' to change and decided to look at a lot of things differently. I relearned to respect the sanctity of life, even looking at kids differently than I had, and chose to be happier. I still saw things in a dark way when I saw others treating someone badly…the sad part of that is I didn't do anything about it. Just let it go. Now…ain't gonna happen. I see something bad happening to someone else, I'm going to do my best to rectify the problem. That's why I *chose* to go to war against those goons in Colorado."

Ruth had been looking at him surprised and in wonder. She saw a side of Dan he probably had never shown to anyone before, so she got up and going to him, gave him a big hug and said, "You're a good man Daniel Norris, Nemo," and gave him a peck on the cheek and a big smile.

The resupply team returned on time and with loads the valley people really needed. More AT-6s, forty Stingers, and more mortar rounds. They found several thousand rounds of fifty caliber high explosive and high explosive incendiary rounds. Jack had found a container full of twenty-five-pound satchel charges. The complex people were in trouble – they just didn't know it yet.

After unloading the supplies and equipment at the warehouse, the valley residents made a meal of buffalo steaks with all the fixings and joined together in a feast celebrating the safe return of the resupply crew. The three Marines would leave in two days' time to go and attempt to capture one or more of the Colorado people. The Ladies would leave the same day and have a 'ladies' day' out, shopping in Laramie and having a good time. Once again TJ would have DD for the day. It would be another fishing day.

Ruth was up at the prearranged time of 0430 hours, handing DD off to TJ with reluctance. She did need a day off. She and Donna climbed into Donna's truck and pulled out behind the Colorado capture team at 0500 hours, leaving for Laramie and a day of shopping and hoping to see and assist the capture team as they went on their way if needed. TJ stood on the porch with DD asleep and wrapped in his blanket and watched the two teams depart on their missions – Ladies Day Out and The Capture Team. He hoped and prayed he would see the ladies' home safely this evening and prayed the Capture Team would return safely as well after their five-day mission. The plan was if they were successful earlier, they'd return as soon as they could.

He turned and went back inside to get the kid into a warmer environment – early mornings in Wyoming were always cool. Inside, he laid DD on the bunk and placed pillows around him to keep him from rolling off.

After TJ had dressed, he put DD into the ATV and drove to Paradise Valley. Inside the house, TJ put DD on the couch and started a fire then went into the kitchen and made a pot of coffee. He would wait for the little guy to wake up, then feed him and himself, clean up and dress the little guy, then they would head to Lake Owen for some fishing. TJ had already fastened the car seat in the ATV and made sure it was secure.

DD slept for another two hours and woke up hungry and needing a diaper change. TJ was Grandpa-on-the-spot, cleaning the little guy and putting him in a fresh diaper, dressing him in his little hunter's outfit the Marines had 'acquired', and gave him his bottle for breakfast. TJ had toast with peach jam, a pair of sausage patties, and of course, coffee.

After cleaning up from breakfast, the pair left the house, climbed into, and strapped in the ATV, and departed for a few hours of fishing at the lake. It took about twenty minutes to get there, and TJ parked the ATV near the old, dilapidated pier. He hoisted DD up on his back in his kiddie backpack, collected his fishing gear, and hiked to the south western side of the lake where the wind wasn't so bad. TJ could hear the little guy talking about all sorts of things in baby talk and smiled.

TJ readied his pole and casted the bait out. He was slowly reeling in the lure when a lake trout hit the bait and the battle was on. First cast and a fish on. TJ brought the trout in and hoisting the fish up to look at it, saw it was about twenty inches in length. *Good enough* TJ thought to himself and hooked the stringer to the trout. He slid DD off his back and showed him the fish, holding it in front of him showing it off.

"Now that's a trout, DD," TJ said then placed the fish in the lake.

He put DD back on his back and readied his pole again and cast towards a stump. Wham, another strike even before TJ began to reel in the bait. This one was a fighter, much more so than the previous one. This one even made the reel's drag sing as it fought for freedom. TJ played the big fish for almost fifteen minutes before it finally tired enough to be landed. And it was a monster, twenty-four-inch lake trout. TJ had never caught one this size and he'd fished in a lot of areas of Wyoming and Montana.

TJ held the fish up and marveled at the size of the thing. He decided these two fish would more than feed he, Ruth, and Donna, so he clipped it to his stringer and turned for his ATV. He put DD into his car seat and stowed the backpack, fishing gear, and fish, hopped in himself and started the engine.

He drove home slowly, enjoying the scenery and solitude, even though he had DD with him. As they drove through Albany, TJ watched for Zs and saw none. They passed the turn to the Marine's drive and rounded the curve on Highway 11 to the north. TJ floored the ATV. The duo sped along, and TJ was enjoying himself. The little ATV was up to fifty miles an hour, the wind whipping into the cab.

After the exhilarating ride, TJ finally reached the ranger station and opened the door. He took DD inside and put the little man on his blanket in front of the heater, placing two logs on the almost dead embers of the morning's fire, and turned to go back out and retrieve the fish to clean them. It had been a splendid morning. After cleaning, TJ put the fish in the fridge – they would taste great for dinner.

Donna and Ruth did as they promised and stopped at the airport, launched a drone, and flew around Laramie on a recon mission. They saw many Zs out and about, but no black vehicles at all. Bringing the drone back, they packed it and went to town. First stop – a lady's boutique.

They went in Z'd up and ready, brandishing squirt guns filled with saltwater. Ruth knocked on the door and one Z sauntered up to the entrance. Ruth pushed the door in, and Donna gave the creature a long blast of the saltwater. It promptly died and they pulled the corpse out into the parking lot. Back inside, they shopped, laughing, and giggling over the things they saw. Both picked out some jeans and a few blouses.

They left that place and went to the big mart store as Ruth wanted to get as much baby care materials as she could. It always was a good thing to have extra. Several Zs were in the parking lot of the mart, so they drove by them and hosed them down with saltwater to end the threat. Donna pulled up next to the main entrance and they went in.

Donna stood watch and Ruth got two carts to fill. She went down the aisle for the baby products and filled both carts in no time. Together, she and Donna put the items in bed of the truck and relocking the store, pulled out and went to the east side of town to try and radio the capture team to see how they were progressing. It was close to noon, so they broke out their lunch and a few bottles of water for a picnic, sitting in the truck. They tried several times on the radio, never getting an answer from the team – mountain interference.

"Ruth, may I ask you a question?" Donna asked.

"I guess," Ruth answered.

"Are you really okay…I mean, since losing Doug, then Dave, and now Julia, are you doing alright?" she asked.

Ruth hung her head for a moment and after a minute of thought answered, "Yes, I'm doing fine. I do miss Doug a great deal and I feel sorry for little DD since he won't know his father other than what we tell him and the few pictures that are left. And losing Dave and Julia…" her head hung as she ended on that note.

"I'm sorry if I made you sad," Donna said, forlornly.

"No, don't worry about it. I need to talk about it and get my feelings out – it'll do me good. Honestly, sometimes I feel like putting a bullet in my head, but DD brings me out of that funk with a laugh or a cry or a squeal, and I have to smile. The new Doug makes my 'sense' come back if you know what I mean."

"I think I do, actually. When I saw my family torn to shreds by those things, my mother, father and four brothers, I've felt the same way many times. When I met TJ, everything changed. Everything. I don't think about them as much anymore. Don't get me wrong, I still miss my family and love them very much, but they're not the most important in my life anymore…my faith and TJ are. So, look at it this way, DD is your…change."

"That's sweet and I agree. He's my angel sent to heal from God. He's my great reminder of the wonderful man I fell in love with and married. Little DD is the result of that relationship, a wonderful reminder of who Doug and I were together."

Donna shook her head positively, tears streaming down her cheeks, to overcome with emotion to comment. After a few moments, she finally croaked out, "I don't know what I'd do if I lost TJ."

"You'd do just like Julia and I – survive. Wake up every morning and carry on. God will direct us and keep us. He's been with us through everything, after all."

"Yeah, I suppose," Donna said, then, "Come on let's go back to the Ranger's Station. We'll wait for the crew there."

TJ cooked the fish and had made a salad of sorts from the vegetables they had left. He served dinner with a few slices of his bread. DD gummed some of the bread and made a real mess. The three adults laughed watching the kid chow down on the slice. The fresh fish was baked using garlic, onion, and butter as a baste. They loved the dinner. All three had glasses of wine with dinner. For the most part the dinner was a quiet affair with each in their own thoughts, most of which were about the future and the safety of the three Marines, and the future actions of the valley residents when it came time to attack the Colorado complex again.

It was the day the Capture Team was to return, and they had voted for 'comfort food' as their return meal of choice. That is, fried chicken, mashed potatoes with gravy, corn cut off the cob and tomato wedges. TJ had gone to the garage at Paradise Valley and got out two chickens to thaw. Back at the Ranger Station, he readied some potatoes to boil for mashing and got out two bags of their frozen corn. TJ would have everything ready for Donna and Ruth to cook as soon as the team radioed, they were on their last leg home…he prayed. He took out six tomatoes which he would cut into wedges. Fried chicken, mashed potatoes with gravy, corn, and tomato wedges – comfort food – his mouth watered.

TJ got out a bag of flour, some yeast, baking soda, some sugar, and salt and prepared the dough for his homemade bread. It would go well with the dinner. After he kneaded the dough, he cut it into four equal portions and setting them aside to rise. Two portions he would make rolls out of for the night's dinner and the remaining would be baked in loaf pans. By the time they rose and were ready to bake, it would be, he hoped and prayed, about time for the group to return, giving the place a wonderful welcoming aroma for the weary travelers.

TJ was sitting on the front porch of the Ranger Station after cleaning up, watching the day and the road. The valley had been quiet since the destruction of the drone over Cinnabar Park. Everyone was on pins and needles waiting for the call to come from the Capture Team who were scheduled to return this day, successful or not.

Donna had been hanging out with DD, giving Ruth a break for a while and now that the youngest valley resident was down for a nap, Donna went for the front porch of the station where they had set several of their lawn chairs. Opening the door, she looked at TJ and he gave her a nod. That was all she needed, and turning, went back inside to the radio room. Donna picked up the radio mike and keying said, "Recon Team, acknowledge, over."

An immediate answer came over the net, "Recon Team reads you loud and clear, over."

"They're alive!" Donna yelled looking at Ruth who had just joined her. "Sit-rep, over?" Donna asked them.

"Everyone A-Okay, over," Donna and Ruth, overjoyed to hear the news, thought it was Jack on the net.

"What's your twenty, over?" Donna asked.

"Comin' down the hill now, darlin, be there in forty-five, over."

Ruth and Donna both looked up and smiled at each other. "Good news, team, do you have the package, over?"

"Boy, do we have the package…more like packages, over."

"Great news, we'll see you in a bit, over and out."

Dan, Jack, and Jeff, pulled up next to the ladies as they stood with TJ behind them in the station parking lot and piled out of their truck. It was like an old home reunion, everyone smiling, laughing, and hugging. Ruth and Donna congratulated the team on their safe return and the team saying thank you for the homecoming reception.

After the excitement wore off, Ruth asked, "How'd it go?"

"We have news," Dan said. "We still having the powwow tonight with comfort food?"

"Absolutely," Donna said. "TJ said he'd be getting everything together for me to cook so we better get inside soon and start."

"We've got news for you, too," Ruth told them, adding, "but it'll wait until the powwow. Come on in and tell us how it went."

Dan answered, "It went well. Let's talk about it later."

Ruth and Donna led the way, as usual and went inside the Ranger Station. The ladies went to the kitchen to finish preparing dinner and the Marines to the facilities to clean up.

They could smell the fresh bread and knew TJ had made a batch.

The Marines thought TJ would have the drinks ready but alas, he had not. They were surprised to find a bottle of twenty-eight-year-old scotch in the latrine waiting for them. They poured themselves a tumbler and began their cleaning process by sipping scotch first.

Afterwards, the six stood on the porch toasting each other and welcoming everyone home safely, again. "Hey everyone, let's head inside and we'll get dinner on the table," TJ said. Looking at Dan, he asked, "You need to do something for those three in the back of your truck?" referring to the three prisoners he saw.

Dan answered, "Nope, they'll keep…promise."

The house was permeated with the aroma of fried chicken. Donna was mixing the homemade chicken gravy and yelled for everyone to get to the table and take a seat, which of course they all scrambled to do. Once the ladies were seated, the men sat and waited for Donna. She brought the gravy over and sat down and said, "TJ, would you lead us in prayer?"

"Everyone, please bow your heads; Heavenly Father, we thank you for the safe return of the team and our ladies from their day out the other day. Thank you for the fish DD and I caught. We thank you for this food and the companionship we have with each other. Please bless each of us abundantly and see us through the tough times we know are ahead. We thank you for all you do for us, in Jesus' name I pray, Amen."

Dinner was a huge success. Everyone ate their fill. Even DD had a few spoons of the gravy and, of course, wanted more, thinking that was the best thing since Pablum – which it was. As everyone finished eating, plates, bowls, and stemware were moved to the sink and tumblers of scotch or glasses of wine came out. The meeting began with another prayer by TJ, asking for guidance and assistance from the Devine Trio in Heaven.

"First thing, I'd like to hear is what happened here?" Dan asked.

Ruth pointed at TJ and said, "You tell it."

"Well, as you know, after some quiet time with the Lord and not getting clear signals, I backed out of going with you, and as we found out, that is exactly what God wanted me to do because…"

After TJ told his story along with Donna's and Ruth's inputs, the capture team said that was a lot better action, fishing, shopping, and a fish fry, than they had on their mission. Dan began by talking about the uneventful trip down and camping in the school. Jack then talked about he and Jeff heading east, to the north of the facility, and doing a recon that direction and not seeing anything of interest save a few Zs ambling about. Jeff mentioned the animals were particularly unafraid of the humans and that the roadways and buildings down that way were beginning to show considerable signs of aging and neglect.

Jack took over by giving his account of doing a recon of the southern areas with no findings of interest and confirmed the run-down condition of the roads and buildings. He mentioned he could see the stars better down there than he'd ever seen them near Denver, saying the sky was clear and becoming much fresher.

"What about the three out in the truck?" Donna asked.

Dan pointed at Jeff who smiled and said, "I got 'em. I was doing a sneak on the south side and was moving north when I saw this hummer coming down the dirt road, I was near. I used the suppressed nine to take out their right-rear tire and they stopped, thinking they'd had a blowout. They were in the process of changing the tire and not paying attention when I jumped them, getting the drop on them with my suppressed nine. I made them fix the tire then tied 'em up and went back to the bivouac and waited for Dan and Jack."

Dan was next and said, "He did that the second day, so we decided to go ahead and stay and collect more intelligence. I launched a high-altitude drone and flew along the western slope and eastern side of the mountains due west of the facility. I was able to pinpoint the opening Jeff had found last time and took a lot of video of the surrounding area, including that little airport. I did see them launch a drone, but it flew almost due south, maybe a little east of south. I didn't see it come back. I landed our drone and got Jeff and together, we dressed in some heavy camo and got as closed to the entrance as we dared. Both of us took a bunch of photos for us to use in our attack development. I feel we should hit the facility as soon as possible."

After his report, there was silence at the table, everyone deep in thought. The three that went on the mission looked at each other and wondered if they had done something wrong. The three that had stayed behind were in their own thoughts. Finally, Donna said, "I think we need to download the video and all the photos and all of us look them over and individually think about actions to take and ideas for weapons use. We can set a time-limit on the review and meet together again for another powwow in a few days. How's that sound?"

"And after some interrogation time," Jeff added.

Everyone agreed and Dan and TJ got up and went into the library and downloaded the video and photos onto thumb-drives for everyone to use. Once finished with the downloads, TJ handed out the drives to everyone and they broke.

While TJ and Dan did computer work, the ladies, Jeff, and Jack, finished cleaning the dishes and the kitchen. DD was out like a light after having been tossed around by the guys since the team's return, worn out as usual by the caring men. The kid would never have a dull moment in his lifetime as long as the Marines and Sheriff were around. Ruth gathered him in his blanket and quietly went to the room they had in the Ranger's Station to put him to bed.

TJ and Donna went back into the station to view the video, which was about forty minutes in length. Afterwards, TJ said, "That thing will be a bugger to bomb with our drones."

"I agree, and we'll only be able to hit it from one direction, and based on the film, I'd say that would be out of the southwest, around two-five-five degrees or so…wouldn't you?" Donna asked.

"I'd say that was 'bout right," TJ agreed. "We need to see if there are any roads further up the mountain on the west to use as access so we can get a sniper team up there, say with two fifties from a couple of different angles."

"Let's run the photos and see if they picked up anything," Donna suggested.

There were several hundred photos, both aerial and ground shots. If they scanned them all and saved specific shots for further review to an additional file, it would take all night. TJ had one and so did Donna, and each had a copy of the video in their additional files, too, so would review them the following day. "No, I say we pack up, lock up, and rack out after we do something with those prisoners," TJ opted. "Dan?"

"Yeah TJ," Dan answered.

"What are we going to do with those three out in the truck?" TJ asked.

Dan shrugged his shoulders and answered, "Leave 'em. They'll be fine. We can move 'em over to the Malone Underground tomorrow sometime. Let 'em sit out there and worry. I need some sleep," and with that he turned and went into the room the Marines had.

TJ, surprised, shook his head, looked at Donna, and said, "Let's go to bed."

The next morning, that is just what Donna and TJ were doing since they'd risen first, looking at photos. "Look at this one," Donna said. "Looks like an old dirt road or trail on the mountainside. Think that would be good enough? It runs right up to this rocky outcropping here."

TJ leaned in for a closer look and said, "That just might do it. Sorry for being off in my own little world there."

"That's okay, what were you thinking about?" she asked.

"Napalm," was the answer.

"Napalm?" she questioned. "What about it?"

"I know the Air Force base probably didn't have any of that since it was a missile base and only had choppers, but if I remember correctly, we can produce a form of homemade napalm and I was trying to remember what the formula was. But I can't."

"We can make homemade napalm - how?"

"That's what I'm saying, but I can't remember the formula. I remember gasoline was the main ingredient, but don't remember what else we would need to add. I'm thinking maybe Dan and the guys might know. You know Marines. It'll be something for us to write down and remember to ask when they get up. If we can somehow produce some and figure out a way to connect it to drones with an igniter, either the bombers or the smaller ones for Kamikaze missions, that might be a big help and a great force multiplier."

He turned and getting a pad of paper and a few pencils, went into the big open room and sitting again at the table they'd brought, began to write. Donna watched him scribbling furiously for a moment and figured she better do the same so got a pad and began writing.

Later that morning, Dan, Jack, Jeff, and TJ, left to take the prisoners over to the Malone Underground. The Marines had trussed up the three captives very well. They had hoods over their heads and Dan had told TJ they had put ear plugs in their ears so they couldn't hear what was going on very well. He'd also wrapped their eyes with pads and wraps then used duct tape to hold it all on.

They used rope to lower the captives down into the underground. Jack stood watch over the three while Dan, Jeff, and TJ cleared three rooms at the end of three of the hallways to hold the prisoners. They added a single chair in each room. Once they had the rooms ready, they took the prisoners one by one and cut them loose in their new homes. They sat them in the chairs and tied them to the legs and back with an abundance of rope, tape, and bailing wire. They would not be getting loose.

As soon as all three were seated, the Marines and Sheriff began the interrogations. TJ had a baseball bat and would smack the backs of the chairs from time-to-time, to get their attention. Dan would use his finger and forcefully poke them on the chest. Jack pulled their heads back by grabbing hair or with his palm on their foreheads. Jeff just smacked them with the back of his hand. Suffice it to say, they each wanted to do much worse but held back. The four interrogators would do this daily, several times a day at times, until they began to get answers.

Three days later the valley residents met again for a powwow during dinner. The discussions, both as a group and between individuals, went on for hours, late into the evening. The Marines did indeed know how to mix homemade Napalm and gave TJ all the information he needed to make a batch for testing. They would have to come up with something to use as an igniter. A few more good ideas came from the meeting, one of which was to get some lead, melt it and make forty-five or fifty caliber balls and add that to bombs, adding to the shrapnel equation similar to a Claymore mine. Ruth came up with that one explaining if they added the lead balls to the C-4, when it exploded, it would act similar to the mines and send them in all directions once the bomb hit its target.

Everything was suggested, including flaming arrows like the American Indians used in the old west. Another suggestion was to create a huge bomb on the mountain to the west and blow it causing an avalanche to rain down on the tunnel entrance. No idea was ignored. All were considered and discussed.

As the meeting wound down, the best ideas were written on the legal pad Donna was using to take notes. Some, like the napalm, would need testing before the valley residents could use it in action. Several suggestions were made on when to make the attack, but no firm date was agreed upon at this point since more recon of the east face of the mountain was desirable.   They also needed to recon a backup place for staging, a place protected from the prying eyes of a drone was preferable, and it had to be large enough to house at least four trucks with trailers full of supplies, fuel, and equipment.

Now came the time the whole group was waiting for, the report on the interrogation of the three prisoners the capture team had apprehended. First came the report on how they were captured. Dan explained it had been easier than thought as the three men Jeff had captured did not at all expect any other humans in the area, especially one that wanted to take them prisoner. All three were taken completely unawares by Jeff as they left the airport on that dirt road.

The first information Dan shared was about the escape tunnel. It did run directly from the destroyed complex to the entrance Jeff located. It had seven branches, with one other exit on the northern end, and he reported they still had over a hundred personnel ranging from practitioners and scientists to grunts…and a few families with children. There were eight kids - that was not good news.

Two of the prisoners had given up enough information for the team to able to map the underground complex for the group and showed where the families were billeted, where the mess hall was, and where most of the work was done in the complex, the rooms where most of the personnel were during the work hours. They were able to 'convince' the two prisoners to give detailed work schedules and guard change timetables at both the western and northern entrances.

The best piece of information, however, was a hand-drawn map of the underground tunnel system. One of the captives had drawn the schematic of the place giving detailed explanations of what each branch was used for, where the communications room was located and even more importantly where the remaining antennas were located.   Another particularly important tidbit of information was where the three armories were located inside – one near each entrance and one near the work rooms. The second entrance was to the north and would have to be reconed.

Another useful piece of data the captives gave was there were only had five drones left that were capable of offensive operations, or in other words, that could carry missiles. With the load of supplies and equipment the valley residents had just brought back from their foraging mission, the last drones could be taken out as the team now had over forty Stinger missiles. The group adjourned close to midnight.

As Dan was turning for his bed space, TJ asked, "Tomorrow, let's ask them why; why they are attacking us. I think that is something we all want to hear."

Dan nodded both understanding and that it was a good idea, then said, "Goodnight, brother."

As Wyoming is in the springtime, TJ woke to thirty-seven degrees and a clear, crisp day. He was to work on the greenhouses again today and dressed in layers, knowing it would warm into the fifties or sixties by afternoon. He cleaned up and brushed his teeth and went out to find Ruth already up and the coffee ready. He gladly accepted a mug and a kiss on the cheek from her and sat at the table with her.

Everyone agreed they needed to move back into their respective places feeling the danger from a drone attack was lessened. They were sure the Colorado people knew they had rockets and were now wary of the Wyoming valley.

"What are you up to today, TJ?" Ruth asked.

"Greenhouse duty," he answered. "I want to get that done and get some plants in before we have to plant the bigger gardens and crops, before we make the attack on the tunnel complex."

"You really think we can take that place out?" she asked.

"Honestly, I don't know," he answered. "We have no real idea what's underground in that place nor how many people are really in there. The doctor said there were children – a kid gave them the idea for that signal, and they named it after her, the Judith signal. The one prisoner said there were eight of them. I'm not comfortable risking a child's life."

"Then what do you think we should do?" she continued questioning.

"Based on the information we get this afternoon on why they're attacking us, try to talk with them. See if we can come to an arrangement of some kind, like a treaty or something…I don't know."

"You know we've tried to talk to them before and even did talk to the doctor for several days when he was our guest. Everything about him was phony, except that he found the saltwater thing so engrossing. If they're all like him, we'll never talk them into a peaceful solution. I still don't understand that, but that's the way I feel."

"Yeah, too many unanswered questions. Maybe the captives will give us some answers to more of our questions so we can get this resolved."

"That is not a bad idea. I for one do want to know why they're trying to kill us."

TJ thought a few moments, taking a sip of coffee, and said, "I think that is important. But we already know they want to kill others, so they probably won't talk about why – just look at Donna's story. Nor do we have the facilities to keep these prisoners for long. Now that we have them, I'm not sure what to do with them, you know. If we were in Laramie, I would put them in the lockup. But feeding them and caring for them will be a task, not to mention a danger."

"We can build something for that purpose easy enough. And if they don't want to talk any more…well there is no more Geneva Convention so we can…entice…information from them anyway we see fit and the way I feel, I can take care of that."

TJ looked up at her and the look she had on her face sent chills up his spine. He would rather not know what she was capable of and as a law officer, a Sheriff no less, how could he condone what she was suggesting. Even though he wanted answers just as much as she did, he didn't feel using unorthodox techniques to garner answers from another human was the way to go.

He saw her eyes, hard as stone, soften and she looked up at him and asked, "You want some breakfast before you go to work?"

"I was going to fix some, yes," he answered.

"Eggs, sausage, and toast good enough?"

"Yes, ma'am, that'll do. And a full travel mug of coffee to take along."

She got up and cut three slices of bread for toast, got out the sausage and eggs and began.

TJ watched her work and realized he'd seen another side of Ruth one he didn't relish seeing again. Doug's death, and Dave's, and now Julia's, had affected her more than he first thought. He wondered now about her mental state overall. Did the valley need to be concerned?

He got an idea at that point and said, as she served their breakfast, "Did Donna tell you about me going out alone and staying overnight?"

"Yeah, what was that all about? Sounded like you were having a time of it about going on that recon or not."

"That's right. I pray about a lot of things now days, and while reading the Bible back then, I felt I was getting confusing and mixed signals from God. I was frustrated and that frustration led to anger, and as I read through the Bible, God sorta smacked me around a little with His word and several verses I looked at led me to question both my desire to have it out with the Colorado group and to face my own anger and not letting it turn to a sinful thing."

She looked up at him and as their eyes met, he knew she'd received the message he was sending. "TJ, my anger towards those people down there is at least sinful in nature. I know I'm in trouble with Jesus over my feelings for them." She held up her hand as he took a breath to say something and said, "I know I have to learn to forgive. I know I have to reel in this anger and turn it to something else. I know that right now I'm just as evil as they are. The problem is, I know why I'm so angry. I know why my anger is sinful in nature. I've read the

Bible over and over and prayed over and over, and it tells me the same thing over and over – I'm wrong. But that doesn't ease the pain of my – our – loss of Doug, Dave, and Julia," and she began to cry.

TJ stood and gathered her in his arms. His weary eyes not focusing on anything in the room but fixed with a stare to nothingness. His jaw muscles tightened, and he knew what he would do this day. He pushed Ruth back some, reached to the table and got her a paper towel to dry her eyes and said, "Come on, finish breakfast so I can get started."

TJ had the first row of growing tables completed when the three Marines showed up to help. Together they built the remainder of the tables and installed the glass supports in the first greenhouse. The project was nearing completion and TJ was happy with their efforts. Soon, the valley residents would be able to plant and grow vegetables all year long. The four men had already decided they would build two to four more of these structures on the southern ridge for the Marines and Ruth to use, depending on where she decided to live.

The sun was well up when the four men decided it was time to stop work and go 'interview' the captives again. TJ said he would like to go in with each alone as he had some good to excellent interrogation methods, he'd learned in the police business. They had placed the captives in the Malone's underground in individual rooms, in different hallways. They were tied to the chairs they were seated on and hooded. TJ, Dan, Jack, and Jeff discussed methods of extracting more information and the suggestions ranged from pleasant to downright nasty.

"I'm going to go over and begin," TJ said. "Dan, want to tag along as the second? We can play good cop – bad cop…"

"Sure, but I thought you wanted to be alone with them," Dan answered with a mischievous smile.

"I suddenly don't trust myself," TJ answered soberly and honestly, looking each Marine in the eye.

The two hopped into the ATV and left Paradise Valley, taking the shortcut across the valley floor. Once at the

Malone's place, TJ unlocked the underground's hatchway, and both readied their silenced nine millimeters in case one of the prisoners had escaped.

Inside, they went to the first captive, turned on the lights, and stood in the room in silence. The hooded figure's head rose as they entered the room, and they could see the head tilting to one side trying to hear better. On the way over, the two interrogators had decided they would be as silent as possible with the three on the first go around. They wore tennis shoes, making it possible to walk around the rooms quietly. They would interject questions from time to time, from different areas of the room to confuse the captives.

"What's your name?" TJ asked in a pleasant manner. The captive jumped in the chair but didn't say anything. TJ moved closer to the captive's back and said, "You know, if you're nice about this today it just might go well for you."

Dan had moved to within a foot of the guy's front and with a yell, asked, "What's your name?" The guy jumped again, not expecting a second, commanding voice from a foot away.

TJ had a three-foot length of round hickory molding from the house project and used it to smack the back of the chair the captive was sitting in, which made the guy jump again lifting the chair off the floor. TJ then motioned to Dan and they left.

As they entered the second room, the guy in this chair, a big dude with black hair, immediately said, "What do you people want with me? I'm thirsty and hungry..."

TJ eased over and smacked the back of the chair with the hickory staff and the guy jumped in the seat and wet himself.

Dan calmly asked, "What's your name?" The guy jumped like he'd been electrocuted.

"I ain't tellin' you nuthin'," the captive practically yelled. TJ smacked the chair again.

"Oh, come on now, you're the one that told us about the cave and tunnel system," Dan said, "Surely you can give us your name."

"What about my friends? Where are they?" the guy asked.

"They're out walking around with the other zombies because they wouldn't talk," Dan said, quietly. "You're the nice guy. You've already given us some good information, why not your name?"

"I ain't no nice guy, you untie me, and I'll show you what I can be," the guy said menacingly. TJ took a full swing with the hickory this time and nearly knocked the guy over, chair and all.

Dan moved within a foot of the guy and said, "Now, you see, when you're nice we are and when you get...well, bad...we get testy, you know? So how 'bout it, what's your name?"

Breathing heavily, shaking some, the man in the chair remained silent.

TJ and Dan quietly left the room but slammed the door as they left. Dan turned to TJ, smiling, and asked, "You think he's ready yet?"

"Just about," TJ answered. "He'll probably spill his guts next time. He now thinks his two friends are walking around in Zombie-land and that he'll be next. We'll have to convince him of that."

"I think if we show him a table full of torture implements and making a bunch of noise bringing the stuff in next time, he'll sing like a new-born sparrow," Dan said with a snicker.

"Come on, let's go back to the first guy again," TJ said.

The two went back to the room with the captive they began with. Opening the door quietly, they entered the room and TJ right away, smacked the back of the chair with the hickory round. The man jumped in his bindings and screamed.

"What do you want!" the man screamed. "Let me outta here!"

TJ smacked the chair once again and leaning near the man's head said, in a mild voice, "I want your name. It's a simple request. You give me yours and I'll give you mine. Then we'll talk like good people in a community should. How's that? Come on, man, you've already talked some."

"I...I can't," the man said and began crying.

"Who said you can't?" Dan asked him.

"The doc did," the man said. Dan and TJ looked at each other and Dan gave an 'Okay' sign.

"Doc, who…Roche or Miller?" TJ asked.

The man's head lifted up at that and asked, "You know the docs?"

"Yes, we do," TJ said, and added, "And we know Roche is dead."

"Yeah, that guy was a jerk…scary dude," the captive told them.

Now they were getting somewhere. TJ looked at Dan and with a nod gave Dan the go ahead and question the prisoner.

"What about Miller…he a jerk, too?" Dan asked.

"Not as bad, but still a weird, scary dude," he said.

"What makes him weird and scary?" Dan questioned.

"He likes to do things to people…he…he…"

"He what?" Dan prompted.

"He likes to watch the dead ones kill people," the man said quietly. "He enjoys it. And he does experiments on the dead and on live people. I've heard the screams," and he gave a shudder.

"What kind of things?" Dan asked.

"I'm not sure, but we have to clean the mess he's made sometimes if we're on duty with him. It's horrible."

"Then why do you stay?" TJ asked.

"Where else would we go? Those things are everywhere and we're safe in the research compound. We'd still be doing great if those other people hadn't destroyed the above ground complex and the dishes."

"Who destroyed the complex?" Dan asked.

"Don't know, they just hit us one day and blew the tar outta the place. Destroyed the place and two of our last drones along with almost all the remaining missiles. They blew up a connex full of ammo and it put us all on the ground. The whole mountain shook."

TJ gave a fist pump with that revelation.

The man continued, "We only had five drones left when they hit us. We were going to launch one then but...well, you know."

"What were you going to do with the drone?" TJ questioned.

"Fly it back to that valley near Centennial, Wyoming, and try and knock off those people there."

"Why were you trying to knock them off?" Dan asked.

"That valley...Doctor Roche said it's a natural barrier the way the land is laid out so now Miller wants it. Says we can move there and rebuild with little or no threat from the dead ones. He said we could live comfortably and reasonably safely there."

Dan and TJ looked at each other and remembered what Doug had said about Doctor Roche mentioning something like that.

Dan held up a finger and asked, "What if those people living there now welcomed you if you'd just ask?"

The man's head gave a little tilt and a small, negative shake of his head and said, "I don't think they would...they've been pretty touchy every time we've sent someone in to take a look."

"You've sent people there to ask?" TJ said.

"No, not to ask, but to look and do what the doc ordered us to do, uh...to...to kill them," he murmured.

"You don't want to kill them, do you?" TJ asked quietly.

"Not really, it was what the doc ordered, though," he replied. "I even asked the doc once if we should just talk with the people...you know ask them to join us... and he got really angry with us grunts and sent us out for a while. Guy reminds me of Nazis I read about."

"Nazis...?" TJ questioned.

"Yeah. I read about them in school. They were evil and did all kinds of things to the Jews and Gypsies...killed millions of them...didn't you know that?"

"Yes, we know about the Nazi movement and what they did in World War Two," Dan replied.

"Doctor Miller reminds me of them and that Doctor Mengele guy, or whatever his name was. Seems like he does a lot of stuff on people and those dead things like that guy did to the Jews."

Dan and TJ looked at each other with concerned looks. TJ held up a finger and thinking for a moment, asked, "Why are you talking to us now?"

The head under the hood gave a tired sigh and said, "I'm tired of it all. I just wish we could live in peace…you know, get along with everyone that's left, start over kind of like…you know what I mean? Live our lives and get by. Get along with each other. There's not that many of us left in the world."

"What if we said we would let you go and you could live with us, peacefully, and in relative safety, as member of our little community?" TJ said.

The man's head slowly rose and after a moment of contemplation, began to nod positively. He quietly said, "But I know you won't. You can't trust me. I wouldn't."

Dan said, "I'm going to take the hood off your head and let you get a look at us." Dan slowly took the hood off and the man squinted his blue eyes in the light, then looked up and saw TJ.

"You've got a badge on…you a cop?" he asked.

"I'm Sheriff Thomas Gerill, sheriff of Albany County, Wyoming," TJ explained.

"This is that valley the doc wants, then, isn't it?" the captive asked almost in a whisper.

"Yes, it is," TJ answered.

"Mister," Dan asked, "give us your name."

"Phillips…Donnie Phillips. I'm from South Carolina."

"I'm Daniel Norris, born here in Wyoming. I'm a Marine, and a cowboy. Sheriff Gerill was born here in Albany County. He's a Ranger."

"Snake eater, huh, well I'm in the Army. Airborne…I guess now I'm just a grunt working for the doc. I figure there ain't no Army or anything anymore."

"What did you do at that complex?" TJ asked.

Donnie Phillips looked at TJ and said, "I was assigned there almost ten years ago. Assigned to the security detachment to pull guard and other duties as assigned. Just a grunt doing grunts work…a gofer really. We were directed to keep our mouths shut about the place and never talk about it to anyone…not even family. We had to sign paperwork saying we wouldn't talk or else."

"Or else what," Dan asked.

"They'd execute us," Donnie Phillips answered.

"How many people are left in that complex?" TJ asked. "I'm asking because we've killed a great many of you and figure you've got to be running low on people by now."

"Yeah, you've busted us up pretty good. We sent people out and they don't come back. At all. You must have some good security around here 'cause you've knocked off everyone we've sent up here. How're you killing the drones?"

"Right now, we're asking the questions so, again, how many folks are left in the complex?" TJ prompted.

"I figure around fifty…not counting the kids – there's eight of them," he answered.

"Eight kids live there?" Dan asked wanting to confirm the number for sure.

Phillips looked at Dan and said, "Yeah, and I'm worried about them. The doc eyes them kind of hungry like. Gives me the willies just seeing him look at them. Reminds me of those Nazis every time I see him looking at them."

"You said the doc does things to live people…where does he get the people?" TJ asked.

"Oh, just around as we find them. If we can't capture them, then they have us kill 'em. When we do capture them, the doc takes them and…and we clean up what's left." Again, Phillips shuddered and shook his head.

"Why don't you just lock up the doc and live peacefully with everyone?" Dan asked.

"He's got all the power," Phillips answered with fear in his eyes. "If we don't cooperate, we're taken and treated like those we catch. He's got several other scientists working with him and they're all…sick is the best word," Donnie said disgustedly. "There's always one or two of them in those locked up areas where they work. They have to wear bio-hazard suits in there so must be some nasty stuff in those rooms. Anyway, if we give them any grief, they'll release heaven only knows what to kill us all."

"They would really do that to you?" TJ asked.

Phillips' head whipped around, and he had an unbelieving look on his face and exclaimed, "You really don't know these people. They kill for fun - don' t you get that! They ENJOY hurting people!" he practically yelled.

Dan motioned for TJ to step out into the hall and together they left the room, leaving Phillips alone to look at his surroundings. Once in the hall and the door closed, Dan whispered to TJ, "We need to find out if those people ever leave the facility and if so, where they go. We can ambush them. What do you think?"

TJ smiled and opened the door and the two went back inside the make-shift cell. "Phillips," TJ asked, "do those people ever leave the complex, and if so, where do they go?"

"No good. Every time they leave, they have a fire-team with them and it's a powerful one. The Sergeant Major usually goes along," he answered dejectedly.

"We've taken care of your fire-teams on several occasions; don't you know that?" TJ commented.

Phillips looked at him and slowly nodded. "My friends will be with them - I don't want them hurt or to die. Not anymore of them; we're so few now."

Dan knelt in front of Phillips and looking him in the eye, man to man, said, "If you were on our side, the side of peace and peaceful living, you could point out the bad guys and we could take them out. Then you could talk to your friends and get them to go along with us for a peaceful existence. The more of the scientist guys we take care of, the better for all of us it sounds like."

Phillips stared at Dan, thinking about what he'd just said. TJ tapped him on the shoulder and looking Phillips in the eye said, "Those other two that were with you, were they your friends?"

"One was, yes," was the sad answer, he thought they were dead.

"You think you could have talked them into going along for the peaceful side of things?" TJ asked.

"Just my friend, yes," again.

Dan looked up at TJ and he nodded so Dan said, "Your two friends are still alive and okay. Just in other rooms. We're not the bad guys here and I think you see that don't you?"

"Yes," was the one syllable answer with a positive nod of his head.

"You want to give it a try – talking them into joining with us to get rid of the 'Nazi' types so we can all get back to living our lives – peacefully," TJ invited.

Dan interjected with, "Earlier you said if you were in our shoes and asked for trust, you wouldn't trust. How about now? All we want is to live in peace, to live our lives in a manner God intended."

"You believe in God?" Phillips asked.

"Yes, we're all Christians here in the valley," TJ answered him.

"I'm a Christian, too, and it really shakes my faith, seeing what these monsters do to people. I have a lot to answer for when the time comes. I pray and ask for forgiveness often. We're not allowed to be religious at the complex, but about half of us left are Christians. My friend you have is and secretly, we have Bible readings sometimes."

"What's your favorite verse?" TJ asked.

"Besides John 3:16, I really like Psalm 46:10, where is says, 'Be still and know I am God.' When I'm on guard duty outside I like to think about that while looking at the stars and wonder about Him, Jesus. It's scary and hard to believe He spoke all that into existence and makes me feel rather small."

TJ stood up and smiled, knowing exactly what the man meant as it was just a few days prior TJ had read that very verse. He looked at Dan who stood up and said, "What?"

TJ pulled his pocketknife, opened it, and cut the bindings from Phillips' feet and hands, stood back up and said, "It's trust time. Last week I was having a terrible time wondering about a few things and took my Bible and went to a spot I know and did some reading and praying and that very verse, Psalm 46:10, played an important part in the decisions I made then. So, it's trust time and I want to trust you. Do you want to trust us?"

"Yes, may I have some water?" Phillips responded.

"I'll get you a bottle," Dan said and left the room. He returned a moment later and handed an unopened bottle to Phillips, who opened and drained it. "Thank you," he said handing the empty to Dan. "So, my friend is alive?"

"Yes," TJ answered. "We're serious about living peacefully. All we want is to be left alone to live our lives as best we can. We have a nice living right now and are trying to make things better. But with the attacks from your people, we fall behind in our efforts for survival. You say you have children at the complex. We do, too. I don't want any children hurt anymore, do you?"

"No," Phillips responded with conviction.

"So, again, it comes down to trust," TJ said. "I'm willing or I wouldn't have cut your bindings. You say you're Christian and we are too, so we're putting our trust in God and in you. What do you say?"

Phillips looked at the ground, thinking.

Dan asked, "Did you know a guy named Chet...Chet Bost?"

Phillips looked at him with disgust and said, "Unfortunately. He's a real looser. Went AWOL several months ago and we all said good riddance. He said he was Christian but wasn't at heart and ratted a few of the guys out to the docs. That didn't go well. We wanted to kill him. Anyway, he's gone, but I knew him…why?"

Dan said, "He showed up in the valley and we took him in. Found out later it was a mistake as he stole some weapons and ammo, food and supplies and a truck and took off. We ran into him again when he ambushed us near Cheyenne. He won't be bothering anyone anymore."

"He's dead?" Phillips asked expectantly.

"Yes," Dan said.

"Good riddance," Phillips said with finality.

Dan looked at TJ and motioned for the door. Out in the hall, Dan asked, "You're sure about this?"

"Yeah, I think it's time to make peace with those that we can," TJ answered. "After what he said about Psalm 46:10, I saw him in a different light, and I think we need to bring him in…along with the others if we can."

Dan looked at the floor, nodding. Looking back at TJ, he motioned to the door and they went back inside. Dan motioned for TJ to take the lead.

"So, what's the verdict," TJ asked him.

"I'm in," Private Phillips answered quickly. "Not sure about the other two - even my friend - but I'm in. If you say we can take out the science types and keep my friends alive, then I'll help out as much as I can," he ended with conviction.

"Okay, we're going out and discuss this. You sit tight and we'll let you know. We'll have to get the approval of the others in the valley, but we'll give you a fair shake. You hungry?"

"I could eat. I could use another bottle of water, too, please," Phillips answered.

"Be right back," TJ said.

He and Dan left and went to the front foyer. TJ put together a few snacks for Phillips, got two more bottles of water, and took them to him. After closing and locking the door he went back to the foyer where he and Dan left, going back to the Paradise Valley.

There, they called everybody together for a quick meeting and told everyone about Phillips and his decision to help out. The trust question was the first issue and Chet's example brought up again and again. The first official valley vote by anonymous written ballot was taken that night. The results were five to allow Phillips in and one against. The proposal to admit him into the community passed and was accepted by all, although reluctantly by one. The provisions of acceptance would be worked out which included where he would live.

The next item of discussion brought a heated argument. That was the possible acceptance of the other two prisoners. The discussion went on for several hours and the valley residents finally called a halt to the proceedings late in the evening, adjourning to their rooms since everyone decided to stay in the valley.

Chapter 7: Amends and Awakenings

The next morning found the three Marines and Sheriff heading for the Malone Underground facility to check on the three captives. The four would give the news to Phillips about his acceptance, with reservations, to the valley population.

As they entered the Malone complex, they gathered in the foyer and prayed together before proceeding. They asked God for guidance and strength with what they were about to do. After they said Amen, they went to the room that held Phillips and entered as a group.

Phillips was seated in a far corner and said good morning to the group. TJ was first to speak for the valley residents and said, "Good morning to you, too. We've come to let you know that after a meeting of the valley residents with much deliberation, and I do mean a lot, we voted to accept you into the community."

Phillips drew in a deep breath and slowly let it out and said, "Thank you, Lord," and then to the men, "I thank all of you and hope I can be a model citizen for your group. I want just what you do – to live in peace and safety if I can. And I'll do all I can to protect that safety and peaceful existence as best I can. That, I promise before God and you."

"That's good to hear because there are a few of us that would just as soon shoot you as look at you. But we've elected to let you join our community so, let me introduce you to Jack Kagel and Jeff Jablonski."

Jack and Jeff stepped up and shook hands with Phillips, both giving him stern looks. Phillips noted they were all four packing side arms for this visit. He wondered why and asked.

"It's the day and age," TJ answered. "We have firearms on our person more often than not these days. Safer to be prepared then to take the risk."

"I understand," Phillips said with a nod of his head. "I wish it weren't like that, but we've been dealt this hand and we have to learn to live with it come what may. I still think we can live our lives as we wish, but we need to be prepared, just as you said. It's like living anywhere, you have to be ready for the conditions. It's like folks living in Alaska – they always have to be aware of the bear threat, but live their lives as if it'll never happen, although prepare for such an eventuality."

"We've discussed that very issue several times and have used Alaska and the bear threat as an example," TJ said smiling. "Since we've accepted you, how about talking to the other two guys and see if they'll come on board, too."

"One might – for sure the other will not," Phillips explained. "He's into this anarchy stuff and loves the danger. He fits right in with the doc's plans and loves to go out 'hunting'," he said giving a quote sign with his hands.

"Hunting for deer and food?" Jack asked.

"No - people. Like you, for instance," Phillips said in a matter-of-fact tone.

"Which one is he?" Jeff asked with a grim look.

"Big guy, black hair, gruff and tough acting but a big woose if you ask me," Phillips answered looking at Jeff. "He's the typical bully and probably a coward at heart."

"What's his name?" Jeff asked.

"Mason, Howard Mason," Phillips answered.

"He in the Army, too?" Jeff asked.

"Yeah, Staff Sergeant," Phillips said.

"What's your friend's name?" TJ asked.

"Timothy Sandoval, Tim. He's pretty cool and he's Army, also," he answered.

"Okay, we're going to go have a talk with them first," TJ said. "We've brought you some food, so you eat. You like coffee?"

"I'm in the Army…what do you think…" Phillips replied smiling.

"Okay then; here you go," TJ said. "We'll be back to get you in a bit."

The foursome left and locked the door. They talked in the foyer and decided to take on the hard-core Mason, first. As they entered the room where he was held, TJ immediately smacked the back of his chair with the hickory rod, then ripped the hood from his head. The light was blinding at first, but Mason, after blinking rapidly and squinting, could see the four men standing in front of him, crinkling their noses at the smell.

TJ began. "Morning. You sleep well? You stink a bit." A glare met him for answer. "Good, then we'll begin. My friend here," motioning towards Jeff, "is clairvoyant. He's going to touch you and after a bit, will give us some information about you. Is that okay with you?"

Another glare.

TJ hefted the hickory, letting Mason see it, and walked around behind the captive, who tensed, anticipating a blow to the back of the chair. Instead, Jeff stepped over and placed his hand on the captive's forehead and looked into his eyes, making his best impression of a mind reader, opening his eyes to their widest and staring into Mason's.

After a moment, Jeff said, "Sergeant…no…Staff Sergeant…Army type. Mean. Enjoys hurting people. Mason…? A brick layer…no, name…Mason is his name."

Mason's eyes were now open to their fullest, showing his amazement at Jeff's ability.

Jeff continued, "Hammond…no…Harold…no, that's not right, concentrate," he said looking deeper into Mason's eyes. "Yes, Howard…his name's Howard Mason, Staff Sergeant, United States Army," and acting the part, released Mason's head and feigned tiredness, stepping away.

Dan was next, asking, "So, Sergeant Mason, you really like to hurt people?"

Mason's head shook from side to side, his eyes still wide and looking at Jeff.

"My friend," pointing to Jeff, "is never wrong. Your name is Howard Mason, right?"

A positive shake of the head from the captive was the only answer Jeff received.

"Then you do like to hurt people, right?" Dan probed.

"It's my job," Mason answered.

"Your job is to hurt people?" Dan asked. "Who orders you to hurt people, or do you just enjoy doing it on your own?"

"The doc, er, Doctor Miller…he tells us to go get people and hurt them…kill them or catch 'em and bring 'em back to his lab," Mason said hesitantly.

"Who's Doctor Miller?" TJ asked, tapping the back of the chair with the hickory stick resulting in another jump from Mason.

"He's the boss…the commander of the complex," Mason answered turning his head to look at TJ.

"Is he in the Army, too?" Jack asked.

Mason focused on Jack and answered, "Yeah, he's a Colonel."

"How many men are under his command?" Dan asked.

This time Mason held his tongue, giving Dan a look that said he wasn't going to talk. Dan looked at TJ, who drew the hickory stick back and smacked the back of the chair. Mason jumped again and tried to turn in the seat, but the bindings held. TJ motioned for Jack and together they left the room. TJ told Jack to get a bucket of water from the creek and bring it in and pour it over Mason's head.

TJ entered the room again and immediately smacked the backside again. Mason jumped once more and gave a guttural moan, his anger rising. Jeff stooped down in front of Mason and with a slight, satisfying smile on his face, said, "My, you are one for the books, aren't you?"

The rhetorical question went unanswered. TJ moved around to the front and motioned for Dan and Jeff to come closer to him and he explained, in whispers, what Jack was going to do and for the three to move back, one into each corner and one in the middle of the wall in front of Mason and just look at him. This they did and waited.

Mason stared back with hate, and if looks could kill, that one would have killed the three valley residents. Mason heard the door open and close. He tried to look behind himself but could not see Jack, who looked up at the three men standing in the positions against the wall. TJ gave him a slight nod and Jack poured the freezing cold creek water over Mason's head.

All four could hear the intake of breath as the icy liquid hit Mason. His eyes popped open wide and the surprised look on his face was one for the books. Jack stepped back and waited, while Mason sucked in huge amounts of air after the shock from the freezing water.

"Now that you've bathed," TJ began, I'll ask again. How many men are under the Colonel's command?"

Mason tensed and looked up with hate in his eyes, giving no other answer but the look.

"It's a shame you won't answer our questions," TJ told him. "There is a lady in our group. She's pretty angry. And that anger stems from you, or one of your comrades, killing her husband in one of your attacks. She's waiting for her turn with you…we won't be in here with the two of you while she…asks…her questions. In fact, we won't even be in the neighborhood 'cause we don't want to hear your screams - know what I mean?"

The hateful look broke just a little, but the defiance remained.

"If you'd answer our questions like a man, you'll remain a man. If you know what I mean. See, she really wants at you and she's given us some pretty specific orders on how we are to leave you if you don't answer our questions," TJ explained.

At that, the three Marines left the room and returned, bringing in…things. First was a table that Jeff and Dan set up in front of Mason, and Jack covered with thick plastic. Next, Jeff brought in several ball peen hammers and set them on the table. Jack followed with several knives and Dan placed several wood chisels on the table next to the knives. Dan added several pairs of pliers and a hemostat. They made sure Mason saw each implement as they placed them on the table.

Next, the Marines took Mason's shirt off, his boots, socks, and his belt. Then, Jeff came in again with several lengths of rope and taking the first, tied it around Mason's right ankle, and ran the rope through a ring in the wall to his right. Jeff gave Jack the nod and Jack took one of the knives and cut the rope holding Mason's right foot to the chair. Jeff immediately pulled with as much force as he could, bringing Mason's right leg out and to the right, fully extended. Jeff tied off the rope and moved to Mason's left side, and they did the same thing to Mason's left leg, leaving the man in a seated position with legs spread widely.

TJ took the remaining length of rope and tied Mason more firmly to the chair, wrapping several lengths around his legs and upper torso, tying it off in the back.

The four men all walked around to the table and looked at Mason, and TJ said with a sad expression, "OK, pal, we'll be leaving in a few minutes, when she gets here."

That's the moment Ruth said from the hallway, "Is he ready?"

Mason practically screamed, "There's fifty-one adults and eight kids in the complex. With me fifty-two."

Even though he answered, the four men began slowly filing out of the room as if it were too late.

Mason screamed, "What do you want to know? I'll tell you anything!"

TJ reared back and smacked the back of Mason's chair as hard as he could. Mason screamed manically and foam flew from his lips. He was more than ready to answer any questions they wanted to ask.

An hour later, with all their questions answered, they untied his legs, retying them the way they originally had been, removed all the implements and the table. Ruth walked around in front of him and said with a disgusted look, "You're one lucky individual. I'm sorry we weren't able to get more acquainted." She turned and left the room, closing the door quietly.

Back in the foyer, the five stood together and chuckled. They spoke together for a while and went to Phillips' holding room and entered. They introduced Ruth, who didn't shake his hand, but did give him a stare that wasn't pleasant. TJ told him they wanted him to introduce them to his friend, Sandoval, and together they went to another hallway and the room holding the third prisoner.

As they got to the door, Dan pulled his handgun and took off the safety and said, "Don't make any sudden moves and don't touch the prisoner…period. We'll do the talking and you speak when told to do so…understand?"

"Yes," Phillips gave the one syllable answer and a slight nod of his head.

TJ opened the door and stepped into the darkness. Sandoval's head snapped up when he realized more than one person entered the room. Dan turned on the lights and Jeff ripped the hood from the seated captive, who squinted and blinked rapidly in the sudden brightness. Once his eyes were accustomed to the light, he looked around the room and with a surprised look, rested his gaze on Phillips.

Dan began with, "Good morning Mister Sandoval."

Sandoval looked at him and back to Phillips and gave a nod of his head.

"Don't look at Phillips, look at me," Dan said. Sandoval's eyes went back to Dan. "I said good morning."

"Morning," Sandoval answered almost as a question.

"You see we have Mister Phillips with us. He's decided to become a part of our little community. Mister Mason is not as…amenable to that as Donnie here. Now we're here to ask you some questions and we brought Donnie along to help us. You see he's not tied up…he's for the most part, free."

Sandoval looked at Phillips, who nodded his head in agreement. He looked back at Dan.

"Donnie tells us you're a Christian; that right?" Dan asked.

"Yes, sir, I am," Sandoval answered with conviction.

"You'll be happy to hear then, that all of us in this room are Christian and have no desire to bring harm to you or anyone else. Do you understand that?"

"Yes, sir, I do."

"Good, then we've jumped the first hurdle. I'm going to ask Donnie to explain to you what is going on and what we would like to ask you. Donnie," Dan said, giving the floor to Phillips.

"Tim, he's right," Phillips began. "We're all Christians in this room and they want just what you and I and the others want. To live in peace and safety. Man - brother - they want us to join them. They don't want to hurt us. They've just been protecting themselves when the doc has had us attack. Obviously, they're good at it 'cause we know the results. They have Bible studies and church, and they pray together. They really want what you and I and the others want. Honest, brother, I'm serious."

TJ stepped forward and said, "Hi, Mister Sandoval, I'm Sheriff Thomas Gerill, of Albany County, Wyoming, and he's telling you the truth. He's given us some useful information and we now know that you were just following the orders of Doctors Roche and Miller. I was in the Army, too, a Ranger. You remember the UCMJ?"

"Yes, of course," Sandoval said.

"Remember it says we could say no to unlawful orders?" TJ prompted.

Sandoval's eyes narrowed and he tentatively said, "Yes."

"Do you feel the orders Miller gives you are wrong?" TJ continued.

"Yes," said with more conviction.

"I'm here to tell you they are, and you can resist and even disobey those unlawful commands. It's not a crime to say no and refuse to obey. We want the attacks on our valley to stop. We want to live in peace and not have to worry about being attacked by humans. We have enough to worry about with the zombies, bears, lions, and weather conditions. We're behind in our planting of our spring gardens and crops. Being attacked at odd times is jeopardizing our survival and we're quite frankly tired of it and want it to stop.

"Donnie tells us there are more Christians at the complex that think like the two of you and we do. We really want peace. We're tired of all the killing, but make no mistake, we will protect ourselves even if it means wiping out every human in that complex. We don't want to do that, but we will if necessary. We want you to join us in our efforts to stop the evil and bring peace to the area."

TJ looked at Phillips and gave him the nod, and he said, "Tim, I think they're sincere. You and I and the others don't like doing what the doc tells us to do. And we know he treats those we capture badly. It's gotta end, brother, and I think we can end it with these folks' help. What do you say?" Phillips said holding out his hands, pleading.

"What would you want us to do?" Sandoval asked.

"Join us and help us rescue the others in the complex and the children there," TJ explained. "Help us bring them out into a peaceful world. We'll set you up here in the valley and we'll live together, work together, plant together, hunt together, and be a community of peaceful people again. What do you say?"

Sandoval looked at each person and stopped when his gaze fell on Phillips. Donnie said, "Please, Tim, please join us. You notice I said us. That's because I'm one of them now," pointing at the others. "I want you and the others to be with us, too."

Sandoval took a deep breath and let it out slowly and said, "I'm in. What can I do to help?"

TJ looked at Dan who nodded. The two looked at Jeff, Jack and finally Ruth, who, surprisingly said, "Cut him loose."

Jack took his knife out and cut Sandoval's bonds and let the young man stand. He asked for some water and was given a bottle. After he downed it, he asked, "Can we pray together, please?" The seven gathered together and gave thanks and asked for God's assistance in reaching the others in the complex and getting them out safely.

After the prayer, each introduced themselves to Tim, shaking his hand, even Ruth. He looked at them a bit fearful as he didn't know what was next. Donnie didn't know as well. Tim looked at TJ and asked, "What's next?"

Donnie immediately asked the same question, "Yes, what's next for us?"

TJ looked at Dan and said, "I think we need to take them and introduce them to the others, fix them some real food and explain what's going on since the last drone attack."

Tim interjected with, "There was another drone attack…when?"

"Almost two weeks ago," TJ answered. "We've moved away from the places we lived in to a more remote and we think secure area for the time being." He looked at Dan again and said, "Want to go?"

"Yeah, I think that'd be okay," Dan answered. "We need to let the others know what's going on and these two need to clean up and eat. We have enough clothing to give them a change. At least they'll smell better." The whole group chuckled at that.

TJ motioned for the door and the seven filed out and went to the portal. Donnie and Tim both inhaled great gulps of fresh air once outside and got the first view of the valley.

"This place is beautiful," Donnie commented.

"You ain't seen nothin' yet," Jeff told him.

They all piled into TJ's truck and headed for the Ranger Station. Once there, they introduced the two newcomers to Donna and DD, showed them where to get cleaned up giving them toiletries, towels and letting them pick out some clean clothing to wear. Donna had asked them what they wanted for breakfast and went with Ruth and DD to fix the meal. TJ, Dan, Jeff, and Jack all went for the coffee.

The six valley residents watched the two newcomers inhale their meal after saying a blessing. They thanked the Lord for deliverance and for joining the valley community. After eating, they asked for more coffee and thanked the ladies and DD profusely for the great meal as they had not had fresh eggs in years.

After filling their mugs, TJ began the story of the valley. The conversation lasted through several pots of coffee and everyone said their piece, including Ruth. Tim and Donnie's questions were answered as much as possible, with some questions not answered as yet for security reasons. By noon everyone had become quiet and with stories told and explanations given, the residents prepared lunch.

Donnie and Tim said they would like to go with TJ and help with the underground green houses, so after lunch, the three Marines, TJ and the two newcomers left the house to go to work.

Chapter 8: Plans, Strategy, and Tactics

It had been two months since Privates Donnie Phillips and Timothy Sandoval had joined the valley residents. Staff Sergeant Mason was not as fortunate since his continued combative attitude towards the valley residents became more and more vehement. Since he was a lost cause, and since Jesus says in the Bible, in three places no less, to 'shake the dust off your feet' when they don't accept you or your testament about Jesus.

So, TJ and the Marines tied him up, double hooded, and driven to the western side of James Town, Wyoming, and dropped him in a dead-end canyon. They cut the bonds on his hands, leaving the hoods and his legs tied tightly, and as they drove away, threw hand grenades behind them to keep his head down long enough for them to get back to I-80, without him seeing. They had dropped one canteen and a knife and left him to his fate.

The original six residents had the pair of privates' move into the home on Highway 11, the one that would be so difficult to defend, and had given them one nine-millimeter handgun with three magazines, without a suppressor, and one twelve-gauge shotgun with fifty rounds for their defense against Zs if necessary. They'd been given more than enough food and water to survive on and had even been provided a generator that ran a small refrigerator and a freezer outfit.

Donnie, being from South Carolina, was the son of a farmer so knew farming and had already become a valued member of the community. His input on crops and how to grow them had saved the valley residents valuable time, resources, and energy as they wouldn't be making too many mistakes with a knowledgeable farmer helping out.

Tim, on the other hand, was from a barrio in San Francisco, California. He was one of the lucky ones from the gang infested area, whose mother and father had really cared about their children and raised he and his sister in a good Christian home and environment. He and his sister were two of the few to get out of the barrio and live good and morally secure lives. After high school, he joined the Army, following in his father's footsteps.

The two newcomers had sat in on every valley meeting and added their input on issues and had provided detailed information on the complex so that now the valley residents knew just about every millimeter of the underground facility in Colorado, including where the northern entrance was. The privates had assisted with the completion of the two underground greenhouses at TJ's place, Paradise Valley, and had been big helps with clearing and planting of several fields for crops. They had been involved with the weekly Bible studies on Wednesday nights and attended church on Sundays. They had become members of the valley population, with Ruth even accepting and befriending the two.

One morning, Dan and TJ were walking the crop fields looking for sign animals were damaging the crops and talking. TJ was the first to bring up the Colorado complex, "We need to get it done."

Dan looked at him and said, "I agree. Full moon is tomorrow night, so we have a few weeks to prepare. Jack, Jeff, and I have been mixing napalm and putting it in those plastic fifty-five-gallon drums we scavenged. Ruth's been melting lead and making forty-five and thirty-two caliber shot to add to the bombs. Jack's been shopping in Laramie and wants to go to Cheyenne."

"What's he looking for?" TJ asked.

"More drones and remote-controlled cars and trucks," Dan said. "He says he can rig them with canisters of napalm, drive them down the tunnel entrances, and create havoc inside the underground system."

"That's a novel idea," TJ said. "I'm glad he's on our side."

"The idea actually came from Donnie," Dan explained. "Jack's just putting it to the test. Donnie say's he was an expert with the remote-controlled gizmos and would be more than happy to steer them into the complex."

"You know, the more I think about that, the more sense it makes, and I wonder why we didn't think of it before. We could add C-4 and really make some noise inside."

"The only bad thing is what the kid said when we suggested that."

"What's that?"

"The stuff in the labs. They're not sure what the scientists are doing in there, but since they all wear biohazard suits inside those areas, I bet it's something we don't want to let out so maybe using C-4 isn't the answer."

"Sure, it is…after we clear all the humans out, we can put in as many drums of gas, and napalm as we can, then blow it and let it burn. That should take care of the issue I would think."

"I think we'll have to discuss that a lot before we blow something like a bio-lab. We might need to go to another military base somewhere and get some real napalm and thermite to make sure we get it all. We could even go inside those areas, with suits on of course, and set napalm and thermite in the rooms themselves. It just depends on what we find out is in there."

"To do that we'll need to grab one of the scientists. Guess we'll need to do that next trip down."

"Two weeks then for final recon, grabbing one of the scientists and anything else we'll need. I'll call a powwow for night after next and see if Donna will make us a feast of some kind."

"I'll spread the word. Crops look good so far; let's head back," Dan said turning for the ATV.

As the two turned, they heard a swooshing sound from the south and looked up to see a smoke trail heading to the southeast. Someone had fired a Stinger, but the disturbing thing was the second vapor trail coming from the southeast, heading towards the Marine's hill. Almost immediately, a second Stinger vapor trail rose from Marine Hill and streaked towards the southeast.

The first Stinger blew and the two could see flaming wreckage of a drone begin falling to the earth. The second was streaking towards the missile the drone had fired and blew as the two seemed to touch each other. The incoming missile's vapor trail continued on its northwest trajectory and impacted on the dirt road leading to Dan's home.

Dan and TJ looked at each other and ran to the ATV. They sped to Highway 11 and turned for Marine Hill. Once there, they found Jack standing there with a satisfied smile on his face and holding another Stinger.

Jack looked at the two as they got out of the ATV and said, "I'm an ace now. That was number five."

"You okay?" Dan asked him.

"Yeah, I got down just in time. Looks like my second missile knocked theirs off course just enough to miss your place. Put a nice hole in the drive, though."

About then, another ATV pulled up with Ruth and Jeff inside, as did a truck with the two privates. All four poured out and ran up to the trio standing together. The only person missing was Donna, and she had DD over in Paradise Valley. Questions flew and answers were given by Jack, who again proudly announced he was an ace.

Dan asked for quiet and told everyone about the powwow at Paradise Valley in two nights with dinner. Everyone agreed and since the excitement had died down, the privates got back in their truck and headed down the hill. Ruth took the ATV and headed out. Dan stayed with Jack and Jeff, and TJ headed home in his ATV.

Donna met him on the porch holding her AR-10. She had on her vest and was ready for anything. TJ got out of the ATV and explained the event to her, and that Jack was now an Ace. Then he told her about the powwow and asked about a meal for the occasion.

"Well, since Jack made history for the valley," she mused, "it should be something he likes, and his favorite of mine is comfort food so how about fried chicken, mashed potatoes, gravy, and corn? You can make a batch of home-made bread for the occasion."

"You know I'm always in the mood for your fried chicken," TJ said with a smile. "How's DD?"

"Sound asleep in his bouncy chair. The boy is like you in a lot of ways, goes and goes then drops."

TJ laughed and pointed to the house and they went inside.

Everyone came over to Paradise Valley just after noon on the day of the powwow. TJ and Donna had set up the tables in the great-room and had set out paper and pencils for everyone. As folks arrived, TJ poured their favorites and invited everyone to have a seat after some social time together and once again hearing the Ace tell his story.

"Please bow your heads everyone," TJ began and said a prayer asking for guidance and clarity on the actions they needed to take. "Okay," TJ began, "in just about two weeks we'll be in a sliver of a moon phase, so Dan and I want to take a team to Colorado and do several things, first of which is a recon of that western ridge above the tunnel entrance. We'll be looking for suitable sniper and fighting positions. We'll also be looking for areas closer to the entrance for the drone flyers and drivers to use safely. Thanks to Donnie and Tim, we know their schedules for guard changes and such, and we feel they may be ready for an outing that we want to take advantage of and see if we can capture one of the scientists for intel."

Dan took over and said, "We figure we'll take five on the mission, TJ, me, Jack, Jeff, and Tim. We'll pack for ten days but will only stay as long as necessary. Ruth, you, Donna, DD, and Donnie should move into the Ranger's Shack again until we're back. As soon as they figure out that we're around, they may launch another drone to attack here. You'll be safer there."

"I know how to use Stingers," Donnie said. "And after Jack got that last one, they only have three or four of those things left. Not sure how many missiles though."

"That's all well and good and you'll have ten Stingers at your disposal at the shack, but we still feel you'll be safer there as our homes are prime targets. Just look at what happened the other day. If Jack hadn't been Johnny-on-the-spot with the Stingers, my home and probably Jack, wouldn't be here now. Better safe."

Donnie shook his head positively. Ruth and Donna said their agreements and said they would pack for the stay.

TJ then said, "If we capture one of the scientists, we'll treat him like we did Mason and scare the dickens outta him. It may not take as long since this person most likely won't be a professional soldier. But we need to milk him of as much information about what is in those laboratories as we can. We need to know if fire will kill the things in there and if napalm and thermite will do the job. If so, I plan to make a trip to Fort Carson, near Colorado Springs, to look for military grade napalm and thermite explosives…and anything else we can find that's useful. I think we should all go on that trip and make the most of it, taking at least five trucks with trailers and loading them to the max, and if we can get the big rig started again, we can haul that flat-bed trailer down and fill it. That'll give us a nice load of materials.

"For that mission, I plan to go to Sidney, Nebraska, then head south, going the long way around the complex for safety's sake. I don't want them to know we're going to Fort Carson. We'll take Highway 113 south to Sterling, then turn west on I-76 all the way to southern Denver, then south on I-25 until we get to the fort. I know exactly where the bunkers are there, and we'll go straight to them and load up. We'll pack for a three-week outing, and hopefully only need ten days or so.

"I want everyone to make a list of items needed to be gathered on both trips. Anything and everything is acceptable at this point in our lives so don't skimp. If you think of it and we can find it, we'll get it. Good enough?"

Nods from everyone around the room. "Questions, comments, suggestions?" TJ asked. "None? Let's get started then," and he grabbed a pad of paper and a pencil and began to write.

By dinner time, the eight adults had quite the list of items to watch for. More AR-10s and magazines; a few high-tensile, heavy draw-weight crossbows with which to use for big game, including man; every drone and remote-controlled car or truck that could carry a load; more lead for Ruth; and the ingredients for napalm were top on the list.

As they sat around the table, TJ asked Tim to pray, and the young man gave a heartfelt prayer for the valley residents and the missions ahead. Dinner was surprisingly good, even better than usual and of course, DD got his chicken gravy.

After dinner, Donnie and Tim volunteered to help Donna and Ruth with the dishes and cleanup. The four men poured themselves scotch and went out on the porch to enjoy the evening air and silence the mountains brought this time of night. They sat in the Adirondacks, each keeping silent in their own thoughts.

After a while, Jeff broke the silence saying, "They're just about out of drones now. They must think we have radar or something since we've knocked so many down. It was indeed fortunate that Jack saw that last one coming and acted. Great action, brother."

"Thank you," Jack answered.

"That was great," TJ added. "It was a God-thing."

"Here-here," Dan said quietly.

The four sipped their scotch in silence once again until Donnie and Tim came out with tumblers of scotch themselves.

Discussion soon followed about the first mission and how those two would proceed.

In the end, they all agreed to watch after doing the recon for the sniper and fighting positions and wait for a convoy to come out. Almost every time a convoy left the facility, at least one of the scientists was along for the ride if nothing else but to get out of the facility and get some fresh air and scenery change. Neither private could remember not having one on a supply run.

Donnie said the big fans that power the air breathers in the cave system would portend the convoy's departure as the exhaust from the vehicles would be sucked out of the tunnels rapidly. Once they heard the fans, they would get ready to move to an appropriate spot to spring their ambush. They had already selected the most likely positions based on the private's advice, knowing the direction of travel always taken.

The guys finished their scotch and broke with the Marines taking the lead and heading out with the Army in tow. TJ went back inside and told the ladies he was heading for bed, so they broke up their conversation, Ruth getting DD and heading for her room and Donna followed TJ. The quiet took over the valley.

Eight days later the little convoy of two vehicles and five men departed after many goodbyes and kisses. Dan and TJ were in the lead vehicle with TJ driving. Jack drove the second vehicle, Jeff as shotgun and Tim in the back seat. Dan had prepared a Stinger and had it sitting on the back seat just in case they saw a drone. No more chances, they would shoot at the first opportunity.

The team drove south on Highway 287 until they reached Livermore, Colorado. There, they would make camp and do their scouting and recon. The complex entrance was about eight miles to the south so wouldn't be a long flight for the high-altitude drone. Dan and TJ would launch it the next morning and search for both the sniper and fighting positions for the attackers.

Since they'd used the elementary school as a bivouac building before, they decided to use it once again. It provided ample space and had reasonable accommodations to hide their trucks and trailers. Not only that, but it also had ample space to launch the drones and would probably be a likely position to launch from on the day of the attack.

They arrived at nine in the evening as planned. TJ wanted to arrive in darkness so as to not attract too much attention from a drone if one happened to be aloft. They had already removed the taillight and trailer light bulbs so break and backup lights wouldn't be seen, and they didn't use the headlights at all. They unloaded the gear they would use to sleep in, cook with and the drones for the next morning's mission. They fixed themselves a quick dinner from MREs and bedded down shortly afterwards. Dan took the first watch.

The next morning after breakfast, Dan and TJ launched the high-altitude drone. This model without a payload had a flying time of almost forty-five minutes and it took only a few minutes to travel the eight or so miles to the tunnel entrance. Hovering at eight thousand feet AGL directly above the entrance, they scanned the area to the east, south, west, and then north, videoing the areas and taking still shots of interesting spots that needed further review. TJ moved the drone to the west and hovered above Highway 287 and shot video of the ridges just west of the entrance. He saw what looked to be a small ranch house or farmstead to the southwest of the entrance and gauged it to be about a half-mile away. It would be a good place to have a sniper's position as it appeared to have a line-of-sight view to the entrance. It would have to be looked at from ground level and would be one of the missions for the evening.

Moving to the south, TJ found an area directly south of the entrance that looked promising. It was about three quarters of a mile distant from the entrance and would be a good place for a mortar, another sniper with a fifty, a few Kamikaze drones and maybe even a bomber or two with napalm.

Now they needed to find two positions for the main remotely operated vehicle (ROV) force, which would include drones and ground vehicles. They needed to be relatively close to the entrance, especially the one that would have the ground based ROVs carrying demolition and napalm explosives. The most logical place was a homestead to the southeast, approximately a quarter mile from the entrance. It would pose some significant dangers for the person there, and the terrain for the ROVs was prohibitive at best by the looks of it.

Dan nudged TJ, pointing at the battery life, and with ten minutes of power left, TJ headed for the bivouac area, landing the drone with less than a tenth battery power remaining. That was close. He went out, retrieved the drone, and brought it inside, removed the small card and place it in a protective sleeve, then in a box they'd brought for the keeping the cards safe.

"What do you think about that place to the southeast of the entrance for the ROV station?" TJ asked Dan.

"Dangerous to say the least," he answered. "I'm not sure about the terrain for an ROV either. Looks rough through there. I honestly think whoever draws that mission will need to be closer because of the battery life. We'll at least have to play with that and see how long they last with a load."

"Too bad we didn't have an F-16 with a few two-thousand pounders to drop," TJ thought out loud. "That would be the ticket."

Dan chuckled and said, "Wishful thinking, dude."

TJ chuckled, too, and said, "Yeah, two of those would take out both entrances and problem solved.

"That would be great if it weren't for the kids and the others that didn't want to be there," Dan said.

"We gotta get a convoy and grab a scientist and maybe talk a few others into joining our ranks," TJ said. "The more we have the better it'll be when we really attack."

"Yeah; Tim? Can you come over and talk with us?" Dan yelled across the room.

"Sure, on my way," Tim answered. He came trotting over with a smile and asked, "What's up?"

"How sure are you the friends you have in there will join us when the time comes?" Dan asked.

Tim gave a confident smile and said, "Very confident. We've all talked together about leaving there, but with so many of us, it would be a difficult thing to do all at once. They'd know something was up and we'd wind up dead…or worse."

TJ and Dan looked at him with serious expressions and Dan said, "We really need to hit one of their convoys and grab a scientist and talk a few of your friends into joining our ranks."

"Sure do," Tim agreed. "As soon as we see them leaving, we can act, launch a drone, and watch which way they go and set up from there. With me on the spotting scope, I can tell you whose driving and whether they're friendly or not and if so, shoot the engine to stop them. If not, I say shoot the driver. The science type will most likely be riding shotgun and everyone else in the follow-on vehicles. Don't worry, guys, we can do this," he ended with a smile and a wink.

"Real confident, aren't you?" TJ asked.

"Yes, and for good reason," Tim answered. "The human world is in dire straits and we know it and pray about it every chance we can get away with it. If we can stop these jerks from killing more people, then my friends in there will all agree and join our ranks. You can count on it," he said with determination.

Dan and TJ looked at each other and Dan said thanks. The kid went back to what he was doing, leaving TJ and Dan looking on. "You know," Dan pondered out loud, "if I was a betting man, I'd bet we have better than even odds of coming out on top of this operation if the others are as confident as Donnie and this one," nodding in Tim's direction.

TJ smacked him on the arm and said, "I think you'd win that bet my good man." The two laughed and got up to launch another drone.

Dan was flying this time and launched the drone with no problems. He flew the craft to the southeast so they could search for the northern entrance. The privates had given them enough information so they would be able to find it, pinpoint it, and send Jack and Jeff to sniff around for a closer look.

Dan found the entrance with no trouble as it was located just to the southeast of a dam that held a reservoir in check. The tunnel itself was to the southeast side of the dam, and a dirt road was clearly seen coming from the aperture. They found several excellent positions for both sniper and fighting positions that were reasonably close and provided excellent cover for the whoever held the positions. They would have Jack and Jeff check out all three positions they'd selected and choose the best two from their reconnoiter.

"Jack…Jeff, would you come over and take a look at these?" TJ asked the two.

They sauntered over and agreed the positions were good ones and marked their approximate positions on their maps. They would check them out that night when they began their recon mission.

"You two should try to get some shut-eye," Dan told the two. They agreed and after some water, they both turned in for a nap.

Tim came over and asked what TJ and Dan were looking at and Dan explained and showed him the positions. "Those are good spots," he told the two.   "How close are they?"

TJ pointed out all three were within a half-mile of the tunnel and had easy line-of-sight angles. Dan said that since there were now eight fighters in the valley, they could man all three positions if they thought it necessary.

"I think Donnie and I should be near the Tunnel West as that is where more of the personnel are," Tim suggested. "When we had guard duty at Tunnel North, we had to be driven there in the golf carts since it was the 'out of the way' position. We could put…say, Jack, Ruth, and Donna on this one and the rest of us take the west entry."

"Ruth will be with the west group as she's the best drone bomber pilot we have. She can hit a dime from five thousand feet," TJ commented. "Donna's good with a fifty, so putting her on the north end with one of those and a mortar would be good."

"I agree," Dan said. "Jack, Donna and one of you two should be enough to take care of the north entrance. Once you've taken out or captured the personnel there, you can enter the complex and use the ROVs to recon. It'll be best having each of you at an entrance so we'll have someone familiar with the terrain, and you might be better suited to talk someone into joining our ranks instead of fighting us."

"Sound thinking," the young private complemented Dan. "I think I should be on the northern side as I used to volunteer for duty there. I'd go swimming in that reservoir, not that I was supposed to, just did. I like swimming," he said with a wry smile.

"You better go turn in, too. You'll be going out with me tonight so get some sleep," TJ told him, as Dan turned the drone for their landing pad.

The five turned in and slept until six that evening, getting up and eating and preparing for their recon that night. The three Marines and TJ would be taking suppressed nine-millimeters and all of them would be carrying M-4s with full loads of ammunition. They all had an array of the grenades, fragmentation, and smokes, and each had a long-bladed combat knife. All five had night vision goggles (NVGs) with belt-pack batteries giving them more than sixty hours of continued use capability if needed.

At ten o'clock that night, the four men of the recon teams climbed aboard TJ's truck. Jack drove and with no lights, pulled out on their six-hour mission. TJ and Tim would be dropped by Jack at the pre-arranged point then continue to their parking spot. TJ and Tim would recon the northern tunnel and Jack and Jeff would take a look at the spots found by drone earlier, checking for suitability for fighting positions.

TJ and Tim slipped out of the truck and quietly closed the door, waiving to Jack and Jeff as they pulled away. The pair left behind donned their NVGs and turned to the east, following the track of a dried creek bed. Keeping low, they crept along making as little noise as possible, pausing from time-to-time, listening for danger. They finally crossed a man-made canal that was dried up and climbed a small rise to the north. They lay on the western side of the rise and looked across the reservoir.

TJ saw the glow of a cigarette burning and pointed for Tim, who gave a thumb up that he'd seen the sentry. They watched and ensured there was only one guard on duty, which the two privates had assured the valley residents was standard procedure.

TJ motioned for Tim to back away from the top of the rise, and at the bottom, said, "You lead since you know this area - which direction?"

Tim smiled and with a wave for TJ to follow, lead the way around the small rise and low-crawled over the reservoir's dam. On the north side, they crept along the base of the dam until reaching the far eastern end. Here, Tim low-crawled up the embankment and slowly raised his head and peered over. He studied the area and after a few moments, with a wave of his hand indicated he wanted TJ to join him.

TJ crawled up and just as slowly, raised his head above the lip and peered over. Tim reached out and pointed towards the tunnel entrance, where the sentry could clearly be seen with their NVGs, enjoying his cigarette. The pair watched the man for several minutes. Tim finally motioned for TJ to back down the embankment and there, said, "Shift change will be at midnight, about ten minutes from now. What do you want to do?"

TJ thought a moment and whispered a question, "How long do you think it'll take us to get to that first place to check out for a fighting position?"

Tim did a quick mental calculation and said, "Fifteen minutes or so, unless we run into trouble."

"Let's hope and pray not...lead on," TJ said, smiling and pointing.

They crept across the dam once again and turned to the south. After ten minutes, they crept up to the home in question. It was, of course, dark. It and the five outbuildings the property held were all dark. The NVGs did their work and the pair saw everything clearly. They moved around to the west side of the home and found a nice flat area that would be a perfect mortar position and spot to launch drones. TJ looked at the house and looking back at Tim, saying, "Let's find a ladder that'll let us get up there."

Not finding one lying around, they entered the open door of the first barn. Inside they found several ladders and picked one that would allow them to reach the home's roof. Carrying it out, they found some rags and using some bailing wire they found, wrapped the upper ends in the cloth. This would allow them to quietly place the ladder and climb up.

On the roof, TJ took a range measurement to the tunnel entrance - about seven hundred, forty yards, or so. This would do for a mortar and fifty-caliber rifle position. And would be suitable for a drone launch spot. TJ took several other range measurements and motioned for Tim to go back down. At the bottom, TJ got out his notebook and made several notations on the ranges he took, then drew a map of the home, outbuildings, the dam, and the tunnel entrance. Time hack, twelve-fifty, or in military lingo, zero, zero, fifty hours.

"Let's head back across the dam and see if we can figure out a way to capture that sentry," TJ said to Tim.

Tim nodded and stepped off, leading the way back. Once again, the pair slowly low crawled to the top of the embankment and peered over.

Tim immediately grabbed TJ's arm, and both froze. The sentry was looking their direction with weapon held in a port arms position. Tim whispered, "That's Corporal Shirley Capelli. She's nice and Christian. She hates this place more than I do."

"You think you could talk her into leaving and joining us?" TJ asked.

"All I can do is try," Tim replied. "She and I got along okay, and we secretly prayed together on several occasions. If you look, you'll see her Bible in her cargo pants pocket on the right."

"Okay, how to you want to approach her?" TJ asked.

"Let me think about that for a minute. She'll have to check in with the NCOD here in a few minutes, after she's done, I'll go."

TJ shook his head, and both continued to watch the corporal. She was still looking their direction, rifle up in port arms, and they could tell she was attentive. Both wondered if they'd made some noise or something that caught her attention. Neither moved a muscle as she gazed their way.

After what seemed an eternity, she finally looked to the west, then to the south, let her rifle down on its single point sling, and moved back to the tunnel entrance. She pulled a radio from her chest rig and obviously made a call, probably the check in that Tim had mentioned. After the radio call, she sat in a chair, opened a bottle of what appeared to be water and drank.

Tim backed down the embankment some, removed his NVGs, vest, sidearm, and placed his rifle on the pile. He was now weaponless save for his fighting knife. He scooped up some dust and dirt from the ground and rubbed it on his face, hands, clothing, and hair. He looked at TJ and smiled. The kid looked a mess. He gave TJ a little wave and turned to the south and crept away.

TJ watched him go and several thoughts went through his mind. One was a thought for God to take care of the kid and let him get this done safely. The next was he hoped to himself that the kid wasn't about to blow his cover and yell, bringing out the garrison to confront the lone Sheriff.

Tim climbed up to what appeared to be an old dirt road and turned towards the tunnel, walking as if he didn't have a care or worry in the world. As he crested the slope of the hill, the sentry yelled, "HALT!"

Tim froze and the corporal approached with her weapon ready to fire. TJ had brought his rifle up and had the crosshairs on her the whole time. If she would make a threatening move, he would drop the young lady in her tracks.

The corporal approached to within fifty feet of Tim or so and stopping, said, "Identify yourself or be fired upon."

"Shirley, it's me…Tim…Tim Sandoval, don't shoot me, lady," Tim said, haltingly.

"Tim…we thought you were dead," she said running up the hill to him. She hugged him and stepping back said, "What happened to you guys?"

"We got hit down at the airport and Donnie Phillips and I were captured. I think Mason was killed, at least I haven't seen him, so I figure he's dead. Donnie's fine last I saw, but I escaped and made my way here."

"You're a mess," Shirley said, reaching for her radio.

"Don't make that call…please," Tim pleaded with her.

She paused, with the radio midway to her mouth and asked, "Why not…you know I need to call this in?"

"Shirley, you hate this place just as much if not more than I do, right?"

"You know the answer to that better than anyone."

"Yeah, I do, and that's why I'm asking you - begging you - to not make that call."

"You gotta give me a real good reason not to," she told him with a stern look.

"Shirley, you trust me?"

"Timothy, what's wrong with you? You know I trust you…what's wrong?"

"Please don't freak out and please don't use that radio," Tim said holding up both hands to her palm out.

"You're really making me nervous, Tim. What's going on?"

"Please don't freak out and don't shoot either," Tim said, turning and waving for TJ to come out.

Shirley looked in the direction Tim was motioning towards and saw a tall man rise from the back side of the dam. She readied her rifle, as did TJ. "No, please," Tim said. "Please hear us out. What you hear in the next few minutes will change your life. Please, Shirley, please hear us out, I'm begging you as a Brother in Christ."

Shirley lowered her weapon and gazed at Tim with a questioning look, then looked back at TJ who was now walking towards the pair, hands out, palms forward.

"Evening, ma'am, I'm Sheriff Thomas Gerill, from Albany County, Wyoming," TJ introduced himself and held out his hand to shake hers if she would.

She looked at Tim and he said to her, "TJ's a Christian, Shirley, and a real good man. He and his people have taken Donnie and I in and we're doing great. They're all Christian and real good people. Please listen to what we have to say…please," he implored.

She looked back at the tunnel entrance then back to the two men. They could tell she was thinking this through and after a moment of thought, she looked at Tim and said, "It's only because we're both Christian and I know you Timothy Sandoval, that I'll listen. What do you have to say?"

Tim began and after about twenty minutes of explaining and telling Shirley about the valley, Tim finally asked her the question of the day, "So, we want to know if you want to join us? Become a member of our community like Donnie and me. We want to live in peace and security. What do you say?"

She stood there with her weapon pointing at the ground, looking at the pair with an expression that showed confusion. A minute later she said, "I can't desert. I can't just leave, that'd be desertion, and I can't do that."

"Miss," TJ began, "I was a Ranger in the Army and had two tours in the desert. What the doc and his scientists are putting you through is unlawful. According to the UCMJ, you are well within your right to leave. You know their orders are unlawful and, according to Tim and Donnie, you know what they do to people. You know they've tried to kill us on several occasions and have killed several of our valley residents, including the father of our only child. That's murder in the sight of the law, and since I'm a Sheriff, I should know. You would be well within your right to leave."

Tim broke in then and said, "What about it, Shirley? Come with us and you can pray and read your Bible anytime you want. They even have church on Sundays and a gathering on Wednesday nights. We're planting crops and growing food, taking care of livestock, and living a peaceful existence there. It's great! Please join us."

She stood there, and they knew she was undergoing a major battle in her mind. She looked back at the tunnel entrance then back to the two men and said, "Stay here, I'll be right back." She turned and ran back to the chair, took out the radio and lay it on the seat, pulled her fighting knife and cut her left hand with it and let the blood drip and run, smearing it on several places on the chair and the ground, then turned and ran back to the men. "Let's get outta here, fast," she said with a grim smile.

Tim jumped to her and gave her a big hug. TJ held out his hand and she took it, gladly this time and with a smile. Together they crept along the west face of the dam and practically ran back to the highway to wait for Jack and Jeff. It was just after 0220 hours.

Ten minutes before four in the morning, TJ could hear the truck approaching so he stood and raised his rifle in his right hand, the signal all was well. As the truck pulled up, Jack and Jeff could see there were three people and all three were holding rifles. Jack suddenly stopped and Jeff jumped out and pointing his rifle at the trio, asked, "TJ, what's going on?"

"Put that rifle down, Jeff," TJ said. "We've got a new member of the valley to introduce you to. The trio approached the truck and leaving it running, Jack stepped out, and he and Jeff went to the front.

"Jack Kagel and Jeff Jablonski meet Corporal Shirley Capelli," TJ said. "She's agreed to join our community. Shirley is a Christian. Shirley, these two are Marines and had tours in Vietnam."

Shirley held out her hand and shook their hands and smiled at the two and said, "Marines, huh, well I guess we all can't be perfect."

That started it and TJ knew then Shirley was instantly accepted. The banter continued as they climbed into the truck. As the banter died down, TJ looked at Shirley and said, "That was a smart move with the blood on the chair and ground."

"Blood," Jack said, "what blood?"

"I cut my hand with my knife and smeared it on the chair and a little on the ground," she explained. "I scuffed the ground a little giving the impression I was carried away to the south, then left with Tim and TJ."

"Smart…that'll give them something to think about," Jeff said with a smile.

"I'm sure they're already wondering where I am since shift change was at four," she said with a devious smile.

"Well, we'll be at our camp here in a minute and you can talk about it all you want with everyone. Dan will be very happy to meet you," TJ said to her.

"Dan?" she asked.

"He's the other Marine," Tim answered her.

"Not another one," she kidded. That started the banter again and TJ couldn't contain his smile. He knew they probably wouldn't get anything done that day that he wanted to get done. It would be well worth an extra day in the camp.

Back in Livermore, Dan heard the truck approaching and getting his rifle, just in case, he stepped out of the building and stood with the rifle held aloft in his right hand, the signal all was well. The truck pulled in and he could see it held five people and he wondered if they'd captured another prisoner. Much to his surprise and delight, he was introduced to Shirley.

He immediately began asking questions and TJ told everyone to get inside and they would talk there.

"I'm hungry," Tim said.

"Me, too," Jeff concurred.

"As am I," Shirley said.

Dan broke out a case of MREs and everyone selected their choice of meals. They made a circle and sat together, and TJ asked Shirley if she wanted to say the blessing. She was overcome with emotion so much that Tim took the lead and said the prayer. Shirley continued to cry after he'd said Amen, and the men all edged to her and comforted her. The relief she felt was overpowering and she broke into a prayer, thanking God for leading her to this group of Christian men. The men joined in, thanking God for leading her to their group. After several Amens, the group spread back into the circle and quietly began to eat.

Shirley continued to cry some and looked at the men while they ate. They, too, looked at her. TJ saw that she had dark brunette hair, and deep brown eyes that took in everything. She looked to be in her mid-twenties and was about five feet, three inches tall or so. A very pretty young lady.

She asked many questions while they ate their meal and the Marines asked just as many. She was extremely interested in the valley and asked where she would be living. Dan and TJ looked at each other and nodding in quiet agreement, TJ said, "Ruth has plenty of room at her new place and I'm sure DD would love to have you there."

"DD?" she asked.

"He's our one and only child in the valley – we're his uncles and grandfathers," Jeff said with pride. "He'll love you."

"How old is he?" she asked.

"About eighteen months old now, crawling into everything," Jack said. "He's the most inquisitive baby I've ever seen."

"Sounds wonderful," she said, smiling. "How many people in the valley?"

"Nine with Donnie and Tim," TJ told her. "Ten with you," he added with a smile.

"How big is the valley?" she asked.

"I suppose ten miles from north to south by six or seven miles from east to west," TJ answered.

"You all live in the same area?"

"No, Donna and I live on the western slope, against Centennial Ridge. My ranch is called Paradise Valley. The Marines live on Marine Hill to the south, and Ruth and DD live to the east of them, about a half mile or so. Just to the north of Marine Hill, right on Highway 11, Donnie, and Tim moved into a house there. It's about two miles from my place to the southeast."

"Sounds wonderful," she said. "I can't wait to see it and meet everyone else. I hope they receive me as well as you have."

"You'll be a big hit with Ruth and Donna," Jeff said. "I guarantee it."

"They have ladies' days out," TJ said.

"Really…like to go shopping or something?" she asked amazed.

"Or something is more like it," Jeff answered. "Last time they took squirt guns and went hunting zombies in Laramie."

The look on her face told them all she didn't understand and the four from the valley laughed. TJ finally explained and she said, "I remember when the doc came back and told us about the saltwater. We were amazed. They began experiments almost immediately."

"Experiments…?" TJ asked.

"Yeah, using saltwater on the dead we'd captured for them. He and Doctor Miller did horrible experiments on both the dead and on the living we captured. Doctor Roche hasn't come back from whatever it was they were going to do."

"He won't ever be going back," Tim said.

"Huh?" she queried.

"He's been taken care of, Doctor Roche that is, a while back," TJ answered. "He and his team attacked the residents of the valley, and they killed him and his whole team. We'll have to let them tell you that story sometime."

It got quiet in the group after that, and they ate in silence. After their meal, they collected the refuse and Dan told Shirley she could use his sleeping area if she wanted, but she refused, saying she was too keyed up to sleep.

"You can watch us do an aerial recon if you'd like," TJ told her. "Dan's going to fly and I'm assisting. Be happy to have you watch if you'd like."

"Sure, why not," she said.

"Night, I'm pooped," Tim said and headed for his sleeping spot.

Dan took the drone out and once back inside, fired up the viewing screen. Shirley sat to his left and TJ on his right. Dan started the drone's engines and let them warm a minute, then lifted off into a hover at about fifty feet and made sure all the systems were in the green. He then rose to over nine thousand feet and headed to the southeast.

"What are you looking for?" Shirley asked.

TJ answered, "We're looking for suitable fighting positions around the two tunnel entrances. Tim and I found one before we met you last night and it's good. We're looking for other suitable areas today and maybe go out again tonight to take a look at a few."

"Fighting positions?" she inquired.

TJ and Dan looked at each other and Dan, looking back at her said, "They continue to attack the valley using drones with missiles. They killed one of our residents, Julia, a few months back and almost got Jack, but he'd been over helping TJ with a project when the missile hit his house. We're tired of it and going to make an all-out effort to stop it by attacking the complex. If we have to, we'll kill everyone in there. Trust me, we'd rather not and would like to talk more of your Christian friends and anyone else that wants to live in peace to come out and join our valley community instead of having war with them. Doctor Miller and the scientists are toast as far as we're concerned."

"You're here doing recon," she commented as a statement rather than question.

"Yes," Dan agreed. "We're looking for suitable position for snipers, mortar pits, and places to launch our drones from. We have drones we call Kamikaze drones and others we can use as bombers. We now have bombs that are HE and others that are HEI, and now have napalm."

She looked down at the floor hearing this and they could tell she was having second thoughts and mixed emotions.

TJ said, "We understand your torment. Tim and Donnie had some also. But they're with us now and ready to do battle. We're not going to just attack without warning, like you're friends have been doing to us, but wake them up with a few well-placed bombs, then using a loudspeaker, like a public address system or something, give them fair warning. Those that would like to leave the complex and join us are more than welcome. The others…"

"I'll help," she said. "I can use the loudspeaker to try and talk them out. I know Tim and Donnie will, too."

"Yes, they've already said they would," TJ told her.

"About twenty-five or so of our Christian friends will want to join us I think."

"Wow, twenty-five. I don't know where we'd put twenty-five people."

"They'd sleep on the ground in the valley if you'd give them the opportunity. We've talked about deserting many times."

"It wouldn't be desertion," TJ said. "It'd be doing the right thing. The leaders of the complex are the ones in the wrong. In your hearts and minds you know it. That's not desertion."

TJ looked at Shirley as she'd become quiet, and he could see she was off in her thoughts. He asked her, "What are you thinking?"

She looked at him and said, "I was just thinking about how we could get the message to the others."

TJ was surprised by the answer and asked what she meant.

"I think we should do the same thing as you did with me. Wait until we see another one of our friends on guard duty, entice them out, explain the situation and the des…er…leaving for the right reasons plan, and coordinate an attack that'll cover their mass exodus. I think that would save a lot of time and effort on our part and they would probably drop a few of the bad people along the way. Once they're out, we can launch the full attack."

TJ quickly stood and said to everyone, "Guys, gather round and listen to this." Once everyone had gathered, he had Shirley explain her idea to them. Tim had a grand smile on his face when she'd finished and Dan, Jack, and Jeff were mulling it over in their minds. The plan was too good to pass up. It was perfect and Dan said so.

TJ looked at the group and almost thought it comical as they began speaking to one another adding ideas to her plan and to the final attack plan. He shook his head and stood getting everyone's attention and said, "Okay, we have an excellent plan thanks to the Corporal. Shirley, Tim, Jeff, and I will go out at ten tonight and put it into effect. Get your gear ready – Jack, outfit Shirley with whatever she needs for her kit if you would – eat and hit the sack. Dan, please write a note to our Brothers and Sisters inside the complex. We'll give it to the person we talk to tonight. Sign it Staff Sergeant, USMC. That'll get their attention. Okay, people, let's get to it."

The group broke with Jack taking Shirley in tow and heading for the locker in the truck that held the extra equipment. The rest going on the mission readied their own gear, ate if they wanted and hit the sack. Dan said he'd wake everyone at nine.

They nicknamed the mission Operation Freedom Flight and left the bivouac on time and by midnight TJ, Shirley, and Tim were looking over the lip of the dam watching the shift change take place. The man that took over the guard duty was a tall guy with what appeared to be longer than normal arms.

"He's six foot-seven and weighs about ninety pounds it looks like," Tim commented with a quiet chuckle. "Nickname's Stretch. Real name is Private Daniel Donnaghan. He's Irish and will let you know it. Has red hair and blue eyes and is meaner than a guard dog with a porterhouse steak. He'll be easy to bring into our group. TJ, give me the letter from Dan and I'll get ready to go."

Tim backed down the embankment and like before, got dirty, put the letter in his shirt pocket, smiled at the two and started to leave when Shirley, stopped him. "I should go, too," and dropped her gear and dirtied up like Tim. They both looked at TJ and he simply nodded and smiled.

The pair turned and moved to the east using the same route Tim had taken last time. TJ eased his head up over the lip of the embankment to watch and saw 'Stretch' looking to the west. TJ also noted there wasn't a chair near the guard station any longer.

Shirley and Tim sauntered down the dirt road and as they came into view, Stretch said, "Halt," and the pair did so with hands raised. The tall private approached the pair with weapon held ready and as he neared, recognized the two and a huge smile broke on his face. "I thought the two of you were dead," he practically yelled.

"Quiet, you nut," Shirley said to him and gave him a hug. Tim held his hand out and they shook hands.

"What happened to you two? All the blood last night scared the tar outta us," the tall man said.

Tim began and Shirley added, and motioned for TJ. As TJ approached, Private Donnaghan became nervous. Shirley put her hand on him and told him everything was okay.

TJ came up and held out his hand and said in introduction, "Hi, I'm Sheriff Thomas Gerill, from Albany County, Wyoming."

The tall private switched his rifle in his hands and shook TJ's. "You're a Sheriff?"

"Yes," TJ said.

"He's a Ranger, too," Shirley said.

"You're a snake eater?" Daniel asked in awe.

"I made the cut," TJ answered.

Daniel looked at the three and asked Shirley, pointedly, "What's going on?"

She explained again and Tim produced the letter, giving it to the tall private. During the conversation, all three commented on the plans with Daniel, who stood there looking between the three and the letter. After some time thinking, Daniel said he'd do it.

TJ said, "Then let's gather and pray asking God for direction, strength, and courage to face the upcoming battle." The four gathered and they all said a short prayer together. When TJ said Amen, the four broke and TJ held his hand out once again. The tall private shook it and TJ said, "God be with you."

"And with you as well, thank you, sir," Daniel replied. He shook Tim's hand and Shirley gave him another hug and they separated.

As TJ and Shirley eased over the lip of the dam, Daniel nonchalantly ambled back to his position. As he neared his assigned spot, a very muscular man in uniform, obviously the Sergeant Major, stormed out of the cave's entrance and yelled, "Where have you been MAGGOT?"

Daniel jumped and was instantly petrified but sprang to attention and had the gumption to reply, "Had to take a whizz Sergeant Major, that's all."

"You know to call someone if you need to use the head...drop and give me fifty...NOW MAGGOT," the Sergeant Major yelled.

Daniel dropped laying his rifle across his hands and began doing the commanded number of pushups. He finished and rose to an attention position with his rifle at port arms and taking in gulps of air, looked at the Sergeant Major, and waited for who knew what.

"Good enough, maggot," the Sergeant Major said. "Next time it'll go much, much worse for you. GET MY DRIFT?"

"Yes, Sergeant Major," Daniel yelled back, trembling at the thought if the man had been thirty seconds earlier coming out of the cave.

The big man turned and stormed back into the dark recesses of the cave entrance. Poor Daniel stood at his post shaking, from the thought, the effort of doing fifty pushups and from the unexpected verbal lashing from the Sergeant Major. Sergeant Majors were not ones to fool with – ever. They ate privates for a snack.

This particular one was simply coldhearted. He was unforgiving and just plain mean. He was a true sadist and loved to torment his juniors. Not to mention he was always present when the doctors and scientists took apart human beings. He was known to 'use' the women while they were anesthetized, awaiting whatever it was the Doc's did. The thirty or so Christians in the complex avoided him as best they could.

He was a big man, well over six feet and more than two hundred pounds of muscle. He sported a horseshoe hairline and for the most part, almost always wore his hat to cover his baldness. The hair he did sport was at best, grey, spotted with the black it once was. He was always in a crisp, heavily starched uniform. He wore a 1911, .45 caliber sidearm at all times and most thought he probably slept with the thing on his hip. Along with it he wore a K-Bar Marine combat knife.

STRACK is what he was called. The word is an adjective. It refers to a military person who has perfect uniforms and behaves far above the normal standards set for one. The vast majority of people given that handle was for the most part very professional military personnel. Normal people that were called STRACK were consummate professionals in all regards – dress and appearance, attitude, the way they treated and handled others. This guy looked the part but was far from the professional the word really related to.

His quarters were immaculate. No dust was to be found. Not even in the hard to see corners or along the desk and cabinet borders on the floor. Everything was in its place, just so.   Every uniform hung precisely two inches from its neighbor. Underwear in the drawer precisely folded six inches square, the undershirts precisely eight inches square, and the handkerchiefs precisely four inches square. His socks were tucked into themselves creating a near perfect four-inch ball and lay precisely next to each other.

Suffice it to say, the man was scary. He would be the one 'unknown' the valley residents would have to worry about when they made their final attack. He would be the wild card, the joker that would rear its ugly head at the most inappropriate time just like he did with Private Donnaghan at the cave entrance.

Back at the bivouac, TJ explained all had gone well and said they'd told Private Daniel Donnaghan they would be back in thirty days and asked that he tried to be on duty that night. They would discuss final plans for the exodus then and adjust the plan as necessary. In the meantime, Daniel would get with his Christian friends, and showing the letter, explain the upcoming operation, and tell them to get ready. It would be five to six weeks before the action actually began.

The homecoming was jubilant indeed and as expected, Ruth took Shirley in with no fuss at all other than to say Shirley needed some new clothes and looking at Donna, said Road Trip. The girls laughed. Donnie and Shirley hugged tightly, and he said he was so happy to see her. That night the valley residents put on a feast for the new person and the prayer before dinner lasted almost fifteen minutes, with everyone praying through their tears.

After dinner, they sat together talking and discussing the future. TJ called for a powwow to plan, strategize, and go over tactics. They now had eight fighters and Ruth with DD. They would split forces and have four at each tunnel entrance. Planning was going to be a long process.

It was late in the evening when they cleaned up. TJ took Shirley up to the Underground, showed her around, and let her decide which room to use for the time being, since Ruth and DD were staying in the guest room. She asked if she could use the tub and of course, TJ said certainly and offered some wine also. She declined. TJ told her to take her pick from the storeroom clothing and shoes, and said goodnight, turning for the stairwell. Shirley stopped him and gave him a big hug and began to softly cry. TJ held her for a moment, and she apologized and broke away, turning for the tub.

"Goodnight, Shirley, and welcome to Paradise Valley," TJ said. She stopped, looked back with a small smile, and nodded in agreement with tears streaming down her face. TJ said, "Tomorrow morning, get up early and go out the eastern hatchway. You'll fall in love with the view, I promise. God bless and goodnight."

Chapter 9: Actions

Shirley got up early the next morning feeling more refreshed than ever after the best night's sleep she'd had in years. She donned a robe TJ had given her and making her way to the kitchen, made a pot of coffee. After she'd poured herself a mug of the steaming brew, she climbed the eastern portal and stepped out to a scene she would never forget. It literally took her breath away as the morning had broken with a partly cloudy sky that was a fiery red and orange with the sunrise above Sheep Mountain. It was one of those rare Wyoming days with no wind.

She was almost breathless as she turned in a full circle looking at her surroundings and the beautiful vista the valley brought to her eyes. She praised God in prayer for the view, praying that it would last forever. She saw elk, deer, turkeys, the cattle, and some sheep out in the flats. Birds were everywhere and chipmunks skittered about, busy with life. From time-to-time she would remember to breath and was overjoyed by what she beheld.

TJ stuck his head out of the hatch and said, "Good morning, I see you're as touched as we all were by the view."

She looked at him with a beaming smile and said, "Good morning to you, too, and yes, I'm breathless by this. Look at that red sky over that mountain!"

Climbing out and standing next to her, he said, "That's Sheep Mountain and it's almost ten miles long from north to south," he said pointing out the ends. "Look at the elk and deer down there."

"I've seen them and some turkeys, too," she said. "This is wonderful."

"Now you know why Doug Sutton named this place Paradise Valley," TJ said rather sadly. "In his memoir, he said he sat up here for hours just looking at God's handy work and reading his Bible."

"Sutton; he the man that made this place?" Shirley asked.

"Yes. He was killed a little over a year ago in the attack that also killed Doctor Roche and his team. Apparently, nearly fifty people died that day in the battle, along with Dave Malone, my good friend and deputy sheriff. Dave was a good man and from what I've read and seen, Doug Sutton was, too. Ruth misses him something awful and little DD will never know his real Father, even though he has four surrogate fathers now…well, maybe grandfathers," he said with a chuckle.

"I'm sorry to hear about their deaths," Shirley replied morosely.

"Yes, it's sad," he commented. "They did live good lives and were Christian men, so we know we'll see them again. Doug called this place Paradise Valley, comparing it to The Garden of Eden I suppose."

"TJ, this place is spectacular. The facilities and home are wonderful, too. I'm so glad you and Tim pulled me from that quagmire. I hope and pray all our friends decide to join us. I prayed for them up here this morning."

"I always feel closer to God when I pray from up here. It just seems like the perfect place to talk with Him, you know."

"Yes, now that you mention it, I did feel closer to Him. The vista…it's just perfect."

"Artwork only He can paint."

"Yes…yes, that's it exactly," Shirley said with a beaming smile looking up at TJ.

"How are you feeling this morning, by-the-way?" TJ asked.

"Wonderful. I slept better than I have in years…literally. That bath was…I don't know…soothing I guess is the word. I no sooner than hit the sheets then I was out like a light. I didn't wake until the alarm woke me. That was unusual. I usually wake several times a night since we've been sleeping in a cave for a long, long time. And I'm always worried about people that work there. Scared of them, I guess. I looked out that window and saw the horses and cattle by the barn, the pigs and the chickens, and the mountain to the west," she said, pointing. "It's all so gorgeous."

"I told you, you would be impressed by the views here. You should see it after a fresh snowfall. Everything white with the green from the pine trees showing through, the animals moving through the snow. Every view from up here is spectacular and I've never seen the same thing twice."

"Everyone is going to love it here," Shirley said looking him in the eye, "TJ, I know everyone is going to help. I know in my heart every one of our Christian friends will fight to get out of that complex and away from the sinister things they do there. Not one will falter. And when they come here and see this place…" she said turning shaking her head and looking at the valley, "they'll never want to leave. We'll make a swell community, I'm positive of that."

TJ smiled at her and said, "I just bet you're right. Come on, go back in there, get cleaned up and dressed and come on downstairs. We'll have breakfast and I'll give you the grand tour of Paradise Valley and the rest of the Centennial Valley." He turned and climbed down through the hatchway.

Shirley paused and did another full circle taking in the view, then climbed down the hatchway. Closing and locking it, she noted the weapons and ammo stored in the compartments next to the hatch and her mind came back into focus. They were still in danger and that saddened her. She shook her head in defiance, however, and climbed down to clean up.

Downstairs, Donna, Ruth, DD, and TJ were preparing breakfast when Shirley came down. Ruth said, "Good morning," and gave her a hug.

Donna did as well and said, "How do you like your eggs?"

"You have real eggs?" Shirley exclaimed.

"Fresh every morning," Donna said with a smile. "How do you want yours?"

"Over easy, please," Shirley said.

"Bacon or sausage?" Donna asked.

"Bacon, please," she answered.

"Toast?" Ruth said already making some in the toaster.

"You have bread?" Shirley asked.

"TJ makes it once a week," Ruth answered. "You should be here on baking day – the smell – woohoo!"

"May I have two slices, please?" Shirley asked.

They all laughed, and TJ said, "You can have four if you want." He invited her to sit down at the table and taking her coffee mug, refilled it with a fresh dose. He sat with her and watched her as she watched Ruth and Donna make breakfast, fascinated.

TJ couldn't help but laugh and DD took up the laughter, too. Shirley got up and lifted the youngster into her arms and sat back down with him in her lap. He was all smiles and giggles as she tickled him.

After she was finished with breakfast, Shirley commented while patting her stomach, "After that meal last night and now this, I'm gonna gain fifty pounds."

"No, you're not," TJ said. "This valley doesn't have a big grocery store to go buy more goods anymore. We have to provide for ourselves and that means work. You'll earn your keep here in the valley. We all do. God has blessed us very well so far and we thank Him frequently for the blessings He gives us. But don't think it's an easy life here because certainly it is not. That being said, come on and I'll give you the grand tour. Okay to take Shirley on the grand tour of Paradise Valley and the valley beyond, Donna?"

"Get," she answered with a flick of her hand.

"Come on then," TJ told Shirley.

He showed her the house, the root cellar, the armory, and the library. Outside they went to the garage first and he showed her all the things out there. Then he took her to the barn and showed her the animals, the tack room, and how to gather eggs. They went out the back and he introduced her to Dusty and the animals in the pasture and pointed out where the cattle and sheep pastures were. Then to the underground greenhouses. She had a multitude of questions about them and marveled at the produce already growing within. They walked down the lane to the gate, and he explained the defenses that Doug and Dave had built. She was amazed by it all and the ingenuity of everything.

Back in the garage, they got in the ATV after getting Z'd up and left. He let her open the gate with the remote and they sped through. TJ turned left and headed towards Centennial. Gave her the tour of town and drove her up to the Ranger Station and getting out, showed her the pump and took her inside and explained about the supplies and equipment kept there, and that the place was one of their bug-out positions. She was impressed with their preparations for just about anything.

Leaving the station, he sped through Centennial once again and continued east to the Highway 11 juncture and turned south. He turned in at the dirt trail that led to the Malone complex and underground. He showed her the aftermath of the ambush and what was left of the Malone home. He showed her the portal to the underground but didn't take her inside, saying they would do that another time.

They headed down the road Dave and Doug had made and back on the Highway he stopped at the two privates' home. After the hugs and back slapping, Donnie and Tim showed her around their place and offered a cup of coffee which was not turned down. They all sat on the porch on the east side and looked out over the valley to the north and enjoyed the company, the coffee, and the view.

TJ said they needed to get along, so they said their goodbyes and left for Marine Hill. TJ showed her Jack's destroyed home and as they pulled up, Dan and Jack came out of Dan's house and waved. TJ pulled up and getting out, saw Jeff coming down the hill, waving. Shirley was hugged by all of the Marines and another cup of coffee was forced upon them. (Well, not really.)

They sat together sipping their coffee and talking. Shirley told them about the vista she'd seen that morning and all three of the Marines said they'd all had the same experience and knew what she'd gone through.

"This whole place is so beautiful," she told them. "I can't believe that someplace like this exists in the world."

"And you can pick any empty home out there you want and live in it," TJ said. "I'll take you up to Albany next and you can see the places there. A few are beautiful."

"Looks like we'll have to round up more horses since we may have a transportation problem before long," Dan commented.

"Horses," Shirley said. "I never dreamed I'd be riding horses for a primary mode of transportation," she mused with a shake of her head.

"Gasoline is getting hard to come by now," TJ told her. "We're fortunate as we've got two tanker trucks with about fifteen thousand gallons left in each and that should last us a while. Diesel is really hard to come by. After we get done with the complex, we'll take a run over to the refinery over in Cheyenne and see if we can get another truck or two full of fuel for the valley. We may need to go over to Sinclair, Wyoming, since that is the next closest refinery and see what we can scavenge there. That would be a trip for the whole crew to take."

"What do you mean by the whole crew?" she asked him.

"We would take as many of us as possible for several reasons. We'd probably take at least every trailer with a fuel tank and fill those so that means five trucks. We would take as many of us as could go so we would have enough people to drive tanker trucks back if we found some, which is a high probability. So, we would need all of us. And if we get a bunch of your friends to join us, we could take three people per truck and we'd bring back as many tankers as we dared. If we were able to bring back five or six or more tankers with fuel, we'd be set for quite a while. And with what we get from Cheyenne…well, we would be sitting pretty for a long time from a fuel standpoint. Then we would have more than enough time for us to round up more horses and get a healthy herd going."

"Where would you find more horses?"

"All over Wyoming and western Nebraska, too. Maybe northeastern Colorado. We'll have to put a tristate roundup on the list of things to do. We can do that for cattle, pigs, and sheep too, if needed. With the elk and deer populations getting so big around here now, cattle are not as important as they used to be. And with the buffalo herd getting so large to the southeast, we shouldn't have any problem with meat gathering for quite some time to come."

"There's buffalo nearby?"

"Yes, there was a small herd of about five hundred animals at a bison ranch on the Colorado/Wyoming border south of Cheyenne. Dan, Jack, Julia, and Jeff ran into the herd several months ago and Jeff, shot a monster."

"Yeah, and those steaks were great," Jeff commented. "There were over a thousand animals in that herd. It took a while for all of them to cross the highway in front of us. It was a sight, alright."

"Wow. We'll be able to live here nicely, I think…all of us, and peacefully, too."

"God willing, that is our hope and want," TJ replied.

"Here, here," Dan said.

Jack and Jeff rapped their knuckles on the table signifying their agreement.

"We better hit the trail," TJ said. "I'm sure the ladies want to get with Shirley and discuss their shopping spree, which will probably be tomorrow I'd say. And I'll be happy to have DD all to myself again. Maybe we'll go fishing again and I'll catch a bunch for a fish fry sometime."

"Hey, I want to go," Jeff spouted.

"Me, too," Jack said.

"I bet Donnie and Tim'll want to go, too," TJ said. "We'll stop by and ask. If so, I'll bring the big truck. If the ladies do go tomorrow, I'll pick you two up after they leave. I'll give you a holler on the radio later and let you know a time."

"We'll pack a lunch so don't worry about food," Jeff said.

They said their goodbyes and climbed in the ATV. TJ drove down the hill and went back to Donnie and Tim's place and they said they'd love to go fishing. TJ told them to turn their radio on about five and he'd let them, Jack and Jeff know the time he'd pick them up.

On the road again, TJ sped up to Albany and showed Shirley around. She loved one home on the north side of the hamlet. It was a log cabin affair and as they cautiously entered, they found it was a two-bedroom home with a loft. It had a full bathroom upstairs, a half-bath downstairs, and a nice kitchen. It had a basement with ample storage room and a small work area. Outside, they found a pump and once TJ got the lock off of it, found it was operational as after a few pulls on the handle, fresh, clear water poured out. TJ cupped his hands and drank some and said it was good. So, the place had water, too.

The home had a detached garage and two other outbuildings. The garage was empty but would hold a good-sized truck and an ATV if they found one. That was on everyone's 'wish' lists. There were tools everywhere for gardening and home repair and upkeep. The first outbuilding had equipment for cutting wood and yard work implements, including a riding lawn mower.

The second outbuilding was obviously a 'she-shed' as it was decorated with a women's touch and Shirley loved it. She looked at TJ and asked, "Can this place be mine?"

"Sure…why not," he answered. "We'd have to find you a radio so you could keep in touch with the valley, but this is a nice place. The only worry I'd have besides the Zs, would be animal threat. Those would be about the same, actually."

"Animal threat?" she asked him.

"Bears, mountain lions, wolves, that kind of thing. You'd have to be prepared for them just as much as you would for the Zs."

"Ah, I get it. I really like this place, though. I could live here, and if I can get one of those chainsaws running, I can cut enough of this standing dead timber around the place to last quite a while. Over here, I could make a garden big enough to supply me with vegetables and things. And I know I can shoot deer or elk for meat."

"Not to mention as a member of the valley residents and working together, you'll get vegetables from the fields and meat from the butchering of beef and the pigs. That's a given. We'll dig you a root cellar to store food in and put in an underground greenhouse for you, say over in that area. We can dig that out fairly easily."

"This all sounds so good…it's almost like I'm in a fairy tale dream and will wake up in that cave any minute."

"Nope, this is as real as it gets, kid."

She laughed at that and said, "Thank you."

"For what?" he asked.

"For calling me a kid," she said chuckling.

"Come on. We'll head back to Paradise Valley and get you with Ruth and Donna. As they turned, TJ stopped and turning back to the house, said, "Miss Capelli, I present you with your new home. May you live in it peacefully and in safety for as long as you desire. We'll have to get everyone together and have a proper home blessing before you move in."

She stood there looking at TJ with a speculating look on her face and after a moment said, "Thank you. I'm kind of stunned by everything that's happened in the last few days…you know?"

"I know exactly what you mean. I was just as stunned when Ruth gave me Paradise Valley. I still don't believe it. Sometimes I stand still wherever I am, kind of in a trance at the wonder of it all."

"Ruth gave you Paradise Valley…why?"

"She said it gave her too many memories. Had me read Doug's Last Will and Testament and said I could have it all. She and DD moved in with Julia, Dave's wife, in that house to the east of Dan's, the one that was destroyed by the missile. That's when Julia was killed. Now Ruth lives in that house southeast of the one that was destroyed. She's only staying with us because of bringing you back. It was a very special occasion to say the least."

She looked at him and smiled, beaming. "I'm very happy to be here," she said.

"Hop in and let's go."

They drove back to Paradise Valley and Ruth, DD, and Donna were on the front porch as they pulled in.

Ruth was first to speak and asked Shirley, "So, what do you think of it all?"

"I'm speechless," Shirley answered shaking her head with the wonder of it all. "The whole valley is so beautiful, the river, the creeks, the animals, the fields, the trees - everything. I just don't know what to say except to thank God for leading me to you all and this…this…Paradise Valley."

They all laughed at her as they knew exactly what she was talking about. Donna broke in and started talking about shopping and weapons and ammo they would need to take. TJ shook his head and went inside, poured himself a mug of coffee and headed out back to the greenhouses to prune and pick now that the plants were producing, thanks to Donnie's input.

A little more than an hour later, Donna came out and grabbed him in a bear hug and kissed him deeply. "I miss you," she moaned.

"I miss you, too," he said and returned the kiss with another. They hugged together for a while.

Donna ended the moment saying, "Ruth is fixing lunch. We need to get in there." She turned from the hug and led the way out.

Just before they went inside, TJ leaned over and quietly said to her, "Maybe we can take a bath together tonight."

She gave him a knowing demure look and smile and ran up the back stairs into the house. TJ followed.

It was early the next morning and Donna brought the truck they were taking into Laramie up to the porch steps. They loaded weapons, ammo, a picnic lunch, extra water and food items and enough equipment for several days, even though they planned to be back by late evening. Ruth brought out two super squirters filled with saltwater and Shirley asked what those were for. She nodded when she got the answer.

TJ had already radioed the other guys about the fishing trip and was packing his truck for the days outing. DD sort of knew he was going with Uncle TJ for a day trip and was excited. All their gear, weapons, ammo, and food were packed and ready. TJ picked up DD and stood near the trucks waiting for the ladies to leave.

Donna came over and gave him a kiss and the three ladies climbed into their truck. TJ waved as they pulled out. He closed the house up and drove with DD in his car seat over to Tim and Donnie's place and picked them up, then went to Marine Hill. Dan insisted they have a mug of coffee before leaving. As men do, they discussed fishing methods and baits while sipping the brew.

As the men got up to leave on their outing, Dan motioned for TJ and said, "I'll keep close to the radio and listen for the girls. They should be okay. You guys have fun."

"What are you going to do?" TJ asked.

"I'm going to open the back door so I can hear the radio if it goes off and sit in an Adirondack and read. I'm putting on a tee-shirt and some shorts and sit out there barefooted and soak up some sun while reading. I feel vitamin D deficient. I'll keep my M-4 and a Stinger handy just in case. I just may sip some of the good scotch while I'm at it."

"Man, that's tough to beat," TJ said, tossing the thought around in his mind, wondering if he should bow out of the fishing trip and go back to Paradise Valley and do the same on top of the Underground. But he shook his head and told Dan to have a nice day, climbed in the truck with everyone else and headed out.

The men returned with nineteen Rainbow trout that were more than twenty inches in length. Enough for the valley residents to have a very nice fish bake some evening. After cleaning the catch and laughing at Dan's sunburn, TJ, DD, Donnie, and Tim left, with TJ dropping the two Privates at their place. They invited him in for a tumbler of scotch and he agreed. They sat on the back porch, boots up on the rail, DD in his bouncy chair, overlooking the valley and sipped their drinks and talked.

TJ told them about Shirley finding a place to live up in Albany, and suggested they take their vehicle up and look for one up there. It would be to everyone's benefit and mutual protection if they did so. The two said that was a good idea and agreed to go up the next day and said they would drive to Paradise Valley and get Shirley to go along. TJ thought that was a good idea.

He finished his scotch and collecting DD, said his goodbye and left for home. As he was opening the gate, the ladies pulled in behind him with an overloaded truck full of stuff, probably lady 'stuff'. He smiled and pulled up to the garage, got out with DD and the bag of fresh fish and headed towards the house.

The ladies pulled up to the porch steps and getting out, were still gabbing about who knew what. TJ was smiling as he mounted the porch. Ruth took DD, giving him a hug and kiss.

"How'd you do?" TJ asked. That brought a flood of talk about this store and that one, this dress and those jeans, these boots, and those shoes. He nodded throughout the conversation on the porch. He told Shirley about going with Donnie and Tim the following day and she thought that a wonderful idea. She said she could take a load of her goods along and put them in her new house. TJ laughed at that, thinking about how he was when he first moved into Paradise Valley.

Donna asked, "You guys catch any fish?"

"A boat load of better'n twenty-inch Rainbow Trout, enough for a valley fish bake. We caught nineteen of the things and had a swell time."

"You didn't have a boat, did you?" Ruth asked.

TJ chuckled and said, "No, just an expression. We did have a good time. And, while we were gone, Dan got a sunburn. You should see him – he's red as a beet."

They laughed and commented they'd like to see that. TJ reminded them they would tomorrow at the powwow, saying they would meet together at one o'clock the next afternoon and begin the process of planning. That revelation sobered the group, and the ladies broke to unload a few of the things they'd brought home from Laramie.

That process started, TJ asked, "So, did you have a good time with the squirt guns?"

Shirley immediately said, "That was the coolest thing I've ever seen. I was skeptical when the doc told us about that but that was neat. And quiet! The dead just dropped as if their lights were turned off. I found several squirt guns in Laramie and brought them for my place. I've got to tell everyone about that when they get here. We'll have to go to Cheyenne and get more of them for everyone."

Donna, Ruth, and TJ laughed at Shirley. She was so excited about everything going on, like a kid at Christmas. It was a pleasure for the three to see her acting this way. She was so vibrant and expectant for her future after living in a military regulated underground complex for so long. She now had all this newness at her disposal. It was refreshing to witness.

It was time for dinner and TJ opted for a sandwich, some carrot and cucumber spears and taking his plate, headed for the Underground.

"What's he going up there for?" Shirley asked the other two ladies.

Donna responded, "He goes up there for some serious thinking. He always does that before a powwow, to think and write down his thoughts. He's probably grabbing his bottle of eighteen-year-old Macallan and taking it with him to the eastern portal. Its best to leave him be when he's in this kind of mood. He'll be okay. What would you like for dinner?"

"Those carrots and cucumbers looked good," Shirley answered. "Do you have the stuff to make a salad?"

"You bet, come on and we'll go out to the greenhouse and get some lettuce, fresh spinach, and tomatoes, and we'll make a great salad," Donna said, leading the way.

After dinner, the ladies cleaned up and Donna said she was tired and going upstairs to check on TJ. Up in the Underground, she paused and getting a tumbler, climbed the eastern hatch. At the top, she looked out and saw TJ sitting in an Adirondack chair and looking to the east. She gave a little 'ahem' and when he looked at her, she held up the tumbler and said, "I've never had Macallan before, mind if I join you?"

He smiled and said, "Not at all, come on up. The view is spectacular again. Look to the west."

She turned, looking that direction and the partly cloudy sky was orange, and red as the sun set. Another beautiful view. She turned to TJ and proffered her tumbler, and he poured a finger of the rich, amber liquid. She smelled it and took a tentative sip and said, "Much smoother than I thought it would be. I figured I'd be hacking up a lung after a sip."

TJ chuckled then said, "No, this is very good scotch and surprisingly smooth. I like it a lot. Most of the time I drink a Glenlivet or Glenfiddich and sometimes, if we find some, Dalmore single malt. All of them are good, but this one" – holding up his tumbler of Macallan – "is the best by far in my opinion."

"It is good, thank you. You mind if I sit out here and enjoy the view?"

"Not at all. Actually, I was just about to head back downstairs. I know you're tired and probably want to rack out soon. I'll leave you to your thoughts…here, you can have this chair. It's already warmed up," he said getting up and gathering his things. He offered her another finger of the scotch, but she declined and sat on the chair. TJ gave her a kiss, said good night, and climbed down the hatchway and went downstairs.

A little after noon the following day, everyone began arriving for the powwow. TJ and Donna had set up tables and chairs on the porch for everyone and had set out paper and pencils. Of course, TJ had the scotch out – not the Macallan – and Donna and Ruth had put out several bottles of wine, mostly white, and a Zinfandel. It would be a pleasant afternoon.

By one o'clock, everyone was seated and ready to go. TJ opened with prayer and the valley residents got down to brass tacks. They discussed the cave system and commented on the layout and how difficult it would be to clear the whole thing.

"I still think we should drive a couple of those ROV things in there with a couple of pounds of C-4 each and collapse the tunnels," Jeff said. "That would seal them in, and we wouldn't have to worry about them anymore."

"But what about our friends?" Donnie questioned. "Can't we give them a chance to get out first?"

"That's one of the reasons we're here," TJ said. "We told – what was the tall guy's name again?"

"Daniel Donnaghan," Tim said.

"Yeah, Daniel – anyway, we told Daniel to talk to his friends and show them the letter Nemo wrote. When we go back in twenty-seven days from now, we'll find out the answer. If they want to jump and come live here, we'll do our best to get them all out safely."

"How?" Ruth asked.

"Leave that up to us and our friends," Tim said.

Donnie added, "We'll know as soon as we see Daniel if we're good to go. If so, they'll already have a plan. We'd been discussing that before the three of us got out of there, so I know that since we made contact, they've been planning something. Daniel will give us the low down when we see him."

"What about the others?" Tim asked.

"That's what we were doing on the last outing, finding suitable fighting positions. Since we'll have eight fighters, we can have four at each tunnel entrance. TJ, Tim, Shirley and Dan at the northern site and Donnie, Donna, Jack, and Jeff at the western entrance. We'll have two mortar positions at each with about a hundred rounds each, and a fifty at each with ten mags or so each giving them over a hundred rounds. Each of those positions will also have Kamikaze and bomber drones ready to fly. Dan, how many drones you think?"

"I'd say five of each at each position should do, and Ruth can have a bunch back at the bivouac to use when needed," Dan answered.

"Good, sounds good," TJ said, thoughtfully. "We have four thumpers and four hundred rounds for them. So, we need to start a weapons list with ammo requirements. Dan, would you be in charge of the napalm mixing?"

"Yep, with Jack and Jeff helping," he answered.

"Me too, I used to make it back home to kill fire ants," Donnie said.

"Okay with me," Dan said.

"Tim and I can gather and ready weapons and ammo if it's okay…I feel like a fifth wheel here," Shirley said, meekly.

"That'll be fine," TJ said, smiling. "You two can break down all the weapons, give them a once over, clean 'em and let us know if any need work."

"What about the other trip we talked about before?" Jeff mentioned.

Everyone at the table became quiet at that. The three from the complex knew nothing of the proposed trip to Fort Carson for more war fighting supplies. Dan and TJ looked at each other and they both looked at Ruth.

"What?" she said.

"You seem to be the best judge of character, what do you say?" TJ asked.

After she looked each, she spoke, saying, "They're good people. I trust them."

"Okay, there it is," TJ said instantly accepting her counsel and continued, "we'd talked about making a major excursion to Fort Carson, south of Colorado Springs, for more supplies and equipment like real napalm and heavier shoulder-fired missiles. We talked about taking the flat-bed truck down and loading the thing."

"I was stationed there," Tim said to no one in particular.

"Then you and I both know the lay out," TJ said to him with a smile. "I know where the ammo and weapon bunkers are."

"Yeah, they're easy to find," Tim added. "The AT-6 missiles are there also, probably several thousand of them."

"Good grief, that many?" Jeff asked.

"Yeah, with that many troops, you need them if you deployed," Donnie said. "Those things, although cumbersome, are worth their weight in gold in a firefight, especially if you're in an urban combat situation. They do a number on the inside of a building."

"I don't know about napalm, though," Tim said. "Never saw any of that at Carson. That's primarily an Air Force weapon, not Army."

TJ jumped in at that and said, "I figured that and wondered if that air base north of Carson would have some."

"Probably not since it was geared more toward intel gathering rather than offensive capabilities," Tim said. "All they had there were Lear jets and space weenies."

"Space weenies?" Ruth asked.

"What they called the Space Operators, they controlled satellites and stuff up there in space – among other things," Tim answered her pointing up. "They also had NORAD and the Cheyenne Mountain complex, where the real intel guys were. Wonder if any of them are still in there."

"Another time - let's get back to Fort Carson and talk about what we want and when or need to go," Dan said. "Do we really need more AT6s? We have a half dozen of the things, not to mention all the Stingers we got from Guernsey. We've got enough ammo to shoot for ten years and not use it all up, and there's still more at the base in Cheyenne. We just need to come up with some inventive ways to get explosive devices inside that tunnel complex."

"That's why I wanted to go to Fort Carson and see if we could find some thermite to use," TJ said. "That would be a real force multiplier if we found some."

"Why don't we just make our own?" Tim offered.

Everyone seated around the tables looked at him with questioning eyes. Dan broke the spell asking, "We can make our own?"

"Sure," Tim answered. "We have more than enough stuff to make…well as much as we want, really."

"Okay, what's the formula?" TJ asked.

"All we need is some rusty metal, which I've seen loads of around here, and some aluminum," Tim explained. "We shave the rust off metal and sand and scrape the aluminum into powder, then mix the two. Presto, thermite."

"You're kidding," Ruth said.

"Yeah, I agree, you're kidding," Donna said.

"No, here, I'll show you," and he jumped up and went to the barn and came out with a rusty horseshoe. "Someone seen or have a soda can lying around I can have?"

TJ got up and went inside and came out a moment later with an aluminum pointer and handed it to Tim.

"This'll do nicely," Tim said and drew his pocketknife. He scraped some rust off the horseshoe and then did the same with the pointer, then mixed the two components together. "Anyone have a match?" he asked.

Dan produced a box of stick matches and gave them to Tim.

"Perfect," he said. Thinking a moment, he said, "I need to get a rock," so he went back out into the yard and found a piece of flat stone, set it in the middle of the front yard, got his mixture and poured the substance into a small pile on the rock and said, "Ready?"

Everyone said some form of yes and he lit a match and dropped it into the mixture. He then jumped back as the resulting fire was intense and made the audience jump as a unit. The rock split into two pieces the heat was so intense.

"There you go," Tim said with a smile.

"We'll have to be really careful with that stuff," Jeff said.

"No foolin'," Jack agreed.

"Okay then, that makes you in charge of thermite production, and ways to use it since you're our expert," TJ said to Tim once he was back on the porch. "Heavens, boy, that just about gave me a heart attack. Is it really that easy to make?"

"You just saw it," Tim answered. "We used to make it back home and fry ant hills. About a pound of it mixed together would burn for several minutes and…well it bakes an ant hill permanently."

"Remind me to never get him mad at me will ya?" Jeff said to no one but leaning towards Jack.

Everyone around the table erupted in laughter. "Okay, that cancels the Fort Carson trip then," TJ said.

"I'll second that motion," Ruth said, and they laughed again.

The meeting lasted another hour and assignments were handed out. Everyone got copies of the aerial videos of the tunnel entrances and fighting positions from the earlier mission on thumb drives. Everyone was to review the films and give their opinions in a few days' time to TJ, who would drive around in the ATV and collect suggestions. Another powwow was scheduled in five days for final thoughts and possible changes or additions. After that, physical preparations would begin in earnest. The meeting done, the men put the tables and chairs away and the ladies began dinner, which was baked rainbow trout, fries, salad, and home-made hush puppies.

The guys stood on the porch with fresh tumblers of scotch, except for Tim and Donnie, who drank beer they'd scavenged in Laramie. They hadn't developed a taste for liquor as yet. Discussion revolved around Tim's knowledge of making thermite and he used the time to brag on himself.

"We can collect the two components separately and keep them separated until we need them mixed together. I suppose, from listening to you talk, that you have drones that can drop bombs?"

"That's right; they can carry four each that weigh no more than two point five pounds each," Dan explained. "We can use a pound of C-4 surrounded by a pound and a half of thermite and drop it. Would that do?"

"Geeze, I guess," Tim said incredulously. "That much would burn half-way to China, and really make a mess."

"What if we could transport, say, up to five pounds of it on an ROV with C4 as the igniter," Dan continued. "Do you think it would take out all the biohazard stuff in the labs?"

"I don't really know, but it would burn the facility something awful," he answered, then, "Shirley might know. She was closer to the scientists and their work than I was."

TJ opened the door to the house and called Shirley to come out. Once outside, they asked her the same question and she said it would, but that it would have to be extremely close to the labs to work best. She added that it would have to be a big and extremely hot fire to do the job.

"Okay, thank you, Shirley," TJ said to her. "How much thermite do you think you can make in five weeks?" TJ asked Tim.

"With three or four of us working, fifty…sixty pounds or so…why?" he returned.

"Fifty pounds would melt the entire place, wouldn't it?" TJ asked.

"I reckon so," Tim answered. "Man, that would be a hot one. I wouldn't want to be anywhere near that when it went off. Like I said, we burned a pound or so, on the ant hills and that made quiet the blaze. Fifty pounds…whew, I don't want to see it."

"Great. That's your mission in life to make as much as you possibly can in the next five weeks. Got it?" TJ directed.

"Sure, can do," Tim answered. "Donnie and Shirley can help."

TJ nodded his head in agreement and the ladies yelled that dinner was ready. It was. It smelled wonderful. The fish tasted splendidly, and the table was cleared of food in no time at all.

"I'm stuffed," Donnie said leaning back and patting his belly.

Ruth, Donna, and Shirley, taking DD along, got up and went into the living room and sat down. "I think that's our hint to do the dishes, guys," TJ said getting up and began to clear the table.

Moans from several of the other men around the table could be heard and TJ smiled. But everyone got up and gave a hand and the dishes and kitchen were cleaned up in no time. Afterwards, they adjourned to the front porch and collapsed on the Adirondacks. "Lord in Heaven, thank you for that meal," Jeff mumbled. "That was great."

"Indeed," from Jack.

"Yes, indeed," from Dan.

"It was good, thank you ladies," Tim said.

"It was the fish," TJ replied.

"No, it was the company," Jack said.

"It was everything," Dan said with finality.

"Okay, I'll agree with that," Jeff said.

"I'm going to sleep for a week – man, I'm stuffed," Tim said again.

"We're all stuffed," Donnie added.

"Jack's out," Jeff said.

They all looked, and Jack was asleep. Several of them chuckled. Jeff got up and tapped his friend until he woke and said, "Come on, buddy, let me get you home to bed."

Dan rose also and held his hand out to TJ. They shook and Dan said good night to everyone. The three Marines got in their truck and left. Donnie looked at Tim and the message was sent and they, too, said their thankyous and farewells and departed. TJ went back inside and told the ladies the men had departed and that he was going to bed, gave Donna a kiss, patted DD on the head and went upstairs. The ladies stayed up until almost midnight.

The next morning, Donnie and Tim showed up early to pick up Shirley and take her and her goods to her new home. They skipped breakfast and drove to Albany for a day of looking around and selecting a new home for the two privates.

The trio went straight to Shirley's place and helped unload her things. Both men liked the home site she'd selected. Once the truck was empty and the tour of the place was done, they went driving around and found a nice place Donnie picked out to the south of Shirley. Tim picked one almost due west of Donnie's, but up the mountain some. It too, was nice and had several outbuildings.

They drove to the home on Highway 11 and collected the few things the guys had there, including the small refrigerator and generator. These, they decided, would go into Donnie's place for the time being, and back in Albany, they unloaded, and each explored and settled into their new homes.

The three met at noon at Shirley's and made a lunch. They sat out on her front porch and ate and discussed their new digs. Shirley produced a pad of paper and a pencil and said, "Okay, what do you need for your places?" They made three lists and decided to take a day to go shopping in Laramie.

Donnie was writing on the list when they heard an engine coming up Highway 11. It had to be one of their new friends, but just in case, Donnie and Tim readied their M-4s that Dan had 'issued' to them. Once their rifles were ready, they each moved to opposite ends of the porch and waited. It was not long before they saw Dan's truck pulling into the drive.

The trio relaxed and Shirley waived as Dan and Jeff got out of the truck. "You're just in time for fresh coffee," Shirley said to them, smiling and waiting at the top of the porch steps.

"Well pour away, girl, and don't keep us waiting," Jeff said with a smile and giving her a hug once he reached the top step. Dan followed suit and Shirley turned to go inside to pour them a mug.

"What brings you Marines up here to Army Land?" Donnie asked.

Dan chuckled and said, "I like that…Army Land. I guess it goes well with Marine Hill to the east, huh," he said shaking proffered hands from Donnie and Tim.

"We'll keep the rivalry going as long as we can," Tim said with a snicker. "What do you guys need?"

"We brought you three a Stinger each for those targets of opportunity that just might fly by," Dan said. Jeff shook hands with the guys, leaned against the porch rail, and accepted a mug of coffee from Shirley as she came out, saying thank you.

The five sipped their coffee for a moment then Dan continued, "We figure with you three up here in Albany, if you saw or heard a drone you could take it out. They don't know you're here so it would be a surprise to them, not to mention they'd lose another drone and maybe a few more missiles."

"That's good thinking," Tim said. "All three of us know how to use them so we're good there. They only have a few more of the drones, but I really don't know how many missiles they have left. They would be in the big armory in the eastern tunnel."

"I have a question for you three," Jeff said. "Is that tunnel system all on one level, or are there more levels below?"

All three looked at him and Shirley spoke for the trio, saying, "As far as I know there is only one level. We can draw the layout more precisely for you if you'd like. It's like a giant triangle with a center line. The center tunnel has branches, where the labs are. I never saw any other levels and the only elevator I knew of was the one destroyed at the surface compound."

"That's good," Dan said with a smile. "If they'd made another level or two, we'd be at a much greater disadvantage. Still, it will be a tough nut to crack. Now, tell me about your new homes."

They sipped their coffee, and the trio detailed their three homes. Shirley took them on a tour of her place and afterwards, they put their used mugs in the sink and said their goodbyes. Dan and Jeff left for Marine Hill, telling the trio they needed to put radios on their shopping lists, with antenna and cable for guy wires. He also told them to get as many water cans and bottles as they could find. Shirley and Tim had pumps in their homes, Donnie did not. He did have a functional one in the front yard, however.

Back at Marine Hill, Dan and Jeff gave Jack the news about the complex only being on one level as far as the three Army pukes knew. Jack said he would run over and tell TJ as he was going over to help out with some building project TJ had going for the greenhouses and grabbed his hat to head out.

Over in Paradise Valley, Jack met up with TJ and told him about the information the three Army pukes told Dan and Jeff. TJ laughed at the 'pukes' reference and Jack said, "Oops, forgot you're Army."

"No offense taken, I relate to that anyway," TJ chuckled. They worked on the greenhouse project and finished at lunch. Donna had made soup and had some crackers out along with iced water. Jack told them about Dan giving Stingers to the pu…he quickly changed to kids…and that they were going into Laramie the following day for water containers, radios, antennas, cable for guy wires, and whatever else they needed for their new homes.

"I hope they check with Ruth," Donna thought out loud. "I think she said she needed something that they might be able to pick up for her."

"I'm sure they'll check with everyone before going over," TJ said. "Jack, thanks a lot for the help today. That saved me at least another day of work. I really appreciate it."

"No problem, glad to help out," Jack answered. "We need to help each other as much as we can to get by now. And I can't help but let my mouth water thinking about the vegetables that are coming outta those things. Mmm, mmm. Can't wait for more," he ended with a smile.

"You and me both, brother," TJ agreed. "I really want to see those strawberries go wild...and the peppers, and...well, everything."

Jack and Donna were both laughing at him and Jack coughed out, "I can't wait to get in a couple over on Marine Hill. We'll really have some stuff then. By the way, how are the crops doing out in the valley?"

"Not bad, wanna go take a look right quick?" TJ asked.

"Sure," Jack agreed.

"Not without me, you don't," Donna said getting up and clearing the table.

The three Z'd up as usual and got in the ATV. TJ took off down his lane and crossed the road. He went through the aspens slowly as the elk frequented the lush grass under the aspen canopy. Today, however, they didn't see any at all. They didn't see any deer, birds, cattle, or sheep grazing in the area either. TJ thought it strange until pulling out of the grove into the first field and saw why.

Thirty to forty Zs had congregated in the first field, which was a corn crop, the plants just then reaching ankle height. As soon as the Zs heard the ATV, they all turned in mass and in that ungainly gait of theirs, making their way towards the trio uttering that rasping growl. TJ slammed on the brakes, narrowly missing a pair of the creatures and Jack jumped out and made short work of those two with shots to the head from his M4.

Donna was out next and racking a round into her M4 began sending rounds into the nearest creatures ambling their way. TJ quickly followed and began firing himself. Even though all three were firing, Zs continued closing in on the trio. Jack dropped his first magazine, now empty, and loaded his second.

"Look to the right, Jack!" TJ yelled as more Zs poured from the trees. Now the three were facing close to a hundred of the creatures, all heading their direction.

Donna yelled, "I'm throwing a grenade, get down!" She pulled the pin on the first of two grenades she'd pulled and threw it into the nearest mass.   Jack and TJ had already dropped down as she threw. She dropped, and when the small bomb went off, got up and yelled, "Second one going out, keep down!" and pulled the pin and threw it into the mass to their right.

The first grenade had dropped several and disabled several others, who were now crawling towards the humans on severed, contorted, and fractured limbs.   Jack rose and continued pouring fire to his right and TJ, in a kneeling position, fired to the left, with Donna standing again firing to their front.

At the report of the first grenade going off, Dan and Jeff jumped from their Adirondack chairs and looked to the north from where the sound had come from. They saw the flash from the second grenade explosion long before they heard the sound, and both ran to get their weapons and ammunition. If one of the valley residents was using grenades, then they were in trouble and needed help.   The two grabbed extra grenades and ammo and throwing everything in their ATV, started, and pulled out not bothering with seatbelts.   They flew down Marine Hill, turned left on Highway 11, then right on the dirt trail they'd cut to the fields.

They both knew the action was out near one of their crops. As they entered the aspen stand, they could now hear the gunfire and knew that at least three of their friends were in trouble of some kind. They came to a curve in the dirt trail and ran headlong into several of the Zs, hitting two with the ATV.

Jeff drew his nine-millimeter handgun and began shooting at the few Zs they'd run into with well-aimed head shots. He'd dropped two when Dan opened up with his M4, shooting away from the direction of the other rifle fire not wanting to take the chance of hurting or killing one of his friends. They had dropped those Zs that were around them and could see more heading their direction through the aspen stand.

"Jeff, get in and we'll try to get to the others!" Dan yelled.

Jeff, continuing to fire at the Zs, scooting backwards into the ATV then yelled for Dan to floor it, continuing to shoot all the while. They leaped forward, running over several zombie bodies and were able to break through the aspens and the sight that met their view as they did so was shocking. What appeared was over a hundred zombies or more converging on Donna, TJ, and Jack.

Dan stopped the ATV and as he did so, Jeff slid out and inserting a fresh magazine continued shooting with his M4. Dan quickly did the same and now five shooters were dropping Zs in almost every direction. Dan continued to move towards the other three, firing as he moved in their direction. As he neared, he looked at Jack and yelled, "Where did all these things   come   from?"

Jack yelled back, "No idea; they surprised us as we came through the aspens."

Jeff had moved over to the four and now they moved as a team, surrounding TJ's ATV, with their backs to it and firing outward in a circle action. Jeff yelled out, "Does this feel like Custer's last stand to anyone else but me?"

TJ yelled, "We need to get outta here, but keep firing."

Zombie bodies littered the ground around the five humans. Donna had switched to her shotgun and was dropping two or three at a time with the buckshot, tissue, blood, and gore flying from the creatures as she fired. Others were dropping with horrible wounds that would have been severely incapacitating to a human but did little other than to hamper a Zs progress struggling to get to and satisfy their desire to consume the humans.

TJ had had enough and yelled for everyone save Donna to get two grenades out and throw them. When everyone was ready, he yelled for them to throw and drop.

After the eight thunderous explosions in close proximity, the five got up and resumed fire. By then, Shirley, Donnie, and Tim had arrived in Donnie's truck and added their weapons to the firing. With eight shooters, it didn't take much longer to thin the herd and almost eradicate the threat.

When the shooting died down to a trickle and the smoke, dust, and debris settled, Donnie yelled, "Where did they all come from?"

"We don't know," Jack answered firing at another Z staggering out of the aspens.

TJ, Dan, Jack, and Jeff fixed bayonets then went around sticking the Zs that were down but not out or giving head shots to end the threat. The carnage was horrible to see and smell. Tissue, blood, and heaps of bodies littered the ground. The crop in this area was ruined. The eight people stood looking at each other and several were still heaving in great gulps of air trying to settle their adrenalin-fueled, quivering bodies down.

Jack stood there with his rifle hanging almost to the ground, spent. He would sleep soundly that night. Donna was rubbing her ears trying to get the ringing to quit. TJ was covered with gore as several of the things had gotten so close to him, he was sprayed with blood and tissue as he shot them. Dan and Jeff were covering the humans with their rifles up and at the ready. So too, were Donnie and Tim, and the four shot stragglers from time to time. Shirley ran over to Donna and they embraced, giving each other mutual support.

TJ, after catching his breath, tiredly shuffled over to Dan and said, "What do you think of this? We haven't seen anything like this in a long, long time."

"I haven't a clue," Dan answered his friend. "How did you find them?"

"We didn't. Jack wanted to come down and see the crops after we'd finished the greenhouse and we ran into a bunch of them and had to stop. We had no choice but to start shooting and that just brought more. They just kept coming," he said exasperated, shrugging his shoulders, and shaking his head.

"I pray God in Heaven helps us if we have to do this very many more times," Dan prayed aloud.

"Amen," from Tim, who had joined the two. "Where do you suppose they all came from?"

"I've already asked that question," Donnie said.

"We don't know," Dan answered anyway.

"I'm wondering if someone has put one of those Judith frequency things around the valley somewhere and that's what's drawing them in." TJ wondered aloud.

"I was wondering the same thing," Donna said easing up to the group.

TJ reached out to her and they hugged. "I'm glad you're alright," he said, hugging her tightly. "You handled yourself very well today."

"Ears will never be the same, but I'm okay overall," she said. "Thank you."

"Your ears will improve with time," Dan told her. "Sadly, we've all gone through these many times before," he said indicating the other two Marines.

"I haven't and I don't want to anymore," Donna said morosely.

"Me neither," Shirley agreed. "I've never seen this before and don't want to get in that kind of situation again."

"This happen often out here?" Tim asked.

"Couple of times, but rarely, thank goodness," TJ said.

"They really know how to crash a party, don't they," Donnie commented. "Is the crop ruined?"

"'Fraid so," Jack answered.

"Crap," Donnie said dejectedly.

The next day, the six men, using trucks with trailers, gathered the gruesome bodies and dumped them in a ravine on the back side of the airport. There were well over two hundred of the things. The men were taking a break, having a mug of coffee, and watching the area after dumping the last of the zombie bodies into the gorge.

"I remember reading in Doug's manuscript about a time he, Dave and the kid, Erskine, had a battle with the things over on Highway 11," TJ, leaning against a truck said. "They killed over a hundred in that fight, and it was just the three of them."

"Yeah, but didn't they have machine guns, if I remember right," Dan said.

"Yep, one on top of the truck they were in," TJ commented.

"Maybe we should mount a Bravo on top of a few of our trucks," Donnie said.

"A 249 would be better," Tim commented. "Belt-fed shotguns would be even better 'n that if there was such a thing."

"Man, could you see the damage a belt-fed, semi-auto twelve-gauge with buckshot would do to a group of these things?" Jeff asked.

"Ugly," Jack said.

"TJ?" Donnie asked.

"What's up, Donnie?" TJ answered.

"You have a 249 we can have to experiment with on my truck?" he asked.

"As a matter of fact, I do," TJ said with a smile.

"Gee, thanks," Donnie said, smiling back. "I'm going to try and mount it on the cab of my truck."

"I'll help," Tim volunteered. "Might need to do some welding…TJ, can we borrow that welding outfit in your garage?"

"Certainly," TJ answered. "Better yet, why don't you just do your experiment in the garage at Paradise Valley? Everything is there you'll need."

"That'll be swell," Tim said with a smile. "There's that old axle off that riding lawn mower at Shirley's we can cut one wheel off of and use the other as a swivel for the gun. We can weld the axle end on the truck, bracing it someway, and affix the gun to the wheel. That'll make for a 360-degree field of fire."

"Now you're talkin'!" Donnie exclaimed. "We can make and mount a can holder on the axle shaft and load belts into it." Tim eased closer to Donnie and they continued their conversation on how to fabricate the gun mount.

The other four men stood or sat listening and quietly thinking about that. TJ had finally had enough and said, "Come on, boys, we have more work to do back in the valley. Let's get to it."

They were climbing back into the trucks when Donnie, pointing, said, "What's that?"

TJ looked up at the young man and said, "What?" and seeing Donnie pointing, looked the direction of the point. From his stance on the ground, he couldn't see anything, so climbed up on the door jamb of his truck, and looked again in the direction Donnie was pointing. What he saw made his blood run cold and sent shivers down his back. "It's a horde!" he practically yelled.

The other men's heads in the group all turned towards TJ and saw him looking down into the valley the locals once called The Big Hollow beyond the airport. Several climbed up onto the trucks to see what TJ and Donnie were looking at, the others grabbing weapons, and saw that a great horde of Zs had gathered in the valley. Dan, reached into his truck and grabbed a pair of binoculars and looked closer at the mass of bodies.

"Which way they headin', Dan?" TJ asked.

"Looks like they're amblin' to the southwest, towards Lake Hattie," Dan replied.

"Everyone, jump in your trucks and follow me," TJ yelled. He jumped into his truck, started it, and pulled out, slinging dirt, grass, and gravel, not waiting to see whether the others were coming or not. Donnie held on for dear life and the others were following not too far behind.

TJ sped out of the airport gate and turning left onto Highway 130 sped to the west. Near the big hill that led down into the Centennial area, TJ pulled off the highway and crashed through a gate to a small ranch that was on a promontory overlooking the great expanse of the valley beyond. He braked hard coming to a sliding stop next to the home on the property. He got up on the door jamb once again and using his binoculars, looked at the horde in the valley below. There were several thousands of the creatures heading to the southwest, towards the southern slope of Sheep Mountain.

Donnie got out and was standing on the opposite door jamb looking out over the valley as the other three trucks pulled up sliding to stop also. Everyone got out looking down the valley, several with binoculars.

TJ said, "Dan, take a look over near the southeast slope of Sheep Mountain."

Dan swung his binos that direction and the sight he saw immediately made him angry. He looked over at Tim, who was riding with him, and handing the binos over the top of the truck to the young man said, "Take a look at what your friends are doing."

Tim, timidly took the binos and bringing them up to his eyes and looking in the direction Dan was pointing, saw two black hummers. They obviously had the Judith signal transmitters attached to the vehicles as the great horde was following them. There was no doubt.

"That has to be some of the others and maybe a few of the science types with them," Tim said.

Donnie asked in a disbelieving tone, "What…what did you say?"

TJ handed Donnie his binos and told him to look. His voice quivered in disbelief as he said, "I can't believe our friends are doing this. It's gotta be some of the others."

"Dan," TJ said looking at him, "Time to Z up. Full loads and everyone we can muster. How many of those AT-6s we got left?"

"I think around a couple dozen," Dan answered.

"Get six and every grenade we have for the thumpers. Everyone, listen up," TJ said in his official Sheriff's tone. "Bring as much ammo as you can carry. Everyone, bring a full load out with M-4, shotgun, and nine-millimeter. Bring every grenade you have. We meet on Marine Hill in ninety minutes. Move it," he ended and jumped into his truck.

Donnie gave TJ his binos back and went to another truck, where he and Tim jumped in, and trading out with Jack, who got in with Jeff and they all sped back to the valley to prepare. TJ flew up his drive into Paradise Valley, honking the horn in short blasts, alerting Donna something was up. He quickly explained what was going on and they both ran into the armory to begin loading.

In Albany, Tim and Donnie stopped at Shirley's long enough to explain things to her and the three broke and collected their arms and munitions.

Jack sped to Ruth's new home to the southeast of Marine Hill and explained to her what was going on and told her to pack herself and DD and get to the Ranger Station for safety until they returned. She immediately began to pack DD's things, her weapons, ammo, food stuffs, and extra water.

Jeff and Dan practically flew up Marine Hill to their homes and began loading munitions. It was about a half-hour later TJ and Donna pulled up, and as they got out, the Marines could see they were fully Z'd up, chest rigs with grenades hanging in several additional loops.

"I know you have a plan, TJ, that's why I didn't ask questions back there," Dan said as TJ and Donna strode up. "What are we going to do?"

"We need to get over to State Road 47 and just before we crest the south side of Sheep Mountain, do a recon and see where those black hummers will be coming out," TJ answered. "We'll hit them when it's appropriate and stop that signal. Maybe then, the Zs will disperse and any that come our way, we'll take out with the long-range rifles first. We'll use the close in stuff only as necessary. But we have to kill those hummers and everyone in them. Jack, I want you watching for drones and take 'em out if you see one."

"On it," Jack said, turning and going back inside for a few Stingers.

"What about me," Jeff asked.

"You, me, Donna, and Dan will be on long range rifles, as I know you're an excellent shooter," TJ answered. "Maybe the privates, too."

"I told Ruth to take DD to the Ranger's Station for safety," Jack said then added, "Didn't think you'd mind."

"You were reading my mind," TJ said with a smile. "They'll be safe there."

"I told her to set up on the front patio and bring a radio out," Jack said. "Told her we'd keep her informed on the situation."

"Good," TJ agreed. "Where are those kids?" he asked aloud, looking back down towards the highway.

"I packed some food and water," Jeff said.

"Me, too," Donna said, smiling at Jeff.

They could hear vehicles approaching down below and saw the Privates turning up the drive to Marine Hill. "'Bout time," Dan said.

The trio stopped and got out and joined the group. TJ had spread a map out on the hood of his truck and told them the plan, showing them the little-known dirt trails that would get them above the projected point where the hummers would probably attempt to enter the valley.

TJ looked each in the eye and asked, "You're not going to have any problems shooting at those hummers, are you? If so, we need to know now."

The three looked at each other and Shirley answered, "We'll kill 'em. No worries. You just say the word and I'll pull the trigger."

"Me, too," Tim said.

"I'm in," Donnie agreed shaking his head affirmatively.

"They're trying to bring those things over here to kill us so I don't have any problem pulling the trigger on them," Shirley said with conviction.

TJ and the others looked at the three and saw the determination in their faces and knew they would be assets in this fight.

"All three of you trained on the AT-6s?" Dan asked.

"Yes, sir," came a trio of responses.

"Good enough," Dan said and went to the back of his truck, motioning for Donnie and Tim to follow. He gave them three AT-6, shoulder-fired missiles and told them to make 'em count. They put them in the backs of their vehicles.

"How are you three on ammo and grenades?" Jack asked.

"Could use more .556 and 7.62, but have enough nine, twelve-gauge and grenades," Shirley answered for the three.

Jack motioned for the three to follow him and Jeff and together they loaded another five cans of each caliber into their vehicles. If the eight fighters used up all the ammunition they had on hand for this fight, there would indeed be a battle royal going on in the valley to the southeast of Sheep Mountain.

The eight were back together at the vehicles and no more was said, so TJ yelled, "Saddle up," and got into his truck with Donna. They all sped down the Hill and only slowed down when they turned onto the little-known back dirt road. It was thirteen-hundred hours.

Chapter 10: Battle at Sheep Mountain

TJ slowly came to a stop on the west side of a stand of aspens and tall Lodge Pole pine trees. He motioned for Dan to follow and to bring his binos. Together, they slowly and quietly made their way along the dirt trail that passed through the stand of aspens and just before reaching the eastern edge, got down and crawled the last fifteen feet or so.

TJ removed his Stetson and eased his head up looking down the ridge. He could see the hummers over two miles distant to the east and bringing up his binoculars, looked at the two vehicles. He could see speakers mounted on the backs of both and knew they were indeed transmitting the Judith signal that guided the horde towards their valley.

Dan, too, was viewing the scene below with his binoculars when he heard TJ move back from the edge, so he did as well and TJ almost whispered, "Can you sign for the others to come forward with the AT-6s or do we need to go back?"

Dan smiled and got up into a kneeling position, getting Jack's attention and after giving several signals, turned and went back to looking down into the valley below.

TJ watched as Jack gathered the other six, who shortly after gathered weapons and ammo and headed to TJ and Dan's position. The six had three of the AT-6s, two Stingers and several cans of additional .556 and 7.62 ammunition. Donnie and Tim both had shoulder bags filled with grenades. They deposited the munitions on the ground behind TJ and Dan and waited for instructions. TJ gave them a thumb up and turned to look into the valley again.

The hummers had only moved about fifty yards and were still over a mile and three quarters away. He looked to the north and then to the south and Dan, noticing TJ looking around, whispered, "What are you thinking?"

TJ motioned to move back and when they rejoined the group, TJ had them all kneel and looked at Dan and said, "What do you think about capturing one of the hummers, not destroying it, and using it to turn those Zs back to the east and south?" TJ could see Dan thinking about that.

Dan held up a finger for everyone to hold that thought and moved back to the trees. He hadn't thought of that and had to rethink his tactics and look for a better area to spring that kind of attack. He motioned for TJ to come forward and back at the trees, the two looked down and Dan pointed to a farmstead below. "The road comes right through that place," Dan said, pointing, "that where you want to spring the attack?"

TJ looked at Dan with an evil smile and nodded. The two thought a lot alike, and TJ said, "I figure we take out the western hummer with a pair of AT-6s and at the same time, shoot the driver of the eastern hummer. Anyone else that gets out gets shot by our snipers who'll be on that ridge," TJ said pointing to a stand of aspens to the north, "and that one," pointing to another to the south. "We can wax anyone else that's alive as we close with the vehicles, then let the kids drive the hummer down that road to Highway 230 and turn the horde to the east from there."

Dan thought a minute and looking at all the options he and TJ had just discussed, simply said, "I like it. Let's do it."

"It'll take a while, but once we get them to Laramie, we can head them down Highway 287 and get them going towards Fort Collins," TJ said. "Maybe we can use them to help with the tunnel complex."

Dan looked at TJ and said, "You really have an evil mind, you know it?"

"Hey, I'm just looking at options," TJ explained. "If we suddenly have a couple a thousand of those things on our side for a change, we'll really be able to surprise those people in the complex. I just hope we can get the Christian friends of our new folks out in time."

"Sounds like another trip down there to deliver another message," Dan said. "It'll take at least a month or so to get those things down there and we'll have to have shift changes for the hummer we take, not to mention fuel expenditures and the time involved."

"Yeah, that'll be tough," TJ agreed. "Come on, let's go talk to the others and get some advice from them and then pray together. We really need God's input on this."

"I agree with you, brother," Dan said.

The two slid back from the opening in the trees and made their way back to the group kneeling in the trees and told them what they had devised. Several agreed with the proposal and several did not, saying the fuel and time expenditures would be prohibitive. Everyone agreed with that part of the equation, however, Shirley brought up the psychological impact of having a several thousand or so Zs show up at the tunnel complex. She argued it would be like using reverse psychology on them. She, Donnie, and Tim agreed the people in the complex would panic at least.

Then Donnie said, "If we could spring the tunnel entrance doors first, they won't be able to close them, and those things could easily get in at them. That'd be the ticket."

Everyone looked at him thinking about that and wondering how to make that come to reality.

After a moment, Dan said, "We still have several hours before the hummers get into range that we can be comfortable with, so we have time to think all this through. I suggest we pray together and listen and watch and see what God will do to help us here."

Everyone agreed with that and they stood, forming a circle, and holding hands, prayed for a time together. TJ finally said 'Amen', and the group broke into small groups or as individuals went off on their own to think and pray about the situation they were faced with.

After about a half hour, Shirley walked over to where Dan and TJ were sitting together and said, "That Judith signal transmits for quite a distance. If we have to, we can take out one hummer, capture the second, and drive it to Laramie. The creatures will follow even though it seems like a long way. We can wait for a while and go back and drive it down to Fort Collins on Highway 287, and just let them go south. They'll congregate at the signal and be a nuisance to the complex folks. Especially as many as have gathered down there. We could do other things in the meantime, such as getting a message to our friends in the complex and tell them to try and escape, maybe figure out a way to damage the doors so they won't be able to close them, or we can work in the valley." She ended by shrugging her shoulders.

Dan looked at TJ and the two looked back at her. Dan slowly started nodding his head and stood up. TJ did also. Dan called everyone together again and had Shirley give her ideas to the group.

"I still think we need to try and get the people in both hummers to give up," Donnie added. "If we show a good deal of force, they just may do so. They probably don't want to fight anyway."

"I agree," Tim said. "I volunteer to be on the group that goes against the hummers with Donnie. If they see us, and it just may be a few of our friends, we'll have a high probability of taking both without having to fire a shot."

"We can keep those that are not your friends in the lock-up at the Malone place and let your friends into our community," Donna said.

Shirley had a smile on her face as did Donnie and Tim.

TJ had a slight smile on his face as he looked at Dan. Dan gave a slight nod of his head to TJ and TJ shrugged his shoulders and said, "Why not. It's better than just shooting them outright."

Every eye turned to Dan at that point and waited for a decision. He looked up and saw everyone looking at him and he said, "What?"

"We're waiting for your approval," TJ said with a smirk.

"Mine...I'm not the leader here, Sheriff," Dan reasoned. "You are."

TJ immediately said, "Shirley, pick your team and go attempt to capture both hummers. And we'll try our best to not use direct force."

Shirley stepped forward and said, "Donnie...Tim...both of you get AT-6s ready. Jack, I want you on an M4. Jeff...a thumper. TJ...I want you on a 249. I'll have another M4, and everyone have their shotguns available. Dan and Donna...up top here somewhere with the fifties just in case. If someone steps out of a hummer to use a weapon...drop 'em. Let's move, people."

Everyone scattered to prepare for the next move. Donna went to the northern position with her fifty and Dan to the southern side. The six that would make the direct assault, packed their weapons and ammo into TJ's truck and they headed down the mountain to the farmstead to prepare the ambush.

The farmstead had seven buildings and the main road passed within fifty feet of the main house for the place. The previous owners had planted a multitude of cottonwood trees around the place and that provided many places to lie in wait. Donnie, Tim, Jeff, and TJ gathered a few logs and a lot of fallen limbs and lay them in the road so that the hummers would have to move into a single file to pass the small ranch site. That is when the team would spring the ambush. With six heavily armed men and women pointing a wide variety of weapons at the two hummers taken by surprise, chances were the personnel in the vehicles would give up. If not, the six were prepared to open up with everything and end the threat. They would then drive one hummer to Laramie, like Shirley recommended.

The team had some time left and the six gathered and prayed again. TJ got on the radio and told Donna and Dan all was ready and told Ruth what was happening. He then asked if the two snipers had clear firing lanes into the area where they'd narrowed the road. Both said they did and would be ready to fire at the first sign of trouble. TJ said if necessary, they would destroy the lead hummer with an AT-6 and do everything they could to save the second. Donna and Dan agreed and said they would concentrate their fire on the first only. Ruth said she'd loaded additional ammunition in her truck to bring if necessary.

It was getting near four in the afternoon when they could finally hear the engines of the hummers on the road. Shirley gave everyone a thumb up, and they dispersed to their positions to wait. She would spring the attack by standing up in the roadway directly in front of the hummers, with an AT-6 ready to fire. The others would spring into action immediately after she moved and show themselves brandishing their weapons from the west. With three AT-6s, a thumper, M-249 SAW and a M4 aiming at them, it was logical to assume the people in the hummers would give up.

They could see the black vehicles topping the small hill leading up to the homestead and got ready for action. Those with the AT-6s prepared the missiles for firing. TJ racked a round into his M-249 SAW; Jack racked a round into his M4; Jeff loaded a bee-hive round into his thumper; Donna and Dan both chambered a round into their fifty caliber rifles and inserted a twelve-round magazine each. It was a lot of firepower being brought to bear onto two unsuspecting hummers with an unknown number of people inside.

The hummers slowed when the drivers realized they would have to go into a single file to pass through the debris field from the supposed fallen tree. The hummer on the right took the lead and pulled up with the second hummer falling in behind.

The first hummer entered the debris field and as the second hummer entered, Shirley jumped out from her hiding place, brandishing the AT-6. She stood with her legs spread, holding the shoulder-fired missile dead on to the lead hummer which came to a sliding halt in the dirt and gravel creating a dust cloud. The second hummer almost slid into the first the reaction was so fast.

The other five attackers leapt from their hiding positions brandishing their many weapons. It was a tense few moments as they waited for someone in the hummers to react.

Shirley didn't wait and yelled, "Outta the hummers - NOW!"

Donnie added his voice by yelling, "You heard her…outta the hummers…NOW!" and moved forward with his AT6 at the ready, aiming it at the passenger door of the first hummer.

That door slowly opened, and two hands slowly came up, palms out. "Don't shoot," came a meek voice from inside the hummer and the door opened another foot. Two feet wearing combat boots settled on the ground and the hands, attached to arms, came out with a head following. The two eyes that raised above the door were huge and unblinking.

"Donnie…is…is that you?" the voice from the head on the other side of the door asked.

"Who's asking?" Donnie yelled.

"It's me, Daniel," Private Daniel Donnaghan shakily answered. He rose completely from the hummer and Donnie lowered his AT-6.

"Daniel, tell everyone to slowly get out of both hummers and they won't be hurt…NOW!" Shirley yelled.

"Shirley…that you?" Daniel asked.

For answer she yelled, "DO IT…NOW!"

Daniel jumped in fear and seemed to shrink some and leaned back into the first hummer and said something to the people inside. The other three doors slowly opened and people, with their hands raised, got out. Daniel slowly moved to the second hummer and motioned for them to do the same. By then, TJ, Jack, and Jeff had moved within a few feet of the machines and were ready to hose them down with their weapons if any funny business began.

After a moment, the four doors slowly opened, and four sets of hands came out and up. There were eight people all together. Five men and three women. They stood with scared looks on their faces and a few were obviously trembling in fear.

Donnie slowly moved over near Shirley, keeping his AT-6 pointed at the lead hummer, and quietly said to her, "I think we should tie them all up, including Daniel, and put them into two trucks. We can put the four scientists in one and our friends in the other. Take them to separate places and let our friends join us or be held captive and put the scientists in the Malone place for safe keeping."

"Sounds good to me," Shirley agreed. "Let the others know. I'll move these people into a line over by the house," she said, lying her AT-6 down and charging her M4.

Donnie nodded and moved to the other team members and explained what would happen. Shirley told the people from the complex to put their hands on their heads and move in a single-file line to the front of the house. Jack and Jeff moved with the crowd covering them. God help the one that did anything other than move as directed.

Shirley motioned for Donnie, Tim, and TJ to come over to her. Once there, she told Donnie and Tim to take control of the hummers and move the horde back to Laramie. She told them she would be along to pick them up in a few hours, saying she'd pick them up at the juncture of Highway 130 at the gas station. Donnie suggested they would return to the valley in one hummer, thus saving time and fuel. That was agreed upon.

Both, smiling, jumped to the task, and turned for the hummers. But TJ interrupted saying, "I think we should look inside first for anything that might be of use, especially from an intel standpoint…"

"Right you are," Shirley said and moved towards the first hummer. She turned back and told Donnie and Tim to search the prisoners and take everything they had. Both jumped to the task.

Both vehicles were set up to transmit the Judith signal. TJ jokingly commented they looked like a pair of overpriced boom-boxes. The three Privates had no idea what he was talking about and he laughed at his private joke. After searching both vehicles and confiscating the weapons and ammunition they found, along with several pouches of written information which they gave to TJ, the soldiers went back to guarding the captives. He and Dan would go over the paperwork later.

TJ pulled his radio and called for Donna and Dan to come on down, that all was well, and the hummers had been taken without having to fire a shot. That they had captured eight men and women. Ruth came over the net with a thank God. The two snipers quickly policed their areas and loading their fifties in their trucks, headed down the eastern slope of Sheep Mountain to join their friends. As they pulled up to the farmstead, the two hummers pulled out and headed towards Highway 230.

The rest of the crew separated the eight prisoners, with Shirley directing who went where, tied them up and placed hoods over their heads and left, heading to the Malone place so as to not be attacked by the horde that was coming up the hill. The Zs would follow the hummers transmitting the Judith signal. The two privates took the long way around and got back into the valley well after eight o'clock that night, leaving one transmitting hummer in Laramie.

Two trucks broke off from the convoy and headed towards the Malone's place. One truck held the four scientists, tied up and hooded. They would be taken one at a time, down into the Malone underground and placed into holding rooms. Their disposition would be determined later.

It took the better part of an hour to get the four science types into their holding rooms. Each had been placed at the ends of the four halls in the Malone underground, in the furthest rooms down. They would not be able to hear each other and were securely chained to loops embedded in the walls, across the room from the doors. Dan had installed a pair of cross beams on each door from the hallway side as extra precautions against someone escaping. Each prisoner was given a bucket, several bottles of water, a few MREs, and energy bars to eat should they feel the desire. They were also given blankets and sleeping pads for sleeping.

Once all four were securely housed, Dan, TJ, Jeff, and Jack, headed for Marine Hill where they would meet with Shirley and Donna who were holding the other four. There, they would confront the captives and offer asylum or captivity…their choice.

As they pulled up, they could see the ladies still had the four prisoners in the back of the truck. Dan and Jeff got the four captives out and with the help of the two ladies, led the four into Dan's home, and sat them at the table. Once everyone was ready, they removed the hoods, and the talks began.

Shirley immediately went over to Daniel and untied him and welcomed him into the community. She had little doubt he would be a welcomed addition to the valley's population. The other three might need some coaxing and that is what she began with.

"You all know who I am, and you three are my friends, my Christian brothers and sisters," she began. "You've been captured by the residents of the valley that we have been attacking for several years. I want you to know everyone, and I mean everyone, in this valley is Christian, just like you and me. They don't want to fight us. They don't want to kill you and the other Christians in the facility. They want just what you and I want. To live in peace and worship God the way we do. When Donnie, Tim, and I were first brought here, we were afraid just like you are now. But we came to trust these folks and learned they just want to worship God as Christians do, live in peace, grow their crops, care for their animals and families, and live their lives. The leaders we had at the underground complex are the ones that want to destroy these good people. I'm on their side now," she said pointing at TJ and Donna. "We've brought you here because you're our friends. Our Christian friends. This is your chance to join us or be placed with the others."

"Where are the others?" one of the male captives asked.

"I'm Sheriff Thomas Gerill, Sheriff of Albany County, Wyoming, where you are now," TJ said as introduction. "The other four science types are in an underground holding facility," TJ explained. "They're in individual rooms and have been given food, water, and sleeping materials. We mean them no harm unless they create the need."

The three looked at each other and Daniel asked if he could speak. Shirley gave him the nod and he said, "Guys, these are the folks that gave me the letter to show you. They're legit. You know me and you know I wouldn't be saying this if I didn't believe it. I say we join them and help them. They just want to live peacefully, like we want to do."

The three, two men and one woman, looked at each other and the woman asked, "Where would we live?"

Shirley spoke up, "I was able to get a nice home in Albany, as did Donnie and Tim. There are still a bunch of homes up there that would be great to live in." She pointed at TJ and Dan and said, "These men, and the others, gave us everything we needed to survive – food, water, weapons, and ammunition – and have been great hosts. Now they've even given us homes. And more importantly, they've given us community with Jesus as the root for our existence in this valley. Like Daniel said, they're legit and want nothing more than to live their lives in peace. Donnie, Tim, and I, all think the same way and will NOT go back to the complex…except to take it and close it for good."

"What if we don't want to live here?" the other man asked.

"Once we've taken care of the complex – that is destroyed it – we'll give you an opportunity to reconsider," TJ said. "If you decide not to join the valley community, you can leave and go wherever you choose and to help you out, we'll outfit you with a means of travel, weapons, ammunition, food and water and other supplies. We mean you, as Christians, no harm. We only want the best for you, our brothers, and sisters in Christ. It'll be entirely up to you."

Shirley took over saying, "We'll let you stay up with us for the time being in Albany. You two can stay with Donnie or Tim and you, Linda, can stay with me. For tonight, you'll all be staying here with Dan and Jack, and I think Ruth will be coming over in just a bit. Are you hungry or thirsty?"

Nods from all three put Dan into motion and he made six sandwiches, cut some fresh fruit, and got out some bottled water for the four and placed the food and drink on the table for them. He then untied their bindings and said, "This should do for now. We really didn't expect guests for dinner tonight. Dig in," he said with a smile.

It was nice to see the three bow their heads and pray first, thanking the Lord for the food and for their lives. They ate in silence, looking from face to face and their surroundings.

Dan and TJ moved away from the table, watching the four eat, and Dan asked, "What do you think?"

"Daniel is in for sure," TJ answered. "He's happy as a lark right now. The bigger guy…I'm not so sure about him. The woman and the other guy will probably stay. She looks eager to be part of our family."

"We do think a lot alike," Dan said with a grin. "I hope they all stay, really. That's what I'll be praying for." The woman at the table turned and looked at him – she'd heard the conversation – and smiled at the two.

TJ elbowed Dan and they laughed.

Ruth came in with DD and asked, "What are you two laughing about?"

That just made the two men laugh harder and louder. "Nothing, Ruth, nothing at all."

Ruth looked at the four seated at the table and asked, "Who's going to introduce us?"

Shirley stepped forward and said, "Ruth and DD Sutton, meet Daniel Donnaghan," who jumped up, stepped forward and proffered a hand to shake, "and this is Sergeant Linda Ballard, Privates Vito Loguzzo and Dino Granillo."

Surprising Dan and TJ both, the other two men rose and proffered their hands for Ruth to shake, and both said they were glad to meet her.

Linda Ballard, a five-foot seven-inch brunette with brown eyes chose to stay seated but offered to take DD, which Ruth allowed, then shook the hands of the two men.

Private Vito Loguzzo was five-foot, ten inches, about one hundred eighty pounds, close-cropped black hair, and dark brown, almost black eyes. He had a nice smile and his eyes sparkled as he looked at DD. "I haven't seen a baby in a long, long time. He's so…small."

Everyone laughed or chuckled as Ruth said, "You won't think like that after holding him for a while."

Private Dino Granillo, also of Italian descent, was a stocky man, five-foot six inches in height and probably knocking on the door of one hundred ninety pounds of solid muscle. His hair was blacker than night and close-cropped. His eyes took in everything and he reminded Dan of himself in some respects.

The two men sat back down after the introductions and Linda gave DD back to Ruth, who sat in the spare chair at the table.

"So, have you three decided to join our little community in the valley? I figure he is since he's standing with Shirley," she said pointing at Daniel.

"We really haven't decided as yet, ma'am," Dino answered. "This is so new and fast…I just don't know."

"I think it's a swell idea," Linda said. "I'm with Shirley on this and feel wanted already."

"I'm still a little leery," Vito said, rather quietly.

"All three of you would be welcome no matter what," Ruth told them. "We'll supply you with all that you need to survive – homes, food, transportation – you're even welcome to attend our make-shift church services we have. We want nothing more than to live in peace, worship the way we do, grow our crops, and survive. I want my son to grow into a young man and I want him to have the same liberties and freedoms I once enjoyed. Because of you and the others in the Colorado complex, we no longer have that kind of security. Because of you and the others, we have to be constantly on our guard just to survive. Because of you and the others, my husband and his best friend are dead. And for a reason or reasons I still cannot comprehend. But you need to know, that I forgive you for the destruction you've wrought in our lives. It only saddens me to know you had a part in the vicious attacks on our community."

"We were ordered to do the things we did," Vito said, with a sadness in his voice that was touching. It was not difficult to tell he truly regretted what he'd been part of.

Looking down, Dino said, "I had a hard time agreeing to the things we did. And yes, we were ordered to do them."

"You could have refused to obey the orders since they were unlawful," TJ said.

"No. No, we couldn't," Linda said morosely and fearfully. "We would have had terrible things done to us if we had. You don't know what those people would have done to us. We've all heard the screams and had to clean the rooms afterwards. You just don't know."

"Sir," Dino continued, "she's right. They did horrible things to people we captured. They didn't care about life…anyone's. When we learned Doctor Roche had been killed, at heart we were all ecstatic. I prayed in thanksgiving at the news of his death. I know that is probably wrong, but the Lord knows it was with the right intentions. That man needed to die…to be erased from humankind."

Vito added to the conversation saying, "I knew exactly what they would have done to us. I was in there once when they took a kid apart. He screamed and screamed. I still hear his screams at night and can't sleep because of them. It was horrible. They made me witness the event. Said I'd be better off if I knew what they were doing, using the tissue from the living to try and correct what they had done to create the plague."

TJ and the three Marines' heads popped up and they stood straighter at that and TJ said, "What do you mean 'they' created the plague?"

Vito looked up with tears streaming down his face and said, "Yes, sir, they made the plague. They said they did it to 'thin out' mankind. But it backfired on them and created the living dead things. Now we all have to live with that and worry everyday about surviving."

This revelation brought every valley resident in the room to their feet. They looked at each other and saw the seething anger in each other's faces. TJ's hands had rolled into fists and they clinched and unclenched. He wanted to tear apart the scientists as did the others. The four newcomers were awed and fearful by what they saw and knew to keep quiet at this point as one of the valley residents might have taken out their ire on the foursome.

Dan and TJ stared at each other, knowing now that someone had made this plague and let it loose on mankind. They couldn't do anything about that now, but they could prevent anything else like this or what they'd just heard about from ever happening again.

Headlights shone through the windows and most of the people from the valley grabbed weapons and charged them, going for the door. It was Donnie and Tim, returning from Laramie in one of the hummers. The other one, they'd left in Laramie, facing south on Highway 287, blaring the Judith signal for the horde to converge upon.

As the two came into the house, the smiles on their faces turned quickly to concern, as they saw the others and Donnie asked, "What's wrong?"

TJ answered by telling them what Private Loguzzo had told them. The two looked at Vito with surprised looks on their faces and asked him if that were true. He confirmed it was and they looked at him as if they'd been run over. Tim leaned back against the wall and began to cry, mumbling something about his parents and little sister. Dan walked over and put his arm around Tim's shoulder and tried to comfort him some.

"Wait a minute," Dan said, quickly adding, "didn't they say it started somewhere in Africa? If that's true, then they couldn't have made it," he ended looking at Vito.

"Actually, you're right, sir," Vito told him. "Doctors Roche and Miller, and the Sergeant Major took a trip to South Africa, they said on a fact-finding mission. They were also going on a photo safari somewhere, too. They brought back some fabulous photos. Anyway, they had infected a few of their safari workers and that's how it started. They did it on purpose."

TJ, staring at the young private, in his most serious Sheriff's tone, said, "You four need to make up your minds right now. Do you want to become members of the valley community? If not, we'll be seeing you on your way." He was dead serious.

Daniel was first and standing and facing TJ said, "I'm with you. I'm with you when you go down to destroy the complex in Colorado, too. Nothing I'd rather do now that I know what they've done."

Linda rose from her seat, tears streaming, and said, "I'm with you also. No matter what, we'll take that complex down and rid the planet of their existence and destroy every notation about that plague and its existence. Most of me wants to kill 'em all, but the Christian in me comes out, too."

"Remembering Joshua in the Bible, sometimes God uses the weak to clean house and I think that's us," Dino said standing also. "I want to be part of your community. I want to be part of the team that goes in and cleans God's creation. He'll be with us, I know it."

"Well said," Vito said almost in a whisper. "I want 'em all dead. I know that's wrong, but I do. Those people murdered billions of innocent people – children...." He stood up and looking TJ and Dan in the eyes said, "I pledged my life to Jesus a long time ago, now I pledge my allegiance to you and the people in this valley and pledge to protect them and this place as best I can for the rest of my life." He took a step towards the two and held his hand out. TJ and Dan both shook his hand, then he turned to Jack and Jeff and shook theirs.

Ruth stood up and said, "Then we welcome you with open arms. Tomorrow night we'll have a celebration…over in Paradise Valley?" she asked quickly to Donna.

"Most certainly," Donna said. "We'll break out a bunch of buffalo steaks and fresh vegetables, wine, scotch, beer if you want."

Ruth said, "I'll make a cake."

Jeff said, "I'm cooking the steaks."

Jack said, "I'm tending bar."

The mood had turned thanks to Ruth saying celebration. The earlier tone was still just under everyone's skin, however. Even though the mood had changed for the better, they all had it in their minds they would be going to war again - a nasty war – and this time it would be a war of vengeance and eradication.

TJ, Dan, Jack, and Jeff got together for a moment and prayed together as men. All four were angry beyond measure at the news Vito had shared about the plague that had decimated mankind and especially their friends and families. It was man-made by evil men and women in the Colorado complex. None of them could fathom the realization and were confused by the idea someone would do such an immoral thing to humankind. They all prayed for easing of their anger and that it would not turn to something sinful. They prayed for calming and wisdom for their future actions. They rejoined the group after their prayer.

They talked about the upcoming celebration for almost another hour. Ruth took DD and left for their home and Jeff left for his place. Shirley, Tim, and Donnie, collected Linda, Daniel, Dino, and Vito, and in two trucks, headed for Albany for the night. TJ and Donna said their goodnights to Dan and

Jack and left for Paradise Valley. Even though the mood had lightened, no one slept well that night.

The Battle for Sheep Mountain was over without a shot being fired. But the news the battle brought, sealed the fate of those in the Colorado complex. The people left in that compound would either capitulate or die - probably the latter. No quarter would be given.

Chapter 11: The New Absorb Into the Valley

The full moon rose over Sheep Mountain, bathing the valley below in an eerie, creamy light. The shadows were long in the moon's glare, giving testament to the clarity of the night sky. Since billions of humans had died from the man-made plague, the planet and the atmosphere surrounding it had repaired itself in amazing ways. The sky had become clean. There was no more man-made light blocking out the starry masses in the heavens. The Milky Way could clearly be seen once again. The air had become fresher, no longer smog ridden. Animal populations had increased. The trees and grasses were greener. Water in the lakes, rivers, and streams had become refreshing to drink once again.

It was Sunday, and everyone had gathered in the front yard of Paradise Valley. TJ was going to share a Sunday message and began with an opening prayer. After the prayer, TJ took a few extra moments and looked at everyone seated in the yard. There were now thirteen people living peacefully in the valley. TJ looked each in the eye, smiling, and began, "A few days ago there were only seven people in the valley. Now we're thirteen. What a blessing. The six new members have seen all that we have and know we are blessed abundantly by God, Jesus, and the Holy Spirit. Our crops are planted and growing. Our animals are healthy and vibrant. Our youngest son, DD, is a blessing and joy. And that brings me to the Sermon on the Mount that Jesus gave. If you have Bibles, please turn with me, and read in Matthew, chapter five, verses one through twelve, The Beatitudes. Jesus is speaking and says…," and TJ read the scripture aloud while the others followed along in their Bibles.

After he finished reading, he paused and let the words from their Lord and Savior sink in. The valley residents all could relate personally to several of the passages, and a few to all of them. TJ looked up at the people seated and said, "We need to rejoice and be glad. We need to be thankful. We need to be satisfied and content. But we cannot – not yet. We still have a persecutor. We have an enemy. One that has and will again try to kill us and take our home for their own. We have fought what I feel is the good fight on several occasions and have survived. We keep living, surviving, and waking another day to face whatever God has instore for us. And with His, Jesus', and the Holy Spirit's help, we'll pull through the next time we have to face danger."

"I think…no, *I* know, we're all blessed. Blessed just like Christ says in His Sermon on the Mount. Blessed because we mourn.   Blessed   because   we   hunger   and   thirst   for righteousness. Blessed because we've been merciful. Blessed because we're peacemakers – or want to be. Desperately. We do want to live in peace and harmony with all others," and several Amens could be heard coming from the people. "We, as Christians, are called to live a morally and ethical life. That is a tall order, and we all know it. It is hard to say the least. It is very hard at this juncture of our lives. We face danger every moment of every day. You all know the list of those dangers and where they may all come from. Jesus warns us later on in chapter five about an eye for an eye, and that we need to love our enemies. I agree with Him. We all should and we should all try to live our lives in that manner. He taught us to forgive and also that if we didn't forgive, we would not be forgiven by the Father and be punished ourselves. That is a hard message for us since we want to go and rid the world of the terrible people in the Colorado complex."

TJ looked at everyone and they had looks of expectancy on their faces as they waited for him to continue. "Even Jesus got angry and using a whip, ran the money changers out of His Father's house. So, I look at that and see Jesus fighting a righteous fight against evil. Frankly, *I* feel that when we have to fight to save our own lives, then we're justified in God's eyes. *I* feel that we are doing right. And now that we know what these people are capable of, *I* feel that we are right and that we will be looked upon by God as doing the right thing by ridding planet Earth of this threat."

TJ took a moment to formulate his thoughts and continued, saying, "I feel that when we go and attack the Colorado complex, we'll be doing right, the right thing for us and the rest of mankind. We'll be saving lives, including our own," and a few Amens could be heard. "The attack won't be a wrong thing, it'll be the right action, at the right time, for the right purpose," and many more Amens rang out.

"All of us need to pray," TJ continued. "All of us need to read the Bible. Ask for the Triune God's assistance. Beg Him for help. If any of you get an unsettling feeling about what we're planning, please let everyone else know. But pray, everyone. Pray like you've never prayed before."

TJ looked at everyone and quietly said, "Bow your heads with me now and pray. I'll start and if you feel the need please join in and pray." He bowed his head and began to pray.

Evil still lurked upon the surface and below the surface of Mother Earth. It had been two months since the Battle of Sheep Mountain and the sermon TJ had given. The valley residents had captured eight of the individuals from the Colorado underground complex during that one-sided battle. Four had chosen to join the valley population and four, the scientists, were kept separated in holding rooms in the Malone underground.

Because of the circumstances, Dan, TJ, Shirley, and Donnie took a trip down and delivered another message to the Christians in the complex advising them the rescue attempt would be put off for a while longer, to keep their faith strong and pray continually. The valley residents knew it would be a difficult time for the complex folks, but at this point it couldn't be helped. The attempt would be made later in the year.

The four science types had been grilled almost incessantly since their capture. TJ and Dan, the Sheriff and Nemo, had tag-teamed the four and felt they had extracted all the information they would ever get from the nerd-like scientists.

TJ, Dan, Jeff, and Jack were standing together in the foyer of the Malone underground discussing what to do with the four. Each had lost a significant amount of weight and was gaunt and pale looking having not been out in the sunlight since their capture. Not that they were starved – on the contrary, they had been treated quite well. It was the constant stress the Sheriff and the Marines had kept the four under during their incarceration. They had not seen the sun during their entire stay in the valley, thus the milky skin tone they now wore.

"We should do them like we did that Mason guy," Jeff suggested, "put hoods on them and drive a long way off in some direction and drop 'em off."

Jack looked at his long-time friend and comrade and said, "At least they'd have a chance, huh?"

"Yeah, I suppose," Jeff replied, looking sheepishly at Jack. "Leave 'em with a sidearm with one round, let them make the choice, but not anywhere near here."

TJ broke in with, "Let's just take 'em out somewhere and drop them off and good riddance."

"I'm with you," Dan agreed. "We'll take 'em in a truck and drive out west and drop 'em off out there in the desert somewhere."

"Muddy Gap," TJ said.

"What…Muddy what?" Jeff asked.

"Muddy Gap, Wyoming," TJ responded. "Little spot…"

Jeff interrupted, "Yeah, yeah, I know where Muddy Gap is, just don't get your drift."

TJ looked at him exasperated and said, "Take them up there. Drive north on 220 and turn into the first dirt road we see. Drive in ten miles or how ever far we can and drop off the first one. Drive back out to 220 and find another dirt road up the way and drive in again and drop off the second. Then, drive back to Muddy Gap and head west on Highway 789 and do the same thing with the last two. We'll give 'em a side arm with one round, two bottles of water and some food and leave 'em."

"We'll take a trailer with fuel, put two in the bed of the truck and two on the trailer, tying them on real good," Jeff said. "Should take us the better part of two days I'd think."

TJ looked at Dan who was obviously having thoughts about something and asked, "Dan, what are you thinking?"

Dan looked at TJ and asked, "Doesn't Highway 220 come out in Casper?"

"Yeah…so," TJ answered.

Dan looked at the floor again and a moment later said, "Then I think we should drop the first two on Highway 789, come back to Muddy Gap and head north on Highway 220, dropping off the last two somewhere, then continuing on to Casper. I say we take two trucks with trailers and tanks and make a big loop. We can stop at Guernsey and get anything else we can find, then down in Cheyenne stop at the Air Force base and look around there, too."

"Okay, I'm startin' ta like your thinkin'," Jeff said.

"Me, too," Jack agreed. "It should be us four and them four, two in your truck bed," pointing at TJ and Dan, "and two in ours," he commented pointing at Jeff.

"When do we leave?" TJ said with a sly grin.

"Three days," Dan said with finality. "We have to finish planting that new crop first. We have to get that in before we do anything else."

"Deal," TJ said. "Come on, fellas, let's get to work.

The morning of the third day since their discussion, found the four, saying goodbye to Donna, Ruth, and DD, then getting in their trucks and heading to the Malone underground. Everyone had agreed upon the plan and the 'kids' were to look after things while TJ and the Marines were away.

Daniel had moved in with Tim. Vito and Dino found another place nearby, and had moved in. Linda moved in with Shirley and they had begun a new community in the hamlet of Albany, which they began to call New Albany.

They had agreed to keep watch over the crops and the animals and lend a hand as necessary with Donna, Ruth, and DD. The six had made several trips into Laramie for supplies and furniture and had even made one trip into Cheyenne and brought back another full tanker truck they'd taken from the refinery. The four men had cut enough firewood it seemed to last two winters from the standing dead trees after the beetle kill almost a decade before.

It was late in the afternoon when the six piled into a truck and left Albany for Paradise Valley. They had been invited for dinner and didn't hesitate in agreeing, since they were all fans of Donna and Ruth's cooking talents. They remembered the feast they'd had when Linda, Daniel, Dino, and Vito had joined the community. That had been a swell party that had lasted well into the early morning. They had all stayed at TJ's place and slept for most of the next day.

As they approached the gate, Daniel, who was driving, honked the horn and the gate swung open. Near the steps to the porch, they piled out of the truck and were welcomed by Donna, Ruth, and DD. They would be having fried chicken that evening and the six had mouths watering because of the aroma flooding the home as they entered.

Shirley and Linda immediately began to help with preparing the dinner and the guys stayed out of the way in the living area, playing with DD. Ruth watched the foursome and knew DD now had three big brothers to depend on for company. They were helping him learn to walk and talk better. The kid would be two years old in a few months.

"Ruth, you alright?" Linda caringly asked.

Ruth looked at her and said, "Yes, dear. Looking at DD playing with the guys saddens me just a bit…even though I'm happy they're here."

"If you don't mind me asking, why does it make you sad?" Linda asked.

"It's been two years now since his father was killed and I still mourn some around this time of the year," Ruth sadly stated.

Linda looked down at the floor, not saying anything. She knew it was the group from the Colorado complex that had killed Doug and Dave. She finally looked into Ruth's eyes and sincerely said, "I really am sad that I was once part of that group. I'll never be able to forgive myself for what they've done, knowing that in some way I may have had a part in their actions."

"I don't feel that way and certainly do not blame you or any of you six," Ruth said, placing a comforting hand on Linda's shoulder. "You all were following orders, not knowing the real story. You were ordered to do things you thought right because of misinformation and I cannot blame you for that. And for that reason, it's easy to forgive you all and accept you into our lives."

Linda's meek smile told Ruth she understood, but the tear that flowed down her cheek said she was deeply saddened and sorrowful by the past.

Donna broke the spell by yelling, "Chow time!" That brought a chorus of comments from the front room as the men gathered DD and noisily made their way into the dining room.

Daniel helped Ruth sit down and as he sat, she asked him to say the blessing for their dinner, which he was happy to do.

Ruth and Donna thoroughly enjoyed the evening. After dinner and after the dishes and kitchen were cleaned up, by the guys no less, they all sat out on the front porch and talked about their past and what they had wanted to be if the world had stayed the same. Baseball player, auto mechanic, businessman, get married and have kids, open a nursery were just a few of the 'would have done' things talked about. Donna said she would have wanted a ranch somewhere and never dreamed of anything like Paradise Valley. Ruth talked about her desire to be a nurse.

It was getting late, so the young folks said their thanks and goodbyes and piled into the truck and headed to New Albany. Ruth and DD turned in. Donna, picking up a bottle of wine, made her way up to the Underground and opening the eastern portal, wrapped up in a mink blanket and sat in one of the Adirondack chairs sipping wine and watching the stars. It was a bright, night sky with a waning moon rising in the east. There was almost no wind. Donna prayed for TJ and the Marines and thanked the Lord for the view…for the hundredth time.

TJ and Jack were in the lead truck. They were heading west on I-80, driving to Rawlins, where they would turn north and go to Muddy Gap. The highway was in fairly good shape out in the desert area of Wyoming. Nothing much grew in the arid country so little had grown through the concrete of the interstate highway.

They had just passed Elk Mountain on their left when TJ asked Jack, "Tell me why you decided to join the Marines."

"I didn't decide," Jack replied, adding, "the draft board did."

"You were drafted," TJ stated, knowingly.

"Yeah, I still remember getting the letter…'Greetings from the President of the United States…' it began," Jack recited, chuckling. "I went through boot on the island - not a Hollywood Marine. I hated most of it. Anyway, I was immediately shipped to Vietnam, arriving in country eleven days before the Tet offensive in '68. It was the first day of my second week in country when I remember the Top coming into our hooch and yelling for us to gear up that we were moving out. He said to draw extra ammo and grenades that we were going into the fight at Hue City. I had an M-14 with seven mags – weighed a ton – and the supply sergeant gave me four bandoliers of ammo and four more grenades. It was a heavy load.

"We were in urban combat and I was scared outta my mind. We were walking in a line sorta, clearing an area in the city. We couldn't see each other very well and only caught sight of each other at the junctures of roads and alleys. The squad I was assigned to got hit in an ambush and we scattered. B-40 rockets were sailing all over the place and bullets were like we'd kicked a hornet's nest, buzzing and cracking by incessantly. I just lay there in a little depression, shaking like a leaf. I was really scared, actually cried. Anyway, the fire lessened and I jumped up and ran around and got behind a building. It was on fire. I saw an open area and it had a fountain thing in the middle, a park, or something. I saw a grunt lying there, wounded, so I ran over to him. He was hit badly in the abdomen and it stunk something awful. He was still alive and looked at me with the strangest expression."

Jack became quiet and TJ looked over at him and with the faraway look on his face knew he was vividly remembering the incident in his mind's eye. TJ gave him a moment then said, "Were you able to help him?"

Jack snapped out of his thought and looking at TJ said, "No. He was too far gone. But I remember his face…his eyes. He wasn't afraid to die. His eyes were filled with confidence. You know, the guy looked at me and said, 'Don't worry, I'll be fine.' He actually smiled at me. Smiled! He knew he was dying, but he looked at peace and he really looked confident. I couldn't understand his look…why he wasn't afraid and pleading for me to help him, but he was more worried about me, telling me not to worry over and over, that he was going to be just fine.

"Finally, he reached into his dungaree pocket and brought out a little brown book – it was a Bible – you know, those ones that's the New Testament, with Psalm and Proverbs added…anyway, he wrapped my bloody hand around the little book and said, 'You're the one that's scared. I don't need this anymore. You need it much more than me'. That's when he took his last breath and died. He died looking content if you can believe that. That's when I became a follower of Christ, and a Christian, I guess. I read every single word in that little blood-stained Bible – every single one of them," his voice trailed off quietly.

TJ noticed Jack had bowed his head and looking at him, saw a tear running down his left cheek. TJ refocused on the highway, chewing on the inside of his cheek to control his emotion. It was quiet in the cab until they reached the turn at Rawlins.

Two days later and after dropping the scientists off in barren, way out of the way areas, TJ and the Marines were pulling into Guernsey. They went straight to the ammo bunkers and since TJ had the keys to the locks they'd installed, he walked down the line of bunkers unlocking the doors while Dan, Jack, and Jeff went inside to search for supplies and equipment they might need. They specifically wanted more C-4 and any thermite grenades they might be able to find.

After several hours of searching, even going to other areas of the base and looking around, they felt they'd had enough of nothing and departed for Cheyenne. All they'd found were several boxes of detonators, which would come in handy. They decided to stay in an old hotel that evening just to the south of the base in Cheyenne.

The two trucks pulled into the parking lot of the hotel close to ten that evening. The four men waited and watched and not seeing any movement or danger, climbed out and went inside to clear the building. Using their suppressed nine millimeters, they had three run-ins with Zs which resulted in some frayed nerves and four very dead zombies. After dragging the corpses outside, the four found rooms and settled in for the night. The hotel had electronic locks on all the doors and since the power was out, they all had popped open. The men used the inside locking mechanisms to secure their doors for the night and they slept well.

The next morning, they woke and after cleaning up, ate MREs for breakfast, in the hotel's breakfast nook, laughing at the food choices for their morning meals – chili and beans, chicken and rice, beef stew and chicken teriyaki.

"I'm glad he's riding with you," TJ, pointing to Jeff said to Jack.

"Whys that?" Jack asked.

"Those chili and beans ought to hit around three or so…the windows work in your truck?" That statement brought laughter from the group.

"That ain't right," Jack snickered.

"I'm glad I'm riding with you," Dan said to TJ, "'cause I have experience with that result." More laughter.

The four finished their banter and their breakfast and loaded up for the base. They went in on the west side where they'd made the cut in the fence line and opened the bunkers to begin their search. They found several more cases of grenades and were fortunate enough to find one that held thermite grenades. Those were most welcomed.

They loaded the materials on the trailers and drove down to the supply complex to see if they could find anything they might need. Inside the building, they saw the stains on the floor from their first entry of the place. TJ asked a few questions and got muted answers as the three Marines pondered their first time here with Dave and Doug.

They broke into every locked locker and crate they found. Frustration was beginning to set in when Jeff yelled for the others to come to where he was. Once there, everyone looked into the large, armored bin Jeff had opened after busting the lock off. Inside were smaller boxes with explosive placards pasted on the tops and sides, indicating they held M-183 demolition charges, the equivalent of a World War II satchel charge used to destroy bunkers and such. Jeff stood there smiling, looking like a cat that had eaten the family parakeet.

The four began carefully loading the crates of kits into the trucks and in just a while had them all loaded. They continued the searching of the supply facility and not finding anything they really needed, departed close to noon.

Happy Jack Road was showing the effects of nonuse and the way was slow going in spots. Trees and shrubbery had grown through the asphalt making the way difficult. They saw elk, mule deer, and antelope in abundance. The animals had no fear of the men or their vehicles and simply turned and looked at them as they passed. They were seeing this kind of behavior from all the animals now since the demise of the majority of humankind, they had lost their fear of man and looked upon them as a curiosity.

TJ got that feeling he always did when he passed the sign, denoting they were passing into Albany County once again. He always felt like that was his homecoming announcement, seeing those signs. He pointed out things to Dan, telling him what they were and why they were named the way they were.

As they were driving through the picturesque countryside, Jeff came over the radio saying, "Jack's looking pretty green back here," ending with laughter.

TJ and Dan looked in the rearview mirrors and could see Jack's head out the driver's side window. Both knew the chili had kicked in and Jeff was breaking wind. They both began laughing.

Turning down I-80 and heading west, they found the interstate highway through the canyon to be in disrepair, slowing their descent through the pass. TJ commented to Dan that soon the roadways would be difficult to negotiate. Dan, agreeing, said that they needed to get the Colorado task completed quickly since it looked like they would soon be back in the dark ages when it came to motorized travel. Both laughed.

"That just might not be such a bad thing, really," TJ commented.

"Why do you say that?" Dan asked him.

"Vehicles won't be able to get around very well anymore making it less likely we'll be attacked from the ground. And if someone wanted to make an attack, they'd have to have a lot of horses or ox or something to haul equipment and supplies. I think we'd see that coming from a long way off."

"Hmm, I haven't thought of it that way, but you're right. Someone would have to go through a lot of trouble to get to us looking at the topography of the valley. I can see why the doc wanted the place so badly." Dan gave TJ a sideways glance and jokingly said, "You ain't as dumb as I thought you was."

TJ smacked him on the upper arm and gave a pouting look and said, "I'm tellin' on you."

The pair of 'old' men laughed. The two had become brothers and were willing to do just about anything for each other. Their laughter began to die down as Dan followed I-80 west down the mountain.

"What was the worst time for you in your Army career?" TJ asked.

"I have to say it was during the Tet Offensive in '68. Bad stuff. I was with a unit that was ordered to take out some gun emplacements on a couple of hills to the northwest of Khe Sanh. It was some intense fighting, even some close quarter stuff. We lost a lot of good men in that fight. I guess the only good thing about it was we were sitting on a small hill waiting for orders to move out when the ammo dump went up on Khe Sanh. Man, that was a sight. Made fourth of July shows meek at best. I felt sorry for the guys down there when a Staff Sergeant came up and said the VC had hit the tear gas storage area."

"You're kidding," TJ said.

"No, really made a mess on the base for a while. I got hit on hill 881 south in late '68, clearing out mortar positions," Dan said. "Hurt a lot. I was awake when I got choppered out to a medical unit but woke up in Germany a week or so later. From there went to Bethesda, Maryland, to the Navy hospital. Finally sent back to duty and a second tour in the Nam where I met those two nuts back there," he said pointing with his thumb to the rear.

"Man, that must have been tough," TJ sympathized. "I talked with Jack some about his time in country. Great yet unusual story he told me."

"He told you the Bible story…" Dan knew.

"Yeah," TJ answered with a grin then quickly changing the subject said, "I was at an FOB when I was hit. We got shot at almost every day and mortared at least once a week if not more; ugly spot. I guess we've all seen a bit too much," TJ mused.

"I suppose. Here's our turn," and Dan pulled onto the lane going up to the house in Paradise Valley and honked the horn. The gate opened and they pulled up to the garage and got out.

Donna, DD, and Ruth came out to greet the men with Donna jumping into TJ's arms and kissing him. In the house, the guys poured themselves some scotch and stood in the front room, wanting to stand after sitting in the trucks for such a long time. The girls shooed them out onto the front porch and Jeff was the first to pull up an Adirondack and kick back with his booted feet up on the rail. Ruth came out and looked at the men and told the other three to sit down.

"Uh oh," Dan said, "this sounds ominous. What's happened?"

After the three had joined Jeff, sitting in Adirondacks, Ruth cleared her throat and said, "Donnie, Tim, Vito, and Dino, have gone on a mission."

"What mission?" TJ asked, concerned.

"They took it upon themselves to go to Fort Carson to get more war fighting materials."

All four men sat up at the announcement.

With hands up, Ruth said, "Now don't jump to conclusions, guys. They talked it out and made some good preparations. They came over and talked to Donna and me first and had Shirley and Linda with them. We all agreed on their plan and they should be back in four days. They took two trucks with trailers with tanks and enough weapons and ammo to fight a good-sized war."

She paused and no one spoke for several moments. Dan broke the tense moment with, "What specifically were they going for?"

"Specifically," Ruth said using Dan's term, "...they're going for more Stingers, AT-6s, C-4, and Thermite...even though they've produced almost twenty pounds of the stuff themselves."

"We found some thermite grenades and some explosive units like the old satchel charges from World War Two," TJ said.

"They were going to collect anything else they could, like more 240's and 249's, M4s and whatever weapons they could. They said they knew Fort Carson very well and knew right where to go and how to get there without going through Denver and Colorado Springs to reduce the risk. They showed us the route on maps and Donna and I thought it was a good, well thought-out plan."

"You think they'll be alright?" Jack asked.

"I do...and Donna as well," Ruth answered.

"We going to follow?" Jeff asked the others. Silence was what he got as an answer as everyone was thinking about that.

"No," TJ said. "I trust Ruth's judgment implicitly. We stay here and prepare for the assault like we planned. Ruth and Donna feel the Army pukes' plan was good and I for one feel we should give them the benefit of the doubt, just because Ruth says. If we follow, it just may bust their confidence in themselves and their decisions. They're adults and know the risks even more than we do perhaps. So, I say we give them the chance to prove themselves."

"What if they've taken our stuff and gone back to the Colorado complex and told them all our plans?" Jeff, always the suspicious one asked.

"Then they've written their own tickets I'd say," Dan said with finality.

"I don't think they would do that," Jack said. "The only one I'd doubt would have been Dino, but he would have acted alone, I'm sure."

"I don't doubt any of them," Ruth added. "I'm sure we'll see them in a few days with loads of materials we can use and probably need."

Donna stepped out and looking at the group, knew the men had been told and waited a moment to see the temperature of the group. Not seeing any seething, red-faced stares, she announced that dinner was ready for everyone to come inside and wash up.

As usual, Jeff was first up saying, "I'm for that."

The next morning, Dan, Jack, and Jeff arrived a bit before nine to help TJ with unloading the supplies they'd gathered on their trip. The explosives went into the storage locker in the garage and the grenades and boxes of detonators went up to the armory in the Underground by ATV. They cleaned weapons and vehicles and around noon, the Marines said their goodbyes and went back to Marine Hill.

TJ stayed in the garage doing minor maintenance on his truck and the ATV, wanting to keep those vehicles in top running condition, especially now since the roadways were getting so bad.

Donna came out and said, "You're not too unhappy with the guys from New Albany, are you?"

"Not really," TJ answered. "I guess they felt they needed to do that to feel wanted and useful. I guess I'd do the same thing if I were in their shoes."

"They really do want to fit in around here," Donna said. "You should have seen them. The whole time you were gone, one or two of them would drop by every day and ask if we needed them to do anything for us. They worked the crops, too, and that Vito, he's really good with the animals. They seem to flock to him. Dusty really likes him."

"That's good, I'm glad they were helpful...and wanted to be it appears," TJ said.

"I feel they want to fit in...be members of the family, and badly enough that they'll just about do anything to stay in the Valley."

"Well, I like having so many minds around now. There's fourteen of us now – can you believe it?"

"Well, in two weeks or so we just may double in size if our plan pans out for the Colorado campaign."

"Wow, can you believe over twenty people…and Christians, too."

"From what Shirley has told me, we may be closer to forty. We can really have some services then. I'd say that every Sunday will become a day of worship, rest, and community with a potluck every week." That brought chuckles from both.

"Jeff'll love that," TJ said laughing more.

"That's mean," Donna said, continuing laughing with TJ. When their laughter died some, she asked, "What are you doing, anyway?"

"Minor maintenance on the vehicles. The roads and highways are really beginning to deteriorate with no use. Trees and shrubs are growing through and becoming a hazard. It took us almost all day to get here from Cheyenne. Happy Jack is getting bad and so is I-80. I told Dan we'd be using horses and oxen soon to transport a crew anywhere. We need to move soon on the Colorado complex, so we'll have the use of vehicles on the roadways. Otherwise, we may just be breaking trail ourselves soon."

"Anything I can do to help you with the vehicles?"

TJ smiled and handed her a shop rag and told her to wipe down the engine in the ATV.

Late in the evening three days later, TJ was sitting on the front porch sipping iced tea when he heard an engine in the distance. It was almost dark, and he wondered if one of the Marines needed something when he heard a horn honk down the lane. He jumped up and inside the house pressed the button on the remote, opening the gate.

Donna asked, "Whose here?"

"Don't know – pull an M4 just in case, will ya?" TJ said.

She turned for the rifle rack near the door and TJ went back outside and watched as two trucks with trailers struggled up the small hill and stopped in front of the house. The four Privates got out of the trucks and stood at the bottom of the steps. Obviously the four were dead-dog tired. Donna came out with a huge smile on her face and TJ stood there with hands on his hips, looking at the four very worn out looking young men.

"Have a nice trip?" TJ asked.

"Yes, sir," Donnie answered. "Brought you some early Christmas presents, too."

"Come on up guys," TJ said, smiling. "What do you want to drink?"

A chorus of 'beers' came from the group and TJ, looking at Donna, saw she already knew and had turned for the house to get some cold ones.

"Pull up some chairs guys and let's talk," TJ said.

"I'd rather stand for a while," Donnie said rubbing his back side.

"Me, too," Vito said.

"Ditto, Vito," Dino chimed.

"Cut that out!" Vito yelled, bringing chuckles from the other three.

Tim shook his head and chuckling, leaned against the rail, crossing is arms and legs and getting comfortable standing.

"Must have been a long ride if you don't want to sit," TJ said.

"Yeah, the roads are getting bad," Dino said.

"We had the same problem getting back from Cheyenne," TJ agreed.

"You guys find anything?" Tim asked.

"We found some detonators, a few thermite grenades, and some of those M183 demolition packages like the old satchel charges. Those will definitely come in handy," TJ said. "Looks like you guys found a few things."

"You won't believe the stuff we found, but can it wait 'till tomorrow to go through it all? I'm beat and just want a beer, go home and get in the rack," Donnie said.

"Man, me, too," Tim said.

"Here, here," Dino concurred.

"Yep," Vito agreed.

"Well, here's your beer, guys," Donna said coming out of the house. She passed them out and the four downed the first cans like water. Each took a second can from Donna and just sipped, letting out a chorus of ahh's in response to the drinks.

Dino burped saying, "Sorry, ma'am."

"Want me to drop the trailer on one of the trucks for you so you can head home in a few?" TJ asked.

Three of the men had sat down in Adirondacks and Tim said, "That would be swell, sir."

TJ smiled and went down the steps and unhooked the trailer on the truck nearest the lane. It would be easier to get out.

He ran up the steps again and the four were getting up and putting their empty cans on the tray Donna had brought the refreshments on and slowly filed by TJ, shaking his hand, hugging Donna, and saying goodnight. They tiredly got into the truck and with a wave, headed down the lane and to New Albany for a good night's rest.

As they pulled away, Donna looked at TJ and said, "Come on, cowboy, I'm tired and want to hit the sack myself."

TJ woke early. Coffee in hand after he cleaned up, he made his way out to the garage and opened the big doors so they could easily unload the trailers. He pulled out the ATV and would use it to ferry some materials up to the Underground.

Donna came out about an hour after TJ had opened the garage and called out to him, "Hey, cowboy…you want some breakfast?"

"No thank you, ma'am, I'm not really in the mood to eat," he yelled back. "I'll take more coffee if you would."

She ran down to where he was and took his mug, gave him a kiss, and took off for the house to refill it. She was back a moment later carrying hers as well. "What can I do to help?"

"Nothing really," TJ said sadly.

"What's wrong, TJ?" she asked him.

"I just can't get over what Vito told us about the plague. It really infuriates me and makes me want to do something drastic and I don't want to do that. I want to go now and take care of the Colorado issue…you know what I mean?"

"Yes, I do, and I feel the same way. I get emotional every time I think about it. I want to go down there right now and clobber 'em."

"We need to call a community meeting soon and plan."

"Yes, I agree."

"We'll need to use the big trucks and a couple of flatbeds to haul all the material down. I want to take enough supplies and equipment to do the job once and for all. End it for sure."

"Yes, I agree."

"Is that all you're going to say – 'yes, I agree'?"

"But I do agree with you. We need a meeting. We need to use the big trucks and do all we can to end this. Period."

The two heard engines and a horn honk, so TJ went into the garage and hit the button to open the gate. It would be the four men from New Albany, coming over to unload the supplies they'd gained from Fort Carson.

Two trucks came up the lane and the whole group got out, Shirley, Linda, Donnie, Tim, Daniel, Dino, and Vito. "We're here," Tim said.

"Morning, y'all," Donna said with a smile.

"Howdy everyone," TJ said.

"You ready for some work, TJ?" Daniel asked.

"Sure. Always ready to do some work," TJ answered.

"Tim…Daniel, would you back up and hook up to the trailer?" Donnie asked.

The two hopped to it and in just a few moments had the trailer hooked up and were backing it to the opening the garage doors had left once they were opened.

"I figure we'll unload the AT-6s first," Donnie said. "That's almost all that is on this trailer. There are a few other things, but we'll get to them in a bit. Where do you want us to stack these?"

"I made some space near the back wall, just double as you stack 'em and it should be enough room," TJ directed. "What about the other stuff…and what is it?"

Donnie smiled and said, "Two crates of five each, Barrett M82, fifty caliber rifles and a case of one hundred, ten-round magazines for them."

"Well, those will really come in handy, won't they," TJ said beaming. "What's on the other trailer?"

"More mortar rounds, more Claymores and the detonator packages to go with them, and six more cases of M4 carbines," Donnie said. "We found a couple of 249's we're keeping up in New Albany. We didn't get any more ammo, other than some fifty rounds since you already had so much on hand."

"The Claymores will be useful," TJ said, still smiling. "How much fifty ammo did you get?"

"I think it was five thousand rounds," Donnie said, smiling.

"I guess we'll be set with that," TJ said very happily. "Let's get it all unloaded.

It took almost four hours to get everything unloaded and stored. The group from New Albany kept an M4 each along with some Claymores to have on hand. TJ fixed them up with ten thousand loose rounds of .556 ammunition and another ten cans of belted M-249 ammo. They would be loaded for bear up in Albany with that allotment.

"We need to find you guys some .308's to have up there for hunting and protecting yourselves from bear and lions and such," TJ said.

"We'll get by with these," Tim said patting the fifty he'd chosen for himself.

"I'm sure," TJ said smiling. "Remember to be back here tomorrow night for the meeting. We'll need all of you to be here to give your input and advice."

Shirley said, "I guarantee you all of us will be here, TJ."

"It's going to be quite the crowd this time what with all of you and everyone else being here," Donna observed. "We'll need to be building a community hall before long I think, just to hold us all."

"We'll plan that for the future, tomorrow will be for one purpose only," TJ said with determination.

"Yes, once we've taken care of the Colorado issue, we can set our sights on community planning and the future," Shirley said.

TJ and Donna, with smiles, nodded and waived as the 'kids' got in their trucks and left to go home to New Albany.

Chapter 12: Updated Plans

"My goodness," TJ said, "I can't believe we've got this many people in here. Sorry about the close communion everybody, but it can't be helped."

Everyone laughed and looked at each other. There were fourteen people in the great room and dining room of the house in Paradise Valley. TJ had brought out every chair they had so everyone could sit together for the meeting. The original valley residents had not seen this many people together at once in quite some time. TJ stood looking at the 'crowd', for to them it was, and marveled.

"I'm glad you're all here and you just don't know how happy I am to have you all together," TJ told the throng. He looked at each person individually and smiling, gave each a nod of his head in recognition. "We've been so few for so long, this…crowd…is a tremendously special event. I praise the Lord we're all here. Please, join with me in prayer to start this meeting."

They all bowed their heads and TJ prayed. Several joined in adding their thanksgiving prayers along with TJ's.

"I hope you all know that in the Bible, Jesus tells us in Matthew, chapter eighteen, verse twenty, and I quote, "For where two or three come together in my name, there am I with them." So, Jesus is here with us this evening and I hope and pray He's going to guide us and give us sound advice…or at least lead us to sound advice for this upcoming operation." TJ looked up and around the room and said to space, "I hope, Lord, that You're comfortable here and happy with us.

"Now, to begin with let's recap. Almost two years ago, an attack was made on the above ground complex in Colorado, utterly destroying that facility. We knew there might have been an underground exit or two but didn't really feel it would be a threat at the time. Almost a year afterwards, we fought off several attacks by humans, by drones, and by zombies of which we were blessed with having come out of the attacks on the winning side…for the most part. Sadly, the valley did lose three important team members, Douglas Sutton, Dave Malone, and his wife, Julia.

"Let's observe a moment or two of silence in their memories," TJ requested.

Everyone bowed their heads and either prayed or reflected. Those that never knew Doug or Dave, or Julia just reflected on what they'd heard and read about the two men, the founder, and builder of Paradise Valley and TJ's Deputy Sheriff, and his wife. All three were heroes in most people's minds, great men and lady, and Christians.

"We've come a long way since the day Doug Sutton and David Malone were killed," TJ began again. "It was a tragic loss when Julia Malone was taken from us. It was a hard time after those days. But we've persevered. We pressed on and with the Lord's help, we've fought and won a lot of battles since then, fighting the battle we hope our Lord wants us to. Now we come to hopefully the last battle. One that we've planned and prepared for, but now, with the addition of several new members in the community," he said indicating the seven newcomers, "I think that with the Lord's help, we have a great opportunity to end one major threat to our very existence.

"Tonight, with your help," he said indicating the new members once again, "we hope to finalize the plan to end the Colorado threat and eradicate all materials about the plague they developed and set upon the world," TJ took in a deep breath and paused a moment to real in his anger at the mention of the pandemic. "If you'll look through the materials we already have, you'll see the photos we've taken on recons of the areas in question. We have, thanks to the new folks, schematics of the underground complex. You'll see it's in a triangle with a center-cut tunnel from the northern peak to the southern tunnel that leads to the western exit and what once was the eastern exit at the complex. That center tunnel running north to south, has five branches, of which two have diagonal cuts that as you look at it on paper, look like two arrows pointing east and west. Those are storage areas.

"We have a lot of M183, demolition block assemblies, and can use them in conjunction with thermite grenades loaded on remote controlled vehicles, or remotely operated vehicles (ROVs), like cars and trucks, you know, the kids' toys. We can load one M183, several thermite grenades on one of the bigger ROVs, with a timer and let them detonate in the tunnel branches. Those should do the trick and destroy the laboratories and storage areas and burn hot enough to destroy any biologics they may be storing there. Looking at the drawings Shirley and Linda provided, I think we'll need at least sixteen of the things. Once they've all blown, we can blow the rest of the tunnels using large amounts of C-4 infused with the homemade thermite Tim and his crew have developed.

"To begin the attack, we'll give an ultimatum. They surrender or die - simple. If they resist, we begin by dropping mortar rounds and bombs using the drone bombers we have. Thanks to Tim and Donnie, we have bombers that now can drop napalm and or thermite charges on a target.

"No quarter will be given. They either surrender or else. Once their decisions are made, those that can make their way out that want to surrender, we'll lead to safety. The rest…well, that will be up to the Lord, but we'll make every effort to see they get to meet Him as quickly as we can."

A few chuckles went around the room at that statement.

"It may seem humorous, but I'm deadly serious. They either surrender or die – PERIOD!" TJ pronounced, slapping the tabletop with his palm making several of the folks jump. "I want it made abundantly clear to the tunnel inhabitants that will be our objective. I want every effort made to get the children out of there safely. Shirley tells me there are eight kids in there. We don't want to harm any children. Shirley and Linda also tell me there are those inside that may try to kill everyone that attempts to surrender, including the children. They have no qualms about ending life, adult, or child. So, we need to act quickly. I suggest we do like we've done before and try to get word inside through one of the Christians in there to get the other Christians and the kids out. And anyone else that wants to surrender. Dan, you're next," TJ ended.

"First thing is to determine a date for the effort. After that, we'll need to do some training. Everyone will have to know how to operate and fire a mortar and a fifty-caliber rifle. Load outs will be the basic Z'd out configuration for everyone. Other weapons will be added by mission assignment. We'll have two mortar teams, two sniper teams, two assault teams and Ruth and DD holding up the rear."

That brought up a round of laughter and applause. Ruth and DD would be what they had already jokingly termed as Camp Rustlers. They, Ruth that is, would mind base camp and have meals and first aid ready as needed, and she would act as quartermaster, handing out ammunition, weapons, and other equipment depending on how the battle progressed. She would prepare meals for the field teams and ensure everyone had a good supply of water.

Dan continued, "The mortar crews will also be responsible for flying bombers and extra training will be done on those with everyone, including Ruth as she can fly a bomber from the main encampment if needed. I plan to have at least three bombers in the air at all times, and at the outset, I'd like to have four flying with two on each entrance. We'll discuss weapon load outs when the time comes. Questions so far?"

Everyone looked around the room and since no one had any questions as yet, Dan continued saying, "Okay, we'll be convoying down in two flatbed trucks loaded to the gills with our war fighting supplies and equipment, along with four trucks with trailers that have fuel tanks. One of those will be filled with diesel for the big rigs. We'll pack for two weeks and hope the operation only lasts a few days once we attack. Best scenario, they'll all surrender and all we'll have to do is demolition. Worse case – we'll have a monumental fight on our hands. If that's the case, we'll start by using the bombers and dropping the loads onto and, if we can, into the entrances, first using napalm, then explosives if necessary. As we drop the napalm, others will be driving their ROVs up as close as they can. Once the fires have died down, we'll give the clearance for you to drive your ROV's inside and detonate them in turn once we have them all in position.

"It sounds simple, but you all know as well as I do that once the challenge is given, all the planning goes out the window and it becomes anybody's guess as to what happens next. We need to be the ones prepared to meet any contingency and that's why we meet together. To think things through and come up with suitable ideas to counter with," Dan said.

He looked back to TJ who said, "Okay everyone, now's the time to think things through and bring up any ideas and suggestions. We'll break into smaller groups in a bit and write your ideas and suggestions on the pads of paper. Write down everything. No idea or situation will be looked at as foolish. We'll look at everything together and decide on the best course of action with each. We begin training in a few days. Donna has lists of who goes where for what training and we'll have the team leaders call their teams together in a bit. I figure it'll take about a week to get everyone trained on everything. In your spare and off time, I ask that you drive an ROV around. Play with them so you get familiar with their capabilities. Put a heavy load on them and drive them around to get the feel of how they handle. It could save your life or someone else's. Practice with your M4s and your handguns. Once the best shooters are identified, they'll be our snipers, and you should shoot often so you know your capability and are familiar with your weapons. If you think you're weak in an area, please ask for additional training. Time is on our side ladies and gentlemen, so if you need extra time on something let us know. We're not in a hurry and I don't want to see anyone get hurt or worse because you didn't know something.

TJ paused for several minutes looking around the room then said, "Okay, Jack, read your sniper team members off and y'all go with Jack to the armory, please."

"Excuse me, please," Daniel meekly asked.

TJ looked at Daniel and said, "What's up, Daniel?"

Daniel looked around the room, obviously nervous and said in a quavering whisper, "I think I need to tell you something about the complex."

TJ, after a moment of hesitation by Daniel, said, "Go ahead, son, let it out."

"I think…I…I mean I feel there is another danger in the complex we need to talk to you about."

"Okay, then, what is it?" TJ asked.

Daniel looked at his counterparts from the complex and finally, with a shrug, said, "There's this Sergeant Major there and he's a real bad guy. I mean a really bad guy. He's what we call STRACK, but only in his appearance. Inside, he's just plain mean and doesn't care about anybody. He's always with the Doc when he cuts up folks and Zs."

Linda broke in saying, "He's a sadistic person, plain and simple. Daniel's right, he's calloused, and has no compassion for others. He's done some horrible things to people we've captured," she ended.

Vito took over then, "They're right. He'll be a wild card we'll need to consider and contend with. He'll do the unexpected for sure and would be the one that would kill those kids just because we show up. He hates Christians."

TJ looked at Dino and asked if he had any more input.

"Only to say Daniel's right – the guy is junkyard-dog mean to a fault. He's sadistic and loves being that way. When we screw up, even in the slightest, he makes us drop and do fifty pushups. We all avoided him as much as possible, but he gets to you eventually and uses his authority over us as leverage, making us do things we would never want to do otherwise," Dino added.

TJ looked down at the table for a moment after this train of thought came through, and finally said, "Okay, we'll take that under advisement for now. Thanks for bringing it up, Daniel. Everyone, if you have anything like that you think we need to hear about, please don't hesitate to bring it up." He paused for another moment and followed up with, "Okay, Jack, call your team," then he sat down.

Jack stood and said, "Donna, Donnie, and Tim, follow me please." The three stood and followed Jack to the armory.

TJ looked at Dan and said, "Dan, gather your mortar and drone teams together…library?"

Dan stood and said, "Yeah, that'll do. Daniel, Shirley, and Vito…come on with me please." The trio got up and followed Dan into the library.

"That leaves us," TJ said to Ruth, Jeff, Dino, and Linda. "Ruth, I guess you and DD can begin your lists of equipment we'll need."

"I'll take him up to the Underground and we'll start the list up there," Ruth said, getting up and collecting DD. "Give me a buzz when you're ready for me to come back down."

"Will do, lady," TJ said. Looking at Linda, and Jeff, TJ said, "We're the assault teams and our call-signs will be Assault Team West, ATW, and Assault Team North, ATN."

"What does that mean?" Linda asked.

"Assault Team West will be at the western entrance, and Assault Team North will be attacking the north one," TJ answered. "You and Jeff will make up ATN and Shirley and I will be on ATW. We'll have M240 Bravos, M249's, fifty-caliber rifles and the usual Z'd out configuration. We'll be going in heavy what with all the ammunition and weapons. We'll be carrying extra grenades and we have the responsibility of driving the ROVs into the tunnel complex from each entrance. That means we need to experiment with the ROVs we have to see how far they'll go with a load.

"The tunnels are awfully long, so we'll need to specifically test for mileage while carrying a load. According to Shirley, the east-west tunnel is about five miles in length, the western tunnel is about four miles, and the eastern is a bit more than that. The central tunnel with the five lab tunnels branching to the east and west is around five and a quarter mile. Those are our primary targets for the ROVs. They'll have to go from your positions to each of these tunnels. The ATN will have the shortest route - Shirley and I will have a long way to go so we'll need the ROVs that can haul the most the farthest."

TJ handed each a drawing of the tunnel complex showing approximate distances and said, "Shirley tells us that each of these five tunnel branches have doors that are sealed by negative pressure. What does that mean to us? We cannot just blow the doors with a charge and thermite. We'll need to blow the doors using an ROV with an M-183 charge, then follow up with another with thermite grenades wrapped in C-4 to get the fire going hot enough to kill all the biological material they're experimenting with in there. I'm thinking we'll need at least twenty ROVs to get the job done. That'll give us enough to allow for a few backups just in case. We can send in any extras and let 'em blow just about anywhere to collapse the tunnels and start more fires. I'm thinking one person drives and the other covers their position. If we find that we have no real danger of being attacked in our positions, we can all drive ROVs inside and let 'em rip remotely. There's only four of us and I feel we'll need at least two per tunnel. That means we'll have to blow the centermost lab tunnel first and the others as we can. I'm not sure how much resistance we'll face, but we'll have to cross that bridge when it happens."

"Questions – observations - ideas?"

Dino, snickering, raised his hand and TJ said, "Go ahead."

"I drove ROVs a lot when I was a kid, even raced in local events back home," he said. "I know how to…reconfigure an ROV to use something like tracks on a tank. They'll be able to climb over just about anything within reason, like debris and stuff. That'll give us some additional trust in the systems."

"That'll be a first priority, then, along with training on driving the things in rough terrain, which we have an abundance of around here," TJ said. That got chuckles from everyone again.

"You know," Linda said, "I recall Fort Carson having the bigger ROVs. The military grade vehicles that carried weapons like the 240 and even one that carried the 40-millimeter grenade launcher that was belt-fed. I'm not sure where they kept them, but if we could find some of those, I feel it would be worth another trip down there to get 'em."

Jeff and TJ looked at one another with knowing looks. Each knew exactly what she was talking about. They would have to discuss that with the group at least. Jeff said, "TJ, write it down and we'll bring the idea to the group and get input. I'm for the attempt."

TJ said while writing, "I am, too. I think it would be worth the risk to have a few combat tested ROVs on our side, especially if they have artillery."

Dino said, "I agree with you TJ. If we could find two with 240s or thumpers, that would give us platforms to cover the smaller vehicles while we get them into position to blow. If we're fortunate enough to score one with a forty on top, we can use it to blow the doors and then send in the little guys with the thermite charges."

"I like the kid's way of thinkin'," Jeff said looking at Dino and smiling. "He's got a good idea going there."

"Yes, he does," TJ agreed, also looking at the kid. "Okay, if you think of anything else, no matter how far-fetched it may sound write it down and present it to the team the next time we meet. Think about the ideas we've already talked about and write down any revelations you have on making our jobs – and those of our comrades - better and easier."

In the armory, Jack brought his team in and said, "I picked you guys because I already know you're good shooters and won't need that much training. Each of us will have a fifty of our choice, and a Remington SPXS .308 caliber sniper rifle. We'll also have our basic Z'd out loads so we'll be going in quite heavy. Probably need two or three trips dragging sleds to our positions to get all the weapons and ammo into position.

I'm going to talk to TJ and suggest we also have a few kamikaze drones in each position to fly around if we're not firing our primary weapons. That'll give us some additional firepower and we may be able to assist the other teams.

"Tonight, I want each of you to pick your weapons. All of us will have ten additional mags each for the fifties, giving us over a hundred rounds of fifty caliber ammo to give as gifts. That's a lot of firepower to bring to bear on an enemy. Each of us should take sixty rounds of .308. Each position will have additional bags of loaded .556 magazines also. Like TJ said, we're giving no quarter, so the more ammo the better. Be generous with the amount of rounds you send down range," he said with a smile. "I'm bringing my thumper with me just because - I like those. If we get into a situation where we have to move to flank or maneuver to attack directly, it'll come in handy."

"Can I take one, too?" Donnie asked. "I know how to use one pretty good."

"I'll say he can," Tim said.

"If TJ'll agree to both of us having one then absolutely," Jack told him.

Donnie looked at Jack, then at Tim, and shrugged his shoulders and said, "Go ahead and ask."

Jack looked at the two and said, "What…what's wrong?"

"Nothing's wrong," Tim answered.

"Then what?" Jack probed.

"Go ahead," Donnie prompted Tim.

"We…er…I was - can I ask you a question? I mean it ain't personal or anything…I, that is we…uh…were wondering about something, that's all," Tim stammered.

Jack's shoulders slumped some and his face took on an almost disgusted look and his eyes focused on Tim's and he said, "Get it out…now."

"We…I was wondering about Dan and TJ," Tim said almost in a whisper.

"What do you mean?" Jack said, head coming up, now probing with his eyes and a questionable look.

"They both are good men – don't get me wrong – and both seem to be the leader around here," Tim finally stated. "That's the issue. Which one is really in charge?" he asked, his eyes locked on Jack's, pleading.

Jack took a deep breath and slowly let it out, nodding his head, understanding their dilemma, and said, "That's a tricky question. I suppose it depends on what's going on at the time. You gotta understand…Dan was a leader in the Marines. He was in charge of a platoon most of the time, the 'top' as we called them, and was even company senior noncommissioned officer a few times, so he's used to leading and being in command. TJ, on the other hand, is the Sheriff of this county after all. He's the authority in the whole county, maybe even the whole state, kinda like the surrogate governor I suppose. This is his county…his state…so, you see it kinda depends on the circumstance, I guess. If it has to do with our area, then TJ gets the nod, if it's a military issue then we all go to Dan. We really don't have a…an ultimate leader…other than our Lord in Heaven."

Both Tim and Donnie looked at the ground thinking about what Jack had just said and Tim, looking back into Jack's eyes, said, "I can dig it. I understand about those two. Nothing's really been decided on who the boss is so to speak but, depending on the circumstance that would dictate who we go to for advice. I get it."

"Yeah, me, too," Donnie added.

"I get it also," Donna agreed with a smile.

"Come on, you three, let's get back to the weapons," Jack said, smiling and shaking his head.

The four selected their fifty-caliber and Remington sniper rifles. These would now become their personal firearms and would be kept close at all times until the crisis was over. They carried their weapons out to their vehicles then went back inside and drew M4s, nine millimeters, and for Jack and Donnie, with Jack's okay, M79, thumpers, and hauled these to the trucks.

"Ok, now the hard part," Jack said. "Each of you goes back inside and gets ten magazines for your fifties and seven each for your nines, and M4s. Donnie, get a thumper vest. Once you have them in your vehicles, go back inside and get a can each of .556, .308, nine-millimeter, fifty-caliber ammo, and two belts of twelve-gauge shells. Donnie, get ten rounds of forty HE for training. Let me know when you've loaded the ammo in your vehicle, I'll be in the kitchen."

Once they had loaded everything, they reported to Jack in the kitchen. He was sipping a bottle of water and as they came up, he smiled and motioned for them to sit at the table. He sat also and said, "Okay, we'll start tomorrow morning, so have a good breakfast of some kind. It'll be a long day and I guarantee you'll sleep well tomorrow night. I want the two of you," indicating Donnie and Tim, "at my place on Marine Hill in the morning as training begins at 0700. Report in full combat gear and all your equipment in one vehicle. Once you've picked me up, we'll go get Donna then head to our place of training. You know where we cut wood up above Centennial?"

Everyone said they did, so Jack continued with, "That's where we're going. Dan, Jeff, and I have already set some things out for us to use as targets."

He noticed the three had concerned looks on their faces and he said, "Look, I know you're worried and nervous about what's coming. I am too. We're all going to do fine," he said smiling. "Make no mistake, though, you're going to work your butts off for the next several weeks. And I'll be with you every step…and I'll pray that God, His Son, and His Holy Spirit are with us every step, too." He looked at each in the eye and smiling, said, "Go on, get out in the front room and when TJ's done, go get some sleep. Let's pray together then I'll see you when we start training."

They rose and took each other's hands and prayed. They each shook Jack's hand and Tim, Donnie, and Donna went and sat in the front room. Jack sat back down and waited for TJ, Dan, and Jeff. He thought about the events that were about to unfold and said another silent prayer for guidance and safety for everyone.

Dan, Daniel, Shirley, and Vito got up and had gone to the library. Inside, Dan began by saying, "I know all of you already know about mortars and that's a good thing. It'll take less time for training. We'll start soon. We've already loaded a truck with mortars and ammo, and a few drones for our training like TJ said. In a few minutes, we're going to go into the armory and select weapons – an M4, a nine-millimeter and a twelve-gauge shotgun – and load ammo for each and that means seven mags for both the M4s and nines, four frags, two smokes and four bandoliers of twelve gauge. From now on, we're on a war footing and we want to see you in full combat gear for every training session. That means fully loaded, or Z'd up as we call it. Starting tomorrow, I'll be in full gear until this thing is over. A war footing to me means being ready at all times.

"In our off time I want you, and I will too, play with the drones. Fly them all over the place, even through the woods and inside buildings. We'll need to be very proficient with them when the time comes. You'll all have batteries and chargers so fly as often as you can. We'll practice bombing techniques using bags of concrete – we've already made up a few hundred of those – and we'll practice filming techniques also.

"We'll have a live-fire exercise in about a week. That means you'll be dropping live bombs and firing mortar rounds and hitting things we've already selected. When training begins, I want you to pick me up on Marine Hill at 0730. I'll have another truck there, the one with the mortars and drones, and we'll go to our area of training. TJ and I went and set targets out already. I think you'll enjoy most of the training, but I'm pretty sure we're all going to sleep very well for the next few weeks." That got some nervous chuckles.

"Any questions?" he asked. There were none so he said, "Okay, to the armory and draw weapons and ammo. Seven mags each for the M4s and nines, four bandoliers of twelve each and don't forget the grenades. I'll see you back by the kitchen table after you've put your gear in your vehicles. Let's stand and pray together. Shirley held out her hands and they all held hands together and prayed. Once they broke, the trio left for the armory and Dan went to the kitchen to wait.

Once they'd loaded everything, they met Dan and he asked if anyone had thought of any questions. None had so he said another quick prayer and dismissed his crew to the front room.

TJ, Jeff, Linda, and Dino, stayed in the great room. TJ deferred to Jeff who began by opening in prayer. Afterwards, he said, "Like TJ said, we're the assault teams. Not very big in numbers and that bothers me and TJ some, but we're it. Shirley told us more may join us when we make our play, but we'll see. Suffice it to say, we're going to train our butts off and be ready to go anyway. Dino, you'll be with me and Linda with TJ. There's a reason for that and we'll get to it later. We're going to have a rough go of it at first because we need to get close enough to use our ROVs effectively. Those things have limited battery power and that's why we need to get close. TJ has acquired more sleds we'll be using to drag our supplies and equipment to our pre-selected positions. That is going to the arduous portion of our mission. I believe it'll take us the better part of two to four days to get everything into position. Why?

"Here, gather around this aerial view of the area. As you can see, from Highway 87 to our position is a little over three and a half miles. From this point here," Jeff said pointing to a farmhouse, "TJ and Linda will have to crawl almost a half-mile, pulling a sled full of equipment along, after hauling it over three miles. You and I," he said, pointing at Dino, "have to haul our equipment a mile, then crawl another quarter mile to our position…here."

TJ motioned to Jeff and continued by saying, "Our training is going to be geared toward strength and endurance. Starting in a few days, we're going to begin a program of daily-daily fitness exercises, including running and strength training. And yes, we'll be crawling and dragging sleds with weights to build those muscle groups and stamina. Jeff and I have laid out a training area that is similar to what we'll be actually hauling and crawling through with our equipment. We're positive it'll take at least two days, and probably most of a third day to get all of our supplies and equipment to our positions – especially ours, Linda. If we need a fourth day, we'll take it."

"That'll be tough for sure, but I have a suggestion that might save us a considerable amount of time and effort," Linda said.

"What's that?" TJ asked.

She pointed at the photo and said, "From here," pointing to a house northeast of the northern tunnel entrance, "it's less than a quarter mile and for the most part, uphill. The tunnel guard won't be able to see us hauling stuff until we get here, and we can use the west side of this dirt road to drag the sleds to our position. We can drive our trucks to this point," again pointing to a house with a large structure, probably a pole barn, "and park them inside this building and haul the equipment from there."

TJ spun the photo around, so it faced he and Jeff. They both leaned over for closer looks and TJ said, "You're sure the guard won't hear the vehicles?"

"If we go on a windy day – I guarantee they won't – and there's never been more than one guard on duty at a time," Linda said. "We could pull in here," pointing again, "at noon on a cloudy and windy day and no one will be the wiser. We could rest until dark and begin hauling equipment then. It may just take one evening, maybe two, to move everything."

"Why cloudy and windy?" TJ asked.

"They usually didn't fly the drones on days like that," she answered.

"I like it," Jeff said. "It would save us a load of time and effort and you two won't be so drained of energy for the assault." TJ looked at Jeff with a concerned expression and

Jeff followed up with, "TJ, you know as well as I do as soon as the first shot is fired, the plan goes out the window. From that point on everything will be determined by the actions of the enemy and our reactive counter measures to their efforts. If it takes you and Linda three days to drag stuff, you'll be beat and almost combat ineffective. Using her idea ups your odds immensely."

"You know, we could stop by this house," Dino said pointing to the photo, "and cover the trucks engine compartments with heavy blankets to further muffle the sound. That would give us a far better advantage."

"The kid's got something there," Jeff said. "The basement in my place had fifteen or twenty of those heavy moving blankets truckers used as covers and padding. Those would work very well, and we could cover the trucks with five or six of those things and they'd really be quiet."

TJ stood and looked at his three companions. He gave a little unsure tilt of his head and said, "Okay, you've sold me for the most part. Linda…Dino…great ideas and real time and effort savers. I'm willing if you are," he said directly to Linda.

"Saving that much time would be worth the effort," she said. "If we do this, then I suggest all four of us do all the hauling at both locations. If we're hauling four sleds of equipment one way, we might be able to cut even more time off the effort. That way we may only need two days to prepare. If we need a third, it was already written into the plan, wasn't it?"

"Yes, it was," TJ said with a grin. "Great ideas folks. Okay, I'm in. We'll put your plans into action. After training, we'll meet again with some iced tea and finalize this part of the plan.

Once everyone had gathered in the main room, TJ said, "One last thing folks…Donnie, Dino, Vito, and Tim…I want you to get into that hummer tomorrow and go to Laramie and get those Zs headed south. Make sure you're Z'd up well and have extra ammo and grenades on hand. If you need two days, go ahead, and take the time but get back here as fast as you can…we have a lot of training to take care of. We'll all begin the training the day after you get back. Okay everyone, let's pray together, then have a goodnight's sleep."

Chapter 13: Training Camps

The morning of the third day since the meeting that included plan changes, Jeff and his sniper team members, Donna, Donnie, and Tim, had made their way up to the place on Centennial Ridge above the ghost town of Centennial, where they cut wood for the winter. He showed the team the view overlooking the valley and the guys, who had not been up there yet, thought it was beautiful. After the novelty wore off, Jack had them get their weapons out and set them up about thirty yards apart. They would be firing the fifties first and shooting at preset targets down in the valley.

Donnie was the skeptical one and said so, "There ain't no way I can hit anything down there from up on this mountain."

Jack chuckled and said sarcastically, "That right..."

"Well sure, that's a long way down there," Donnie said.

"Sure is," Jack agreed then motioned for his crew to follow him to the edge behind a formation of rocks. "You see that little brown box-looking thing way over there, this side of the creek and just north of Highway 130?"

Donnie and Tim, squinting, both said they did.

"That's where Doug Sutton shot and killed two people that were shooting at them up here," Jack told them. "One was by that box thing, which is a pump cover, and the other was in a hummer parked back by the creek in the shade of those trees. He killed them both and shot five times. Two misses and three hits. One hit was to take out the hummer. When we did the ranging, the shot that killed the person in the hummer was one point eight-two miles from here. Now, what were you saying about it being too far?"

Both Donnie and Tim's eyes were huge and the looks on their faces registered surprise. Finally, Tim turned to Jack and said, "Almost two miles and got them both?"

Jack simply nodded, smiling the whole time.

"I gotta try that," Tim said. "What's first?"

"Okay, then, go to your rifles and get comfortable with them," Jack instructed. "I'll help you set the shoulder foot and you can adjust everything else. All of you take a magazine with you."

The three raced to get magazines and prepare their rifles – everyone liked target practice. Jack helped to adjust the butt plates to their shoulders using the monopod foot adjustment. He told each to put in ear plugs and use the earmuffs as the explosion the rifle made when fired was a tremendous noise. Next, he told them to insert magazines and chamber a round, which they did.

Talking loudly so they could hear him, Jack said, "I want each of you to find targets below that are marked with red and orange paint. Each will have a number, one, two, or three, which you drew earlier and are positioned in front of. Give me a thumb up when you find yours."

Each quickly gave him a thumb up, and he continued saying, "Donna, you drew number one so you're first to fire. I'll spot for you so don't worry about where the bullet hits, I'll let you know. Anytime you're ready, you may fire."

Jack watched Donna snuggle into her rifle and watched as she took a deep breath and fired. He watched as the heavy bullet hit several yards in front and almost fifty to the left. He told her where she'd hit, and told her to adjust and fire again, which she did. This time, she hit just to the left and above the target. He told her where she'd hit, and she adjusted once again, and he told her to fire. This time, she hit the target about four inches high but centered.

"Nice shot – hit," he reported. "Donnie, you're number two, so go ahead, and fire your first round."

Donnie, too, snuggled into his rifle and taking a deep breath, let out about half of it and squeezed the trigger. The bullet hit just in front of the target.

"Good shot, but a little short, by about five yards. Adjust your sight and fire another round," Jack directed.

Donnie made an adjustment, sighted, and fired. The round hit in the center, just on the bottom edge of the bull's eye. "Good shot, hit on the bull, low, but center. Nice going. Tim – you're up."

Tim's first shot hit the target high and right. Jack told him, and his second round was nearly a center bull hit. Jack about wet his pants he was so excited, yelling, "Great shot!" Almost dead center. I knew I picked the right people for this job. Now, look out beyond your targets and you'll see your second set. Once you have them spotted, give me a thumb up." In rapid succession, they did so, and he told Donna to go ahead.

Her first shot hit the lower edge of the target and he told her where the hit was. She made one small adjustment and fired again, hitting the bull in the right lower quadrant.

Donnie was next and he fired, hitting the bull on the left edge, but centered. Jack told him and Donnie, making one small correction, fired his second round and hit the bull squarely in the middle. Jack gave Tim the go-ahead and his first shot was a hit, center right on the bull.

"Great shooting you three," Jack congratulated them. "I knew I'd picked the right people for the fire-team. Okay, to the north, looking through your scopes, you'll find an old truck out in that field just west of the creek…find it. He waited a moment and got three thumbs up from the trio. "That's your target. Empty the magazine you've got in your rifles into it - light it up."

Jack focused his binoculars on the old truck and had to back up some from the concussion of the multitude of rounds going off at the same time. The old truck threw pieces of itself all over the field. Great spouts of dust rose from the ground beyond the old vehicle as the rounds passed through it and impacted the earth beyond. When the three had empty magazines, the truck looked like a kitchen colander.

"Donnie," Jack asked, "What do you think of distance now?"

"I guess these things can reach out there a way, huh?" Donnie said rather meekly. They all chuckled.

"That truck…is one and a quarter mile from here," Jack said looking at Donnie as his head whipped around and looking at the truck again, his face with a surprised look.

"Wow, and we all hit it…a lot!" Donnie practically yelled.

All four laughed.

"Good shooting, people," Jack congratulated them again. "Okay, team, you've each fired ten rounds so should be feeling fairly sore right now. If you can shoot like that with a fifty then you'll have no trouble with a .308. We'll shoot those another day and sight them in good. Pick 'em up and we'll go back and clean 'em up. I'm going to buy all of you a beer."

Back-slapping and hugs were going around as the trio put their rifles in Jack's truck. Jack was satisfied with their shooting and with their acceptance of each other on the fire-team. The first day of training was a resounding success.

TJ, Jeff, Linda, and Dino studied maps and photos, and discussed options for attack all day the first day of training. The second day, they played with ROVs, driving them all over the front and back yards of Paradise Valley, laughing a great deal. They played tag with the remote vehicles and raced back and forth up and down the lane.

The third day found them packing the ROVs with payloads of different weights and getting the feel of the heavily laden vehicles as they went up and down hills, over rocks, small tree limbs they'd cut for the purpose, and once again racing the vehicles up and down the lane. Laughter fostered the mood and teasing about whom was the best ROV operator poured out. Each was better than the others, of course.

Day five found the assault teams once again buried in maps, photos, and hand-drawn schematics of the underground lab complex in Colorado. TJ had previously called a special meeting of all the folks that had been inside the complex and had them gather in the library to put on paper everything they could remember about the place. Based on that information, they had an almost perfect diagram of the underground complex along with approximate tunnel lengths and distances added. It would be used to lay out a close-quarter battle arena mimicking the Colorado complex. Specifically, they would build a mock-up of the complex for training purposes. The only sections they would build to near specifications would be the two areas they would specifically attack. The valley residents would begin constructing the CQB training area the following day in a field they'd selected east of Sheep Mountain.

Ten days later found Dan, Daniel, Shirley, and Vito, back at the airport training range they'd set up for their mortars. Using the south side of the airport was good as the explosions wouldn't spook the animals nor upset the other residents of the valley. The targets were down the ridge in an arroyo bottom that was sandy and rocky, with little chance of fire starting from the exploding munitions.

As with every day of training so far, the foursome began by running around the parameter of the runways. That equated to almost a ten kilometer, or six-mile run. Taking a few minutes to let their bodies recover after their jaunt, and sipping water from their canteens, the four sat quietly enjoying the peaceful time.

Shirley broke the silence saying, "It sure is a beautiful day today, huh."

"Yeah, no wind hardly and that's a blessing running around the runways with all this gear every day," Daniel said.

"You never did like running," Vito said.

"It's okay, but I can do without it," Daniel retorted.

"Easy, team," Dan said to the three. "Don't get your panties in a bind now."

The three broke into laughter at that. Dan got up from where he was sitting and looking around, didn't see any Zs about and went to the back of the truck. He pulled out a two-wheeled dolly and then began putting a few crates of mortar rounds on to take to the firing area. It was about fifty yards in front of where they parked the truck.

He walked past the three young'uns going to the 'pits', when Daniel yelled, "Dan, get down! Drone!"

Dan dropped flat as did the three. Dan yelled back asking, "Which direction?"

"Your nine o'clock, out about two klicks to the southeast," Daniel yelled back.

"Vito, can you pull a Stinger out?" Dan yelled, since Vito was closer to the truck doors.

Vito low crawled back to the truck and opened the back door. Every day they'd brought one Stinger for just such an occasion and he withdrew the weapon and activated the seeker head on the missile. It immediately gave a whine and Vito knew the weapon was good to go.

"Daniel, point to the thing," Vito said, looking at Daniel from the side of the truck.

Daniel pointed to the southeast and up about forty degrees. Vito looked and finally saw the drone heading right at them. He lifted the missile and activated the radar mechanism, and the Stinger immediately gave a tone indicating it had a lock. Just as Vito fired, he saw a smoky trail leave the drone, heading their direction. He yelled, "INCOMING! Run west!" and dropped the missile launcher and ran to the north himself, seeing Shirley and Daniel jumping up and heading west.

Dan stayed down when he heard Vito yell and covered his head. He was about thirty yards from the truck.

The Stinger struck first since it was much faster than the Hellfire missile, and hit the drone blowing it to pieces. The drone-fired Hellfire missile struck just behind the cab of the truck, at the midpoint, and exploded after passing completely through the vehicle. That was the good thing as the result of the explosion sent most of the debris and shrapnel to the southeast. That included most of the exploding mortar shells from the truck.

The cab and engine compartment lifted up and crashed just short of where Dan was lying. He was hit with several pieces of shrapnel in his back and the backs of both legs and was grazed on the scalp by another piece that knocked him unconscious.

As soon as they heard the explosion the three running to the north and west dropped flat. And good thing they did so as the exploding mortar rounds were sending fragments in all directions. All three were hit. Daniel took several shards of shrapnel to his right side, right arm, and leg. Vito was hit twice in the right leg and once in the arm.

Shirley took the worst of the hits, being hit in the abdomen, her upper right chest and just above her right ear. She was out cold and bleeding profusely from all three of her wounds.

It took several moments for Daniel and Vito to shake off the concussion affects and as Daniel rose, he yelled, "Shirley's hit!" and crawled over to her. He immediately began first responder actions and placed dressings over the head wound and the abdominal wound. He wasn't sure, but the chest wound might have been a sucking chest wound so he covered it with plastic, then sealed it with tape and wrapped a bandage around her torso to hold it in place.

Vito heard Daniel yell about Shirley and looked, seeing Daniel was administering first aid, he looked for Dan and saw him lying unconscious. He struggled to his feet and staggered over to Dan and seeing the head wound bleeding, yelled, "Dan's hit, too! I'm on it!" and knelt next to Dan to administer first responder treatment.

Once Daniel saw that Shirley looked out of danger and breathing on her own, he checked himself and dressed his wounds. He looked over to where Dan and Vito were and yelled, "Need help?"

"No, I got it!" Vito yelled. "He's bleeding from a head wound and has several hits on his back and legs. How's Shirley?"

"She's out cold and that's probably a good thing," Daniel yelled back. "She's got bad head and chest wounds and another in her abdomen. I think she has a sucking chest wound, but she's breathing okay for now. What are we going to do?"

"Hang on, I'm hit, too," Vito yelled back. "Can you come over and help me with my arm?"

"On my way," Daniel yelled and got up sluggishly and staggered to his friend. "Oh, man, you got hit good on the arm," he said pulling another battle dressing out of his first aid kit. How's your leg?"

"Huh, oh, man, I didn't know about that 'till now," he said surprised. He pulled another battle dressing out and wrapped his leg while Daniel finished dressing the wound on his arm.

Dan moaned right then and tried to move but Vito put his hand on him and said, "Don't move Dan, you're hit and we're working on you now. Stay down, brother."

Dan slowly shook his head and moaned, "What about the drone?"

"I got it, but it got us, too," Vito said. "Hellfire hit the truck. Shirley's hit bad and Daniel thinks she has a sucking chest wound. She's stable for the moment. All four of us got hit. I got hit in the arm and leg and Daniel's hit in his side, arm, and leg. Shirley has a head wound, the sucking chest wound, and an abdominal wound. You got hit in the head, back, and legs, but not too bad. Got a headache?"

Dan actually chuckled and said, "Yeah, feels like I was on a bender last night."

Vito and Daniel laughed. "He's going to be fine," Vito said to Daniel.

"I'm going back and check on Shirley," Daniel said and got back up and limped back to her. She was still out cold, and he figured that was a good thing. He raised her feet and put her in a shock preventative position. She was breathing okay, but he was concerned as her color was awfully pale. He took her pulse and it felt thready as her heart was beating rapidly. He remembered from his buddy care class to position her on her injured side when a chest or abdominal wound was present, so he rolled her onto her right side. She took a deeper breath once he moved her, and she moaned.

"Shirley, if you can hear me, this is Daniel. Don't move, girl, you're hit and hurt pretty bad. Stay still, okay?" He was worried about her and yelled over his shoulder for Vito to come over as soon as he could.

The truck was still burning sending a black smoke cloud into the sky and from time-to-time another mortar round would cook off. The drone had crashed about a mile away and Daniel could see a smoky tendril rising into the sky from there.

The exploding munitions had finally stopped. Daniel stood and going over to the wreckage, found what was left of his field pack and he found Shirley's and dragged both over to her. He put her feet up on one and dug in his pack and pulled out his poncho liner and covered her with it.

That was when he heard the vehicle approaching.

"COVER!" he yelled to Vito, who dropped next to Dan.

Daniel pulled his nine and chambered a round. He looked back and saw Vito doing the same. Daniel reached over Shirley and pulled her sidearm and chambered a round in it as well and waited with both side arms aimed in the direction of the sound.

It was a great sigh of relief as Vito yelled to him, "It's TJ! Looks like he's got Jeff, Jack, and Ruth with him."

Daniel about passed out from the relief of hearing that news. TJ's truck slid to a stop next to Dan's destroyed vehicle and they piled out with weapons ready. TJ saw that Vito and Dan were both bloody and ran over to them, dropping to his knees he asked, "What happened?" as Jeff, Jack, and Ruth slid to a stop next to him.

"Drone got us with a Hellfire," Vito said, and then looking to Ruth, said, "Shirley's hit bad, but can you help Daniel?" he asked her pointing.

Ruth gave a little groan as she looked and saw a blood-covered Daniel working on Shirley who was also blood covered. She dashed over to the pair as did Jeff and together they worked on the two while TJ and Jack worked on Vito and Dan.

"Where's the drone now?" TJ asked Vito.

"I got it with a Stinger," Vito said. "Just as I fired, it fired and…well you see the resu…" He didn't finish his statement as his eyes went back into his head and he passed out. Jack caught him and gently laid him down next to Dan and arranged him into an anti-shock position.

"TJ, this ain't good," Jack said. "I'm going to drive back and get more help and more vehicles. These folks are hurt bad."

"Leave us everything you can and have Tim, Donnie, and Dino, get Stingers and get ready for more drones," TJ said.

"Got it," Jack said and jumped up. He threw everything out of the truck he thought they might need including the first aid kit, jumped in, turned around, and floored the thing for all it was worth. He was doing almost a hundred miles per hour when he started down the hill towards the valley and got on the radio. "Paradise, Paradise, this is Jack, you there?"

"Go ahead, Jack," Donna answered almost immediately and happily.

Jack told her to alert Tim, Donnie, and Dino, and told her to get all the medical equipment she could that the team was hit badly. He didn't let up on the gas until he slowed for the turn to Paradise Valley. Once on the lane, he saw the gate already open and flew through, skidding to a stop in front of the house. Donna was already on her way out with two bags slung over her shoulders and threw them in the back. She flew back into the house and came out a moment later with a Stinger and several M4s over her shoulders and put them in the back also.

She jumped in the front passenger seat and said, "Floor it," which Jack did with a stomp of his foot. "Linda has DD," Donna said as they turned onto the main road. "What happened up there?"

Jack spun the tires in the dirt and sped back to Highway 130, where he really floored the truck once he hit pavement, he answered her question saying, "Drone attack. Hellfire missile hit the truck and all four of them are hit; Shirley's hit real bad with a head wound, sucking chest wound, and an abdominal wound. Daniel has several wounds as does Vito, who passed out from blood loss as we got there. Dan has a head wound and several wounds on his back and legs. Daniel and Vito did first aid and that probably saved all their lives." He was flying past the junction with Highway 11 and noted another truck pulling out behind them. He correctly figured it was Linda with DD and would be along to help.

He also knew Donnie, Tim, and Dino would be at Marine Hill with Stingers before they reached the top of the hill. He was glad Donna had thrown another one in the back seat for their own protection. He looked over at her and she was praying. He drove on, mashing the gas pedal for all it was worth.

Back at the airport, TJ and Jeff were working furiously on the three wounded the worst. They had moved Dan and Vito over next to Shirley, so they could better treat the trio. Daniel was sitting against TJ's truck, watching. Every so often, either TJ or Jeff would stand up and scan the sky, especially to the south and southeast watching for drones.

Jack and Donna pulled in and screeching to a stop near the casualty collection point, jumped out with the packs of medical gear. Donna knelt next to Shirley and asked TJ, "She looks pale, she breathing okay?"

"So far," TJ answered, grimly. "She's coughed a few times and moaned a few times but is unconscious. She hasn't woken since we got here. The head wound has stopped bleeding and I looked and pulled a small piece of shrapnel out and redressed the wound. That should be okay. The chest and abdominal wounds have me concerned. I don't think it's a sucking chest wound but left the plastic on just in case. It looks like a piece of shrapnel hit one of her ribs and lodged between two of 'em.

"The abdominal wound…I don't know. I looked but couldn't see any metal or anything so it must be deep. I don't know how much damage has been done inside. Do we need to look?"

"Yes, I have some probes in the pack so I'll see if I can follow the wound track," Donna said. "Jack, would you open that pack for me, please?"

Jack opened the pack and began placing instruments and things on a blanket he'd spread out. Donna pointed at one pack he pulled out and he handed it to TJ, who opened it.

"I need gloves, Jack, please," Donna asked, "and one of those big bottles of betadine in the other pack, thank you." She sounded so serious and professional suddenly.

TJ handed the gloves to her and watched her put them on. Next, she asked for four-by-fours and had TJ open the pack for her. She reached in and pulled the sterile pads from the pack and Jack knelt next to her with the betadine. She told him to open the bottle and pour the liquid onto the four-by-fours, which she then used to swab a large area around the abdominal wound. She did this several times hoping it would create enough of a sterile field for her to do what she had to do.

She sat back on her legs and looked at TJ, taking a deep breath said, "Please pray for both of us."

"I been prayin' ever since I got here, darlin'," he responded.

She looked at him and gave a strained smile and motioned for the probe pack which TJ opened. She reached in and took one of the sterile probes out and taking another deep breath, spread the wound opening with her gloved fingers. Shirley groaned a little, but Donna continued, slowly inserting the device, following the wound track. She'd gone in about an inch when she felt metal and said so. She directed Jack to get another pack of instruments from the backpack and after he opened it, selected a sterile eight-inch straight Kelly hemostat. She opened the locked forceps and slowly inserted the instrument into the wound until she felt the metal. She spread the forceps wider and tried to clamp it onto the metal. It took several attempts, but Donna was finally successful locking onto the piece and ever so slowly pulled the shrapnel from the wound. Shirley moaned once again and Donna, TJ, and Jack, all looked at their patient with concern.

Donna looked closely at the metal fragment and finally said, "I don't see any fecal matter, so I don't think her intestines were perforated. I certainly hope not as if they have been, there's not much we can do for her."

"I can," Linda said, standing there holding DD. That made the three startle and jump as they didn't realize she had arrived.

"What do you mean, you can?" TJ asked.

"I was a vet tech before I joined the Army and assisted with surgeries on animals many times. I've even closed intestinal wounds and closed abdominal wounds before," she explained, then added, "But I agree with Donna, if there is no fecal matter on that piece of metal, then the likelihood she has intestinal damage is small. We'll see in about three days, however."

"Why three days?" Jack asked.

"That's about how long it'll take for infection to set in from a fecal…leak," she explained.

"Oh," Jack responded.

"Do we just wait?" TJ asked.

"That's about all we can do at this point…unless…," she ended.

"Unless what," from Donna.

"If we anesthetize her some way, I could do an exploratory and see if there is any damage," she explained. "If not, we'll close her up and she, from her abdomen that is, should be okay in six weeks or so if infection does not set in. The chest wound…Donna, you should see if you can get the shrapnel out of there also."

Donna nodded and looking at Jack, said, "More four-by-fours and betadine, another probe and another hemostat, please."

When she had everything together, she once again cleaned a large area around the chest wound, inserted the probe, and noted the piece of metal was very shallow so she got the forceps and slowly pulled the fragment out. She took suture material and closed the wound, bandaging with fresh, sterile dressings and bandages. She then closed the abdominal wound in the same manner. Once she was done, she checked and cleaned the head wound and using suture material closed it. Afterwards she cleaned up the area and looked up at TJ who had the strangest look on his face.

"What?" she asked him.

"I'm going to call you Doc from now on," he answered with a satisfied smile.

"That was really great, Donna," from Daniel who had joined the group.

"Yeah, a real trooper," Dan said from his spot. He had regained consciousness enough to watch what had transpired. "If I yell for a corpsman, it'll be you I'm yelling for, Doc."

Jack put his hand on her shoulder and smiling, said, "That's the biggest compliment a Marine can give to a corpsman, Doc. You're a hero."

"I think somebody should check on Vito…he's still out," Daniel said to the crowd.

Donna jumped up and Linda went over also. The bandage on his leg wound was soaked through with blood as was the bandage on his arm. Linda folded up a shirt that was hanging out of a pack and put it under his armpit, while Donna cut the bandage away and started working on the arm wound. She pulled a small piece of metal out and closed the wound with sutures, redressed with several layers of four-by-fours and bandaged the arm using an elastic wrap.

"That should slow the bleeding some on the arm," she said to Linda. "Now the leg."

They did the same thing on the leg and this time, had a hard time getting the metal fragment out of his muscle. It had twisted as it entered and was buried deeply in the tissue. It took her several attempts, but finally removed the almost two-inch sliver of metal. It was definitely a piece of mortar round as it was painted OD green and had yellow lettering. She set it aside and probed for more metal and finding none, closed the wound with sutures and redressed and bandaged it. She covered him with a blanket and went back to Shirley.

"She moved her head a minute ago," TJ said. "I'm praying she'll pull through."

"Add Vito to that list, he's lost a lot of blood," Donna said, apprehensively.

"How are we gonna get them back?" Daniel asked.

They all looked at each other with blank stares. They didn't have any litters or anything that came close.

TJ finally broke the spell saying, "Jack…Jeff…Linda, go over to the airport terminal and see if there is a first aid room or something and see if they have litters or a gurney, would you?"

"We're on it," Jack said and headed for his truck with Jeff and Linda in tow. They drove to the terminal and knocking loudly on the doors to see if any Zs were inside, waited. Sure enough, several of the creatures ambled towards the front door. The three prepared their side arms and Jack opened the door. As the creatures drew near, the three opened fire and dropped seven of the things. They waited for a few more minutes and then went inside.

Jeff found a marquee plate on the wall and it directed them to a nurse's station where they found not only a gurney, but more medical equipment and supplies and four military-style folding litters. They took it all and drove back to the site.

TJ, Jack, Jeff, Donna, and Linda all helped to get Shirley onto the gurney. They covered her with blankets and put her in the back of Jeff's truck. Dan and Vito were put on litters and placed in the back of TJ's truck. Daniel got into the back seat on his own. Once everyone was on board one truck or another, they left the scene and headed for Paradise Valley, which would be the make-shift hospital for the time being.

They put Shirley in the library. Dan was put in TJ and Donna's bedroom and Vito in the guest bedroom. Vito woke and said his leg was hurting badly. Donna sent TJ for a bottle of scotch and gave the young man a two-fingered shot with two extra strength aspirins. He was going to sip the scotch, but Donna said to down it. Poor kid choked so badly he almost threw up his aspirins. After the coughing spasms passed, he settled down and after several minutes, looked at Donna and grinning, said, "That's much better."

She gave him another two fingers of scotch and said to sip it down in the next half hour. She moved over to Dan and inspecting his wounds, cleaned, redressed, and bandaged them, gave him a double which he promptly downed and then sipped the refill to take his aspirins. He would be fine in a few days.

Daniel finally had his turn with the 'Doc,' and she sutured his wounds after pulling fragments. She gave him scotch and aspirins also. He was able to get around and hadn't lost very much blood so was out of danger. They were worried about Shirley and Vito. Shirley because of the risk of infection, and Vito, because he'd lost so much blood. Donna knew that once he fell asleep, he would most likely be out for ten to twelve hours if not longer.

She stayed with Shirley, constantly feeling her forehead for any signs of a fever coming on. They had electronic thermometers, but she really didn't trust them. She very much wished they had one of the old mercury thermometers from the past. The one they were using said her temperature was 99.2 degrees. That could be normal for her. They'd have to wait and see.

TJ surprised her with a plate of fresh fruit, crackers and cheese, and some cucumber spears. He'd brought her a glass of sweet tea also, which she promptly drained. He smiled and took the glass and refilled it. She had not realized how thirsty and hungry she had become and was thankful TJ had remembered for her.

Jack, Jeff, and Linda decided their welcome was over and left around midnight. Jack had assured TJ that there would be an all-night watch put into effect for the time being and Stingers would always be ready. Ruth and DD moved back into the Paradise Valley Underground to help with patient care which was much appreciated by Doc Donna and TJ.

The next morning, TJ stepped out onto the front porch for a few moments of peace and quiet and to sip his coffee. He was stunned, as when he stepped out, he found to his amazement every valley resident in his front yard. Most were watching; several were praying, and a few reading Bibles. It was the most touching thing he'd ever seen and almost moved him to tears.

It had become quiet as soon as he stepped out, so he moved to the front step and said, "It's going to be a while, but I think they'll all pull through. Pray especially for Shirley and Vito. They're still critical." He turned to go back inside but hesitated and turned back to the group and said, "Thank you all for the support. I love all of you." He turned quickly and went inside as he didn't want the folks to see his tears of pride and joy.

Training had come to a complete stop since the drone attack at the airport. The valley residents kept three of the four patients in Paradise Valley for an extended time. Daniel, the least injured of the four, was out on his own with instructions to watch for infection and to take it easy for a week or so. At the first sign of a fever or wound discharge, he was to see Doc Donna, Linda, or Ruth immediately.

Dan was healing nicely as was Vito. Dan's head wound still caused him to get dizzy if he got up too fast or moved to the side quickly. His back and leg wounds were going to be an irritant but wouldn't limit his movement. Vito's leg would take time to heal. The blood loss was still making him fatigue quickly. It would be days, possibly two weeks, before he felt anywhere near back to normal. Dan would be released within a day or two with the same instructions as Daniel.

The operation as a whole was put on hold much to the chagrin of TJ. The only positive from the attack was he and his team were now augmented by Jack and his team. They were proceeding with building the close quarter battle (CQB) area and the construction project was making progress. TJ and his three team members were already taking runs with the ROVs, testing their endurance in the CQB, and learning their different capabilities and ranges. The information they were collecting would be beneficial to the overall effort. In the end, they would have a live-fire exercise and detonate several of the ROVs in the areas where they planned doing so in the actual complex. Not only that, but the teams would practice dropping bombs using the drones. They wanted to be as proficient as they possibly could with everything, and training together as a team was the key.

The drone attack had destroyed Dan's truck, and along with it, three cases of mortar rounds and two mortar tubes, several M4s and a pair of twelve-gauge shotguns, not to mention the ammunition for each and the magazines. The valley still had two more complete sets of mortars and about three hundred rounds of ammunition. The M4s, shotguns, and ammunition for each could be easily replaced from the supplies on hand in the valley.

It had been ten days since the attack and all four of the mortar team members were doing much better. Even Shirley was up and about, although moving slowly because of her abdominal wound which would take longer to heal. She and Vito had been very fortunate in their recovery. Dan and TJ both said it was due to the quick actions of Vito and Daniel. In addition, the ministrations of both Doc Donna and Ruth, who constantly fussed over the pair, cleaning their wounds, putting on fresh dressings and bandages, and giving them antibiotics from the supplies on hand they had scrounged from local pharmacies. Too, it was due to God's good grace they healed.

The prayer from the valley residents had something to do with it as TJ was quick to tout.

Dan still experienced dizziness from time-to-time and his back and leg wounds itched something fierce. Daniel…was Daniel. He always seemed to not be bothered by his wounds or by the fact they had been attacked. His easy-going demeanor left most of the original valley residents wondering if maybe some of his mental ammunition was laced with blanks. Jeff was the one who said that Daniel's elevator didn't go all the way up. But they loved the kid and enjoyed having him and all the others around. Truth be told, the young man was just a real easy-going kind of guy.

The valley community was growing and that was an exceptional thing in the days they were in. They had grown from seven to fourteen in only a few months – their population doubling in size. And, considering what they knew about the underground labs in Colorado, they just may double again or more before too long. Because of the drone attack, TJ and Dan had decided to ask the new 'kids' if they wanted to try and get a few more of their friends out before the attack. He called for an all-valley powwow that would take place at Dan's home on Marine Hill.

The three Marines grilled elk and deer steaks and roasts for the dinner, and served it with salad made with fresh lettuce, spinach and kale, freshly chopped radish, and tomatoes from their garden. Ruth had made cookies. Dinner was served with iced water and tea. The Marines had set out a huge plywood table on sawhorses and covered the thing with sheets. Lanterns were set out on the makeshift table and everyone laughed and kidded with each other, and played with DD, passing him from person to person. The two-year-old loved the attention. The prayer for the meal was given by Shirley.

After dinner, Dan used his butter knife and tapped his glass calling for everyone's attention. "I hope all of you have had as good a time as I have this evening," he began. "Thank you, Shirley, for that lovely and heartfelt prayer for dinner tonight.

I'm sure we all agree on that. I feel the Lord has had direct input on our wounded warriors' wounds," he said pointing at the new scar on his head. "TJ and I decided to call this meeting for an important reason."

"Just a few months ago, we were seven people in this valley, and feared for our lives and for our very existence every minute. With all the attacks we've gone through and losing three of our loved ones, we were low on hope…if you know what I mean. Then, through a miracle, in just a few weeks' time we doubled in population. We are now fourteen," he said smiling and looking at all the new faces.

"From what you newer folks have told us, there are more in the Colorado complex that would in all likelihood join our little village, and that's what this meeting is about. TJ and I talked for quite a while the other day, and we feel it may be time to make another trip down there and see if any of your friends want to attempt to escape and join us. That being said, I'd like to open the meeting up to discussion, so if you have any thoughts on this, now's the time," and Dan motioned to the group and sat down.

Shirley was first and said, "I'm still busted up some, but I'll go."

"Let's do it," Daniel quickly agreed.

"I'm in," Tim said.

Vito said, "I know at least three that would boogie in a second if given the chance…I'm in, too."

Jeff said, "I'll drive."

"Me too," from Jack.

"I'll be camp gofer," Ruth added. "DD can issue smiles." That brought laughter from everyone.

Donna quickly said she would help Ruth and DD.

Linda said, "I think we should approach it like we did with Daniel, send in a note with a plan for the escape. They would have to plan their portion of the exfil, and we would be ready on the outside to cover and with vehicles, food, water, whatever, and haul it back here."

"I'll do whatever I can," Dino said.

"I'm in, too," Daniel finally said, but hesitantly.

"Why are you hesitant, Daniel?" Dan asked.

He shrugged his shoulders and said, "Just seems dangerous to try something like that is all."

"Everything we do now is dangerous," Dan said to him in a gentle, fatherly way.

Daniel looked up at him and said, "I guess so, huh?"

TJ motioned for Dan and Dan pointed and gave a little upward flick of his head at him giving him the nod to continue. TJ stood and looking around the table and seeing all the faces looking at him, said, "Dan and I did talk a long time over this. We know it'll be dangerous. They still have three or four drones we know of and that is a very real danger. And we're not sure of any other capabilities they may have, and the warning you gave about the Sergeant Major – he seems like a wild card and unpredictable. You seven new folks have given us as complete an understanding of their capabilities as you could, and we appreciate it to no end. They still may have something up their sleeves we don't know about. And for one, I'm worried about their biological capabilities. Knowing now they're the reason we faced this worldwide pandemic it makes me wonder what they may do to us if we're successful with this escape plan. Maybe they'll load up a drone with a biological weapon and fly it over the valley."

Daniel meekly raised his hand and every eye turned to him. TJ said, "Daniel…you have something to say about that?"

"Yes, sir," almost a whisper.

"Okay, son, let's hear it," TJ prompted.

He sat there with his head down for a moment, unsure of himself, but finally lifted up and actually stood. He looked at everyone and suddenly his face seemed to change, to harden, and said, "Then I say we don't give them the opportunity. I know they have that capability and have wondered why they haven't chosen to use it yet. It may be because they want this valley, and if they use a biological on it, then they can't have it, if you know what I mean. What I'm saying is, we get a note to them like Linda said, but as soon as the last one that wants to come with us is out…" he hesitated.

"Go ahead, Daniel," TJ prompted.

Daniel looked up again with a serious look on his face, took a deep breath, and said, "As soon as the last one is out…we attack with full force. Blow the crap outta the place and fry everything and everyone in there."

Dan and TJ looked at each other and smiled as that was the gist of their plan. TJ, with a big smile on his face said, "Daniel, you've hit the nail on the head as that was what our plan actually calls for. You're very perceptive, young man," TJ said, beaming. "So, everyone is for this, right?"

A chorus of yesses and pounding on the table arose from the twelve. Even Tim and Dino stood and raised their fists yelling 'yeah, yeah, yeah,' and immediately many separate conversations began around the big table.

Dan motioned for TJ and the two moved off for a bit and Dan said, "I bet you and I weren't the only ones thinking about this, huh?"

TJ snickered and said, "I'm not taking that bet because I'd lose. You want to try to plan tonight or let them blow off some steam, get some rest, and have another meeting with a select group tomorrow?"

"Let 'em blow off some steam," Dan agreed. "I'll tell the group the plan and have the team leaders along with Ruth, Linda, Daniel, and Tim, join you and I up on top of the Underground tomorrow for a lunch meeting, say elevenish?"

"Sounds good; come on, let's join the festivities," TJ said, then, "You have any eighteen-year-old lying around?"

Together they went inside and came out with tumblers of scotch and joined in on the conversations going around the table.

The discussions went past midnight when Dan stood and announce a halt to the gathering, stating everyone needed their rest, especially Shirley and Vito. He then told them about the lunch meeting the following day and everyone broke, cleaning up and heading to their own homes. Donna drove back to Paradise Valley since TJ had the scotch.

The valley became quiet shortly after that, save for the animal noises and the gurgling of the rivers and creeks. A lone coyote was yelping to the north out in the valley; elk were bugling to the west and up on Centennial Ridge; a cow wailed down in the pasture and a single whinny from a horse sounded in the valley bottom near the river.

Daniel stepped out of his place and looked at the night sky with the millions and billions of stars and heard the animal sounds. He breathed deeply and stretched. He enjoyed living where he was and loved having the friends he did. He silently prayed a prayer of thanksgiving for them, the other residents of the valley, and thanked the Lord for steering him to this place, this paradise valley indeed, a true land of milk and honey. He decided he could live here comfortably forever. He stretched once again and took in another deep breath, looked at the night sky once more, smiled and with a light-hearted step, went back inside. He was resolute in his decision to rid the world of the threat from the Colorado complex, and in the process help to create a peaceful existence for everyone in the valley.

Chapter 14: Discussions, Decisions, Duty

By one o'clock the next afternoon, the eight met on top of the Underground, and had already made several decisions about their mission. They had opened in prayer and had asked God for guidance and success. TJ brought his Bible and turning to Paul's first letter to the Corinthians, chapter nine, read verses fifteen through nineteen, "$_{15}$But I have not used any of these rights. And I am not writing this in the hope that you will do such things for me. I would rather die than have anyone deprive me of this boast. $_{16}$Yet when I preach the gospel, I cannot boast, for I am compelled to preach. Woe to me if I do not preach the gospel! $_{17}$If I preach voluntarily, I have a reward; if not voluntarily, I am simply discharging the trust committed to me. $_{18}$What then is my reward? Just this: that in preaching the gospel I may offer it free of charge, and so not make use of my rights in preaching it. $_{19}$Though I am free and belong to no man, I make myself a slave to everyone to win as many as possible."

After he read this, he closed and set his Bible on the table, looked at every face at the meeting and said, "What this means to me, especially verse nineteen, is like Paul, I'm free, and I chose to make myself a slave in the effort to free as many as possible and bring them not only into our family, but into God's family. Just as Jesus says in Matthew chapter twenty-eight, it's my duty. Later on, in the same letter from Paul I read, he says that whatever we do, we need to do it for the glory of God, and also says that we should not be seeking our own good, but the good of many, so that they may be saved. After reading this I prayed and got a really good feeling that we're now doing the right thing. I actually felt relief, and as I stood from my praying, I felt invigorated and energized. I wanted to go right then and do this.

"I hope all of you feel the same way as I. If not, pray. Then pray some more. We're going to save our brothers and sisters and bring along any others that want a better life. I am at peace with the decision to rid the planet of the threat from the Colorado complex scientists.   We'll have our own scientists, but they'll know God and know that His science is perfect and that they can only prove it with their attempts to replicate or do things better through their endeavors.

"Dan and I suggest we load the trucks and get everything ready. Once that's done, then we take a day or two off and have a church service together, a pre-launch feast here in Paradise Valley, and then a full day of rest and relaxation before we deploy. Everyone in agreement with that?" Yeses' and nods from everyone. "Dan…" TJ ended.

"Okay, everyone, we need…"

The discussion led to decisions and with pencils to paper, they wrote those down. They added supply and equipment listings for everyone and every team. They planned as much as they could and by four o'clock, were satisfied.

Linda, Shirley, Donna, and Ruth would pen the letter to hand off to the remnant in the lab complex. Daniel, Tim, Linda, and TJ would be the ones taking the note in and handing it off to one of their friends and fellow Christians on guard duty. If the guards were not one of those people, they would return every night until there was one. While this was going on, the other people would drag the supply laden sleds and equipment to the areas chosen for the mortar and sniper teams. Once the note was delivered, the plan would go into effect on the third night afterwards. This would allow time for word to spread and a plan to be made for the escape attempt.

The teams would be ready for the lab Christians to escape from just one tunnel, or from both ends if necessary. Either way, they would be prepared. The note would direct the escapees to be the ones on guard duty that night. It would tell them to ignore sounds they heard as the teams would get

ROVs as close to the entrances as possible. Once the signal, a red laser being flashed on a wall near each guard was seen the escape process would begin. The guards would be last out and return a signal to the teams with blinking a flashlight twice. Allowing the escapee's time to move, five minutes after they make their break, the attack would begin in earnest. Additional arms and ammunition would be held in readiness for any of the escapees who wished to add firepower to the fray – they would be a welcomed addition.

TJ stood at a bit after four o'clock and said a closing prayer, blessing all the valley residents, asking for the protection of the complex Christians until the rescue attempt, and asking for God to guide them in their efforts to free them and anyone else that might want to get out of the underground lab. Everyone shook hands or hugged, and they broke up.

Back downstairs, Donna asked, "How'd it go?"

"It went great," TJ answered. "Here's the plan…" He went over the whole thing with her, Shirley, and Ruth, and all three said it was a good plan.

Ruth asked, "When do we go?"

TJ looked at her and said, "We figure another three or four days to work out any bugs the new folks might come up with. That'll give everyone time to think about supplies and equipment to take, you know, how much of what and so on. I told them to tell everyone and for all of us to write things down. I told them we'd pack here and that Dan, Jack, Jeff, and I, would get the vehicles ready. We'll take two flatbeds, the one with the fuel tanks and another, and five other trucks, two with trailers. We'll convoy down to that little town where we stayed last time and move supplies and equipment from there.

"Once we begin moving equipment, we'll have a person in the backs of the trucks with a Stinger ready to go at a moment's notice. We've decided to not take any chances. We're setting up and supplying sniper team south first and that position will be manned from then until the operation is complete. If anyone tries to launch another drone, they'll take it out before it leaves the ground as from their position, they can see that airport. We'll be giving them incendiary and armor piercing rounds for their fifties, and some of the combination armor piercing high explosive rounds. We're hoping those will cause a fire or an explosion and permanently disable or destroy the drone.

"So, ladies, get your minds going and start writing down ideas and things for supplies and equipment. We'll have another valley meeting in three days and compare notes and ideas. I want to get this over with and done as quickly as possible. Fall is just around the corner and we'll need to be doing the harvest and canning, the butchering of beef and a few pigs, hunting for elk, deer and maybe a buffalo, and getting ready for winter. We've got to cut a firewood load or two also."

"I think you guys should go over and get another buffalo or two," Ruth agreed.

"I feel that's a good idea, and I know just the Marines for the job," TJ said smiling. The ladies all laughed.

Four days later, Dan and TJ had every list and all the ideas consolidated into two comprehensive listings. The letter had been written to pass along to the Christians in the complex and sealed in an envelope. It had been compressed down to three pages, front and back, and gave the lab residents a clear understanding of what was about to happen and how they needed to respond on the third night after delivery of the letter.

The only thing the letter didn't do is tell them how they would plan their own movements inside the complex. They would need to do that on their own. One idea formulated from Daniel, was to have the lab residents signal on the second night how many and where they would be exiting from, either the western or northern portals. That was a great idea and was immediately written into the letter.

TJ and Dan, the following morning, drove the two flatbed trucks up to Paradise Valley and backed them in the area to the west of the garage. They next brought in their pickup trucks and attached trailers to both and backed them alongside the two flatbeds. Now the valley residents would begin bringing supplies and equipment to be packed and TJ had cleared out the garage so the supplies and equipment could be stored there until loaded onto the trucks.

Dan had drawn up a listing of who was riding with whom and had himself and Jack riding in one flatbed, Daniel, and Jeff in the other, with TJ leading the convoy in one of the pickups hauling a trailer. Donna, Ruth, and DD, would be in TJ's pickup, followed by Tim and Shirley, then Donnie, Vito, and Linda. Dino had decided he would drive the fifth truck alone saying he would have plenty of company on the return trip. Everyone got a kick out of that positive thinking testament.

Jack had the sky-watch duty the next morning and found him sitting in an Adirondack up on top of the Underground with a Stinger across his lap. Binoculars up and watching the sky, primarily to the south and southeast, and from time-to-time to the west towards Cinnabar Park, watching for drones.

He had just lowered the binoculars when he heard the eastern portal opening. Looking down, he saw Donna coming up with a plate holding a sausage and egg sandwich, cucumber spears, and tomato wedges. She had a napkin for him and a mug of coffee. "Hey, Marine, thought you might be hungry," she said with a smile.

He stood and helped her climb out and said, "That, my lady, is most appreciated."

"Chivalry will get you everywhere," she said with a giggle.

"Now, now, missy, just another way to say thanks," Jack said.

"Seen anything yet?" she asked him.

"Just beautiful scenery and a few animals," he replied. "Saw a pair of eagles out near Cinnabar, and a bunch of Turkey Buzzards were circling to the north. I wondered if something had died up there. Other than that, it's been quiet."

"That's a good thing," Donna said. She kept watch, taking his binos while he prayed, then ate his sandwich and veggies.

"This is great," he said. "I love eating up here – shoot, I love just being up here at all. Paradise valley is a great name for this place. The whole valley is paradise if you ask me. Have you noticed how green it is now? I can't get over how green everything is getting and how fresh the air has become. The water tastes better and there's so many animals now. It makes me wonder if this is the way it was when the first settlers arrived, you know, before the industrial revolution set in."

"Yeah, I agree with you, Jack," Donna said. "I've noticed many changes in the past few years. Everything is…well…changing for the better. Everything. Have you noticed the aspens in the fall? So golden, really vibrant in color. I've never seen them like that before and like you, I could sit up here and just look at the view for - well ever. You know?"

"Yes, ma'am, I do know. I guess the planet is repairing itself. That being said, I've also noticed the roads becoming much worse to drive on. Trees and shrubs and grasses are growing through. The frost heaves are much worse now. This trip may very well be the last we take using the vehicles, unless we make dirt roads I suppose and go around the highways. Not sure what we'll do about the bridges and overpasses when they begin to collapse."

"Yes, I know what you're talking about. I think we need to get a grader and smooth out the lane and our drive before too long. It's getting bumpy if you ask me. TJ and I were talking about building a wagon for going back and forth to Centennial for supplies and things. I thought it a good idea. Soon, we'll need to go on a roundup and collect horses and other draft animals to help with transportation. TJ said we need to start watching for solar panels and things like windmills for power. We'll be relying on wind, water, and solar power for all our home uses before too long."

"We should collect candles and things like fuels in the little cans…I can't remember the name of it. Anyway, stuff like that. I think we should take the ATVs and scour the countryside looking and inventorying everything in houses around the area and collecting things we'll need sooner rather than later."

"Have you been drinking any of the water in creeks around the area? I have and it's refreshing. I think all the pollutants are out of it now so even when we run out of bottled water, I think we'll be okay. I've been keeping all the empty bottles and will refill them here soon.

"Yes, it's much better. I went for a dip in the river the other day. It was marvelous. Cold but very refreshing. Woke me up like you just don't know. It was invigorating to say the least. I noticed the fish – there were more of them and they were larger than I'd ever seen. I want to go back to Lake Owen and fish some more and catch a bunch. We can cook them up and can them for the winter. I'm thinkin' we can do the same with vegetables, beef, chicken, pork, elk, deer…just about anything."

"I'm making jars of stew and soups right now and putting them up for winter. I made a big batch of buffalo-barley and vegetable soup the other day and put up almost thirty quart jars. I'm going to do the same with vegetable beef, vegetable chicken, tomato, and just plain vegetable soup. I should have several hundred, quart jars done when I'm through. I figure like you, we could put up beef, pork, chicken, fish, and other game the same way."

"I'm thinkin' turkey noodle soup for me. That sounds really good."

"Now that does sound good," Donna said with a thoughtful look on her face.

"We need to put up a bunch of everything for the new folks as well. I mean, hunting and fishing will do, but they'll need other sources of nourishment."

"The first year will be tough to say the least, but with the Lord's help, we'll get through. Next spring, we'll have to concentrate on getting two or three more of those underground greenhouses put in. Our two are going nuts growing things."

"Yeah, TJ was showing me around in them the other day. Those strawberries are really good."

"You stay outta my strawberries. TJ's on my list for that."

Jack began laughing then, that kind of laugh that comes from deep within. Donna joined him and together they laughed it off. Jack brought the binoculars up and took a look around the sky and satisfied no dangers were near, turned and said, "Thanks a bunch for brunch. You're a doll, you know that?"

"Thanks, Jack, I appreciate it," Donna said taking his plate and going back down the portal.

Jack sat once again on the Adirondack and resumed his duty, watching for airborne threats to their peaceful existence. He contemplated their conversation and suddenly realized they had been talking about their future. A future. What they would be doing in the winter and the following spring, planning in their minds what they would do to further their survival in the new world they lived in. He smiled, beaming, and thanked the Lord. He knew he would be there for the spring planting and building projects. Life in the valley would be good once again, peaceful, and tranquil.

Chapter 15: Action Stations & Contact

The equipment and supplies were loaded. The fuel tanks full and ready. Food, water, and most importantly, coffee, had been packed and loaded. They had prepared for a fifteen-day mission. If it took longer, they would resupply from the surrounding area and Charlie Mike, as the Marines are want to say, continue mission.

TJ stood at the top of the hill on his driveway, looking out into the valley, deep in thought. Dan walked up beside him and said, "What's the problem?"

TJ looked at him and said, "Nothing, really. I was just thinking if we'd thought of everything and can't think of anything else…you?"

"Nope. I think we're good. You ready to depart?" Dan asked.

TJ, still gazing out into the valley, nodded affirmatively, but said, "For some reason I gotta bad feeling about this suddenly. Can't put my finger on it, but somethings got me uncomfortable."

"Pre-combat jitters, that's all," Dan said. "It happens to all of us, a little doubt setting in and suddenly the feelings get compounded by the smallest things. Don't worry, Jack and I feel good enough for all of us so let it go."

"Yeah, I've noticed a kind of change in Jack…what's up with that anyway?"

"He's been swimming in the river almost every day and says he's a changed man because of it."

TJ shivered visibly and said, "Oh man, that must be freezing cold. Is he for real?"

"Yep. I went with him one day and watched him get in. I get goose bumps every time I think about it. You ready?"

TJ finally looked at Dan and said, "I guess." The pair turned and found, to their surprise, the other twelve residents standing there staring at them. TJ thought quickly and said, "I guess it's time to shove off. Come on over and lets gather together for prayer."

The residents joined hands and TJ began praying. Several other residents prayed also and after a time, Dan ended the prayer asking God to lead and guide them in their endeavor and to bless everyone with abundant life. Once he said 'Amen', everyone looked at TJ and he raised his hand with his index finger pointing upwards and rotated it in a circle. The population of the valley mounted their trucks and started engines.

TJ pulled out, followed by Dan, then the others. By mutual agreement, they decided they would go down Highway 287, so TJ turned for Laramie. They would be wary of any Zs lingering in the area after the 'boys' had led the horde to the south. They had hoped the mass of creatures had already gone through Fort Collins, and too, hoped they had taken care of a few unwanted people from the lab complex.

Highway 130 was still doing fairly well. They needed to slow down in a few places, but for the most part went along at fifty miles per hour until they pulled into Laramie. Taking a right off of I-80, they headed south on Highway 287. This highway was in a real state of disrepair. Not so much as trees and such growing through, but from disuse and frost heaves. Having to slow and go around several of these, they finally pulled into Tie Siding near noon and TJ called a halt for a break and some lunch.

The young members of the group explored the few building that remained standing and brought out things they may need in the future, such as candles and canned fuels, and for Doc Donna, a real thermometer. They put all the canned and dried goods they found in a central location and would pick it up on the return trip.

Dan and TJ began making sandwiches. Donna and Linda were slicing apples and Ruth and DD were getting out water bottles. Dan, TJ, Donna, Ruth, DD, Jack, and Jeff, sat in the shade together under some trees and ate their lunch. Small talk resulted in a conversation about building another three underground greenhouses, two near the Marines, and one up in New Albany for the kids.

After he finished his sandwich, TJ lay back and closed his eyes. As the crow flew, they only had about another twenty-five miles or so to go before reaching the place they would bivouac. They wanted to pull in as close to dark as they could so as to not draw unwanted attention from the complex. This time of the year, it didn't get dark until around eight thirty or so in the evening. They would depart Tie Siding at eight, allowing plenty of time for exploring and napping.

TJ woke when he heard one of the truck's engines start. He looked up and saw Donnie, Tim, Vito, and Dino, heading down a side road. "Where are they going?" he asked.

"To explore the ranch houses they can see," Ruth answered pointing. "One down that road and another across the highway. They're bored so went exploring. They'll be back in an hour."

"They Z up?" TJ asked.

"To the hilt," Ruth answered, "and Donnie has one of the silenced nines."

TJ chuckled and lay back down to continue his nap.

The young men had entered the first house and found it unlocked. No Zs were in the place so they went right in and began to look around. Tim found two baskets and said if they found anything, they could put the stuff in them.

Donnie looked on top of a hutch and found an old Sharps, forty-five-seventy caliber buffalo rifle and two boxes of shells. "Man, I'm going hunting with this thing," he said showing off his find to his friends. It was a single-fire, breech loading rifle with a heavy octagon barrel. A real prize the others said. Donnie took one of the big bullets from a box and dropped it in the breech.

"It's like loading a cannon or something," Vito said, snickering.

"Seems like it, huh," Donnie said as he closed and locked the breech. "This thing'll really give a Z what for, huh?"

"No foolin'," Dino said. "I wouldn't want to shoot that thing, man. Probably dislocate my shoulder."

"You always were a wimp, Dino," Vito commented with a chuckle. Dino playfully smacked him on the shoulder and the foursome laughed.

They collected the canned and dried goods and, in a work shed in back, found several boxes of nails, screws, nuts, bolts, and washers, and put them in the baskets in the back of the truck.

Another building sat across the dirt track from the house that had a line of old vehicles, trailers, and farm equipment so they headed that way to look around. Inside, they found more nuts, bolts, nails, screws, and such, along with some welding equipment and materials, and an anvil. These they put in the truck.

They climbed in and left to go to the other place across the highway. There, they found a nice house with four out-buildings. This would take a while, so they split into two groups to cover more ground.

Tim and Donnie chose the house and the big barn. Dino and Vito would take the other three out-buildings. The house didn't really have too much to offer. They did find a Winchester thirty-thirty, which Tim claimed. The few canned and dried goods they put in a box they found and after putting that in the truck, went to the barn.

There, after opening the door, they found the barn held two trucks, both covered in a thick layer of dust and all four tires flat on both, most likely from lack of use. In one stall they noted an old buckboard and the tack to go along with it, hung upon stakes on the wall to the side. It too, was covered in dust. They would tell TJ about that. Looking around, they found that the place was just another barn, with tools that catered to taking care of livestock and gardens. Finding nothing else of interest they left and went back to their truck.

Dino and Vito entered the first outbuilding and found it held farming implements. Things like hoes, shovels, machinery parts and pieces, an electric motor that went to nothing they could find, and a multitude of ropes and pulleys hanging from the center crossbeam. Nothing caught their interest, so they left.

The second building held rotting plants and seeds of some kind. It smelled horrible, so they left it almost immediately. The last building held all kinds of tools and had a large, heavy-duty workbench. The bench had two vises, one on either end, which they could see had once been used a lot. The bench top itself was heavily stained from oils and grease and what appeared to be coffee stains. A large, stained aluminum coffee cup with a dent adorned one of the vises.

"We'll have to tell TJ and Dan about this place – they may want to come back and load up all these tools later," Dino said.

Vito nodded and pointed to the door and they left. Getting in the truck, Donnie asked, "You guys see anything good?"

"Yeah," Vito said, starting the truck, "that outbuilding over there has a bunch of tools and stuff in it. We'll tell TJ and Dan about it. They may want to come back and get all that stuff one of these days."

The foursome drove back to the group and finding Dan and TJ, told them about their exploration, showing off the rifles, and telling them about the barn find with all the tools and things and about the buckboard, which TJ took keen interest in.

Eight o'clock came and the group remounted and started vehicles to pull out to their final destination. It took forty minutes to cover the remaining twenty-five miles to their bivouac area and once inside, closed the doors and began unloading their sleeping gear and food preparation kitchen supplies. They would prepare a nice meal for the evening and the four going out on the mission tonight would rest after eating as they would be departing on their mission at thirty minutes past midnight.

Everyone was claiming space for sleeping. TJ and Donna, lay their pallet close to Ruth and DD's. The New Albany folks all bunked together in a corner of the building and the Marines set up their area near the doors…of course.

At midnight, TJ, Dan, Donnie, Linda, and Tim, got up and the four that were going on the mission to deliver the letter, were getting Z'd up. They would be going fairly light since they already knew the route and area.

Donna kissed TJ, and said, "You be careful, Sheriff."

"I will, darlin', see you in a while," TJ said, smiling. He got up and headed for the truck they would be using on the run.

At the truck, TJ asked Linda, "You have the letter?"

"Sure do, TJ," she answered, patting her left shirt pocket.

Dan met him at the door and motioned for the others to join them. Once everyone was close, he whispered, "Let's pray," and they all bowed their heads. He prayed for God's work to be done that night, protection, and blessing for the four going out, and that the guard would be one of the Christian friends and would be receptive to the letter and escape plan. After he said 'Amen', he hugged Linda and shook hands with Donnie and Tim. He looked at TJ, put his left hand on TJ's right shoulder and held his right hand out for TJ to shake, and looking into TJ's eyes, said, "God be with you and keep you, my friend."

TJ did the same as Dan, and shaking his hand said, "Thank you, my friend. Tell Jack and Jeff I said to keep their powder dry for our return."

That got a smile from Dan and they parted. TJ got in the driver's seat, started the truck, and without turning on the lights, pulled out of the building and turned right onto Highway 287. The drive to their parking spot would only take fifteen minutes or so. TJ, being cautious, had already unhooked the brake lights and as they approached the parking spot, he slowed to almost a crawl. Every head inside the truck resembled radar domes rotating in all directions, searching for danger.

TJ finally stopped. Interior light bulbs had been removed so no lights came on when the doors opened. Prior to that, TJ quietly told everyone to lock-n-load their M4s and sidearm. Once everyone was prepared, he nodded and they all exited the truck, activated their night vision goggles, and immediately set off on their almost four-mile journey.

They had planned for an hour to make the trek and in actuality made it in fifty minutes. They rested and watched on the bank of the reservoir, peering over the top edge of the dam. They could see the guard standing near the tunnel entrance. He was looking to the southwest.

TJ motioned for the three to follow him and he climbed the embankment up to the dirt road they had used previously. He knelt and motioned for the three to get close and kneel with him. He whispered, "Everyone take a deep breath and let it out slowly. You ready to do this?"

The three nodded they were ready, and he whispered, "Give me a minute to get set on the dam and then go. God go with all of you and keep you, I'll be waiting for you." All three gave him a thumb up, smiling, so he nodded and turned for the dam.

TJ got into position and with his M4 ready to fire in case of trouble, waited and watched the guard and for the three that by then, had begun to sneak down the road towards the tunnel entrance.

He finally saw the three moving to his left and watching the guard, saw that whoever it was still looking to the southwest. TJ looked in that direction, but didn't see anything, so continued watching the guard and tunnel entrance.

TJ could now see the three had stopped and were conversing. He assumed they were talking about who the person was and put his M4 sites on the man standing guard, hoping, and silently praying the guy wouldn't react in a harmful manner towards his companions.

He noted movement to his left and saw Linda, slowly stand with her hands held high, palms out, and start to move towards the guard. It only took a few moments for the guard to hear her and spun, bringing his weapon to bear on the person approaching him. He was about to yell halt when Linda quietly said something to him. He quickly lowered the weapon and looked back at the tunnel entrance, making sure no one was coming and then stepped out to meet Linda.

The two stood near each other for a moment then the guard gave her a hug. TJ and the others were relieved beyond measure when that happened as they knew they had run into one of their Christian brothers.

TJ watched as the two continued talking for several more minutes, the guard constantly looking back at the tunnel entrance. Finally, TJ saw Linda unbutton her shirt pocket, remove, and give the letter to the guard, who quickly folded it again and stuffed it down his shirt.

TJ saw the man put his hand on Linda's shoulder and saw their heads bow, knowing they were praying. TJ joined in silently, praising God for a successful mission. Only thing left to do was get away and back to the bivouac area safely.

He watched as Linda hugged the guard and turned to leave. The guard turned and strolled slowly back to his position near the entrance, looking as if nothing had happened. Linda reached Tim and Donnie, and together they made their way back to TJ's position.

TJ backed down the dam face as he heard the trio approaching. All three had beaming smiles on their faces and Linda, not being able to hold back, grabbed TJ in a bear hug. She had tears streaming down her cheeks and said, "He was so happy to see me. They're all ready to go already – there are nineteen of them that want out along with the eight children- and figured we would be back for them. They've already made plans and said they'll be coming out of both entrances.

TJ, it's going to be great – all of them want out." She hugged him again.

"Come on, then, let's get outta here, and tell the others," TJ said, turning to the west and moving rapidly for the truck.

After the nearly four-mile hike back to the truck, all four were beat. They stood at the truck and downed bottles of water while putting their weapons away. TJ got in the driver's seat and started the truck, so the others climbed in. He put the vehicle in gear and pulled out. It only took them a few minutes to drive back to the bivouac, and as they pulled up to the door, it opened, so TJ pulled right in.

The four tired valley residents dragged themselves out of the seats and made their way to the front of the truck. There, they faced the entire valley group, and smiled. Linda gave a thumb up and said, "They all want out and have already made plans for their escape. They'll be exiting from both exits." With the fourteen they already had, that would make forty-one people, living humans, in the valley. Ruth, Donna, Dan, Jack, and Jeff, all had beaming smiles on their faces.

The four, after back-slaps, handshakes, hugs, and prayers, collapsed on their sleeping mats and pads and promptly went to sleep. TJ slept till noon, the others several hours longer. TJ woke to the aroma of freeze-dried beef stew being warmed up. It was Donna, preparing it for him to eat. Once it began steaming, she stirred it for a few more minutes on the fire then cut him a slab of bread from a fresh loaf he'd baked and spread what looked to be butter on it.

"Is that butter?" TJ asked her.

"You're awake…yes, it is," she said with a smile.

"Where in the world did you get butter? I haven't had butter in…in…in years!" TJ exclaimed.

"Ruth and I learned how to churn butter and made our own," she answered. "I found a book in Doug's library that gave instructions on how to do it and together we made a bunch for this trip. Here, eat," she said handing him the bread and a bowl of stew.

TJ smelled the bread and butter and marveled at the aroma. He prayed then took a large bite and savored the taste. "Mmm, this is great," he moaned in delight. He was very hungry and dove into the stew and asked for a second chunk of bread and butter.

Donna smiled at him while he ate, enjoying the fact that they now would have butter for cooking, and that TJ loved it on his bread.

"You love it, don't you?" she asked him.

"You bet your sweet bippy, girl, this is wonderful, thanks," he said and took another large bite. "The stew is good, too."

"Don't talk with your mouth full," she scolded.

He looked up at her with his cheek packed with the bread and butter and mumbled, "Bmumphgff, sumpffamhph guudd…" and smiled.

"You're horrible, you know that?" she said with a giggle.

He just smiled at her with his cheeks bulging and held his spoon up to her loaded with stew.

She turned and walked towards Linda's sleeping area.

By the middle of the third day, all the equipment, ammunition, and other supplies, had been dragged to the mortar and sniper positions. Shirley, even though still somewhat uncomfortable with all the movement, did very well helping to haul the equipment. That night, the same team as before would make their way to the northern portal and get updated information from the inside. All was ready on the valley teams' side, and they needed to know if the complex folks were ready to make the attempt to escape and when.

Everyone else went back to the bivouac and waited for the answer. Jack, Donna, and Donnie got together and went over their plans once again. They talked about bombing tactics, sniping procedures, and ROV deployment. Tim and Donnie would fly drones into the caverns and do the kamikaze thing to a few areas. They had been practicing that and had become quite proficient flying drones with loads in tight spaces around the valley. Before they broke for the night, they prayed together asking for God's guidance, help, blessing for TJ, and the others out on their mission, and for their safe return.

Dan, Shirley, and Vito, did the same, going over mortar safety procedures, shell spacing and fire discipline, ROV deployment and drone flying and bombing. They too, prayed before breaking for the night.

Jeff, Linda, and Dino went over their assault timetables and discussed what they would be doing inside with their ROVs. After the initial attack from the snipers and bombers, the two teams would begin their assaults, along with any others from the nineteen that might want to join them. The three hoped many would as they would most certainly welcome the assistance. As soon as the nineteen adults and eight children were out and safe at the assault team areas, the adults would be offered firearms and ammunition. Jeff ended their meeting with prayer.

Donna curled up in her sleeping bag and got as comfortable as she could. She was nervous and apprehensive about the mission that night. She wasn't alone either as Jack and Jeff both, were not too comfortable trying to sleep, and were just as keyed up as she.

TJ, Donnie, Tim, and Linda had finally made it to the dam and eased over the top to look at the tunnel entrance and saw the same guy on guard as before. They watched him for a while and although he looked their way several times, concentrated more on the southwest and west.

TJ motioned for the others to back down the bank and at the bottom, gathered them for a prayer. After the Amen, TJ looked at Donnie and Linda and whispered, "You two know what to listen for and what to say, right?" They both shook their heads. "Please be careful out there and come back safely. Tim and I'll be waiting," he finished and pointed for them to carry on.

TJ and Tim climbed back up the dam face and this time, took their M4s off safe and aimed them at the tunnel entrance.

They looked and saw Donnie and Linda crest the hill and step out on the dirt road and ease down towards the tunnel area. Tim motioned to TJ and pointed to the entrance. TJ saw a second person peering out of the entrance – they had a smile on their face.

It was too late to signal Linda and Donnie, so TJ aimed his M4 at the entrance and selected three-round burst firing. He knew he was about to be involved in a firefight.

Linda eased around the bend and stood there, looking at the man from the previous encounter. She stood there quietly for what seemed to be a long time, when the man finally turned and looked her direction and saw her. He immediately broke into a great smile and looked back to the cave entrance and motioned for the person to come on out.

TJ almost pulled the trigger but saw the person's smile as they exited the cave and waited. He looked at Linda and she broke into a huge smile and ran to the person and embraced him. The other guard kept watch, looking at the cave entrance. TJ relaxed only a tiny bit and watched closely, cradling his M4 and sighting through the sights a few times.

Linda and the two men conversed for almost five minutes. Linda had motioned for Donnie to come forward and he joined in on the conversation. Once the talking ended, the four did a group hug and prayer. It was touching to see the emotional display that came from the two from the cave. Streams of tears flowed down their faces and as Linda and Donnie turned, TJ could see tears streaming down their cheeks. Linda held a thumb up, which was the signal to TJ and Tim that all was well.

When they reached the backside of the dam, Linda broke down and cried. Donnie was wiping tears from his eyes but had recovered, no longer crying. He looked at TJ and said, "They're more than ready. If they could, they'd come right now. They said tomorrow night is great for them if we're game. The children will be coming out with the north entrance group. So, what do we signal?"

TJ looked at Linda, who nodded her agreement. Looking at Tim, who already had a thumb up, he said, "Give 'em one red. It's a go for tomorrow night. Let's move."

Tim gave the signal and slid back down the dam face and began following the other three and caught up quickly. TJ had poured on the coals and was moving out at a brisk pace. The other three kept up and they made the almost four miles back to the truck in record time.

Back at the bivouac, they told everyone to prepare and try and get some sleep as they would be very tired after tomorrow night. TJ ate lightly and loaded the extra ammunition and grenades he wanted for the mission. Once all was ready, he lay back on his pallet and attempted to snooze. Donna joined him and together they tried to nap. It wasn't working so the two got up and helped the others as they could.

The attack would begin at 0100 hours. The first part of the action would be the max exodus of the nineteen adults and eight children who wanted to escape. The first bombs would be dropped as soon as they were safe and from then on, the valley teams' fire and actions would be dictated by measures taken from the complex. They had all agreed that no quarter would be given, and the complex would be completely destroyed...period. Nothing of the materials, either actual biological specimens or the written documentation, would be taken from the place.

At six that evening, they all gathered for a meal, community prayer time, and to rehash their plans for the night attack. By seven, they were all quiet and looking around the room at each other. DD was out like a light, his mother holding him in her lap. TJ wished he were just as out as the kid was but was way too keyed up to even try.

"Time, everyone," Dan said, standing. "Get ready to leave. Make sure you have your ammo and weapons tight. Fresh batteries in your commo gear and NVGs. No noise tonight until the time comes. God bless and keep you all. Jesus is on our side and the Holy Spirit is with us tonight. We do not need to fear. We do not need to worry. Our plan is a good one. Once the nineteen and kids are out…" he hung his head and turned for his equipment. The others looked at each other with a few nodding grimly, and broke silently for their battle gear.

TJ and Donna helped each other with their camouflaged clothing, putting on their Mollie gear and combat vests. TJ slug his M4 over his shoulder on its single-point sling, chambered a round in his suppressed nine-millimeter, racked a round into his sawed-off shotgun and reloaded a round into the tube, giving him nine rounds of double ought buck shot to deliver if needed. He raised his M4, inserted a magazine, and charged his weapon by activating the BAD switch. He was as ready for combat as he could be. He stood with Donna and they held hands, facing one another, and prayed.

They heard a vehicle start, and saw Dan and Shirley, pulling out. TJ raised his hand in farewell and Dan waived in response. Next, Daniel and Vito pulled out and got the same wave from TJ. Next to leave was Jack and Donnie. Tim motioned for Donna and she and TJ hugged and kissed once more. She turned with tears streaming down her cheeks and pulled herself into the truck. Tim started the vehicle and giving TJ a salute, pulled out. Finally, Jeff and Dino got in their truck, started it, gave TJ salutes, and pulled out.

Last to leave were TJ and Linda, who got into their truck, started it, and waved at Ruth, who was lining up drones to fly during the attack. She waived back and gave them a sad but confident looking smile. DD was still out like a light.

The six pairs drove to their assigned parking areas and immediately hiked to their positions. As they arrived, they made short calls to TJ and Dan saying they were in position. It took forty-five minutes for all six teams to say they were in position and preparing. Once Ruth heard that on her comm gear, she readied the first bomber drone and once the lift off order came from Dan, would bring the bomb-laden craft to an altitude of five thousand feet AGL, and fly directly to the little airport. That was to be her first target. She was to crater both grass-covered runways.

It was ten minutes until one o'clock in the morning. Ten minutes until their world changed forever. Ten minutes until their lives would get better or much, much worse…if they lived. Ten minutes until their community possibly grew by more than half. Ten minutes until the rest of their eternity began.

Chapter 16: Actions & Reactions

The teams having arrived at their combat positions began to get ready for action. Jack and Donnie were the first to arrive on their station. Once Jack called in, he and Donnie loaded their fifties and Remington's. Jack snuggled into his fifty and Donnie got under his Remington. They had set out four bomber and four kamikaze drones and had the controls handy for the time they would be readied and flown to attack the northern entrance. Donnie had painted the kamikaze drone controls red and the bomber controls blue.

It had been decided earlier that both sniper and mortar teams would have bomber and kamikaze drones. Along with Ruth's drones back at the bivouac, they would have more than enough firepower to handle most situations outside the tunnels.

Jack looked at Donnie, who gave him a thumb up and a smile. Jack nodded and felt badly for the kid as he felt Donnie had no idea what was about to happen. Jack, with a sad look, said, "Kid, I'll be the one shooting anyone that comes out that doesn't give the signal, understand?"

Donnie whispered, "Sure, Jack, sure thing. I'm ready, though. They said we'd be getting seven folks on our end. I sure hope they run fast."

Now Jack smiled and said, "They'd better because as soon as the last person is out and given the proper sign, the next person is going to feel the might of this thing." He patted the side of his fifty while saying that. "It's five till so get ready."

Donna and Tim, the northern sniper team, had readied their weapons and had also set out their drones and control boxes. Tim had earlier checked all the batteries and made sure they were fully charged. Donna had set out all her magazines for the fifty and a box of loose rounds for her Remington. She would be the shooter on the fifty when the time came, and Tim would be on his Remington. He had already loaded it. He, too, set out the magazines for his fifty and loaded the big rifle. He got under the big gun and settled in, preparing it for firing, then moved over to his .308 and readied it.

"You nervous?" Tim asked.

"Yes, and a little afraid, but I keep praying," Donna answered.

"Me, too. You're shooting first, right?"

"Yes, the first person that exits without giving the proper sign…well, I'll be making the first shot. I hope they all run like the wind."

"Twelve plus the kids are coming our way. Twelve - that's almost the entire population of the valley."

Donna chuckled and said, "That's the only thing I find kinda humorous about this whole ugly situation."

"What's that?"

"We're more than doubling in population tonight. I'm really excited and happy about that."

"Yeah, me, too. I'm excited I'll be seeing my friends again. I think Albany is going grow in size quickly in the next few days."

"That's a real laugh, that," Donna said smiling. She looked at her watch and said, "Five minutes…get ready."

Dan and Shirley immediately began unloading mortar rounds from the cases and shipping tubes as soon as they arrived. They wanted to have fifty rounds each prepared to fire. That many rounds would give them about an hour of shooting time. They both neatly stacked the rounds in a half-moon around the back of their tubes, within easy reach.

Once they began firing, they would have to correct for range and distance quickly and continue fire once on target. They would shift fire as needed. Dan had one Stinger just in case a drone from the complex did get airborne and they all hoped they wouldn't need it. He readied the missile and knew Dan would be doing the same, as would Jack and Jeff. They figured four Stingers would be more than enough to take care of any drones that might get launched.

Shirley prepared her drones and set her painted control boxes behind each. She had eight of the things, four each of the bomber and kamikaze drones. Dan followed suit and set his drones out like she did and moved back to his mortar tube.

"Five minutes, get ready," Dan said. Shirley only nodded and knelt next to her mortar, picked up a round, cradling it in her arms, prayed silently and waited.

Daniel and Vito had set up exactly like Dan and Shirley. The two stood together and prayed for a moment and at five minutes before 0100, they clasped hands in a fierce slap and shake and said together, "Live or die for Christ." Then knelt next to their mortars, prepared rounds and got ready.

Jeff and Dino got into their position just over the embankment from the north entrance. They were just behind the dam and would wait there for the groups that would be escaping. They had additional weapons, M4s and loaded magazines, ready to hand out when the time came.

Together, they readied their grenades – fragmentation, high explosive, thermite, and smokes – and added two pouches with additional frags and thermite grenades for if and when they had to enter the complex.

"Five minutes," Jeff said, and they knelt next to the trail that led up the dam face.

TJ and Linda had prepared just like Jeff and Dino had, then prayed together. TJ looked at her with sad eyes and said, "Five minutes…ready?"

"As I'll ever be," she said with a sigh.

TJ suddenly had a vision of his mother and father, his sister and Jamie, school friends came to mind and memories of happiness living on the ranch of his childhood shot into his consciousness. Many thoughts flashed through his mind – all seemingly pleasant and happier times from his past. He saw his first dog, his first horse, and remembered basic training and Ranger School. Those were not for the most part pleasant memories but were good in that they created for him a new family, his brothers, and sisters in arms.

He turned and looked at Linda for another moment thinking that was what was about to happen, he'll be getting more brothers and sisters, but they would be Christians this time. He gave her a nod then looked towards the entrance of the tunnel from his vantage point and said into his comm mike, "TJ here, Five till; all teams report."

"Sniper team north, ready," Jack came across.

"Sniper team west, we're ready," Donna said.

"Mortar team north, set, God be with you all," Dan radioed.

"Mortar team west, we're green," Daniel echoed.

"Assault team north, set," Jeff said.

"Assault team west, set – go with God everyone," TJ said, then, "Three minutes. Get ready."

The guard at the north entrance looked at his watch. Jeff said, "Get ready, the guard is looking at his watch. He just looked back at the cave entrance." He quickly looked at his watch and it was just a few seconds before 0100 hours. He looked up just in time to see a person exiting the tunnel entrance and saw the sign given, the right hand quickly over the left breast, above their heart, and then pointing to the sky. A Christian for sure. And with him were the eight children.

Jack immediately sighted on the first person out of the northern tunnel entrance but saw the sign and eased off the trigger. Then he saw the kids and immediately felt a feeling of relief. He watched as the man ushered the children to the dam and over the embankment and were greeted by Jeff and Dino, hugging the kids. He watched as Jeff instructed the man to grab a weapon and a few mags, and lead the children to the west, across the dam and to a safe area behind a small ridge. They would await the outcome and further instruction there.

When the first person came out of the western tunnel entrance, Donna and Tim both sighted on the person and immediately held off the triggers as they saw the sign given. The woman had a huge smile on her face as she ran to TJ and Linda's position.

The next man out of the northern entrance had hugged Jeff fiercely. He had a huge smile on his face and said, "Hello, brother, it's so good to see you."

Jeff couldn't help it as the tears began to flow and hugged the man just as fiercely. They separated and the guy grabbed Dino and they hugged together for a moment. Dino pointed to the rifles and magazines and said, "Join us," with tears in his eyes.

The guy picked up a rifle and four magazines, inserted one and charged the weapon and put the other three mags in his pockets, then, as directed by Jeff, climbed to the lip of the dam to cover the tunnel entrance and surrounding area.

The woman out of the western entrance fell to her knees at TJ and Linda's feet. Linda joined her and they said a quick prayer as TJ kept watch. Linda stood and pointed to the weapon cache and said, "Join us." The woman went over, picked up an M4, loaded it and took two more magazines and put them in her two front cargo pant pockets. TJ told her to climb a small ridge to their right and cover the tunnel entrance.

The second and third people came out without any problems and too, picked up rifles and joined the assault teams. Now they were five people each.

The first hint of trouble came from the western entrance as the last four people to come out, came at a dead run. All four gave the proper signs and practically flew to TJ's position. The last to reach him was the guard and he said, "The Sergeant Major is coming up the tunnel. He'll be out here in a minute.

"We've heard about that guy and we're ready for him," TJ answered, then, "West snipers next person out is a tango. Confirmed bad guy so you're cleared to fire."

"Understood," Donna said, and she readied her fifty. Tim was already good to go on his rifle.

They both saw the man at the same time as he came out shooting an M4 towards the people fleeing. Without hesitating, Donna took a breath, let half out, and pulled the trigger on the big rifle. Even with hearing protection the report made both jump in surprise from the rifle's explosion and concussion. Their ears began to ring immediately. Donna looked through the scope and only saw a great red splotch on the rocky wall next to the cave entrance where the man had been. She knew immediately she'd hit the guy and the heavy bullet had made short work of him. She radioed, "Wild Card folded; launching Kamikaze drones, out."

The Sergeant Major had a fleeting feeling of tearing pain as the big fifty caliber bullet tore through his torso. It entered his body just below the diaphragm and the force literally blew him apart. His head, still attached to a portion of his chest and right arm, flew up and onto the top of the ridgeline above the cave entrance and plopped in a heap facing west. The eyes blinked a few times and finally ceased seeing, as it were, a moment later. Close to the end of the battle, the Sergeant Major's head reanimated and began the raspy gurgling all Zombies made.

Tim got the control to one of his Kamikaze drones and started the craft, lifting off a moment later and flying towards the tunnel entrance. Without hesitation, he flew the craft at the door and hit near the center hinge assembly. The little drone, filled with C4 and thermite, exploded in a blinding, fiery blast that destroyed the hinge and so warped the door that no one would be able to close it. This allowed free access to the tunnel system by the ROVs and other drones they would fly inside.

Tim readied his second drone and lifted off. He radioed, "West entrance door disabled, out."

"Copy," TJ answered. "Send in the second and go hunting."

"Roger, already airborne," Tim responded. The craft flew to the entrance and slowed. Tim flew the craft carefully into the tunnel entrance and eased down the shaft. He was looking for people as he knew no more of their friends or anyone else that wanted to be free would be inside this west side. He came to the mid-point and turned up the central passageway and saw a person turn into the first hallway. Tim poured on the power and hit the north wall as hard as the craft could. He saw a quick glimpse of the explosion on his screen before darkness set in. He was certain his craft took out the person in the tunnel shaft.

The northern assault team had a similar event as seven people erupted out of the cave entrance and joined the guard in a mad dash towards Jeff's position. All were repeatedly giving the sign and from way off in the distance to the southwest, heard the report from Donna's fifty. The eight literally dove over the dam's precipice and slid on their bellies almost to the water's edge.

Jeff had his rifle up, covering the eight, but Dino held his hand out and smiling said, "No, it's cool." Then to the eight he said, "Where's the last person?"

Several heads hung and he knew, hearing one of them saying, "Someone shot him down as we were running for the cav…"

That's when they heard the loud report of Jack's fifty. They all ducked, and Jeff quickly climbed the embankment and looking over the top of the dam, saw a large red stain on the wall next to the guard's position, and knew Jack had killed one of the compound's supporters.

At 0100 sharp, Ruth started her first drone and lifted off, quickly climbing to five thousand feet AGL and flew on a south easterly heading. It would take her just under six minutes to fly the almost ten miles to the airstrip.

She quickly found the two runways and turning a little to the southwest, concentrated on the longest and dropped her first bomb, counted two seconds, and dropped the second. The first landed just right of center and exploded on contact, making a crater six feet in circumference and four feet in depth. Dirt and rock rained all around the crater. The second hit dead center and made an almost identical crater as the first.

She flew to the southwest and, making a turn to the east, flew to the shorter of the two runways and dropping the third bomb, counted to two again and dropped the fourth then immediately turned the little craft back towards the bivouac. Those two bombs effectively ended the use of the shorter of the two runways.

"West assault, airport taken care of, both runways cratered," she radioed.

"Copy, airport no danger," TJ answered then said, "Break-break; mortar team west - shell the airport's north side and take out those two buildings."

"Roger, firing in one mike," Dan answered. He and Shirley quickly shifted and aimed their tubes towards the intended targets and dropped their first rounds, his first and hers a split-second later. His hit long and wide left by fifty yards. Hers hit short and just to the right. They both corrected and fired another pair of rounds. The first building, a house, was hit by Dan's round and a fire started. Shirley's round hit between the two buildings and holed both with shrapnel. They dropped four more rounds each and as the last two detonated, they could see both buildings burning fiercely and were for the most part, destroyed.

"Buildings destroyed," Dan said over his comm unit.

"Copy," from TJ.

Ruth landed her first drone in the parking lot and quickly launched her second bomber. This time she flew to a point just southwest of the northern tunnel entrance and in a hover, contacted TJ saying, "Assault north, bomber two in position, standing by."

Jeff quickly radioed her and said, "You're cleared in hot. Blast 'em."

"Roger, turning in for first run now," Ruth said. She turned to the north and going to full throttle, dove for the cave entrance and dropped her first bomb. It impacted just in front of the door and exploded, driving the door inward and shattering the frame. She pulled the drone up and did a circle to the west and hovered.

"Door is down, action?" she asked.

"Put one more in the entrance if you can, thanks," Jeff answered her.

"Diving now," and she put the drone into the dive. She centered the crosshairs on the top of tunnel entrance and at five hundred feet, released the bomb, and pulled up. The bomb hit, bounced for some reason, and then exploded in midair inside the tunnel entrance, sending a fireball down the tunnel ramp, and incinerating another of the complex personnel.

"Clear; bomb exploded inside tunnel," Ruth reported.

"Copy, saw that - clear to the east, break - break. North assault team advancing with fourteen fighters. Children clear and safe. ROVs activated and advancing," he radioed to his comrades.

Every one of the attackers breathed a sigh of relief hearing the children were out and safe. That was the biggest blessing for the mission they all felt. Most said short, silent prayers of thanks for the children's deliverance and safety.

"Drone, come south to the western tunnel entrance, please," TJ called after a moment.

"Turning south, be there in three mikes," Ruth answered.

"West mortar team, assault west here, please begin bombardment of tunnel entrance and surrounding area," TJ radioed.

"Firing in one mike," Dan answered.

"Assault west, west snipers opening up on entrance," Donna said.

"Copy, green light," TJ answered.

Tim moved over to his fifty and the two began sending rounds into the cave entrance. The cave walls being rock, and the floor being concrete, made the heavy fifty-caliber bullets ricochet around and down the tunnel. Both snipers were glad they were not in there.

Dan and Shirley had readjusted their tubes and began dropping rounds on the entrance and the small parking area as soon as they adjusted fire. They would drop ten rounds each.

"North mortars, open up on north tunnel; snipers, green light," Jeff radioed. Almost immediately they heard both the mortars thumping and the fifties going off. Soon, rounds began impacting all around the tunnel entrance and the big fifty caliber bullets were ricocheting all around the tunnel.

The north assault team was lying flat, watching the mortar rounds exploding and sending shrapnel inside the cave entrance and all over the outside. They had lined up several of the ROVs, as a few of the new people were competent 'drivers' of ROVs from their childhoods.

After the mortar barrage ended, Jeff said, "North assault, ROVs out." He moved his control stick forward and his ROV moved toward the cave entrance. He maneuvered the robot to the entry, climbing over the debris from the mortar barrage easily, much easier than he thought he would. Looking at his screen he moved his craft inside. His ROV was fitted with C-4, mixed with lead ball-bearings, similar to a Claymore mine, and would be used to clear the path if any humans were found in the tunnels.

He told the others to stay behind him at least fifty feet and continued on. He came first to the armory door and seeing it was closed, told Linda to bring up her ROV and get ready to blow it. He pressed onward, the others stopping and waiting for Donna to move forward. She parked her ROV against the door and waited for the command to detonate, starting her second ROV, and driving it towards the tunnel entrance.

Jeff saw movement on his screen and saw two men with M4s at their hips easing towards his ROV. They had inquisitive looks on their faces as they saw the ROV, so he detonated the bomb laden robot.

"West snipers cease fire, good job mortar team; west assault team with nine personnel moving in with ROVs. Snipers cover please," TJ said over his comm unit. The time was 0200 hours.

"Sniper's copy," Donna said. Tim readied another drone.

"Mortar's copy," Dan added.

TJ and his team moved forward, carrying their weapons and ROVs. As they neared the tunnel entrance, TJ set his ROV down and activating the control panel, maneuvered the machine over the debris and into the tunnel. He, too, had an ROV filled with C-4 and ball-bearings for anti-personnel action. He saw no one in the tunnel and continued on. His team would have the longest to navigate and he 'hit the gas,' so to speak and drove the craft at its top speed down the cavern. The others quickly followed at a distance.

"West mortars, west snipers, over," Tim radioed.

"Go," Dan answered.

"Detonated a Kamikaze drone in first left shaft from central passageway because of human contact. Be aware there may be debris, over," Tim told Dan.

"Roger, thanks for the warning, over," Dan answered.

He came to the door of the southernmost armory and saw the door partially open so stopped and motioned for the others to stop where they were. Several were close and he told them to back up. As he turned back to the screen, a man stepped out of the armory entrance with an M4 and closed the door. As the man turned, TJ detonated the ROV. He quickly readied his second craft and moved down the tunnel as fast as he could.

He told Linda to park her ROV against the armory door and activate her second unit and get the bomb-laden craft in there.

The northern assault team was making good time with their ROVs and came to the first side tunnel that held labs. Two ROVs were sent inside and parked next to the largest windowed lab. Those ROVs held C4 and several pounds each of thermite. The heat would be intense when they blew.

Jeff had his second anti-personnel ROV activated and had driven it past the first lab tunnel. He was heading for the next side tunnel when he saw two men come out of that tunnel and run to the south. He radioed TJ and said, "Assault team west - two men heading your way, south, in the central tunnel. They were moving fast. Just a heads up," he said.

"Thanks for the warning, we'll be ready for them," TJ said, smiling.

Dan continued on and coming to the second tunnel, eased his craft around the corner and took a look. Seeing no one, he directed the next two drivers to park their ROVs next to the large, windowed labs. In one he saw scientists working. They would know nothing save a moment of intense heat when the ROVs blew.

Dan backed his ROV out and turned to the south, heading towards the third side tunnel of labs when he heard a muffled explosion.

"Those two guys are gone," TJ said over his comm unit.

"Roger," Dan said with a grim smile.

"We're at the first tunnel to the south," TJ added.

"Roger, heading to the third," Dan answered. "We'll be ready to blow 'em in about ten mikes."

"Great job," TJ answered. "We'll be ready in about twenty. Getting close to 0230 so let's say we blow them all then."

Dan responded, "Maybe 0300 so we can get the rest of the ROVs and drones in positions to blow…"?

"Roger, that sounds better; holding until 0300," TJ agreed.

Tim's third drone was in the central tunnel. It had a load of C-4 and thermite and he landed it between two labs and told Dan what he'd done. He launched his fourth and last drone and headed for the tunnel entrance. Dan had told him to do the same thing with his last drone.

TJ sped his ROV down the tunnel and came to the first side tunnel with the labs and storage facilities. He motioned for three of the following ROVs to go ahead and go down the tunnel. One each, parked underneath large windows in labs, and the third sped to the end of the hallway, where it parked against the far wall of the juncture of the storage tunnels and the main tunnel. It was loaded with ten pounds of C-4 and four pounds of thermite. It would be a hot rocker for sure when detonated.

The same type of ROVs would be used in the second lab tunnel with storage. When all of the ROVs were activated to blow, it would be a massive, combined detonation.

"North sniper team, launch your drones and fly them inside. Land in the lab areas, please, over," TJ radioed.

"Copy," Jack answered. He and Donnie activated two of their drones and launched.

TJ moved his ROV down towards the second lab tunnel and eased around the corner and looked. He saw three men speaking together down the hallway. TJ smiled and 'floored' the ROV directly at the trio and hit the detonation button. His screen went blank after a momentary flash.

"Just took out three more in a lab tunnel," TJ radioed. "Second tunnel will be ready in five mikes. Tell everyone to duck at oh-three," TJ said, chuckling.

TJ directed his team to send the other ROVs to their assigned spots. Several were left over, and he told them to split between the two tunnels and the main tunnel.

Jack and Donnie had landed their drones next to large windows in front of laboratories. Both immediately launched their second drones and flew them as fast as they dared to the next set of labs, settling the bomb laden craft as close to the walls as they dared.

Jack radioed, "Drones inside and secure, ready to blow, out."

"Copy," TJ answered.

Dan told his team to place their remaining ROVs in areas along the tunnel path. They now had five more ROVs spread out along the tunnel. They, and the satchel charges they would place at the entrance, would ensure the collapse of the northern half of the complex.

"North sniper team to north assault, you have anyone stationed on the dam?" Jack said on his comm unit.

Jeff stopped and said, "Negative, no one there, just at the tunnel entrance, why?" For an answer, he heard Jack's fifty roar several times. Jeff and his team all hit the ground hunting for cover. "North sniper team, what's happening?" Jeff asked.

"Dam is clear now. Three tangos down," Jack answered.

"Roger," Jeff said.

"West assault, you clear?" Jeff asked.

"Negative, another three, or four mikes, we're in the last tunnel now setting up," TJ answered.

"Roger, north side prepared and we're moving to India Papa now," Jeff said.

"Roger, we'll be doing likewise in four mikes, out," TJ said.

"North snipers, west, you see any other movement?" Donna radioed.

"Negative, how about you," Jack asked.

"Negative also. We're considering bugging out to our India Papa, over." Donna said.

"Roger. Advise against until teams clear and ROVs popped, over," Jack replied.

"Roger, standing by," Donna said. "We're here until they blow the tunnels and labs," she told her partner, Tim.

"No problem, we can hang a while longer," he answered with a smile. "I'm praying and thanking God it's gone so well so far. I really think he's blessed us with a successful mission," he said, beaming.

"I think you're right," Donna agreed, also with a huge smile on her face. "I'll start giving praise and thanksgiving myself."

A few minutes later, TJ radioed, "West assault clear of complex and all ROVs set. West mortar and sniper teams cleared to India Papa. Standing by," he finished.

"North assault copies," Jeff answered. "North sniper and mortar teams are cleared to India Papa. North assault clear, all team members accounted for, standing by, over."

TJ stood taking one last look at the tunnel entrance. He turned and looked at the other seven members of his team and they all gave him a thumb up. He was looking them all in the eyes and said, "North assault, cleared to detonate at 0300. I'll detonate as soon as I hear yours begin, over."

"North assault copies, commencing in one mike, over." Jeff answered looking at his watch. He too, stood and looking at his team, Dino and the eleven new people, nodded once and they all told him to blow it. He gave them a grin, flipped the cover up on the detonator button, winked at Dino, turned to look at his watch, and at precisely 0300 hours, pressed the red detonator button. The first explosion was at the tunnel entrance, which promptly collapsed in a cloud of dust and debris.

As soon as he heard the first bomb detonate, TJ flipped the cover on his detonator and pressed the red detonation button on his controller. The western tunnel entrance collapsed, and a huge dust cloud rose.

For the next several moments, the ground shook repeatedly with the explosions, dropping everyone to the ground. The north reservoir quickly emptied as a fissure suddenly opened in the rocky ground, allowing the water to drain into the cavernous opening caused by the number of titanic explosions. A huge dust cloud and fireball erupted from the complex and several other small lakes and reservoirs emptied. The destruction of the complex was obviously complete as the ground suddenly settled, forming a jagged, deepening bowl. A great cloud of dust and debris began settling to the southeast. It had risen almost ten-thousand feet.

Doctor Miller and his team of scientists felt the explosions getting closer and closer in quick succession. When the charges went off in the tunnel to their north and one to the south, the explosions drove them to their knees.

Miller quickly stood back up and was heading for the door when the charge outside that door detonated sending the ten pounds of thermite in a fiery arch through the lab. His last fleeting thought was one of intense searing pain from the heat as he disintegrated in the blast.

The Sergeant Major's head and arm bounced around during all the explosions going off below it. It growled and gurgled as it flopped about, finally coming to rest viewing the new 'canyon' to the east. It's eyes blinked as it took in the scene, not understanding any longer what or why it was, only that it was hungry for warm blood.

TJ stood on the bluff overlooking the new 'dent' in the earth they had created and knew no one would be coming out of that destruction. The smoke rising into the sky and turning to the southeast attested to the fires raging inside, the C-4, the thermite charges, grenades, and satchel charges having done their jobs. TJ hoped and prayed they did their job well. The materials and information in the complex should never come to light again. TJ, thinking about that, suddenly became overcome with sadness and dropped to his knees and began crying.

Linda ran over to him and asked, "TJ, what's wrong…are you okay?" and knelt at his side.

He looked at her and with tears streaming, shook his head. He began to sob and fell to the ground overcome with remorse and anger at what the scientists had done to their home – Earth. They had killed billions of innocent people – billions!

Linda placed her hand on his back and felt him sobbing. The others gathered around the two and wondered why the tall man was sobbing. She looked at them and said, "Kneel, everyone, and pray. Pray in thanksgiving that we're free and safe. Praise God for our success. Pray in thanksgiving that we're alive and no longer will be persecuted by the people that once controlled us. Pray for blessings and thank the Lord, His Son, and His Holy Spirit for the lives we have and will have because of the actions of this man and a few others. Pray for joy and glad tidings for all of us. Rejoice that the Lord sent these people to bring us out of despair. Rejoice…," she began crying herself and, like TJ, dropped to the ground sobbing. The others knelt and prayed like she'd asked, many dropping prostrate in prayer and sobbing themselves.

At the northern rendezvous, Jack and Jeff embraced as they rejoined. Dino and Donnie did likewise and the others they'd brought out of the complex gathered round. Jack and Jeff knelt and began praying. Dino and Donnie quickly followed suit, and the rest did likewise, even the children.

After almost ten minutes, Jack rose and looking at the others said, "Ladies and gentlemen and children, we've done a good thing for mankind today. I hope all of you were giving thanks to the Lord. We came out of this unscathed for the most part. I'm truly sorry the one was killed inside. It saddens me beyond measure. Our lives are forever changed because of that place - several times over, actually. First by the plague they set upon the world, by the repeated attacks they put the original valley residents through and then the rest of us over the past several years.

"And now they've impacted our lives once again, in a rather macabre fashion, in that we destroyed them and their complex and hopefully all the materials and correspondence about that plague. Our lives very soon will be pleasant. We now will be able to live in peace and in relative safety in the valley to the northwest. Those of you that have never seen it will rapidly fall in love with it as we did. We'll be able to worship together. You'll have your own homes and land to grow crops and raise animals. You'll be able to marry and have children and care for the children we have now – DD needs some companions." Chuckles came from the group and one little girl asked who DD was.

"You'll all meet DD soon," Jack answered. "His mother, Ruth, is the one who was flying the drones that bombed the tunnel entrances to begin the attack. She also took out the airport so no larger drones could be launched against us. Soon too, you'll meet the two surrogate leaders of our community, Dan, and TJ. TJ is the Sheriff of Albany County, Wyoming, where the valley is. We still consider him our sheriff even though we don't really need one these days. The two of them have led us on this mission and they are the ones that developed and implemented the plan. Your freedom is because of their love for you as their Christian brothers and sisters."

"I'm a son of Islam," one of the men proudly said.

"I'm happy to meet you and have you in our community – welcome, friend," Jack continued, stepping over and shaking the man's hand. "We were fourteen this morning. Now we're forty-one people that wish to live in peace. In happiness and health. No one will take that from us any longer. No one. Now, let's gather our gear and get outta here," Jack ended.

Everyone laughed and lending a hand began gathering equipment, loading a lot of it on the sleds to be dragged back to the trucks. Jeff eased over near Jack and nudging him said,

"I ain't never heard you say so many words in my whole life, man."

Jack looked at him, smiled, and jokingly said, "I'm running for mayor. Didn't you know?"

Jeff almost passed out he was laughing so hard.

The five trucks packed with people pulled into the bivouac area and parked outside, even though Ruth had opened the garage doors as they arrived. It was a nice feeling not to be fretting a drone would shoot a missile at them or something. She was holding DD and stepped out as the trucks arrived and began disgorging passengers, left and right. Ruth had a huge smile on her face and DD was oohing and ahhing at all the people. He'd never seen so many at one time. They all gathered and milled around the pair, introducing themselves and shaking hands with DD, tickling him, and getting him to laugh. The children were most inquisitive and had many questions for Ruth about DD.

Talk around the group was furious in nature, everyone telling a story or two, laughing and crying and praying. The talk and banter went on for several hours.

Finally, Ruth called for everyone's attention and said, "We need to prepare the evening meal. Who wants to help?"

Way too many volunteered so TJ and Dan gathered a few of the others and gathered wood for a fire. They would have a bon-fire outside that night and eat together for the first time – in peace and relative safety.

Ruth, Donna, Linda, and Shirley had packed several coolers with frozen buffalo steaks, and several more with fresh vegetables and fruits. They were cooking the vegetables in large pots, steaming some and boiling others. The fruits were cut into slices and arranged on plates for everyone to enjoy. Three large tables had been set up and it would be a large buffet-style affair. Bottles of water were laid out.

Vito and Dino came to TJ and asked him if he'd like to have them stand guard. He thought about that for a time and said, "I suppose we should be watching for Zs. They still pose a clear danger to all of us and a horde coming in would not be in our best interest, so yeah, I suppose so. Thank you for reminding me we still have a danger to watch out for. I'll save you a nice steak for your dinner."

The two shook his hand and went to get Z'd up. As they were leaving the building, several of the new people asked what was going on and when told were surprised, and thanked them for guarding the group. Two of the men, including the man that said he was Muslim, said they would be out in two hours to relieve them. That was much appreciated by the two and asked that they tell TJ.

The two went over right then and told TJ they would be the relief for Vito and Dino in two hours. TJ thanked them and asked them to follow him. He took them over to the flatbed truck with all the weapons and ammunition, and told them to pick out vests, magazines, handguns, and shotguns and to load up with ammunition and grenades for the task of guard duty.

He turned to leave, and the Muslim said, "Thank you for trusting us with this duty."

"You're very welcome, but why wouldn't I trust you?" TJ asked.

"I'm Muslim," came the answer.

"Then I'm very glad to meet you and hope you love living with all of us," TJ told him, shaking his hand.

"You see, I told you," his partner said giving him a punch on the shoulder. "It don't make no difference to them what you are, it's who you are they're interested in. I don't mind if you and I don't agree on our God. We can even agree to disagree on religious topics, but I will always be your friend and now, a neighbor."

The two smiled at each other and continued to Z up. TJ shook his head, smiling and turned to go sit with Donna.

Dinner was smelling grand, and everyone's mouths were watering. Finally, Ruth called out it was dinner time, and everyone gathered for the meal.

It was strange, because for a few moments after they gathered, no one moved. Finally, several of the new folks backed away from TJ and Dan and motioned for them to go ahead of the group.

The Sheriff took a step forward and looking at the children asked in a gentle voice, "Who's Judith?" A sweet little girl, with reddish-blonde hair and a fearful look in her eyes, slowly raised her hand. TJ smiled at her and gently said, "I hear you're a very special person. I'm happy to meet you." She was beaming when he shook her hand, then he looked at Dan and shrugged his shoulders, saying, "Please everyone, let's bow our heads in prayer, and thank God…for everything." He began the prayer and passed off to Dan who prayed for a moment then said Amen.

TJ looked at everyone and said, "Line forms at Ruth, ladies and kids first then the men. Dig in everyone!"

Chuckles overflowed and the ladies and kids of the group were ushered forward to begin the festivities. As the group filled their plates, they sat as they could and ate. Small talk ensued and many conversations started. TJ did like he promised, and put aside two plates with huge steaks, and stacked them with fruits and vegetables. He sat them near Ruth and told her who they were for and she smiled at his thoughtfulness.

True to their word, the two volunteers relieved Vito and Dino at the two-hour mark. Dino and Vito, once inside, removed their combat gear and got their plates Ruth had been guarding for them. The food was great. The steaks were terrific. The fruit and vegetables tasted better than ever as now they were eating their food in freedom.

When it was lights out time, the children were bunked in the back corner with several of the men and women with rifles keeping watch to protect them if it came to that. They hoped it wouldn't.

Jack and Jeff relieved the two volunteers two hours later and had made a deal with TJ and Dan for them to relieve the pair in three hours. That would carry the guard duty through the night.

The next morning, breakfast was MRE's. No one complained, and at about nine in the morning, everyone loaded up and the caravan set out for Centennial Valley, new homes, and new lives – in freedom and peace. There would be two stops; one in Tie Siding to retrieve the materials left there and one in Laramie, for a rest break.

They arrived in Laramie close to noon and they decided to both take a rest stop and for those who wanted, a lunch break. Several of the men took turns watching for Zs, and it was a blessing they didn't run into any and the group leaders thought the hummers broadcasting the Judith signal had done the trick leading the Zs to the south. The kids were running around the area playing tag, laughing, and having a grand time.

TJ, Dan, Jack, and Jeff loaded the new folks into their trucks and took off for the ranch store and let the new folks shop. They about cleaned the place out, so they dropped their goods off back at the lunch stop, loaded up again and went to the big mart store and let them finish up. Jeff came out after a while inside with two carts filled with footballs, basketballs, baseballs, gloves and bats, dolls, and a multitude of other toys saying the kids needed to have something to play with. There was almost no room for all the goods brought out and the people, laughing at the thought, made it back to the rest area and put all the goods on the flatbed with the other supplies.

They left Laramie at two in the afternoon and went to the valley. At the apex of the hill, before going down into the valley proper, they stopped and let the new folks see their new home from afar. Comments like 'beautiful' and 'spectacular' were many. TJ told everyone to get back on board their vehicles and they would be at his home, Paradise Valley in just a few minutes.

As they turned down the lane, TJ felt a new sense of pride and accomplishment. Their future seemed assured for the most part, now with a major threat eradicated. They would all need to be on the watch for Zs, but that was beginning to be as great a threat as being attacked by a lion or bear. The valley would indeed become peaceful and quiet once again. Now, the community could focus their efforts on building a vibrant home, grow their crops and build things as they pleased, surviving in a peaceful environment. It was a great day in the history of the valley, and possibly of mankind itself.

TJ pulled into his drive and hit the button opening the gate and they pulled into the front yard. Everyone piled out as the vehicles arrived and the looks of astonishment were many. TJ, Donna, Dan, Ruth, and Linda mounted the steps and TJ called for everyone's attention.

"Obviously, we don't have enough room in the house for everyone, much less including the garage and barn," which got nervous chuckles. "Needless to say, you're all welcomed here any time. No kidding…any time," he emphasized. "We'll have a real feast tonight as Dan here and I butchered two of our cattle before we left and put them in the cooler. We're going to make a big fire and roast both on spits - men with Dan and me - ladies with Ruth, Donna, Shirley, and Linda. We'll have dinner in a few hours. Everyone that's not helping with us or inside, if you would, unload the two flatbeds into the garage, I'll open it in a second, and if you would, move the two trucks down the hill into the lane past the gate afterwards. Thanks," and he turned with Dan to go to the cooler and get the beef.

Daniel and Vito directed the unloading of the trucks and moved the two beasts down the hill. When they got back to the front yard, Daniel went inside and hit the button to close the gate. One of the guys asked why, and Daniel told him the place was completely secure from Zs with the gate closed and told him about the fence surrounding the home's location.

"Wow, that must have been a big job for someone," the man said.

"The fence is nothing," Daniel told him. "You haven't seen anything yet. Come on guys, gather around, and sit down in the shade with me, and let me tell you the story about this place. Almost ten years ago, a man named Douglas Sutton…"

Chapter 17: New Beginnings

The sunrise woke TJ, the glare of sunlight seeping into the room through a slit in the curtains since they hadn't closed them all the way the night before. He got up, used the restroom, and brushed his teeth, combed his hair then stepped out onto the balcony. People lay everywhere, sleeping, wrapped in all kinds of things to keep warm. He smiled, stretched, and went back inside to shower, shave, and dress. He did his best to not wake Donna and closed the curtains to keep the light out for her to rest and snuck out of their room.

Downstairs, he found Dan, Jack, and Jeff sipping coffee. Dan saw him and got up and poured him a mug of the brew.

"Thanks, brother," TJ said, accepting the piping hot mug. "What's the plan today?"

The three Marines looked at him and Jeff said, "Beginning a new life sounds good to me."

"Yeah, that'll do," TJ agreed nodding and smiling. "I suppose we can start by driving folks around and letting them pick homes and get them settled. We'll help them any way we can with getting their places ready for winter."

"We've already been discussing that to some degree and that's going to be a tall order since they'll need everything," Jack commented.

TJ nodded.

"I'm sure the first group will invite them all to move up to New Albany," Dan said.

Jeff said, "They already have. Daniel told me last night. I really don't think we'll have any say in where they live. It seems they've all already decided for New Albany. And, really, there are enough homes left up there for them to move into. We'll need to help with water, and probably firewood for the winter, but that'll be fun to do. They can do their own hunting for meat and fish also. The real job will be next spring."

"Why do you say that?" Jack asked.

"Planting crops for over forty people is going to be a chore," Jeff answered. "And we'll need to be building more of those underground greenhouses also."

"And rounding up stray cattle, horses, sheep, pigs, and chickens," Dan added. "Next year is going to be a big one for work."

"God will see us through," TJ said. "We need to concentrate on this winter for now and getting them through safely."

"I agree," Dan said.

"So, do I," from the stairs. They all turned and looked and saw Donna coming down in her robe. "Yes, I'd love some coffee."

Jack jumped up and poured her a mug and offered her his chair at the table as she walked up.

"Thanks, Jack, you're a doll," she said with a smile, sitting in his proffered spot.

Jack turned to make another pot of coffee.

"How many eggs were out there?" Donna asked.

"Twenty-seven," Dan said with a smile.

"With those and what we have in the fridge, we can feed this bunch," she decided. "TJ, get another slab of bacon out and some sausage, would you please?"

"Yes, ma'am," and he turned to go out to the cooler.

"Jeff, down to the root cellar and get a bunch of apples and some green pepper and onions, please."

As he jumped up, he said, "Yes, ma'am."

"Dan, you take roll call out there as they get up, please," Donna asked him. "Make a good list and tell them all that later on we'll be having a meet-n-greet in the front yard with breakfast. Tell them we'll want to hear a little of their stories, too, and to be thinking about that. And grab the first couple of guys and have them set up the tables and chairs out of the garage in the front yard for us to use this morning."

Dan got up, taking his mug along and said, "Yes, ma'am, I'm on it." He went to the library and got a pad of paper and a few pens, then went out on the front porch. He saw that the garage supply of blankets and sleeping bags had been broken out and smiled, knowing that either Donnie or Daniel had done that. Which was fine. He knew TJ wouldn't disagree with their decision.

He stood on the porch savoring the sunlight and coffee, listening to the snores and snorts from around the yard. He saw one of the young men get up a few moments later and sneak down into the trees to relieve himself and as the youngster came back up, Dan motioned for him to come up.

"Wow is that coffee, sir?" he asked.

"Yep. Not sure when you'll be able to get some, but yes, this is coffee. Here, put your name, date of birth and place of birth on this for me. Mrs. Gerill asked me to gather that information for her. Thanks. How'd you sleep."

"Gosh, like a log," he answered. "I haven't slept that well in a very long time. The ground was more comfortable than I thought. Probably because it's free soil, now."

"Yes, indeed, free. Hungry?"

"Yes, sir, I could eat."

"Well, in about an hour, Mrs. Gerill will be serving fresh eggs, bacon, sausage, probably toast with either her strawberry or peach jam, and I'm hoping, coffee for all of you."

"Oh, my, the Lord blesses us in many ways, huh."

"He sure does."

More people began to stir out in the front yard, so Dan asked the young man to have them come up and 'sign in' when they were ready and asked him to get a few of his friends together to set up the tables and chairs from the garage. He watched as the new members of the community began to get up and move around. It didn't take long, he saw, for the men's room and the lady's room to be decided. The lady's claimed the bathroom in the garage straight away and that made Dan chuckle – the guys got the trees as usual.

He was sitting in one of the Adirondacks, when Jack came out with Jeff in tow. "She's kicked us out. Has TJ in there with an apron on and has him cooking and slicing bread for toast. She's like a Sergeant Major or something."

"Closer to a Corporal of Marines, if you ask me," Jeff said.

"You two are nuts," Dan said. Just then the door opened, and Donna came out and told Dan she needed his help inside. As he got to his feet, he saw Jack and Jeff looking away, both doing everything they could to hold back laughs. He followed Donna inside.

A young lady came up the front steps and told them Mrs. Gerill wanted information, and Jeff pointed to the pad of paper. The youngster signed in, smiled at the two Marines, and went back down the stairs.

Jack and Jeff took over collecting the information Donna wanted and within an hour, had everyone's name, date of birth and place of birth on the pad. Counting the children there were over twenty new names to remember and now over forty souls in their little community. The possibility of having to house so many new folks in new homes seemed like a monumental task. Hopefully, some of the ladies, and for that matter, a few of the guys, would bunk together this first year. That would certainly make things much easier.

Donna came out and told the two Marines to come back inside and help serve breakfast. Inside, they found that Ruth, Linda, and DD, were up and DD was already into everything. His awkward attempts at walking were comical to watch.

The smell of bacon and sausage cooking permeated the front yard, and everyone's mouths were watering. The kitchen 'staff' stepped out on the front porch and Dan nodded at TJ, who stood on the top step and called for everyone's attention.

"Good morning," he yelled in opening and received a chorus of return salutations. "I hope you all got some well-deserved rest last night. I want to welcome you, again, to

Paradise Valley and Centennial Valley." He hesitated a moment, looking at all the new faces, and said, "Looking back at the last eight or nine years, and now looking at your faces…well, I'm awfully glad you're here and safe. This valley is your new home if you chose to live here. You're more than welcome to stay as long as you wish, and if you decide to leave, we'll do our best to see that you have everything you need for your journey and survival."

He hesitated once again, for several moments, all eyes upon him in anticipation of what he was going to say next. He could hear the wind in the leaves, the birds singing, cattle in the lower pasture, sheep baying in the distance, and geese in the creek below, and smiled. It was a new day for all of them.

He looked up at the crowd and said, "Today marks a new beginning for all of us - a new life and for many in new homes. We have some difficult times ahead of us and with God's help we'll face those challenges as they come. Today, however, is a day of feasting, rest, and finding homes for all. Please, bow your heads with me as I say a blessing for our morning meal."

"Heavenly Father, we thank you for our safety. Thank you for allowing us to gather together this day. Thank you for the blessings you give each of us daily. Thank you, Father, for the food we're about to enjoy. Please bless it for the nourishment of our bodies so that we may work together in peace. Thank you for your Son's sacrifice for our salvation, and in His name I pray, Amen."

Heads came up and Donna took over and told everyone to form a line. She, Ruth, and Linda had arranged everything so that as someone entered the house, they got a paper plate, plastic ware, napkin, cup, then were served their food, coffee, juice, or water by TJ and the Marines, then stepped out the side door from the kitchen back to the front yard to sit down and eat. The children and ladies went first and then the guys. It was a joyous occasion.

After breakfast, everyone pitched in and helped to clean up, break down the tables and chairs, putting them away in the garage. TJ noted all the blankets and sleeping bags had been returned to the garage storage unit also.

Outside, everyone milled around, talking together in small groups. TJ called Daniel, Vito, Donnie, and Dino over and said it was time to find these folks some shelter and asked if they had any ideas.

Daniel began saying, "We've invited them all to move into New Albany with us…just seemed right. They pretty much agree with us, so I was going to ask you if we could borrow a few trucks and take folks on a tour up there and get started with the rest of…well, our lives."

"I like that statement – 'get started with the rest of our lives.' That's a good line. Most certainly you can use the trucks…all of them if you want and take everyone up at once. Remember to Z up and keep your heads on a swivel. We still face dangers as you reminded me the other night. Remind everyone of the bear and lions up here and that they need to keep on their toes. Let them know, too, that we'll help in any way we can to get them settled and prepared for winter. As far as supplying them, we'll start by emptying the warehouse in Centennial and the Ranger's Station of the supplies and things we placed there before."

"We'll be careful and we've already got our kits ready to go," Dino said. By kits, he meant their equipment to Z up with. "If you don't mind, we'll take the first groups up in just a few minutes."

"I don't mind at all, guys," TJ said. "Thank you for helping them out. If you need our help, you know where to find us."

The four of them shook TJ's hand and turned for the garage and the key box. TJ stood on the front porch watching the action, wondering who would be first to go up to Albany. He understood quickly, however, that the whole crowd was going as they pulled out five trucks and the whole bunch, kids, and all, climbed in. TJ turned and opening the door, hit the remote to open the gate. Donnie waived as did TJ, and the majority of the population of the valley pulled out for New Albany, to look for their new homes.

Dan and Jeff came out of the house and asked what was going on. TJ told them and said he was getting another mug of coffee and relax. The three sat in the Adirondacks, enjoying the quiet after all the hustle and bustle from the morning.

Jack finally came out, supporting a mug of coffee himself, and asked why it was so quiet. The three already sitting broke out in laughter. Dan explained, so Jack sat in the last chair and other than the noises of nature, it was quiet once again.

Ruth, Donna, Linda, and DD came out next. Shirley had gone with the New Albany group. The guys got up and offered chairs to the ladies, and Jeff took DD and began rough housing with him. Donna looked at TJ and asked him what the plan was for the day.

"Well, I told the guys that today would be a day of rest and instead they loaded up the trucks with the new folks and they've gone to New Albany to look for homes. I suppose they'll be gone for most of the day, some may just go ahead and move in. They'll probably be back in a while for their new clothing and things, and maybe some supplies. I figure I'll just go with the flow today. Maybe go back and work in the greenhouses some, weeding and such. I needed to take care of the animals, but Jack and Jeff did most of that earlier when they got the eggs."

"I'm taking the rest of the day off," Donna said. "Someone else can fix lunch and dinner for this crowd."

Linda said, "Shirley and I can do that."

"That's sweet, honey," Ruth said. "I'll be helping. Donna, what's the menu?"

"There's a bunch of leftover beef from last night," she answered. "That was sure good. Thanks guys, for cooking that. We could de-bone it and make a few huge pots of stew, or make beef and barley soup, or vegetable beef soup. We could get the grinder out and make burger out of it and make something like sloppy Joes with it…what's your fancy?

"I vote for all three," Jeff said, adding, "…we can put up the left-overs for the winter in canning jars."

"Ditto on that idea," from Jack.

"I vote for the sloppy Joes," TJ said, more to get a reaction from Jeff than anything. But the stew would be great.

"You would be the oddball guy in the bunch," Jeff began.

Donna quickly squelched any more bickering and pointed to Dan, who said, "I vote for the stew."

"Me, too," Linda voted. "Shirley will, too."

"No proxy voting," TJ kidded.

Laughter from everyone. TJ acquiesced, saying, "Okay, okay, stew would be great."

"The Democratic process still lives," Jeff kidded.

"Okay, okay," Donna said. "Kidding aside, TJ, would you and Jeff go out to the greenhouses and pick a bunch of vegetables – carrots, potatoes, a few onions, and some celery for us?"

"He'd love to," Jeff said jumping up and grabbing TJ's hand, helping him get up. "Come on, old man, let's get to the chores."

"Who you callin' old…" TJ challenged, and the pair ran down the front steps heading to the back yard.

TJ'll catch 'em," Jack said, chuckling. "He'll smack him good.

"Probably cuff him," Dan said and that brought all to laughter.

Quickly getting up, Jack said, "I gotta see that," and took off after the pair.

Dan looked at the ladies and shook his head and they began laughing again. It had been quite a while since they had been able to laugh the way they were. Busting a gut laughing that brought tears to their eyes. Dan sat and watched the ladies as they laughed, and marveled. He was happy their world was changing to something better than it had been a few days earlier. He thought about that and looked around the front porch – no Stingers or M4 rifles lay about. No weapons of any kind. For the first time in years, he knew he was totally safe inside the wire of Paradise Valley. He could really relax and, so to speak, let his hair down.

He stood and looking at the ladies said, "If you would excuse me, ladies, I have something I need to do."

Donna flicked her hand as if dismissing him from her court.

Smiling, he turned and went in the house, went up the long stairway to the Underground, stopped by the den and poured himself a tumbler of Macallan eighteen-year-old scotch, then climbed the eastern portal. He stood on the precipice of the mountain's face and looked out over the valley below, raised his glass and said, "Lord, God, thank you so much for bringing all of us out of adversity, blessing us with our safety, our security, and our very lives. In Jesus' name I pray, amen," and he took a healthy swallow of the fiery liquid. He dropped to his knees and began to cry, more from joy than anything else. He was absolutely overjoyed.

He looked down into the valley and saw the greenery, the trees, the grasses, the river, and the creek. He saw elk, deer, and cattle. He saw geese and ducks, birds, squirrels, chipmunks, and rabbits and thought to himself, *all is well in the world and this valley.* He continued to cry and began heaving in great gulps of air. He sobbed and sobbed.

After several minutes of crying, he finally settled down and felt a comforting peacefulness come over him. He was experiencing a calmness he'd never felt before and savored the moment looking down into the vista below. He turned and gazed to the west and the sight took his breath away. The sun shining through the partly cloudy sky was marvelous, the rays fanning out to the earth. The view from on top of the Underground was spectacular. He felt he was fortunate and blessed to have known Douglas Sutton for the short time he did. Doug's foresight, that came from God, built this place, in this place, at the right time, so people like Dan and the rest would be able to survive.

He stood and walked over to the western portal, watching the sun's rays. The colors were vibrant and pure. He took a sip of scotch and hearing a noise behind him, turned and saw TJ climbing up the eastern portal with a tumbler and the bottle.

"I knew you'd be up here," TJ said with a smile, proffering the bottle, which Dan refused.

"I've got enough, TJ, thanks," Dan said.

TJ sat the bottle down and rising, held out his tumbler and Dan touched his against TJ's. The pair smiled and sipped their scotch.

"Have you ever seen anything so beautiful, TJ?" Dan asked.

TJ gave a huge sigh looking to the east and the west and shook his head, "No...I haven't."

The two stood on the edge of the Underground and looked at the people below as a few of the new folks began returning and wondered what the future would bring.

TJ took another sip of his scotch and said, "I'm not real sure what our next step should be, other than to just let things go as they will."

"I think life will go as God wants it and we'll just tag along for the ride," Dan offered.

"Perhaps so," TJ agreed. "I still feel at a loss as to what's next. I really didn't think about that."

"I don't think you and I have anything to worry about," Dan said. "Those young people down there will do just fine I'd say. They'll probably have more and better ideas than you and I have or will have. We need to let them go. Maybe plant a seed of thought or two but let them go after that."

Behind them came an 'ahem' and they turned to find Jeff's head sticking above the lip of the portal. "Greetings from my lady Donna, who demands your presence in the castle common below, my liege's."

Dan scooted a rock his direction with his boot and the head disappeared down the eastern shaft.

"We've been summoned my friend," TJ said with a smile.

"I guess so," Dan agreed and stepped to the portal.

Down in the great room of the homestead, TJ and Dan stood on the stairs and looked at the people gathered in the room. They had stopped as everyone was looking at them as they came down. Jack and Jeff, Donna, and Ruth, with DD in her arms, were seated in front of the fireplace. Linda, Shirley,

Tim, Donnie, Vito, and Dino were standing near the kitchen and a half-dozen of the new folks were standing with them, the others scattered where they could find room.

Shirley stepped forward and said, "Now that we're all here, we, as a group, want to thank you six for getting us out of that situation. If it weren't for your kindness, thoughtfulness, and Christian love for us, we would probably all still be living in fear. You six saved our lives and we're forever - and I mean forever - grateful. There is nothing we can do to show the gratitude we have for you. All we have comes from God and He let you provide it for us. We just want you to know how we all felt."

The young Muslim man stepped forward and said, "I have never been as fortunate as I am now, and I thank my God…and yours…for the life you've given back to me. Thank you."

The six were humbled. They were speechless. Dan and TJ finally took the initiative and climbed down the remaining stairs and began hugging and shaking hands with the group. Ruth, Donna, Jack, and Jeff got up and did the same.

After the thank yous were over with, TJ looked at Donnie and Tim and asked them, "So what's next, you two?"

"We're building a community up in New Albany," Donnie said. "New Albany will thrive. Most have already found homes for themselves or together. Several of the men are housed together and one home has four ladies."

Tim said, "We'll start collecting food and other things tomorrow. We're sending a team to Cheyenne and would like to take one of your flatbeds and a pickup for the trip. We'll Z up to the hilt and be careful." He looked at Ruth and Donna and said to them, "If you need anything…anything at all, let us know, and we'll find it for you."

"We're going to find more vehicles and go over to the refinery and see if we can fuel up more tankers to bring back. We'll be looking for farm equipment and ranching supplies, too. If we see any stray animals, we'll try to at least write down where we saw them for a possible roundup later on. We're planning on a five-day trip."

"Sounds like you've already got things going well," TJ said. "I love the New Albany handle. A new community. A great beginning if you ask me. How many are going to Cheyenne?"

"Seven…a God number," Tim answered with a smile. "We figure three in the flatbed and four in the pickup. We're hoping to bring back a bunch of vehicles full of fuel and supplies."

TJ and Dan both nodded. They looked at each other and thought the 'kids' had things under control.

TJ said, "You're more than welcomed to use the trucks – they belong to everyone here in the valley. If you need ammo or weapons, stop by here as we have plenty. That being said, all of you need to come by here and pick up a rifle, shotgun, and sidearm, and enough ammunition for all three to get you by for a while. We've pretty much cleaned out the area of weapons and ammo and have a very good supply."

"We've thought about that, too, and have decided to go to Fort Carson again next spring for a shopping trip," Tim responded. "We'll be taking almost every truck we can get, including the two flatbeds if you'll let us, for that one and bring them back loaded to the hilt. We'll also hit food stores in Colorado Springs, if any are left, and bring back all the canned, dried goods, and paper products we can find. Things like that may be deteriorating by now. We'll also get every canning jar and lid we see."

"I cannot argue with you," TJ said. "It's been a long while since deliveries have been made to grocery stores and such. I'm not sure canned goods will be too good for much longer. When you go down there, hit all the sports shops, too, for freeze-dried foods. They last much longer. And if you remember, get all the three-inch deck and dry wall screws you can find."

"I'll put those on the list," Donnie said with a smile.

"How many guys will be left after you leave tomorrow?" Dan asked.

"A few, why?" Donnie asked.

"We Marines are going on a wood cutting expedition and wondered if a few of your men would like to join us," Dan answered.

"I'll let the guys know; when and where do you want to meet up?" Donnie asked.

"My place, say around nine tomorrow morning. We'll probably get done around five or so. We're taking our three trucks with flatbed trailers and loading them up for you folks up in New Albany," Dan told them.

"For us?" Donnie asked, surprised.

"Yeah, you guys need to get ready," TJ said. "The winters up here can be nasty, so we all need to be prepared to keep warm, fed, and dry."

"I suppose so," Tim said.

"We have a list of things we need to check at our own places before winter sets in, we'll share it with you," Dan said,

"What kind of things?" Donnie inquired.

"Your roofs, to begin with," TJ said. "Make sure they are weather ready. Ensure your propane stock is full and ready, as well as your firewood and food pantry – dried and canned goods – things we put up for the winter in canning jars, smoked meats. Check your windows for air leaks and get some six or eight ply heavy-duty plastic to cover your windows as an extra insulator: it creates a dead air space and traps cold air. Your water supply will be very important as well as your sanitation setup. What you're using now may not work in sub-freezing temperatures. A bunch of other small things that looked at now and fixed if needed will save you some uncomfortable time trying to repair it in freezing weather."

"Looks like we have our work cut out for us for the next few months," Tim observed.

"Not months…weeks," TJ said. "I've been watching the weather changes and we may get our first snowfall within the next month the way things are looking."

"How much snow do you usually get?" Donnie asked.

"The biggest storm I've seen around here was in 1985, and they got about forty-five inches up here in Centennial," TJ replied.

"Whoa!" Tim exclaimed. "I'm from Florida and other than the little bit of snow we got in Colorado every now and then, I've never seen snow like that."

"Shoot," TJ continued, "My dad told me about the storm of 1965, and that in seven days dropped one hundred-seven inches of snow. That's almost nine feet of snow, three feet taller than I am."

"We don't need one of those," Donnie breathed.

Dan and TJ broke into laughs. "Yep, that would be a tough one for us," Dan chuckled.

"Just gives you an idea what you need to be prepared for," TJ said. "Heck, we may only see a couple of feet for the whole winter. That's just the way things happen around these parts. We can get mild, moderate, or horrible winters. We have to be prepared for all three."

"Dude, we better get moving and get to Cheyenne and get everything we can find," Tim said. "I'll tell the other guys about meeting you and the others for wood cutting. You have any more trailers we can haul up there?"

The four walked over behind the garage and TJ showed them the additional trailers he had and said they could take their pick. Afterwards, Tim, Donnie, and the others got in their truck and left for Albany.

At 0900 the following morning, TJ pulled up at Dan's home and the men from Albany were already there. All of them save the ones that had gone to Cheyenne. Dan, Jack, and Jeff were standing with them and looked ready to go. TJ stayed in his truck and watched as Dan gave the signal and everyone got into the trucks and followed Dan as he left his ranch.

They drove to Centennial and went up the mountain to the same place they had been cutting wood for a while. They had six chainsaws, so six men went to work felling standing dead trees, and the others used axes and bow saws to remove limbs. TJ had the ATV on his trailer, and they used it and the winch to haul the timber back to a trailer and load. Within an hour, they had their operation down to a science and by four in the afternoon, they had all the trailers loaded. It would be slow going down the mountain.

By five, they were unloading the logs in New Albany, stacking timber near each home the group had chosen to live in. They wound up with eleven cords of wood, not enough to get through a harsh winter, but a very good start.

They made an agreement to go out again two days hence and drop the same amount or more. They would go to a different place, up the road from Albany towards Cinnabar Park. It would make for shorter hauling distance.

That morning, however, broke to cloudy skies, with the cloud cover a deep gray. TJ wondered if they should go or stay inside and do other things for the day and radioed Dan with that in mind. Dan agreed stay close to home and said he would contact the New Albany folks.

TJ got another mug of coffee, gave Donna a kiss and a hug, and headed up the Underground's stairwell. He wanted to check the mechanical room and make sure it was ready for the winter. As he opened the door to the Underground, a flash immediately followed by a thunderclap resounded as if it was just above his head. It made him duck it was so close and so loud. The concussion rattled the Underground, feeling almost like an earthquake. TJ went into the kitchen and peered out the window and saw the angry, steely gray clouds undulating and churning. He knew this was going to be a big storm and watched as lightning struck in the valley to his left. The thunder hit a second later and he knew that bolt had hit within a mile.

The rain soon followed, and it came in torrents, the wind whipping it into what looked like sheets of water pouring. Donna came up and stood next to him and said, "I knew you'd be watching this."

"It's something, from up here, isn't it?" he said putting an arm around her shoulders.

"Yes, spectacular," she replied.

They watched for several minutes. The storm was coming from the northwest, so the rain went by the window to the southeast and cascaded down the mountain. They could see the rain pouring off the roof of their home below, and saw it pouring off the sides of the barn and garage.

Donna looked up at TJ and said, "Looks like we could use a hot-tub bath during this thing. What do you say, cowboy?"

He smiled and took her hand, leading her to the tub.

The storm was still raging when TJ stepped out of the exercise room and back into the kitchen to make them some lunch. Rain was still pouring and as TJ got to the window, he could see the creek below had turned into a torrent and wondered if the bridge would hold. He looked at it and saw that it was doing well so far, but it worried him, nonetheless. He stood there and chuckled to himself, thinking that this year might just bring another banner snow year, if this storm was any indication.

Donna came in with a satisfied smile on her face and asked, "What's for lunch?"

"I'm thinking tomato wedges, cucumber slices, and some of my garlic bread."

"That sounds perfect. I'll make the tea. You want hot or cold?"

"Hot I should think on a day like this."

"You got it, cowboy."

They sat together at the table near the window and watched the storm while eating and sipping their tea. TJ gauged they had received several inches of rain at least and it was still coming down in sheets.

"Are we in any danger from all this rain?" Donna asked with a sudden worried look on her face.

"I don't think so. I'd better go check the mechanical room, though." TJ got up and did that very thing, finding the holding tanks were full and the back-flow water emitter was working as advertised and had water flowing out the relief pipe on the western side of the mountain from the Underground. Just to take a look, he climbed the western portal and slowly opened the hatch and looked to the west and northwest. There was a lightening of the sky that direction so he knew the storm would be letting up and would end before long.

Back in the kitchen, he told Donna everything was okay and that the storm would be letting up soon. They decided to go back downstairs and out on the front porch, they stood together and watched the storm abate and the creek below churning. It was a raging creek now. TJ wondered again about the bridge and about the emergency escape bridge near the southern pasture. Both would probably need some repair after this.

The rain began to let up and slowed to a sprinkle about an hour later. TJ and Donna got in the ATV and went down their muddy lane, stopped before the bridge and looked for damage. Other than several logs and a lot of debris, mostly limbs and such, the structure looked intact. TJ opened the gate, and they crossed the bridge and drove out to the main road, closing the gate behind them. TJ turned left and sped to Centennial and saw where the rain had created furrows in the soil around town, and two places where dirt and debris had washed across the highway.

He turned right onto 130, and quickly came to the bridge over the north fork of the Little Laramie River. That bridge was still intact with quite a bit of debris washed up against its support struts. They would need to clear that soon.

He was about to push on when Donna nudged him and pointed. He looked closer and saw a Z tangled in the mass of debris. It had seen them and was reaching for them. It looked horrible. TJ pulled his M4, made sure a round was chambered and shot the thing in the head. He safed his rifle and setting it in the holder, continued on.

Turning right onto Highway 11, the pair drove to the next bridge, the one where the Great Ambush had taken place. It too had debris and a log jam butted up against the struts. TJ looked closer and saw the far side, the west side, was somewhat washed away, probably from the water diverting from the log jam. They would have to repair that before using it.

TJ backed the ATV up and turned around and pulled back out onto Highway 11 and turned for Marine Hill. Their drive would need some repair as they could see many furrows that had been worn in the ground by so much water.

Dan came out and, smiling, said, "Man, was that a doozy or what?"

"Yes," Donna answered. "It was a mean one. We just came around the long way and the bridges, for the most part, are still okay. We'll need to do some work on the one going to the Malone Underground as it was damaged."

"There's a lot of debris and a log jam or two we'll need to take care of," TJ added.

Jack ambled up and said, "Our pond is full and overflowing to the north a bit. The dam will hold. There's some elk over there in the aspens. Good lookin' group of animals."

"How many in the herd?" Dan asked.

"Fifty or so I'd say," Jack answered.

"Good, I hope they hang around," Dan said.

"We're going up to New Albany and check on the folks up there," TJ said. "Anything you want us to tell them?"

"Want to try and do wood tomorrow or the next day?" Dan asked.

"Next day I suppose to give time for everything to dry out," TJ answered. "This mud would be dangerous with a load. I can meet you here around eight-fifteen or so day after tomorrow then we can head up to New Albany. How's that?"

"We'll be ready. See you two later," Dan said, giving the two a wave as they pulled away.

TJ sped down their drive and turned left back onto the highway. They pulled into Albany and saw one of the guys waiving them down and they pulled into where the old restaurant was. The residents of New Albany had made that into their community house and meeting place. It was well suited for the task with plenty of chairs for everyone and more than enough room.

They parked and went inside and found the entire community discussing damage done to their places and repair work that needed to be done. They were also discussing what they needed to be doing for winter preparation, which TJ, and Donna, found to be good news. Donna noted several of the folks had pads of paper and were taking notes.

TJ asked, "What kind of damage happened to your places?"

One member of the group said, "A few roofs leaking, and one place lost a window due to a tree limb breaking. Nothing really major. We can handle the repairs. How about you guys – any damage at your places?"

"Not any at all at Paradise," TJ said. "We were for-tunate."

"Nor at Marine Hill according to Dan," Donna answered.

"What kind of things are you writing down?" TJ asked.

"Things we need to do to prepare for winter," the same guy said. "Daniel and Tim told us what you said about getting ready for winter and we agree. We sent out the group to Cheyenne and the rest of us will continue to cut wood and forage for food items. Hunters will be going out in a few days for meat. We're considering adding some kind of insulation to the places we've moved into and the folks that went to Cheyenne will look for insulation for us to use. By the way, thank you for letting us use the vehicles. Hopefully, they'll find a few in Cheyenne we can use."

"Did they tell you about plastic on the windows?" Donna asked.

"Yes," he answered. "And we found a roll of six-ply plastic in the house that Linda is staying in, and some plumbers putty in another place. Linda and several other ladies have volunteered to cover the windows for everyone."

"Good, sounds like you're on your way to a comfortable winter," Donna said.

TJ then said, "For wood cutting – we've decided to hold off until day after tomorrow so the muddy roads can dry some more. It'll be dangerous trying to haul a load of timber around in mud, especially coming down the mountain. I'll meet the Marines at their place then we'll swing by and get you guys and drive up the mountain to a place I know about a mile from here."

The group agreed with that then the discussion went to other things, like water and power production. Several ideas were presented and written down for consideration. The meeting continued for another hour and adjourned with everyone having a cup of coffee or hot tea the ladies put together.

TJ and Donna said their good-byes and left New Albany for Paradise Valley. Once home, Donna told TJ it was his turn to cook and he offered to cook pork chops, with carrots, onion, and potatoes. She said that would be good and said wine would go with it. He chuckled and began dinner.

The next day, the Marines, TJ, and Donna, began the harvest, wanting to get the crops they did have in before the first snow. If the rainstorm were an indication, winter would soon be upon them. The five of them were old hats at harvest by now and in no time had several fields cleared of the corn and barley. Next would come the potato fields. Those were always a chore and were labor intensive. The New Albany folks came down and helped with that and it turned into a great community gathering. After the day's labor, the valley residents had a potluck and cook out together.

The crops were divided, and each home received a supply of each for their pantries and root cellars. Several of the homes in New Albany did not have root cellars so TJ and a few of the boys got together and built several, completing the work before winter set in.

Next, TJ drew a map and sent several of the guys up to his old homestead to fill the two trucks they took with apples and any produce from the gardens in that area. They returned that evening with trucks full of apples and vegetables they found growing almost wild in the gardens TJ had annotated on the map. These too, were divided and stored in the root cellars.

The Cheyenne group returned the following afternoon and had indeed found more vehicles and one tanker truck they had filled from one of the large storage containers at the refinery. They stopped by TJ's long enough to let them know that they had had little trouble and only saw a few Zs that needed to be taken care of. They told the pair what they'd found and asked if the two residents of Paradise Valley needed anything. Getting negative answers, the group left and drove to Marine Hill and talked with Dan, Jack, and Jeff, and if they knew if Ruth and DD needed anything and getting negative answers then carried on to New Albany and unloaded. They told TJ they would be putting the tanker truck alongside the old garage across the street from the town hall so everyone would have easy access.

The next morning, TJ and the Marines left for the tree cutting job and collected the rest of the cutters from New Albany. They used the same system as the last time they cut so it was no time at all before the work was back in full swing and by two o'clock in the afternoon had the four trailers loaded to capacity with firewood. This time they dropped off two loads in New Albany, one on Marine Hill, and the last at TJ's place. The Marines would cut two cords for Ruth and DD. They figured one more load such as this one and they would be set for the winter and agreed to meet one more time in two days.

Three weeks later the first winter storm came in. It didn't amount to much but dropped enough snow for everyone to get the message that winter was upon them. TJ and Dan went to New Albany and found the community doing well and had suffered no ill effects from the first winter storm as their preparations had not been in vain.

Two weeks later, TJ was in the Underground working on some weapons in the workroom and noticed it suddenly getting darker and had to turn on the bench lights to see. Curious, he went out and opening the eastern portal, found deep gray and menacing clouds forming to the west and northwest, blocking the sun. The cloud cover went as far as he could see from north to south and east to west, with the cloud cover being almost black to the west. There was very little wind and heavy humidity could be smelled and felt in the air. TJ shook his head and knew they were in for a real storm with this one.

He closed the portal and locked it, then went downstairs and told Donna what he felt was about to happen. They prepared by putting the plow blades on the ATV and truck and backing them with the plow blades towards the door in the garage. TJ got the snow shovels and put one inside by the front door and the other near the kitchen door. The two then began bringing in firewood and stacking it both, in the house, and on the front porch.

Donna was stacking kindling near the fireplace and heard Dan's voice come over the radio. "Dan, this is Donna, what's up?"

"You two see the clouds out west?" he asked her.

"We're already preparing, adding extra firewood inside, and have the vehicles ready to go when needed, plows are ready. Way ahead of you partner," she told him.

"You're funny. We're getting ready here, too, and Jeff is over helping Ruth and DD. This one looks like it'll be a beauty."

TJ had entered and motioned for the mike and answered, "You're not kidding, partner."

"Donna, your voice changed...got a cold?" Dan said, jokingly.

"Yeah, right...cold," TJ said with a chuckle. "You getting ready?"

"Yep, almost done," Dan answered. "Figured I'd go check on New Albany when I get done."

"Okay, let me know if you or they need help and we'll come a runnin," TJ told him.

"Marine Hill out," Dan said. He and Jack got into a truck and left for New Albany. As they entered the little hamlet, they could hear chainsaws going, a good sign the folks were getting ready for the storm.

They saw Dino, and waving at him, he ran over to their truck and told them the community was getting ready, that they had seen the clouds and knew a storm was coming. Dan and Jack watched for a while and decided the hamlet had things well in hand and left.

About four that afternoon, the sky became calm - a bad sign in Wyoming. When the wind wasn't blowing, it was cause for alarm in the Equality State. By six, the flurries began – straight down. At nine, it began to snow in earnest. TJ and Donna were standing on their front porch watching the storm develop and as the snow began falling, they looked at each other, smiled, and went inside. TJ threw two more logs on the fire and they ran up the stairs to the Underground and a jet tub bath, TJ with his scotch and Donna with her wine.

When TJ woke the next morning up in the Underground master bedroom, he thought it was much earlier as it was still dark. When he got up and looked out the big picture window in the room, he was not really surprised to see the sight that met his eyes. The snow was still falling, and heavily, with huge snowflakes raining down and piling up. He smiled and knew he would have some fun moving the white stuff later on.

Donna put her hand on his shoulder, and he started, "Oh, sorry, I didn't mean to startle you," she admitted.

"Just wasn't expecting you, that's all – isn't it beautiful?" he said, smiling at her.

"From up here, yes. But it looks like you'll have your work cut out for you today…"

"It'll be fun as always. I like moving snow with the plow. I don't really consider it work, but something for my play…and artistic abilities."

"You – artistic? I suppose. Can I ride along and watch you create?"

"Why sure you can darlin'. I'm going to get cleaned up and head downstairs. Want a big breakfast and some coffee?"

"What kind of breakfast?"

"Eggs, bacon, toast with jam, and coffee sound okay?"

"I'm in. You go get cleaned up and I'll clean up here. Now scoot," Donna commanded, giving TJ a smack on the behind to get him going.

He took one step, then turned and gave her a passionate kiss. "I'll see you in a bit."

Breakfast was good as usual. TJ had made the coffee and he poured each a travel mug full before leaving the house for the garage and the plow. TJ began the snow removal by clearing off the front porch. He'd do the upstairs patio later in the day. He cleared the steps and stood watching the snowfall.

When it was this heavy, the silence was what got to TJ the most. Heavy snow muffled sound and the world was silent at the moment. The big flakes falling almost straight down was a most unusual sight in Wyoming, and today it was a blessing. If the wind had been up it would be a real mess.

Donna stepped out and stood with him a moment, enjoying the scene. She wrapped her arm around his waist and the two stood there in the silence. She could hear her own heartbeat.

The two were startled by a bird flying by and alighting on the gate next to the barn. It was a Western Meadowlark, the Wyoming State Bird. TJ wondered why the little bird had stayed around, as most of the little birds migrate into the warmer southern reaches for the season. This one must have been part of the few who stayed through the winter months. Strong little birds for Wyoming's winters.

"Did you know the Western Meadowlark was the state bird for six states, including Wyoming?" TJ suddenly asked Donna.

She looked up at him and with a skeptical tone, answered, "No, I didn't."

"Yep, Montana, Kansas, Oregon, North Dakota, Nebraska, and Wyoming. They're tough little birds and for the most part migrate to the warmer southern climates in the winter. That little guy is one of the few that stay behind. He must be a stout little bird to hang around Wyoming in the winter."

"You're just full of trivia, aren't you?"

"Yep. Come on, gal, let's trudge to the garage. I'll lead little lady."

"You'd better, buster. Get going and blaze a trail through that stuff for me." Laughing together, they started their way through the almost two feet of snow to the garage. TJ opened the door and started the truck with the plow blade and began the day's labor of love, moving snow.

Donna bailed after TJ had cleared the front of the house, garage, and barn. He would continue clearing snow from the lane to the main road while she went inside and stoked the fire and made more coffee.

He had just moved over the lip of the hill, moving snow over the edge of the lane, when a snowball smacked the backside of the truck cab startling him. He hit the brakes and skidded a little, stopping the vehicle on the slope. He put it in neutral and set the brake, then climbed out to see what was going on.

He saw Donna standing back a way and waiving at him to come up to the house. By the look on her face, she was concerned about something so TJ turned off the truck and ran to the house. Donna was already inside in the library and told TJ to come in and get on the radio that Dan was calling.

"Dan, this is TJ. What's up, buddy?" TJ radioed.

"Morning. Hey, we have a problem up here and wondered if you might be able to give us some advice," Dan replied.

"Sure, I'll try. What's the problem?" TJ asked.

"Propane system seems to be frozen or blocked or something. We're not getting any heat in the house. None of us are really familiar with a propane system. Got any ideas?" Dan asked.

"Probably moisture build up that froze. Seen that before. It's probably near the main regulator off your tank. You have a wood mallet or one of those rubber hammers?" TJ asked.

"Yep, both."

"Use the wooded mallet and rap the regulator, gently, a few times. Do that to the line also. You're sure the tank has propane?" TJ asked.

"Yeah, it's full. We filled it the same time you filled yours, remember?"

"Yeah, I do. Try tapping the regulator and the line and see if that does it. If not, we may need to remove the line and see if there is some other type of blockage of some sort."

"Okay, will do. You have all the snow moved yet?" Dan said with a chuckle.

"Working on the lane now and should be done in a half-hour or so. How about you guys?"

"Almost down to the highway; Jeff's on it today."

"Alrighty then, let me know if the line clears, out." TJ said. He turned and Donna gave him a kiss.

"Want a refill on the coffee?" she asked him.

"Absolutely, ma'am," he answered then added, "I love it when you read my mind."

Donna poured him a fresh mug of joe and he went back to the task at hand. As he said, it took just over a half-hour to clear the snow out to the road. As TJ pulled up to back into the garage, he looked at the work he'd done and knew if the snow didn't quit, he'd be back at it in a few hours. He backed the truck into the garage, cleaned the blade and swept the snow out, then refilled the beast with fuel. He closed the garage door and went back into the house for another mug of coffee and a warm fire.

It wasn't long before the radio crackled again, and Dan related the wooden hammer trick had cured their propane problem. All was well once again on Marine Hill and the Marines were getting heat.

Three weeks later, another huge storm came in from the northwest. This time, it packed winds topping fifty miles per hour along with it and quickly became a raging blizzard. It would be a bad storm that left over seventy inches of snow behind, with drifts up to twenty-five feet in places. This time it took days for TJ to just clear walkways between the house, garage, and barn.

The bad part about this storm was the animals. TJ had to put panniers on Dusty and Donna's horse, load two hay bales on each and lead the horses down to the pastures holding the sheep and cattle. He would cut the lines and throw flakes of hay out for the animals to eat. He had to make three trips a day so the critters would have something to nibble on.

Communication with the other areas, Marine Hill, and New Albany, was strictly by radio. No one was moving about. The folks up in New Albany were doing well so far and had put in enough firewood and food to last. Several of the men had gone hunting and shot a few elk for the community up there before the storms had come in.

It was during one of these conversations over the radio, that one of the men asked Donna a favor. "Sure, what do you need?"

"Hope I'm not being a pest or anything, ma'am, but...well...I, uh..." he stammered.

"What's wrong?" Donna asked.

"Nothing's wrong, ma'am...I just...uh...I, uh...I want to know if the Sheriff can do something for me and I don't really know how to ask is all," he said.

"TJ's a pretty direct kind of cowboy, so just shoot from the hip and ask. He can take it. What do you want to ask him?" Donna inquired.

"I…uh…I…well, it's like this. I…we…uh…that is…well, Wanda and I want to get married…"

"AHH! THAT'S FANTASTIC!" Donna yelled. "TJ, get in here!" she yelled out to the house.

TJ came running in and said, "What? What's wrong?"

"Nothing. Now you be a perfect gentleman while you talk to him…here," she said, handing him the mike.

TJ looked at her with an inquiring look and taking the mike, radioed, "This is TJ, what can I do for you?"

"Sheriff, this is Matt. You remember me?" Matt asked.

"Certainly, Matt, what can I do for you?" TJ asked again.

"Well, I asked Mrs. Gerill, and she said you were a direct kind of person and to just come out and shoot from the hip, give it to you straight," Matt stammered.

"Yep, that's the kind of guy I am. Just give it to me straight, what's happened?" TJ asked.

"Nothin's happened. We're all okay up here…it's just…aw, shoot…Wanda and I want to get married, sir, and we wondered if you'd be able to do the ceremony…you know, marry us?"

TJ looked at Donna and he had a huge smile on his face. He winked at her and said, "She's not…"

"Oh, no sir, nothing like that…we wouldn't…we haven't…no, nothing like that. We just think it's time we got married, that's all," Matt explained.

"Is she okay with this?" TJ asked.

"She's right here, hang on…"

"Hi Sheriff, it's me, Wanda," she said.

"Morning, Wanda, how are you doing?"

"Just fine Sheriff. I'm a lot better after Matt asked me to marry him. I almost died when he knelt down and took my hand. I cried, Sheriff. It was wonderful," she explained.

"So, you're in agreement to get married?" TJ asked.

"Oh, yes, sir, I am. Everyone here is excited and…well you know, we'll have a million things to think about and get ready, you know?"

"Yes, ma'am, I think I do. You sound happy…is that right?"

"Sheriff, you just don't know. Matt and I really love each other. He said he prayed for days before he finally decided to ask me. Everyone here thinks it's a great idea."

"Wanda, put Matt back on, please," TJ told her.

"Hi, Sheriff, Matt here."

"Matt, you and Wanda and I need to get together and discuss a few things before the event, but I'd be honored to marry you two. Have you set a date yet?" TJ said, beaming.

"No, sir, I just asked her a little while ago. I suppose next spring or something," Matt said.

"Okay, I understand. You two make the arrangements and I'll perform the ceremony for you. Congratulations you two. I'll pray that you have a long and bountiful marriage," TJ said.

"Thank you, Sheriff, you've made our day, out," Matt said, signing off.

"I bet everyone in the place is yelling right now," TJ said, looking at Donna.

"TJ, this will be great. We'll do everything we can to make it a special day for them and our new community. The first marriage in our new community. I'm so excited for them," Donna said.

Throughout the rest of the winter months, Wanda and Matt, TJ, and Donna, made the arrangements for the wedding that would take place right after the first planting, near Mother's Day. The wedding would be on a Saturday and the entire valley would turn out for the festivities.

The men of Albany had gotten together and fixed up one of the homes for the pair and would give it to them as a wedding gift of sorts. It would be fully furnished, stocked with food, and firewood. TJ and the Marines built the root cellar and ran piping for the plumbing from the pump outside. The pair would need to get nothing for their new life together.

The day was rapidly approaching. The snow was about gone, and the valley residents had begun plowing the fields for the planting. TJ and Donna saddled their horses and rode up the river, following Doug Sutton's old trail up to the place where he and Ruth were married by Dave Malone. It was a fitting spot and TJ wondered if Wanda and Matt would like to have their ceremony up there.

Donna said, "I don't think that's such a good idea."

"Why? This place is perfect. It's beautiful," TJ argued.

"I still don't think it's a good idea. This spot was perfect for Ruth and Doug, and I feel it should stay that way for her – that perfect place for them. A place we shouldn't infringe upon."

"I see your point and agree. This should be a place reserved for just that memory then," TJ said, then leaned over and gave his wife a kiss. "Thanks for being you."

"Come on, cowboy, let's head back down and I'll fix you some lunch," Donna told him.

The fields were planted, and work had begun on at least three more underground greenhouses with an additional two more being planned in New Albany. The New Albany bunch had planned a trip to Fort Carson and Colorado Springs. They would take all four of the flatbed trucks and five pickups with trailers, four with gas tanks. Eighteen members of the community would be going on the mission including Jack and Jeff, who had decided to tag along for good measure. It would be an arduous journey, as everyone knew, but would be well worth the effort in the long run.

The mission had changed some as with the new peace, following the attack and destruction of the research complex in Colorado, they would focus on gathering materials for living rather than on destruction. Shopping lists were being made by everyone. It would be a monumental journey. They would be looking at sporting goods stores and large warehouses for supplies and materials. They'd also make lists of products and where they could be found for future outings. The group would be searching for new vehicles to bring back also, and every nook and cranny would be filled with goods.

The day came and the caravan departed. They would be gone for two weeks at least. The others watched as a group as the caravan left New Albany. TJ, Donna, Ruth, DD, and Dan had made a point of going and watching the departure. The community had gathered for a prayer before the group departed. Afterwards, the Marines and Ruth went with Donna and TJ to Paradise Valley and had a brunch, then went their separate ways.

The foraging group returned sixteen days later and had added seven new vehicles, all four-wheel drive trucks, and every vehicle was loaded to overflowing with goods. The team radioed Paradise Valley and the Marines letting them know all the products would be up in New Albany. Everyone gathered there and helped to unload the massive amount of products they brought back. The garage structure next to the community house and the one across the street were packed with goods by the time they were done unloading. The goods were shared with everyone and every pantry was full for the most part.

A feast was put on that night by the New Albany community and TJ opened the festivities with a prayer, thanking God for the materials and the safe return of all the people that went on the adventure.

TJ and Dan got together with Jack and Jeff after dinner and asked them what they'd seen on the trip. Jack started by saying, "Everything is beginning to really show the lack of use and care. Buildings sagged and some walls were collapsing. There were several fires in Colorado Springs, so we avoided those areas. We were surprised by both the lack of humans and Zs. We only had to take out about fifty of the things and they were no big deal, really. Most were showing their age and the rot was gross. They were all skin and bones. Very emaciated and stunk worse than a skunk on a hot day."

Jeff was next saying, "The new folks did great and worked their butts of getting stuff for the community. It was a swell trip overall. We were fortunate and blessed that no one was injured or worse. A few of the buildings we went in were dangerous to say the least. I expected a few to collapse on us just because our footsteps were making noise in the place. It was nerve wracking in a few of the places."

"Hey, did you marry those kids yet?" Jack asked.

TJ answered, "No, but they're getting close. I'm sure they'll announce a date real soon."

TJ had counseled Matt and Wanda on their responsibilities for each other and used several verses from the Bible to drive his message into their thinking. A Biblically based marriage of a couple would be more successful than any other. TJ focused his talks from two letters from Paul, his first letter to the Corinthians and his letter to the Ephesians. He used other verses from Proverbs, the book of knowledge. The pair were very receptive, and the trio laughed many times, especially through the more embarrassing topics. TJ felt the pair were ready and announced he was ready to go ahead.

The day finally came. The first real wedding in the valley was to take place the next day, a Saturday. The morning broke sunny and bright. The sky was clear and blue. The air was crisp and fresh. The aspen leaves were quaking in the gentle breeze, making that soothing sound, seemingly clapping in honor of the event.

Every resident of the valley had gathered. The pair had decided to have an outdoor affair and picked the big meadow a little southwest of Dan's home. It was large enough to hold everyone and Dan, Jack, and Jeff, were honored to have them pick their place for the event.

TJ mounted a podium on a small stage they'd built for the purpose and called the valley residents to order. He opened with prayer and asked God to bless the day, the couple, and everyone in the valley. He thanked the Lord for the lives they had and the lives they would live, and he asked God to especially bless the marriage that was about to take place.

After he said his 'Amen', he asked Matt and his best man, Donnie, to come up. Matt had a huge smile on his face. Donnie looked serious.

TJ looked at the two and looking back at Matt, said, "Are you ready, Matt?"

In a comforting, sincere tone, Matt said, "Yes, sir, I am."

"Then let's get going," TJ said, nodding to Donna.

From behind a partition that was built for the purpose, Wanda and her Maid of Honor, Linda, stepped out. Matt's breath sucked in as he saw his bride to be, dressed in a beautiful white gown. He had no idea where it had come from, but Wanda radiated in it. She was the most beautiful woman he'd ever seen.

As she stepped out, gasps came from the crowd. No one knew she would be in a wedding gown. It had been kept a very close secret between Wanda, Donna, Linda, and, most surprisingly, Ruth, as she had gone rogue and done a singular mission to Laramie, leaving DD with the Marines, and acquired the garment. The three women had fussed and bothered Wanda to no end and made her stand in that dress, sewing the hem, taking it in here, out there....

Matt was decked out in new blue jeans, a white shirt with a dark blue tie, cowboy boots, and had a yellow Columbine flower penned to his left chest above his pocket. Matt's eyes told TJ he was thrilled with what he was seeing, and as Wanda and Linda stepped onto the stage, Jack came up acting as the man that would give her away offering his hand to Wanda, then guiding her to stand next to Matt, and held her hand out to her husband to be.

Matt reverently took her hand, looking at it as if it was precious porcelain. He looked up into her eyes and broke into a huge smile. A tear suddenly streaked down her cheek, but she too, was smiling.

"Valley residents," TJ began, "friends and family all, we gather today in Centennial Valley on Marine Hill for a first of sorts. The first wedding in the new peaceful valley. The first wedding under God's view, in our new community. I have prayed for our Lord to bless this union and to bless their lives, so they live long and prosper to the fullest of His desire for them. It is my great honor and my great pleasure to wed these two, fine people. With that in mind, let's begin…"

"…I now pronounce you husband and wife. Sir, you may kiss your bride," TJ said with a gesture and a huge smile.

The valley residents erupted in yells, hoops, and hollering. It would be one of those events no one would ever forget. People were jumping up and down, arms raised. TJ could see several praying and several with tears running down their cheeks. It was an auspicious moment.

TJ raised his hands, signaling for silence and looking at the two newlyweds, motioned for them to hold hands and face the crowd then said, "Residents of Centennial Valley, for the first time ever, I present to you Mister and Missus Matthew Robinson." The residents went wild again, and many rushed to the center to greet the new husband and wife as they made their way down the aisle. Handshakes, hugs, and kisses were plentiful. Smiles were enormous. Back-slaps actually stung but no one cared. Everyone was happy and joyful for the new husband and wife.

TJ again called for silence and it took several minutes to finally get everyone's attention. He raised his hands in the air and said, "To begin the festivities, let us pray first and thank the Lord for this day and it's event. Everyone held hands and bowed their heads as TJ began, "Heavenly Father…"

After TJ said 'Amen', pandemonium broke out once again. The bride and groom were escorted, dragged was more the word, to the head table, and everyone else sat where they wanted. A banquet had been set up by the ladies and the Marines, that spanned five tables in length. It was a buffet-style affair and after the bride and groom served themselves, the rest of the residents filed through the line.

Elk, deer, buffalo and moose steaks, and roasts were there. Beef and pork ribs, steaks, and pork chops were served. Every kind of vegetable they grew was served fresh and piping hot. TJ had made forty loaves of fresh bread and from the lady's group, fresh butter had been churned. Donna and Ruth had gotten together and baked a homemade wedding cake, both white and chocolate cake, and used stick figurines for the bride and groom on top.

Although not many, there were gifts for the bride and groom, best of which was the home the valley residents had prepared for the pair up in New Albany. They were most appreciative of the gestures. Most gifts were bedding, kitchen items, and tools for the 'man of the house', although the woman of the house was an Army-trained mechanic.

The festivities lasted well into the evening and at nine o'clock, the pair was led by the Best Man and the 'Minister', to TJ's hummer, which had been decked out in a 'Just Married' motif. Everyone laughed and clapped as the groom opened the door for his bride, then went around and got in the driver's seat with the help of Donnie and TJ. Confetti was thrown by everyone as they had lined up down the lane leaving Marine Hill. The hummer was showered with the stuff which included aspen leaves, wheat kernels, and long-grain grass stems.

After the couple had driven away, the rest of the valley residents continued to party well into the night. Donna and TJ left near ten and back in Paradise Valley, drove the ATV up to the Underground and sat out on their Adirondacks and stargazed for a while. TJ went down the eastern portal and poured himself a tumbler of scotch and Donna a glass of wine. They sat together in silence, enjoying the moment.

"You remember the day we married?" Donna asked.

"How could I ever forget that," TJ answered. "The most memorable day and night of my life."

She smiled and said, "Well, cowboy, want to relive the experience?" she asked with a demure grin.

"Most certainly, my dear," TJ answered and rising, offered his hand to her, helping her up from her seat.

The next morning, TJ rose early and showered, dressed, and left the Underground by the eastern portal. He drove the ATV over to Marine Hill to help with the cleanup and found quite the mess waiting. The party obviously went all night as several of the residents were 'camped' out on Dan's lawn. Dan and Jack were already at it when TJ pulled up.

"Mornin' guys, how's things?" TJ asked.

"Not so loud, dude," Dan said, holding his head.

"Ohh, did we tie one on last night, brother?" TJ asked with a smile.

Jack answered for him by saying, "You missed it. He brought up dinner, lunch, and breakfast from the day before yesterday about midnight. It was a sight."

"Shut up…you're not helping at all," Dan complained. "My head is going to explode."

"Where's Jeff?" TJ asked.

"Over there in the aspens – he's still out," Jack answered with a snicker. "I'll wake 'em all up in just a bit with a flash-bang," he deviously said, juggling the item in one hand. "The whole valley will groan," he ended, laughing.

TJ grabbed a bag and began collecting the debris left over from the previous day's activities. It really didn't take them too long to clean up, as the valley residents were most respectful of others' belongings and property. The birds and rodents were taking care of the lane as the confetti used by everyone was edible for the critters.

Jack gave a little whistle, which Dan and TJ looked up for. He held the flash-bang up and had a great big smile on his face. Both Dan and TJ quickly put their fingers in their ears and opened their mouths to lessen the effect of the blast. Jack pulled the lanyard and threw the thing into the aspen stand where Jeff had crashed, and Jack quickly put his fingers in his ears and turned away from the blast site opening his mouth.

When the thing went off, Jeff came straight up and ran to the west. He came to a skidding halt in the meadow and looking around, remembered where he was and why. He turned, looking at his 'friends', who were bent over laughing so hard they hurt.

"You better be glad I'm a nice guy you bums," Jeff said with a snarl. The trio continued to laugh.

The rest of the residents lying about had risen at the blast. Many were holding their heads, and most were covering their eyes from the brightness of the sun. It had been a wonderful celebration the night before, and many were paying the price for the experience.

After the cleanup, TJ, Dan, Jack, and Jeff, sat in the front yard of Dan's place having a cup of very strong coffee. Jeff said, "I wonder how the happy couple are doing this morning?"

"Probably much better than you," Jack said, bring the three to gut wrenching laughter once again.

"You guys are terrible," Jeff complained.

"You should have seen yourself when you came outta those aspens," Jack laughed out. "Your eyes were big as saucers and your mouth was even wider," bending over laughing.

"Paybacks...I'll get the three of you..."

Quickly from TJ, "No...no...no, I just came over to help clean up...I had nothing t..."

"Oh no you don't – you're just as guilty and you know it," Jeff admonished. "You're in for it as much as those two," he said, pointing at Dan and Jack. "Which one of you threw the banger?"

Silence.

"I'll figure it out," Jeff said with a sneer.

The three busted out laughing again and reluctantly, Jeff finally joined in and said, "I guess I woulda done it to you if I coulda." The laughter got even louder at that.

After the joking around finally died down, Dan looked at TJ and asked, "You think we'll be seeing a little more of that now that the first one has broken the spell?"

"I suppose, and I for one, think it's a good thing," TJ answered. "We're building a new community here and we need to make it as good as we can with the good Lord's help. I figure if we do things in a Biblical fashion, it'll be okay with our Father in heaven. We'll need to teach the children we have, and the new ones that come along, about morals and character. We'll need to teach our children and hold each other accountable in accordance with the Lord's Word in the Bible. It's a great road map for life."

"Well put," Jeff said. "I sure want to be one of the folks to teach the little ones. I think that would be a neat thing to do."

"We'll remember that when the time comes," TJ said with a smile.

The summer wore on. Crops and livestock were tended. Men fished and hunted to feed the valley residents. Two more weddings took place and Albany had become a regular little town with everyone helping each other. Overall, the valley was becoming a real Christian community based soundly on Biblical principles.

The Fort Carson trip had been a success save for the run-ins with Zs and horrible road conditions. The trip took longer than expected for that reason. However, the bountiful yield of that effort was enormous. All four flatbed trucks came back over-loaded with goods. The trailers behind the pickups were also, and the beds of the pickups were loaded to overflowing. It was a God's blessing that no one had been injured on the trip and the vehicles had run smoothly. They'd had only one blowout and it had been changed without difficulty. When the team had returned, the entire valley fell out to help, beginning first with a prayer of thanksgiving for both the safe return of the team and the resources they acquired.

The fall harvest was splendid. Everyone had been involved with both the harvest and the canning and 'putting up' of the harvest. Preparations for the coming winter months had gone smoothly and hunters and fishermen had begun storing fish and meats for the community. Jack and Jeff took a group of hunters and had tracked down the buffalo herd and harvested enough meat to last the valley for the whole winter. Dan and TJ had hunted turkeys and were ready for a Thanksgiving celebration, the first official one in the valley.

It was the end of August, when the Robinson's announced they would be having a baby in the spring sometime. That announcement fostered another celebration, and the women of the valley were…well, overly protective of the prospec-tive mother. Springtime was going to be a hoot. Everyone in the valley would be pacing the front yard of the Robinson's place awaiting the news when the time came.

Ruth and Donna had already decided they would be the midwives, Ruth because she had DD. And Donna…well because, she was Donna. TJ and Dan would be the runners for water, towels, and such and keeping the father-to-be in check. Jack and Jeff would ride herd on the rest of the valley. It would be another spectacular event that would include a feast honoring the second birth in the valley.

The first Thanksgiving in Centennial Valley was bountiful indeed and a grand feast was held. Buffalo, beef, pork, turkeys, and fish were served on the great tables the men had built for the event. Vegetables from their harvest were cooked and served. Fresh breads and cookies, pies and cakes were on hand for desert.

TJ was asked to officiate and his prayer, thanking God for their year, was heartfelt. He added a request for a special blessing for Mrs. Robinson and her child, and another for the father for his strength.

The meal was fantastic. Everyone ate their fill. DD was passed around and would sleep well that night as would everyone else. Leftovers were given freely to everyone that wanted them. The festivities ended at seven that evening, and everyone turned in for the night.

TJ and Donna visited with Ruth and helped put DD down for the night. TJ carried the tyke in and put him in his bed. "Kid's getting heavy," he commented. "You feeding him concrete or something?"

"No, he's just going to be big like his dad was I guess," Ruth said with a smile. "He's growing like a weed and walking everywhere."

"I bet he's a handful," Donna said with a grin.

"He can be, but he's a joy to have," Ruth admitted. "He's looking more and more like Doug every day. Going to be a handsome young man in a few years I'm thinking."

"A real ladies' man, huh?" TJ said smiling.

"Yep," Ruth agreed.

"How are you doing over here, Ruth?" TJ asked. "You have everything you need?"

"We're fine, TJ, the Marines keep close tabs on us, so we never want for anything - thank you for asking though," she answered.

"You know if you need anything, just let us know, and we'll do our best for you," Donna said.

"I know that and thank you both so much for all you already do," Ruth answered sincerely.

"If there's anything you want from Paradise Valley, even to move back, just say the word; you know we're okay with that if it's what you want," TJ told her.

"No, the place is yours TJ," she said earnestly.

"I'm still astonished you did that for us," TJ said.

"With all the work you've put into the place, it should be yours anyway," she replied. "Have you done anything else since the last time I was there?"

"Not really, just maintenance," TJ answered. "I've had to do some maintenance in the Underground to keep the pumps and electrical systems going. Just normal stuff, nothing major."

"He's really keeping the place up, Ruth," Donna said. "We're going to refill the propane next week – want us to take care of that for you, too?"

"That would be nice, thanks," Ruth agreed.

"Dan and Jeff are helping so we'll do all of them next week," TJ explained.

"Sounds like you have everything going well," Ruth said.

"Have to with all these young people running circles around us," TJ said. "They have too much energy. But they do have some great ideas for the valley. They're planning to build a school and an infirmary. With the information Doug stored on all those CDs and thumb-drives, they're learning all kinds of stuff and making improvements all over. I think we're in good hands with God and them on our side."

"TJ, Donna," she asked looking directly at both, "you mind if I ask you something?" Ruth asked.

"Not at all, Ruth…what's on your mind?" TJ said in response.

"If something was to happen to me, would you and Donna please consider taking DD into your home as your own?" was the question.

The surprise on their faces was apparent and the sheriff was not surprised often. His face broke into a slow smile and he knelt in front of her and taking her right hand in his said, "Ruth, it would be our honor to take care of David Douglas Sutton. We'll indeed treat him as if he were our very own son. Really, he already is in a way." Ruth hugged TJ, and Donna came over and joined in with a group hug. When Ruth released the pair, she had tears running down her cheeks.

"Now that that is off my mind, here, I have something to show you," Ruth said getting up pointing at TJ.

TJ followed her into a room off to the side she used as a small office. She had stacks of paper and books everywhere. On a desk she'd taken from somewhere in Laramie, she produced an envelope and handing it to TJ, said, "This is my will…of sorts, I guess. It's in my own handwriting, but you'll be able to read it. My penmanship is much better than Doug's was." They chuckled together. "I'll leave this in a lock box," she said and pointed out the box, "and you can show it to folks if they have questions about why you have DD. It contains a letter to him as well."

"Ruth are you okay," TJ, suddenly concerned, asked.

"Yes, I am, TJ. I just want to be prepared in case something was to happen to me in the future. Honestly, there is nothing wrong," she added seeing the doubt in his eyes. "I'm fine. Doug taught me to be prepared and…well, this is me being prepared. I thought about it for a long time and decided on you and Donna for a lot of reasons. And trust me, I almost asked Dan, Jack, and Jeff. I think they too, would make wonderful surrogate parents for DD. But I think if something does happen, he'll need a woman's touch in his life to help him grow into a proper man. I know he'll have the best role model – models – in you, especially, and with the Marines backing you up."

That was the best compliment TJ had ever received, being told he was a fine role model for another man's son to emulate. He was humbled beyond belief and reached out and gave Ruth another hug and quietly whispered, "Thank you."

They broke away from the hug and she said, "TJ, I really do thank you for all you do for us. You and Donna have done much more than necessary to help DD and me. I really appreciate it."

"We love helping out," TJ answered.

"That's all I have for now, TJ," Ruth said, then, "You and Donna want to stay for a snack?"

As they walked back into the living room, TJ said, "Heaven's no, I'm still stuffed from the Thanksgiving dinner earlier. I'm going to have to go for a walk and walk some of this off before I go to bed or I'll be up all night."

Ruth laughed and Donna said, "I'll be joining him as I'm just as stuffed. Ruth, thank you for asking us to take DD. We're very honored by that and I promise you, if something happens to you, DD will have nothing to worry about as long as TJ and I are alive."

"Thank you, Donna. You two are great," Ruth said.

"We better hit the road, cowboy," Donna said to TJ.

He stood and getting his Stetson, said, "Ruth, we mean it, dear, if you or DD need anything, let us know and we'll get on it. Sleep well." He bent over, giving her a hug and a peck on the cheek, saying goodbye. Donna did also and the duo left for home.

Ruth watched as they drove off and closing and locking the door, retired for the evening after checking that DD remained soundly asleep. It had been a fantastic day. A wonderful first Thanksgiving for the community and for her, a relief knowing DD would now be taken care of by a wonderful, loving Christian couple if something were to happen.

Her mind now at ease, Ruth slept better that night than she had since losing Doug.

Spring came after a milder than usual winter. The Robinson's had a baby girl and asked Ruth if they could name her Julia, in honor of Julia Malone. Ruth broke into tears, yet smiled, and said that would be wonderful. DD was fascinated by the baby.

A few months later, one of the other newlywed couples announced another pregnancy. The Centennial Valley population was growing the way God intended.

Planting went well and two more underground greenhouses were constructed. Building began on the schoolhouse and Linda was chosen to be teacher. The Albany folks had grilled everyone - men, and women - for the honor of being teacher. Once the construction had begun, every time someone went to Laramie, or anywhere, books were gathered for the library in the school. Every textbook found was brought back and added.

A church was under construction too, and the valley as a whole told TJ he would be the spiritual leader for the residents. He said he'd do his best and said that his talks on Sundays would come straight from the Bible. One of the men from Albany made a sign, carved by hand into the wood,

'Centennial Valley Christian Church', and below that, 'All Are Welcome'. It would be hung above the doors.

Without realizing it, life had become for the most part, normal and routine, in the valley. Yes, there was no longer any television, radio, phones, pods, or pads, no cable or 'I.T.' support, but life was indeed becoming routine. Even the zombie threat had dwindled to just a few encounters a year. Still, everyone Z'd up before leaving their homes.

TJ's job as Sheriff was rather a moot point. He still held the office and figured he would until the day he died. He thought about handing it off to one of the younger men, retiring the badge to someone else, but being the only adult 'native born' Albany County person in the group, he felt the need to continue in the position.

Dan, not Jack, had been 'elected' as Governor of Centennial Valley, and Jack was his deputy. They handled disputes and were the deciding votes on things like construction and farming or work-related issues. Jeff had become the scrounger. If someone needed something, they would tell him, and he would deliver. He always seemed to be able to come up with what a person needed. He'd found an old Jeep and restored it, and that became his vehicle he used to get things. He built a small trailer to haul behind the Jeep and went everywhere with it. He and Jack mounted winches on the front and back ends of the four wheeled drive monstrosity, and they would literally go anywhere with that thing. He named it 'Tank', and everyone in the valley knew who was coming to call when they heard that rickety old thing.

A ladies' group formed, and they had sewing sessions, making quilts and things, repairing clothing, cooking, canning, and baking for others. They canned fruits, vegetables, and all kinds of soups, chilies, and stews for the winter months, and canned smoked meats and fish also. They would go around and help each other with home maintenance issues and improvements and worked alongside the men during planting and harvest times. Even a few of the single guys sat in on the sewing sessions to learn how to sew. A few of the men got together and made a spinning wheel and a loom for fabric making. The women loved both machines and made fabrics out of llama and sheep's wool. The men who made the machines were the first to receive homemade turtleneck sweaters from the ladies. The ladies group wondered if they would be able to grow cotton, but at the altitude of Centennial Valley, it wasn't feasible.

The way the valley population felt, work in general wasn't a women's or a man's, it was 'our' work and depending on what was going on, everyone pitched in and got the work done. Building, cutting timber for lumber or firewood, planting or harvesting crops, hunting, fishing, sewing, cooking…no matter, everyone pitched in. It was the right thing to do.

The biggest improvement in the valley most felt was the construction of the sawmill. Jeff, on one of his outings in Tank, came across an old sawmill and scavenged all of the blades and spindles to hold them. Once he had those back in Centennial Valley, the 'architects' got together and designed a sawmill. The entire valley population turned out for the building and together had the facility constructed in four days and began turning out lumber on the fifth. This wood would be used to construct the church, school, the community center, and new buildings as needed. Dino and Vito quickly became the experts on wood cutting and became 'carpenters' for the valley.

Ten years after the Colorado complex campaign, the entire bottom land alongside the river and creek of Centennial Valley, had been cleared for crops. A few areas that were once wooded became grazing pastures for cattle, sheep, llamas, and goats. Eleven more children had been born since Julia Robinson's birth, and several more weddings had taken place. Transportation, for the most part, was by horse or by horse-drawn wagon. The valley residents had rounded up many horses, cattle, sheep, goats, pigs, chickens and, oddly enough, llamas. Once a year a party of men went in search of the buffalo herd and would bring back enough meat for the community, supplementing the beef, pig, deer, and elk harvested. Chickens were raised and every home had six to twelve for egg production.

Money was a thing of the past. If someone needed something or needed something built, they brought their needs to the Elders and the Elders gathered the men of the valley and a decision would be reached through sound reasoning. Not everyone got what they wanted.

One of the men, who had gone out scrounging with Jeff, had found an old ham radio set and brought it back to the valley. He and Jeff, with a few others' help, had erected an antenna and had begun broadcasting to see if there were others out there somewhere. Several contacts had been made with survivors in areas similar to theirs - one group in Kentucky, another in Michigan, and several in the Yukon and British Columbia Territories of Canada.

He was broadcasting one day and happened upon a community in New Zealand. That was a happy moment and that conversation lasted over an hour. TJ, Donna, and the girls, along with Dan and Jack, had gone to the home where the radio was and listened in. It became quite the show and they had agreed to connect weekly, allowing everyone to get in on the conversation with new people. Trying to contact new communities suddenly became the new 'fad'.

TJ had retired, handing the badge over to Donnie. He'd earned it. Dan was no longer governor, having turned that over to one of the younger men. Jack had finally lost all of his hair blaming it on the stress of being the vice and he 'retired' shortly after Dan stepped down. Jack let his beard go and it now hung to his chest, giving him the 'Santa Claus' look, which he put to good use every year at Christmas. Jeff…was Jeff. He continued to scrounge for things folks needed and the old jeep, Tank, had been repaired so many times it looked like a patch-work car.

The valley residents had insisted TJ, Dan, Jack, and Jeff, become the Elders of the church and community. They made decisions based on Biblical principles, and taught ethics and moral standards to the children. They had a Biblically based men's group that met every Saturday and taught leadership ethics and morality in those sessions. The four also handled issues such as land disputes or ownership of animals, all from a Biblical perspective. The community had become a model Christian society.

The young man, who was a son of Islam, continued being a man of faith in those teachings. He was treated with the same love and respect all were and was invited to all events the valley had together. He, too, was a model citizen and worked alongside the others in every endeavor.

Ruth had her hands full with DD. He was a rambunctious young man and was always going off on his own to hunt and fish for mom. TJ, Dan, Jack, and Jeff trained him in the 'manly' (mostly Marine and Ranger) ways and the young man was becoming quite the provider (and Marine) for his mother. Overall, he was a quiet kid, and was fierce when he did take out the rare zombie that made the mistake of getting too close. (Did I mention he was mostly a Marine…?) He took his first bear at age thirteen, and his first mountain lion at fourteen, with a spear no less. He let his hair grow and wore it in a ponytail, and usually sported a headband of some sort to hold his hair back when out exploring the vastness of Wyoming and northern reaches of Colorado. The kid ranged far on occasion and would be gone for days at a time. Ruth worried, but allowed him to range as he had become quite the provider for his mother. He would come back from his forays and give information to Jeff and Jack, telling them where important supplies and materials the community might need was located. That always led to an expedition.

TJ and Donna were one of the couples who had a pregnancy. It was an unexpected surprise to both, and when their twin daughters, Danielle, and Denise, were born the valley residents went ballistic with that festival since they were the first set of twins since the pandemic that decimated mankind. Both had raven black hair like their mother, and blue-gray eyes, obviously a mix of mom and dad's. Their skin was fair and would be like their mothers' - they would tan nicely and look like Wyoming cowgirls should. Both Donna and TJ would see to that.

The community had not seen nor had a run in with zombies in over a year, other than the few DD admitted taking out on his forays. They all wondered why but were quite happy with not seeing any of the foul creatures. They were all tired of zombies. Their lives had moved into the realm of routine now and even though most of them still carried at least a handgun or a long-bladed knife when outside, no one had had to use a weapon in anger or for protection in a few years, some for many years, and that was refreshing.

After the final battle with the Colorado complex, they had not been attacked at all and had lived a decade in peace. They had watched the world repair itself, seeing the skies clear and the air become fresher. The roads were now dirt trails for the most part, the concrete and asphalt having become gravel. Most of Laramie and Centennial had rotted and the buildings sagged and collapsed upon themselves, and from time to time, fires would break out in the old towns for some unknown reason. No one had been to Cheyenne or to Sinclair, the fuel depots, for quite some time. There wasn't the need for a trip of that magnitude any longer.

Snow was fit to eat once more and every winter they had an ice cream festival. They drank water from creeks and streams without fear of becoming ill. Vegetables, fruits, wheat, and corn tasted different because they didn't use chemicals, nor were they genetically changed. The men of the valley had constructed a grinding system out of large stones and used the power of the river to operate the great grinding wheels to make flour out of wheat and corn. The people's hearing and eyesight improved over time and they wondered if it was due to being outside and not indoors in front of a screen of some sort.

Douglas Sutton's foresight and ingenuity had become legend in the valley. His Last Will and Testament was on display in the County Building in New Albany, and all could read it from copies made by the students at the school. It was because of his efforts, and the grace of God, that the valley had become what it was.

A lot of things had changed in the almost two decades since the plague turned loose by maniacal scientists had taken the planet by storm and decimated mankind. Two decades of change…for the better.

The grace of God had provided a new and peaceful existence for the Centennial Valley residents.